A Woman Named Sellers

A Witches of Pendle Novel

Sarah L King

ACKNOWLEDGMENTS

First and foremost, my heartfelt thanks must go to my husband
David and my children for their love and support. At the outset,
writing a second novel sounded less daunting than writing the first,
until it dawned on me that my work now had something to 'live up
to' and I began to feel under that level of pressure that one can
only ever place on oneself. I shall be forever grateful for the cups
of tea and beautiful drawings placed tentatively in front of me
during those difficult hours.

I would also like to thank my beta readers Jennifer Adam, Michael
Brown and K.J Farnham for taking the time to scrutinise the novel
and give me such invaluable feedback.

PENDLE AREA MAP

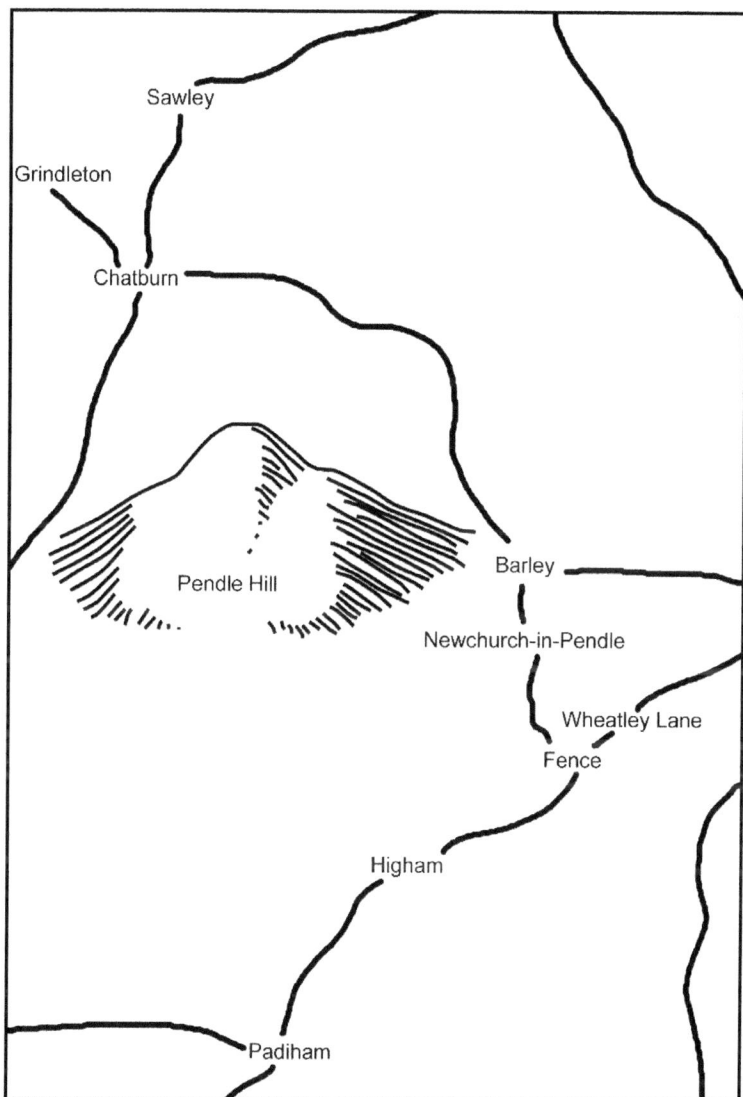

Sawley

Grindleton

Chatburn

Pendle Hill

Barley

Newchurch-in-Pendle

Wheatley Lane

Fence

Higham

Padiham

Part One

1632

1

Under Pendle Farm, Barley
February 1632

Jennet opened her eyes as the winter daylight trickled lethargically into the room. She moved a little and winced with discomfort. Her makeshift bed for the night had been little more than a few blankets heaped on the hard floor, and now her back ached and her hips pained her. The Holgates didn't have room for her really; their home was already filled with several generations of their family, and their cottage, though bigger than the one Jennet had shared with her father at White Moor, was still only a modest assembly of a few rooms. They had taken her in kindly enough, and her cousin George had assured her that they would find better sleeping arrangements in the coming days. Nonetheless, Jennet could sense that she was an additional burden that they did not need. She wished that she didn't have to impose upon her cousin, but she had no choice; apart from them, she had no one else left in the world now.

Wrapping herself up tighter, she screwed her eyes shut and willed herself back to sleep. She wanted to hide there, in that uncomfortable bed, all day. All she wanted to do was sleep, because if she was sleeping then she wouldn't be thinking, if she was sleeping she wouldn't have to remember. Perhaps, she thought as she covered herself in blankets once more, it would be best if she never woke up at all. Then she could truly forget, and be forgotten. Then she wouldn't be a burden to anyone.

"You can't stay there all day, you know," said a voice, interrupting her thoughts. "We've work to do and you're in the way. This is just no good; George is going to have to do something about this."

Jennet turned over to see her cousin, Alice, standing sternly over her, hands placed firmly on hips, a scowl fixed on her lined face.

"Well, are you going to move?" Alice continued.

Jennet studied her cousin for a moment. Until yesterday, she had barely known Alice, and already she felt less than fond of her. At ten years older than Jennet and fourteen years older than her brother George, she was the eldest child of Jennet's uncle, Christopher Holgate and his wife Isabel, and her seniority in the family was not lost on her. She had never married or had any children, but instead chose to live with her brother and her parents in this large, extended household, fulfilling a sort of maid's role. From what Jennet had already seen, Alice undoubtedly worked hard, caring for her parents and more recently for George's wife Ellena, who was heavy with child and greatly weakened by pregnancy. It was her manner which offended Jennet; the way she carried out her duties with such an air of authority that anyone would have thought her the mistress of a grand house.

"Moping will do you no good, you know," Alice advised. "You may as well get up and help me with my duties. I'll soon find you a purpose around here."

"I don't want a purpose," retorted Jennet. "I don't want anything or anyone. Leave me alone."

"Suit yourself," replied Alice. She sounded irritated but was clearly trying to exercise some restraint in the face of her cousin's grief. "You are in the way though, so I shan't apologise if I step on you."

"Fine, I will move," declared Jennet, dragging herself carelessly from her heap of blankets and dumping them in the corner of the room. "I know when I'm not wanted," she added as she swiftly tucked her dishevelled hair under a crumpled coif.

"Oh Jennet, I didn't mean…" Alice started as Jennet opened the door and went outside, allowing the door to slam hard shut behind her.

Outside, the day was forbiddingly cold and bleak, the frost-bitten ground and the heavy sky merging together to form a seemingly endless scene of white and grey. It had been a long winter; the first snow had arrived just after Martinmas and had reappeared sporadically ever since, with the heaviest snowfall occurring during the twelve days of Christmas. Jennet recalled how everyone had enjoyed the snow then, how it had made the Christmas festivities seem even more special and enjoyable. She remembered sitting with her father in their cottage, wrapped up in a shawl, nursing a cup of ale, watching the snow fall outside. All had seemed well then, just a few short weeks ago. Jennet thought about how they had sat together on cold evening after cold evening, enjoying the respite from farm work which the festive season afforded. She thought about how they had talked about nothing much, gossip from the surrounding villages, sharing stories they had heard about folk they knew.

Closing her eyes for a moment, she could hear her father's laughter echoing in her ears. She could see his smile too; his broad grin which displayed the large chip in his front tooth and the gentle creases around his eyes which betrayed his advancing years. It had been just the two of them at Christmas, but then it had always been just the two of them, ever since she had been left at his door at the age of eleven. Now he was gone and she was all alone, again. A solitary tear spilled down her cheek; it felt so hot against the frozen air and she brushed it away angrily.

"This weather had better start to improve," said Alice from behind her. "We'll need to start tilling the fields soon."

Jennet didn't respond. She continued to stare at the desolate Pendle countryside. She didn't want to talk to Alice, or anyone for that matter. She just wanted to be left alone, because that's what she was now: alone. She might as well get used to it.

"I'm sorry, Jennet. I didn't mean to upset you," Alice continued, "I don't want you to feel unwelcome. I shouldn't have spoken to you so sharply; you've had a terrible shock, it'll take you time to come to terms with it."

Jennet bristled. She had buried her father yesterday, and already Alice was talking as though she should forget him. "He was the only person in the whole world who cared for me," she said, her words laden with self-pity. "What am I meant to do now he's gone?"

Alice sighed. "I don't know, Jennet," she replied. "I don't know what you should do. But at least for now, you're with family. I know that you don't know any of us very well, but we do care about you."

Jennet turned and studied Alice for a moment. It was true; she didn't know any of her Holgate family very well. Most of her recollections of them were from her childhood, before she went to live with her father. She could recall some faint, distant memories of feast days spent at Malkin Tower with her Uncle Christopher and Aunt Isabel and their many children running around. She tried not to think about those times. She didn't want to remember them, because such recollections brought other memories to the fore, and before she could stop herself she could see her mother's face, her sister's face, and her brother's face all looking down at her, aghast. She couldn't bring herself to think about those times and so, for many years, she had tricked her mind into forgetting, she had convinced herself that her life had begun on the day she found herself on her father's doorstep at White Moor. Anything that had happened before then was just a bad dream.

"Are you going to come back inside?" asked Alice. "I've plenty to do if you would like to lend a hand."

Jennet nodded. Realising how cold she had grown, she shivered and wrapped her arms around herself. "I suppose I could help," she replied, trying now to be conciliatory. It was no use standing outside, crying and dwelling on the past. At least if she kept herself busy by Alice's side she could be distracted, she could forget herself for a while.

"That's more like it," said Alice, taking her by the arm and leading her back inside.

Inside the cottage it was warm, with the family gathered around a fire which was burning brightly in the hearth. As she walked back in through the door her uncle Christopher looked up, forcing a grim smile in her direction, showing his large gums which were completely bereft of teeth. Drawing a deep, considered breath, Jennet went over and sat down beside him.

"Good morrow, Uncle," she said.

Christopher did not return her greeting. Instead, he sat there for a few moments, staring at her, studying her thoughtfully with his big, yellowing eyes. "You look like your mother, you know," he said finally.

Jennet looked at him, shuddering at his words. She had been expecting this, ever since she had arrived. She had been waiting for him to mention her mother. Of course he would want to talk about her; she had been his younger sister, after all, and Jennet undoubtedly did look like her, with the same blue eyes, the same straight nose and high cheekbones. Even her hair, although dark like her father's hair had been, contained hints of her mother's red colouring. Part of Jennet did want to ask him all about his memories of her, how she had been as a child, how life had been growing up together. She knew a little of her mother's childhood; she knew that her mother and Christopher had different fathers, that Christopher had been born out of wedlock. She knew that her mother's father had died when her mother and Christopher were young. She couldn't remember her grandfather's name, however, or what had happened to her mother and her family after his death. She wasn't sure if she had ever known this, or if in the passing of time, she had simply forgotten. She wanted badly to ask her uncle, but she knew that to do so was to invite other conversations, other discussions about the past which she wanted desperately to avoid.

"I don't talk about my mother," she replied.

"I'm sure you don't," Christopher said after drawing a considered breath. "I'm sure it's hard for you to ever think about her, lass," he added kindly, patting her hand.

"All a long way in the past," Alice interjected, handing him a cup of ale. "Father likes to dwell on his memories these days, don't you?" she teased.

"Well, what else is there for an old man like me to do?" Christopher replied, his tone defensive. "Too old for this, that and t'other. Too old for anything," he added.

"Oh! Here he goes with the self-pity again," retorted Alice, rolling her eyes.

"How old are you, Uncle?" Jennet asked. She could tell by his appearance that he was a good age, his face heavily lined, his slender frame hunched, his voice at times unsteady like his feet. Her mother, had she still been living, would have been in her mid-sixties, and Jennet was sure that she had been his younger sister by more than a couple of years. She shuddered again. She had thought far too much about her mother today.

"Threescore and ten," replied Christopher. "And not long for this world now, lass."

Alice gave an exasperated sigh and frowned in disapproval. "Not this again," she said.

"Not what?" asked Jennet, feeling confused.

"He's talking about the Bible, Jennet. Psalm 90. It says that folk don't live past seventy years, unless they are strong. Or at least, that's what Father takes it to mean. I'd just say that he's lucky to have lived this long; there's many taken long before they're old," Alice said, shooting her father a pointed look.

"Aye, that's right, lass. It's all sorrow, as the good book says," replied Christopher, his mind wandering over the familiar verses. "But Jennet knows that better than any of us," he added, giving

Jennet a meaningful glance, his old eyes staring at her as though he was peering into her morose, grief-stricken soul.

"Right, enough of this idle chatter," declared Alice, touching Jennet lightly on the shoulder. "Jennet, could you help me see to Ellena? She hasn't risen yet this morning."

Jennet nodded in response, keen to leave her uncle's prying conversation and grateful once more for the offer of a practical distraction. She knew that everyone was worried about Ellena; it was one of the first pieces of information she had been given when she had arrived the previous day. Ellena was big with child and very near her time, but pregnancy had made her gravely ill. Alice had said that as the baby's arrival had grown nearer, her health had worsened and she was now very weak, almost bedridden. Jennet had no experience of these matters; she had never borne any children herself, and at almost thirty-two years of age and unmarried, she expected that she never would, but even she could see with her untrained eye that Ellena looked ill. Her face was pale and gaunt, her eyes sunken, her body skinny but for the enormous stomach in front of her. As Jennet followed Alice into a small, dark room, she could hear Ellena's breathing, laboured and unsteady.

"Come on lazy, up you get," teased Alice. "You'll need to eat something, Ellena, and that child will need to be fed."

Ellena groaned in response. "I can't, I can't move," she stammered sleepily.

"Jennet," Alice beckoned her. "Help me lift Ellena up."

Jennet nodded and walked over to the bed. She gasped as she took hold of Ellena's arm; it was so slender it was like touching a child. It was as though the baby she carried had taken the flesh from her bones, as though it was consuming Ellena herself. Now there was almost nothing left, just a weak and skeletal figure fading away before her family's eyes. Jennet winced as it struck her that poor Ellena still had to go through childbed; despite the brave face worn by Alice and Ellena's husband George, they must have been gravely concerned that Ellena would not survive it.

"Come now, Ellena," Jennet urged in little more than a whisper.

Together, she and Alice gently coaxed her into a sitting position and pulled the pillows up behind her back. Ellena gave a brief groan before opening her eyes properly and looking at them both. Alice handed her a cup of ale.

"Drink, Ellena. I daresay that child will have a thirst as well," Alice instructed her.

Ellena gave Jennet a faint smile. "You'll get used to being bossed around, I'm sure," she croaked. "Alice's tone is rough but her intentions are good. She's taken care of me, these past months."

"How's the pain today, Ellena? Do I need to fetch Goodwife Lund for you?" Alice asked.

Ellena shook her head and sipped from her cup. "Don't fetch the Goodwife," she instructed.

"Who is Goodwife Lund?" Jennet asked.

Alice gave Jennet a deliberate stare, as though carefully considering her words before speaking. "She's a kind and knowledgeable woman who lives in Wheatley Lane," she said finally. "Ellena's pregnancy has been a trying one, but Goodwife Lund's remedies have helped ease her discomfort, haven't they Ellena?"

Ellena nodded in response. "Yes. She's tried all manner of concoctions. Some have worked well, others haven't. The one she gave me last week has helped ease the pain in my bones, although it makes me feel a little sick. I'll be glad when this pregnancy is over. I feel unwell and I just want to sleep all the time, but when I sleep I have the most dreadful dreams," she replied, her tone a little melancholic.

"What sort of dreams?" asked Jennet, keen to change the subject. She understood Alice's careful gaze now; Goodwife Lund made remedies, just like Jennet's grandmother, Old Demdike, had done. She was a cunning woman who saw countless women through pregnancy and childbed, women who could not afford a physician, women who would otherwise get no assistance at all. Jennet gulped hard at the thought of her grandmother; another memory upon which she did not wish to dwell.

"Now come, enough of that sort of talk," Alice interrupted them both. "Ill-thinking is bad for the child. I daresay Goodwife Lund is right, Ellena, when she says that you're carrying a girl. She says that girls always make for more troublesome pregnancies. She says it's nothing to worry about, that her herbs and concoctions will see you fit and strong for childbed, and it will all be over soon enough. Now, I will fetch you something to eat. Jennet, will you assist me? We'd best leave Ellena to rest."

Jennet nodded and followed Alice out of the room and towards the hearth and the simple wooden table, upon which laid a few carefully chosen ingredients. Alice leaned against the table and, putting her head in her hands for a moment, let out a long sigh.

"The winter is so difficult," she said, looking up and gesticulating towards the table. "We're beginning to run short of a few things, so I'm afraid you'll find the food here a little plain. I give the best meals to Ellena, of course, although often she doesn't keep them down."

"Alice, tell me honestly, what's wrong with her?" Jennet asked.

"I don't know, Jennet," replied Alice with a sigh. "I've little experience of these matters, but I've never seen a woman with child look so ill and in so much pain. She says her body hurts all the time, and as you'll see, she struggles to keep food within her belly. She is wasting away. I've said little to George about my concerns; he's determined to remain positive for his wife and child, as he should, but I don't see how she's strong enough for childbed."

"What can we do?" asked Jennet.

"Pray," replied Alice, her face grim. "All we can do is hope and pray."

2

Under Pendle Farm, Barley
Early March 1632

Jennet looked out of the small cottage window and watched the men and women working outside as they hurriedly finished the spring planting. The winter's snow had lasted until the middle of February, meaning that the fields, which were usually tilled just after Candlemas, were still not ready for planting when the first of the lambs had begun to arrive at the end of the month. As a result, it had been a hectic fortnight on the farm and everyone who was fit and able had been called upon to help. Even Alice, whose duties normally kept her confined to the cottage, had been called to the fields to assist George and the other labourers. Uncle Christopher, understanding the urgency of the task at hand, had been desperate to help, but had been told by Alice in no uncertain terms that his aged condition prevented him from such strenuous activity and he was safest indoors. Jennet had sensed, however, that such was the importance of getting the fields planted, if there had been any further delay, they would have had no choice but to take up Uncle Christopher's offer of help.

Jennet, meanwhile, had been given Alice's duties. She had protested at first; she was just as able a labourer as Alice, she had insisted, whereas she was certain she was nowhere near as good as her cousin when it came to looking after the household. She wasn't exaggerating either; her father, for all he had taught her about farming, couldn't teach her 'woman's work', as he called it, and he freely admitted that he had failed to have her schooled correctly in this regard. As a result she had only basic cookery skills, and a scant knowledge of the remedies used for common illnesses and complaints. She could prepare a field for planting comfortably, happily even, but she was a poor cook and nursemaid. Now she was being asked to be both, her protest falling on deaf ears. "You'll manage," Alice had said as she headed off to the field on that first frost-free morning, whilst George had simply looked dumbly at her, too distracted by his fields to comprehend what all the fuss was about. That had been almost two weeks ago, and after two weeks of watery pottage for the weary labourers and underwhelming care for the sick and elderly residing in the cottage, Jennet could almost see the admittance that she had been right hovering on Alice's and George's lips. For Jennet it was a bitter triumph; for all that she liked to be proved correct, she also felt acute embarrassment about her shortcomings.

"Wish you were out there, instead of stuck in here? Me too, lass," said Uncle Christopher, interrupting her thoughts. Jennet nodded in response but didn't turn around. She continued to gaze out of the window. She didn't feel like talking, but she suspected that her uncle wasn't going to give her a choice in the matter. She had learned over these past weeks that his seniority in the household seemed to afford Uncle Christopher his own way on most matters.

"Year after year I tilled those fields. I used to work so hard, I thought that I'd end my days out there, not stuck in here, withering away like an old fool who no one has any use for."

"Where's Aunt Isabel?" asked Jennet, determined to keep away from her uncle's favourite subject, his aged and pitiable condition.

"In her chair, sleeping. Where is she always? She only moves if you make her. She's probably worse than me; at least I'm awake most of the time. She used to be a lot livelier, you know, when we were younger. It's horrible, what age does to you," her uncle replied.

"At least you've lived to be so old. You should be grateful," retorted Jennet, feeling exasperated now. It hadn't taken many weeks of living with the Holgates for her to tire of Uncle Christopher's self-pity. "My father's dead, and he was younger than you," she added.

Uncle Christopher nodded in response. "Aye, and your mother too, almost twenty years now since that dreadful business."

Jennet clenched her jaw as she looked out of window. "I told you, Uncle Christopher, I don't talk about my mother," she said firmly.

"You will do, one day," replied Uncle Christopher, placing a shaky arm around her shoulders. "And when you do, I will be here for you, lass."

Jennet stood there, frozen, her eyes still fixed upon the fields in front of her. She refused to turn and meet the old man's gaze. If she did, she feared that she would be unable to stop the words and tears tumbling forth, that she would start talking about her mother, that she would start weeping about what she had done all those years ago.

"You should blame me, Uncle Christopher," was all she could manage to say as she stared stoically ahead, tears gathering in the corners of her eyes.

"You were only a child, lass, how could you have known..." he started, but Jennet didn't let him finish.

"I must check on Ellena," she said quickly as she moved from under his arm and turned away.

She walked into Ellena's room. It was dark and silent. Jennet bit her lip as she realised that she had let Ellena sleep too long this morning; it was almost lunchtime and she hadn't woken her to eat and drink, like Alice would. Jennet sniffed the air; there was an odd smell in the room, a sweet, sickly odour like none she had ever smelt before. Wrinkling her nose in distaste, she walked over to the bed where Ellena slept.

"Ellena," she said, shaking the sleeping woman's shoulders gently to rouse her. "Time to wake up, Ellena. I will fetch you something to eat and drink."

Ellena groaned in response. "I feel strange," she said. "Go away and leave me alone, leave me to sleep."

"You can't sleep all day," Jennet insisted. "You need to eat something. What do you mean, you feel strange? Are you unwell?"

"I don't know," replied Ellena, shuffling uncomfortably, her eyes still only half-open. "I feel odd, like I'm wet. Why are my sheets wet?"

Jennet hurriedly pulled Ellena's blankets back and gasped. She was right; her sheets were indeed covered in water, the sweet smell she had noted upon entering the room emanating from them. "Ellena!" Jennet exclaimed. "Do you think the baby's on its way?"

Ellena grunted. "I don't know," she replied, her voice tinged with panic. "How would I know? I've never done this before."

"Don't worry. Just stay in bed, and try to stay calm," said Jennet, forcing her voice to remain even and ignoring the heat of worry which was rising in her cheeks. "I'll fetch Alice. She'll know what to do."

Without another moment's hesitation, Jennet ran out of the cottage and towards the field where Alice was working. As she ran, a myriad of questions raced through her mind; was it Ellena's time yet, or was the baby coming early? Was the baby coming at all, or was this another symptom of Ellena's illness? Did it matter that Ellena hadn't eaten anything yet today? Why did the water on the bed smell so odd? She wished in that moment that she had more experience of these matters, that she knew a little more of carrying and bearing children, that she knew what to expect when a woman was in childbed. As she approached Alice, breathless, it occurred to her how sheltered her life had been with her father, just the two of them up on White Moor. She knew so little about the world because he had deliberately sheltered her from it and she, having glimpsed the world's ugliness, wickedness and sin as a girl of eleven, had been willing to be sheltered. Yet now, as she ran towards her cousin, struck by the realisation that she had no idea how to deliver a child, she wished she knew a little more of life.

"Jennet, what's the matter?" asked Alice, immediately reading the panic on Jennet's face.

"It's Ellena. I don't know what it is! I woke her, and her sheets were wet, and she says she feels strange and there's an odd smell, I don't know how to describe it…" Jennet's words tumbled forth clumsily.

Alice chuckled. "Oh, Jennet, you do make me laugh. That's all normal for a woman about to go into childbed. Listen, her pains will start soon if they haven't already. I will come inside and start to prepare what we need. Could you go and fetch Goodwife Lund? Do you know your way to Wheatley Lane?"

Jennet nodded. "Will Ellena be alright?" she asked, her anxiety still refusing to subside.

"I don't know," Alice replied with a sigh. "She is weak, as you know. But that is why we need Goodwife Lund. If anyone can see Ellena safely out of childbed, she can."

Jennet walked so fast that her sides hurt and the back of her legs ached. It was easily an hour's walk to Wheatley Lane, meaning it would be at least two hours before she returned to Barley with Goodwife Lund. She didn't know how long childbed normally lasted, if it was hours or days, but she had sensed enough urgency in Alice's instructions to understand that the sooner she fetched the Goodwife, the better. She took the quickest route to Wheatley Lane that she could recall, crossing fields directly where she could instead of opting for the usual lanes, moving as quickly as she could manage. By the time she reached Wheatley Lane, her heart was pounding so hard in her chest from both nerves and exertion that she thought she might burst, and her usually pale face was scarlet and running with sweat.

Looking around and taking a moment to catch her breath, Jennet realised that although she knew her way to Wheatley Lane, she didn't know exactly where Goodwife Lund lived. She began to panic again, realising that time spent seeking this woman was time that Ellena could ill-afford. It was only a small hamlet, composed of a handful of cottages and farms, but like many such hamlets in Pendle the dwellings were arranged sporadically rather than clustered together, meaning that to knock on each door would take a considerable amount of time. Jennet took a deep breath. She would have to ask someone, to pick a door and knock on it and hope that the person who answered knew where she might find Goodwife Lund. As she approached the nearest cottage, she was startled by a noise behind her, like pebbles spinning on the ground.

"You're not from round here." said the voice.

Jennet spun around to see a boy stood behind her. He was small, she guessed around eight years of age, and skinny, with untidy hair and dirty clothes. He looked up at her with dark, knowing eyes. He was just a boy, full of mischief no doubt, but he might be able to help her. "Do you live here?" she asked.

"Might do. What's it to you?" the boy asked.

"I'm looking for someone. If you live here you might know her. I'm trying to find Goodwife Lund; do you know where she lives?" Jennet persisted.

"What do you want her for? You don't look like you've a sick cow needing cured," the boy replied impertinently.

Jennet bristled at this child's rudeness. She'd have given him a clip round the ear had she not needed information from him so badly. "I've a friend...family actually. Someone in my family is in childbed and badly needs the Goodwife's help. Now, do you know where she lives?"

The boy sighed, obviously bored now by his own charade. "Aye, she's up there, on Blackwood Head," he said, pointing up the hill over which Jennet had just come. "Can't say she'll be at home, though. Likes of her roams here, there and everywhere delivering her charms. My father says..."

"Thank you," said Jennet, interrupting the boy. She didn't have time to indulge his interest in idle conversation. "What's your name, lad?"

"Edmund," said the boy proudly, puffing out his chest. "Edmund Robinson."

"Thank you, Edmund. And a good day to you," Jennet called over her shoulder as she lifted her skirts slightly and ran back up the hill.

Breathless, Jennet reached the top of the small incline and the small stone cottage which sat upon it. Without hesitation, she ran forward and banged loudly upon the wooden door. After a few moments, the door swung open.

"Yes?" asked the girl who answered.

Jennet was immediately taken aback. She had been expecting a woman of around fifty, a formidable, knowledgeable looking woman by all accounts, not the pretty, freckled girl of slight build who stood in front of her now, looking at her with her bright green eyes. She glanced momentarily over her shoulder; that boy, that Edmund Robinson, he must have sent her to the wrong house! Little boys should never be trusted to be truthful, she thought angrily.

"I, er…I'm looking for Goodwife Lund. I think I must have the wrong house," she stammered, feeling flustered again.

"That's my mother," replied the girl with a warm smile. "Come in and catch your breath, you look like you've had a long journey."

The girl beckoned Jennet inside the cottage, which was small, but warm and cosy. Jennet removed her shawl; although the weather outside was still cool, with a chilly breeze lingering in the early spring air, she realised that all her running around had made her feel very warm indeed. Jennet breathed in deeply as she detected an unfamiliar but delicious scent; it wasn't like food, but flowers and plants, mixed and ground together into a wonderful fragrance.

"I'm just preparing herbs for my mother's remedies," the girl explained. "She's just gone out but she won't be long. Would you like to wait? Sorry, I just realised I hadn't even asked your name! We have so many people come to the house looking for Mother that I forget my manners sometimes. My name's Grace."

Jennet nodded. "Jennet," she replied. "Jennet Sellers. Your mother has been caring for my cousin's wife during her pregnancy, she's been very unwell these past months and now her pains have started. My cousin, my other cousin, Alice, sent me to fetch your mother."

"I see," said Grace. Jennet thought that she sounded disinterested, but perhaps this was understandable. Grace must have spent all day, every day at her mother's side, listening to lists of what ailed other folk and offering remedies and advice. To her, Ellena was probably just another woman in childbed and nothing really to worry about.

"Are you sure your mother won't be long?" asked Jennet anxiously. "I've walked here from Barley and it's at least an hour's walk back. I fear we will be too late."

Grace laughed loudly in response. "Oh, goodness, don't worry about that! Childbed takes an eternity, especially the first time. Is this her first child?"

Jennet nodded, slightly irritated by Grace's casual attitude.

"Well, it'll be even longer than an eternity then," Grace said. "Mother will arrive in plenty of time, she always does."

Their conversation was interrupted as the door to the cottage slammed and an older, busy looking woman walked in. Jennet breathed a sigh of relief as she realised this must be Goodwife Lund. The woman looked to be around the age of fifty; her face, although pretty and friendly like her daughter's, wore the marks and lines of advancing years, and her greying hair peeked untidily from beneath her coif. She was a short woman with a heavy build, especially around her waist, which Jennet estimated to be at least three times the size of her own. It was no wonder she looked to be sweating; the effort of carrying herself around all day must have been almost intolerable.

"Can I help you?" the Goodwife asked, panting and trying to catch her breath.

"It's Ellena Holgate," replied Jennet. "Her pains have started.

We need you to come to Barley right away."

The Goodwife's green eyes widened slightly as she absorbed Jennet's words. "Goodness. I didn't think it was her time just yet. Grace, fetch my bag of remedies, we must leave at once."

The journey back to Barley took much longer than Jennet had hoped. The Goodwife, for all her determination to get to her patient, was slow on foot and struggled breathlessly as Jennet led them across the rolling fields. At times she clung unsteadily to Grace, who Jennet could hear periodically grumbling about the route she had chosen. Jennet gritted her teeth and tried to ignore the girl's muttering; although Grace had been nothing but friendly to her, Jennet sensed a youthful petulance about her which she found irritating.

"Not much further now," she assured them both. "Tell me, Grace, how old are you?"

"Almost twenty-two," the girl grinned. "My birthday is in the summer."

"I took you for younger than twenty-two," Jennet mused, half to herself.

"That's because she behaves like a silly lass," interjected Goodwife Lund, between gasps.

Grace frowned at her mother before turning back to Jennet. "How old are you, Jennet?" she asked.

Jennet hesitated. She hated admitting her age, but then she had asked the girl first, so it was so only fair to tell her. "I will be thirty-two this year," she replied. "In October."

"Goodness!" Grace chuckled. "Ten years older than me, I wouldn't have thought it. Do you have a husband?"

Jennet shook her head in response and looked away. She disliked revealing her age now because that was always the question which followed. She hated admitting that she had never married, that she probably never would, that she was destined to die an old maid. She hated it even more when people looked at her as though to ask her why not, but never dared utter the words. She didn't glance back at Grace to see if she bore this look upon her face now; she didn't need to, because before she could say anything else, Grace asked the dreaded question.

"Why?"

Jennet turned and looked back at Grace, studying her face as though she was searching for an answer. Why, indeed? What could she say to this young woman, she was little more than a girl in looks and spirit really; what could she say to her to explain why she had never met a nice man and married him? Should she tell her about all those years spent living in sheltered isolation with her father on White Moor? Should she tell her why she chose to hide herself away; that she grew up hoping that the world would forget who she was and what she had done? Would this young woman have any comprehension of how lost she felt now that the only man who had ever meant anything in her life, her father, was gone? Would she understand that Jennet never expected to be happy again, let alone find a nice husband? Jennet sighed, still staring at Grace's bright, innocent green eyes. No, probably not.

"Grace!" Goodwife Lund interjected. "Save your impertinent questions, please. We're almost there, and we have work to do."

The three women walked down on to the small track which led to Under Pendle Farm. As they approached the cottage, Jennet increased her pace, feeling once again the urgency of bringing this woman to Ellena. As she got nearer she called out, "Alice! George! The Goodwife is here!" After a moment, she saw the door to the cottage open. Alice walked outside and walked towards them.

"Alice, I've brought the Goodwife," she repeated.

Alice's face was pale and sombre. She let out a small sob then immediately tried to compose herself. "It's too late, Jennet. You're too late. Ellena's gone."

3

Under Pendle Farm, Barley
Early June 1632

"Jennet! Fetch some more bread, James is crying again," Alice called impatiently as the baby boy began his familiar, high pitched squeal.

Jennet sighed and put her head in her hands. She had only just managed to get the baby girl, Anna, down to sleep and now, no sooner had she started making the family's meal, the other baby was awake. "At the rate these two are drinking milk, we're going to need more goats!" she called back, exasperated.

It had been a difficult few months since Ellena's death. Jennet shuddered as she remembered that dreadful day. She remembered standing outside the cottage, listening to Alice stifle her sobs, her voice trembling as she delivered the terrible news. She recalled how she walked back into the cottage, arm in arm with Alice who, for the first time since she had known her, appeared visibly weak and shaken. She could see in her mind's eye the awful scene as she walked in through the door; Ellena's body, still and lifeless in front of the fire, laid out on a bed of straw as a physician sliced open her abdomen, pulling babies from her womb. She could see George sitting on the bed, his head cradled in his elderly father's arms, both of them turned away from the bloody scene before them. She recalled how Goodwife Lund and Grace had walked in, the Goodwife rushing to swaddle the new-born babies whilst Grace, gasping at the sight of so much blood and gore, promptly fainted. Jennet shuddered again; seeing a woman's body butchered like that had been the worst thing she had ever seen, even if it had been to save not just one, but two innocent lives.

Jennet sighed again as her mind returned to the babies. The Holgate family had been afforded little time to grieve for Ellena; mourning seemed a luxury that they could ill-afford when there were two fragile infants to care for and nourish. Alice, to her great credit, had stepped in to make arrangements very quickly, finding a wet nurse who could provide milk for the babies to sustain them during their first few weeks of life. When it became evident that a wet nurse for two babies was an expense which the family could not afford, Alice expertly oversaw the infants' weaning on to cheaper, more ingenious means of nourishment. As she soaked yet another piece of bread in milk for James to suckle on, Jennet reflected on how Alice always seemed to know exactly what to do, even when it came to matters about which she appeared to have little experience. Over the past few months she had come to appreciate the extent to which Alice held the family together; if George was the head of the household then it was in name only, because on a daily basis it was Alice who took charge of the family's affairs.

Jennet handed Alice the sodden bread and sat down beside Aunt Isabel. The old lady gave Jennet a faint smile and briefly squeezed her hand. Jennet returned her smile just as weakly and closed her eyes. She felt exhausted. She couldn't remember the last time she had enjoyed a full, uninterrupted night's sleep. As she sat there, allowing herself to drift into a light slumber for a few moments, it occurred to her that she had spent so many of her adult years berating herself for not finding a husband and having children, when perhaps really it was a blessing. Childbearing, she had decided, was a dangerous and thankless exercise; at best she would have spent year after year nursing a crying baby, attending to their every need day and night, and at worst she would have ended up dead, cut open on the floor like Ellena. She was certain that she wouldn't marry now, but for the first time in her life she had come to regard this as a narrow escape, rather than a lost opportunity. She wondered if Alice felt the same way, whether she enjoyed caring for these two motherless infants and hankered after her own, or whether to her raising these children was just another task to approach in her usual straightforward, no-nonsense manner.

"Mother, could you hold James and try to settle him for me?" Alice asked Aunt Isabel. "I need to prepare our supper, and Jennet's obviously planning to rest a while before Anna wakes again."

"No, no," Jennet protested drowsily. "I'll assist you now."

Jennet followed Alice wearily to the kitchen. She tried hard to stifle her sighs; she knew that Alice did not take kindly to her suggestions of tiredness, her indications of how completely fed up she felt. Jennet gazed out of the small window at the calm, early summer's day; the plants beginning to bloom, the hedgerows beyond them a lush green. How she longed to go outside, how she longed to be free to roam the beautiful Pendle countryside, to enjoy the summer sunshine on her back as she lost herself in the familiar wilderness. How odd it was, she thought, that during all those years living with her father at White Moor she chose never to wander far, despite being completely at liberty to do so. Now, feeling trapped inside this little cottage with Alice, her elderly parents and two demanding infants, she wanted nothing more than to break free, to run away and never look back.

"Ow!" exclaimed Alice, burning herself on the pot which she was trying, rather clumsily, to remove from the fire.

"Here, let me help," offered Jennet, taking the pot and giving Alice some cold water in which to soak her hand. As she stood there, screwing her face up slightly as the cooling effect of the water soothed her burnt skin, Jennet noticed how exhausted Alice looked, her face drawn and pinched, her eyes dark and heavy. "You need to take better care of yourself, Alice," she ventured, tentatively offering advice.

This time, it was Alice's turn to sigh. "Do you ever feel cross with Ellena?"

Jennet shook her head. This was not a thought that had ever occurred to her. When she thought of Ellena she usually felt revulsion at the memory of her innards spread over the cottage floor, followed by pity for the poor woman that she died in such a dreadful manner, and that she didn't live to see her babies. She could weep for Ellena, but she never felt angry towards her.

"Do you?" she asked.

"Yes I do," replied Alice. Jennet noted that whilst her face was straight and her answer typically direct, there was something about the way in which her voice wavered over her words that betrayed the emotions simmering beneath them. "I feel angry that she died. I feel angry that she left me to take care of her babies."

"Us. She left us to take care of her babies, Alice. You have me, and George, and your mother and father. We're all here, you know," Jennet tried to reassure her gently.

"George and Father are men, what do they know about looking after babies? George is so grief-stricken he can hardly bear to look at them. Mother is too old and you, well…" Alice allowed her voice to trail off, as though she had thought better of what she was about to say.

"Me…what?" asked Jennet, not happy to let the matter lie. She could feel herself grow indignant, the heat rising a little in her cheeks. For the past few months, she had done more than her fair share of feeding, cleaning and comforting, day and night. She had done everything that had been asked of her; in fact, she had never been asked, but she had accepted responsibility for the two little babies nonetheless. Yet, to hear Alice talk, it was as though Jennet had been completely idle while she had shouldered the burden alone. Once again, Alice's haughty, superior air threatened to annoy her.

Alice removed her hand from the cold water and wiped it

gently. "You don't have to be here," she said finally. "You don't owe us anything. You could leave any time you please. You're free, Jennet, whereas I am not. That is the difference between us."

Jennet looked at Alice, open-mouthed. Her first reaction to Alice's words was to protest; of course she wasn't free, she certainly didn't feel free! Then, as the meaning of what Alice had said began to sink in, she realised that there was truth in her words. She had only lived with the Holgates for a matter of months; her position in their home was therefore by no means a settled one. Although she owed them a debt of gratitude for taking her in, she had more than earned her keep during her stay. If she chose to, she realised, she could pack up and leave tomorrow. Alice, on the other hand, could not go anywhere; she was trapped by her own sense of duty as well as the real burdens and responsibilities which rested upon her shoulders.

"I had hoped that I might leave here one day," Alice said wistfully. "Mother and Father are old, they won't always be here. I had thought that once I no longer had them to care for, that I might make a life for myself. That perhaps I might marry…well, that won't happen now. I think that's why I feel angry, Jennet, because I realise now that the secret, vain hopes I once harboured are all but dashed. I suppose I'm not really angry with Ellena. I'm probably angry with myself for being so selfish."

Jennet reached out and touched Alice tenderly on the shoulder. It was somehow comforting to learn that underneath all those layers of superiority and organisation, there was a fragile person who felt keenly the misfortune of her position. In that moment, Jennet discovered a new level of respect for Alice; despite her unhappiness, she shouldered all the responsibility which was flung her way with such confidence and skill. She had never complained, never talked about how she really felt; even now, as Jennet tried to offer her comfort, she began to brush it all off, putting her feelings aside once again and getting on with the essential tasks at hand. Alice was brave, and she was strong. Jennet was about to tell her so, but just at that moment, Anna began to cry.

It was much later in the day when visitors came to the cottage, the early summer sun casting its orange glow through the small windows. Jennet was initially startled by the knock at the door; they never received visitors after supper-time, when George had already fulfilled his evening routine of coming home, eating, and going back out to the alehouse. Lifting Anna on to her shoulder and bouncing her gently as she peered out of the window, a small smile crept over her face as she realised who had come calling. Opening the front door, she greeted Goodwife Lund and Grace enthusiastically, beckoning them inside. The Goodwife and her daughter visited frequently, to check on the babies' progress and to offer advice. Jennet had come to depend on their visits greatly; she and Alice seldom had any other visitors and the Goodwife and her daughter were such cheering, kind folk, it was impossible not to warm to their company. Jennet had even grown fond of Grace's youthful, flighty nature; her own life had become so dull and monotonous over the past months that it was hard not to find such a light-hearted temperament appealing.

"What a lovely welcome!" the Goodwife exclaimed. "Sorry I am so late; it has been a busy day. Now then, let me see those babies," she added, peering at Anna.

"I didn't know you were coming today," said Jennet, handing Anna over to Goodwife Lund who held her up into the light, as though she might be a puppy or a piglet rather than a person.

"Yes well, I see we gave you a nice surprise," the Goodwife replied, smiling broadly. "This little one looks well, although she could do with a bit more colour in her cheeks. Have you had them both outside yet? The air is mild enough, I think."

Jennet shook her head. "No, we have so much to do here. We will try though, if that is what you recommend, won't we Alice?" she asked as Alice walked in, handing James to the Goodwife for examination.

"Hmm," Alice replied distantly, "as Jennet says, we have much to do."

"Jennet," Grace interjected. "Do you recall I told you that it is my birthday this month? It's this Sunday, the tenth of June."

"Hush now, Grace," the Goodwife scolded, as though she might be a small child. "These ladies are too busy to talk about your birthday plans."

"I was only going to ask," Grace persisted, "if you might like to join me in the alehouse this Saturday, to celebrate? And you too, Alice."

"Grace, how on earth do you imagine these two ladies are going to be able to leave these babies so that they can celebrate your birthday with you?" the Goodwife said as she manipulated James's limbs, making him shriek. Jennet always wondered what she was looking for, and what she learnt by handling the babies in such a way.

"Your mother is right, Grace," Jennet began, "but thank you very much for the invitation."

Grace cast her eyes down. "Alright," she said.

"You go," Alice said to Jennet after a moment, swiftly ending the awkward silence which had descended in the wake of Grace's disappointment.

"Alice, are you sure?" Jennet asked.

Alice nodded. "Goodwife Lund is right, we can't both go, but I'm sure one of us can get away from here for a few hours. It seems a shame to turn Grace's invitation down completely," she added, forcing a sweet smile in Grace's direction.

Jennet glanced at Alice hesitantly, surveying the smile which was still fixed upon her face. She recalled their earlier conversation, when Alice had all but confessed her unhappiness. Yet here she was, urging Jennet to go out and leave her, as though to prove that her words earlier had been true, that Jennet could leave whenever she wanted. Jennet narrowed her eyes momentarily, unable to decide if Alice was being utterly selfless, or merely playing the martyr. Either way, she wasn't about to turn down permission to escape the cottage for a while. Perhaps she might even enjoy herself. She couldn't remember the last time she had done anything purely for pleasure.

"In that case, Grace, I would love to come," she said.

4

The Horse and Gate Alehouse, Fence
9th June 1632

Jennet blew a weary breath as she walked into the village. A stifling, sticky heat lingered in the late afternoon air, sapping her energy and exacerbating her tiredness. Despite the warm day she had walked quickly, and now the beads of sweat which had gathered around the edges of her white coif were beginning to run down her red face. She had left the Holgates' cottage much later than intended; just as she had opened the door to leave, James and Anna had woken and one glimpse of Alice's sullen face was all it had taken to make her shut the door again, take hold of one of the twins and fetch the milk required for the umpteenth time that day. Jennet sighed; it was amazing she had managed to leave at all. In the end, it had been Aunt Isabel who had urged her to go, reminding her of her promise to Grace, and assuring her that she would help Alice that evening. Jennet smiled. Contrary to what Alice said, it seemed that Aunt Isabel wasn't so useless after all.

Her pace slowed as she approached the alehouse. She glanced down at herself, a wave of hesitation coming over her as she remembered that this wasn't something she normally did. She didn't go out in the evening; she didn't attend feasts and gatherings like this. Even when her father was alive they seldom went to the alehouse together. Her father had taken the view that ale drunk by women was best consumed where it was brewed, in the home, and that for women the taking of ale in company should be both infrequent and in small quantity. As she walked through the door of the unfamiliar establishment which was to host Grace's celebrations that night, her father's words rang in her ears: "nothing good comes of a woman who spends too much time supping with men in the alehouse."

Jennet glanced swiftly around her, her eyes darting backwards and forwards, absorbing her surroundings and seeking familiar faces. The alehouse was busy, filled with animated chatter, and the occasional burst of raucous laughter. Jennet wondered if everyone there had come to celebrate Grace's birthday. It was possible, of course; in her mother's line of work she would know a great many people throughout the Forest of Pendle. Jennet pondered for a moment on what it must be like to be so popular, so well-liked by so many people. She shuddered then, remembering what it was that she was well-known for and why it was that she shrank back from her infamy, grateful for the shadows she could hide in, the other names she could call herself so that the collective memory of the forest folk was not recalled to her past.

"Jennet! You came!" Grace exclaimed as she ran towards her, greeting her with a friendly arm around her shoulder. Grace was just as warm-hearted as her mother, Jennet thought, as she reflected momentarily upon how she grew fonder of this young woman each time they met.

"Yes, I escaped eventually," she replied, half-joking. She looked around her again hesitantly. She felt so awkward, so uneasy in such social situations. By contrast, Grace was in her element; her pretty heart-shaped face was wearing the broadest of smiles, framed by her chestnut hair which she wore loosely around her ears in the fashionable style. Her green eyes were shining brightly, almost dancing to the music being played in her honour. Next to her, Jennet suddenly felt very plain in her white coif and brown bodice and petticoats.

Grace continued to chatter excitedly. "That's my father, John Lund, over there," she said, pointing briefly towards a short, stout-looking man with the same nut-brown hair as Grace. "I don't think you've met him, have you?"

Jennet caught Grace's father's eye and he gave her a small, friendly smile. "No, I haven't," she said with a small shake of her head. "Do you wish to introduce me to him?" she asked timidly.

Grace tossed her head dismissively and gave an exasperated sigh. "Oh, no. Honestly, he is such a bore. Come, there are much more interesting folk for you to meet. I love meeting new people, don't you?" she asked giddily. Jennet noticed the potent smell of ale on her breath; she had obviously begun her birthday celebrations some hours earlier.

Jennet followed reticently behind Grace as she was marched towards a plethora of smiling, happy faces. Unlike Grace, she didn't like meeting new people; she didn't like the awkward conversation and difficult questions which usually accompanied the experience. Forcing a smile upon her face, Jennet tried her best to make herself appear sociable, reminding herself that she was Grace's guest tonight and she didn't want to come across as surly or ungrateful.

"Jennet, this is Goodwife Dickenson. Goodwife, may I introduce my friend, Jennet Sellers? Jennet has recently moved to Barley to live with her relatives, the Holgates," Grace said.

"Nice to meet you, Jennet," replied Goodwife Dickenson kindly. She was a tall woman, well-dressed in fine petticoats of deep red. Her greying hair was styled fashionably, loose around the ears like Grace's, with small curls set around her long, slim face. When she smiled, the vague creases around her grey-blue eyes grew deeper; a lifetime of happiness was etched on the face of this evidently prosperous woman.

Goodwife Dickenson touched Jennet's hand gently. "So you're one of the Holgates of Barley?" she asked.

"Yes," Jennet nodded, "Christopher Holgate is my uncle." She hoped this nice lady would leave the questions about her family at that. "I have been living with them since my father passed away," she added, hoping that the mention of her bereavement might encourage the Goodwife to suspend her enquiry.

"My dear, I'm sorry for your loss. So your father was…Sellers?" Goodwife Dickenson asked, unperturbed.

"Yes," Jennet replied once more. "Richard Sellers. He…we farmed at White Moor."

"I see. And your mother?" Goodwife Dickenson continued.

"Dead," Jennet answered, trying to force her tone to sound neutral. "My mother has been dead a long time now." She looked Goodwife Dickenson straight in the eye now, trying to decipher if there was any flicker of recognition of who the woman standing in front of her was or, at least, who she had been. If Goodwife Dickenson had pieced together the family connections, however, she kept it well-concealed.

"Do you live in Fence, Goodwife Dickenson?" Jennet asked, swiftly changing the subject.

"No, we live on the heights, just above Higham. That's my husband John, and my son Nicholas," she added as she gesticulated across the room to where her husband and son were standing. "We have quite a large farm there."

"Goodwife Dickenson is so modest!" exclaimed Grace. "Do you know, Jennet, they sell butter to the Shuttleworths - the Shuttleworth family of Gawthorpe Hall! They do very well indeed. Well, I shall leave you two to get to know each other and Jennet, please, fetch yourself some ale. There is plenty to go around!" added Grace as she almost skipped away to another group of women who were giggling nearby.

Goodwife Dickenson took a considered sip of her ale. "So how do you know Grace?" she asked.

"The same way that I suspect everyone else knows Grace – her mother helped my cousin's wife when she was with child. Pregnancy made her very sick, unfortunately she didn't survive it," Jennet replied.

"Yes. I did hear a little about that. A dreadful business for that poor woman, and for you all, I'm sure. I know it upset Goodwife Lund; she hates losing a patient," she replied, "I hear your family sent for a physician to save the babies. That must have cost them dearly. They're fortunate one was nearby."

Jennet nodded. She had often wondered to herself how the Holgates had afforded such an expense, but she hadn't the nerve to ask. That was their business, after all.

"Grace is a good girl, helps her mother, as I'm sure you know," Goodwife Dickenson continued. "She's a little giddy, though. I don't know where she gets all that energy from but I daresay a husband and a few children would calm her down," she added with a wry smile.

"Oh?" Jennet asked, Goodwife Dickenson's comment piquing her interest. Grace had never mentioned any suitors.

"Well, I know of one who would make her his wife. My son, Nicholas, he's a couple of years younger than Grace, but he's told his father that he's sweet on her. I don't know," she said with a sigh, "they're both very young and have a lot to learn. But perhaps, in a few years…perhaps…"

Jennet was no longer sure if Goodwife Dickenson was talking to her, or to herself. She smiled in response, wondering if Grace returned this young man's affections, if she was even aware of them at all. She would have to try and find out, she thought. It would make a change, prying into someone else's life rather than worrying about others enquiring about her own.

"You will have to visit us in Higham," announced Goodwife Dickenson, touching her hand again, this time signalling the end of their conversation. "Come with Grace if you like, my son would be delighted. Any friend of the Lunds is a friend of ours." Jennet gave a little smile in response, wondering if she was being genuine or just polite. She still couldn't tell if this lady realised exactly which cousin of the Holgates' she was, or not.

Goodwife Dickenson caught the eye of another guest and wandered away. Jennet stood by herself again, surveying the room, looking for the faces she knew. She could see Grace mingling with her guests, a broad smile fixed on her face as she shared a joke or funny story with a couple of other young women of around her age. Jennet noticed that two other people watched Grace as intently as she did; her mother, whose expression was one of maternal concern for her bold and sociable daughter, and Nicholas, Goodwife Dickenson's son. Jennet noted the wistful expression on his face as he studied her; clearly his mother hadn't been exaggerating when she said he had fallen in love.

Nicholas, perhaps sensing someone watching him, turned his gaze away from Grace and, catching Jennet's eye for a moment, went a perfect shade of scarlet before looking down and studying the cup of ale in his hand. Jennet smiled slightly, finding his youthful embarrassment charming. She looked away, not wishing to torture him. She glanced around the room once again, seeking other familiar faces. She felt awkward now, standing by herself, and wished that Grace or her mother, in fact anyone in that room, might come over and make polite conversation with her.

As she stood there, pondering her social isolation and contemplating fetching herself a cup of ale with which to distract herself, a sense of being watched crept over her. Instinctively, she sought out the source of her uncomfortable feeling, her gaze settling on a man sitting across the room, surrounded by a large, raucous group of labourers. The man was around her age, perhaps a little younger, with dishevelled, wavy brown-blonde hair, like the colour of the rain-starved lanes in summer. His beard, fair like his hair, was fine enough to betray a strong jawline and defined cheekbones. He was dressed simply, his shirt loose around his neck, revealing a skin colour which could only be obtained through a lifetime spent working outdoors.

Noticing her returning his stare, the man did not look away but smiled boldly at her. Jennet felt the colour rising in her cheeks, unsure whether to look away modestly or continue to return this stranger's gaze. Her father's lecturing words about the pitfalls of alehouses were ringing in her ears once again. He was probably watching her right now, shaking his head and furrowing his brow in paternal disapproval.

Before she could decide what to do, the man got up and walked towards her. She stood there, frozen on the spot, her mind racing. This wasn't something she did either; she didn't talk to men she didn't know, and certainly not in the alehouse! Men, like so many other things in her life on White Moor, had always been a mystery to her. She had never been courted; no man had ever come to the cottage and asked for her hand in marriage. Her father had never encouraged her to seek a husband; instead, he had protected her, providing for her long after the time when a young woman would normally leave home and marry. Now, this man was coming to talk to her and she had no idea what to say to him. Her cheeks felt so hot that she was certain they must have looked crimson against the rest of her pallid complexion.

"William Braithwaite," said the man as he stepped forward and offered her his hand. Jennet immediately noticed his accent, which differed from the familiar Pendle tongue.

"Jennet Sellers," she replied, taking his hand briefly.

"I presume you're one of the birthday girl's guests?"

"Aren't we all?" Jennet replied with a shy smile.

"Aye, that we are," said William with a small sigh. "Can I fetch you a cup of ale?"

Jennet nodded. As he walked away, she glanced momentarily out of the small window. It was dusk outside now, the sun a blur of red and grey in the sky, and she realised she must have stood by herself for some time.

William returned with some ale and handed it to her. "So how do you know Grace?" she asked, feeling quietly pleased with herself for taking the initiative in the conversation.

"I don't really. I came with the Dickensons. I work for them. Well, at least some of the time, anyway. What about you?" he asked.

Jennet took a considered sip of her drink. "I met Grace through her mother. She attended my cousin's wife when she was with child." She decided not to mention Ellena's terrible demise or the fact that she was now caring for the woman's babies. This was a light conversation between strangers, after all.

"I see. So you live with your cousin?" William asked.

Jennet nodded. "Yes, in Barley. The Holgate family, if you know them? George Holgate is my cousin."

William shook his head. "I don't know many folk from around these parts, I'm afraid."

Jennet smiled. "Yes, I did notice your accent. Where are you from?" she asked, taking the opportunity to satisfy her curiosity.

"Whitehaven, in Cumberland," he replied.

Jennet shook her head slightly. She had never heard of the place, but then, she had heard of few places, except those immediately in and surrounding Pendle. Further afield, the only places she knew were the important ones: Lancaster, York, London. She knew Cumberland was further north, which explained this man's strange accent, but that was all she knew. She wondered then where Whitehaven was exactly, what it was like, what the people were like. She didn't normally give much thought to anything beyond the Forest of Pendle, and doing so now made the world feel suddenly large and strange.

"My family has always lived near Whitehaven, though it is much changed now," William continued. "It used to be little more than a village, owned by the priory at St Bees. Then King Henry got rid of the monks and the abbots and...well, things have changed, haven't they? Now the village is growing and is fast becoming a busy port. Master Lowther, he's the landowner, he's got plans to build a stone pier and export goods to Ireland." He glanced at Jennet's bemused face. "Sorry, I'm going on a bit, aren't I? I tend to find that once I start talking about home, I can't stop," he added with a grin.

Jennet smiled back. "It's alright, you obviously miss it. Why did you leave?"

William sighed. "I wonder that myself sometimes. I plan to go to London, but it is a long way and a great expense so I stop wherever I can find work along the way."

"What will you do in London?" asked Jennet. Her tone was incredulous, she realised, but she couldn't help it; she felt suddenly fascinated by this man, his ambition and sense of adventure.

"I hope to find work in the Law. Find a lawyer willing to take me on as his clerk, perhaps. Who knows what will happen; London is such a big place, full of possibility."

"The Law?" Jennet asked, that incredulous tone persisting. "Can you read?

"Yes," replied William. "I was fortunate to be apprenticed to a stonemason who educated my mind as well as my hands. Before I left Whitehaven I worked for Master Lowther, and it was he who gave me the idea of the Law. He was admitted to the Inner Temple, that's one of the Inns of Court where you study to be a lawyer. He told me so many stories about his time there, in London. He's a clever man," he added.

Jennet nodded. It was clear that William thought a lot of this Master Lowther; that this man had, inadvertently or otherwise, acted as a sort of mentor to him. Jennet tried to avoid the masters of this world. She had learnt early in life, and to her dear cost, that coming to the attention of a master, or worse, being useful to a master, usually didn't end well for ordinary folk. She shuddered, unwillingly recalling those dreadful memories of her childhood once again.

"You're very easy to talk to, you know," William complimented her, "but I think it's me who's doing all the talking. Tell me more about yourself, Jennet. You mentioned you live with your cousin?"

Jennet took a deep breath. Her story wasn't nearly as interesting as William's story, or at least, the parts she was willing to tell weren't that interesting. She told him the usual tale, the one she told everyone who asked; the one which contained enough detail not to seem enigmatic but which avoided the revelation of who she really was, which little girl she had been. William expressed sympathy for her losses and showed interest in even the most mundane details of her days spent with Alice and the babies in the Holgates' cramped cottage. They talked for hours, William sharing stories from his life in Whitehaven and Jennet reciprocating, as far as she was willing to do, with anecdotes from her quiet life on White Moor and the busy household she now lived in. In the end, when there was only them and a handful of others left in the alehouse, it was Grace who interrupted their conversation, inviting Jennet to stay at her parents' cottage for the night.

"Do you go to church, Jennet?" asked William, as he too got up to leave.

"Yes, sometimes," replied Jennet. "Why do you ask?"

"I was curious, that's all," said William, with a small, mysterious smile. "A conversation for another time, I think," he added, taking her hand and kissing it gently. Jennet blushed at the gesture. She could see Grace's face out of the corner of her eye, open-mouthed, eyes wide with incredulity. "I hope I do see you again," he said finally, looking back up at her.

"So do I," said Jennet, trying her best not to sound flustered. "It was a pleasure to meet you, William."

Jennet spent the walk back to Wheatley Lane deep in thought. Grace, who initially tried to ask her a hundred questions about the handsome man who had occupied so much of her evening, was met with a wall of silence and eventually gave up. Jennet felt dizzy, perhaps because of the ale – she had lost count of how many cups William had brought her – but also because her mind was racing over the details of her evening with him.

In so many ways, William was just an ordinary man. His experiences had been like that of so many other men; apprenticed as a boy, trained as a mason and now scraping together whatever living he could manage. Yet at the same time, he was so unlike other men; he was learned, ambitious, adventurous, amusing. He had met people like Master Lowther, folk who had seen a bit of the world and had taken the time to share it with him. Seeing the world through their eyes had spurred him on to want to see more of it himself. Jennet shuddered, remembering her own encounters with a man of learning, remembering how in awe of him she had felt.

Jennet suppressed these thoughts, turning her mind back to William. He was undoubtedly very handsome; his eyes a lovely shade of green, his smile broad and open. A chill ran down her spine as she remembered how he kissed her hand so deliciously at the end of the evening. She touched her hand now, as though to hold the kiss upon it, to not let it go. He wanted to see her again, she thought with a smile. And she wanted more than anything to see him again.

As she approached Grace's cottage, however, her smile faded. As much as she had enjoyed his company and conversation, she had spent the entire evening omitting details of her life, editing her stories to present herself in a certain way. She couldn't let William know her better; for him to know her well would be for him to discover all the details of her life, her past, the awful things she did. That was the real Jennet Sellers, not the bland, fictional account she had provided this evening. She spent her adult life hiding from who she was, and that was why she could never get close to this man, or indeed any man. That was why she could never fall in love, she realised, because surely no man would love her if he knew the truth.

5

Under Pendle Farm, Barley
August 1632

"Hurry up, Alice! I can see Grace coming up the lane," Jennet called to her cousin.

Alice marched briskly back into the room, where Jennet was hovering impatiently by the front door. "There," she declared, clasping her hands together, "both babies are sleeping. Hopefully they will afford us some peace for an hour or two. I think they're becoming easier, don't you? They eat and sleep so well these days."

"Hmm," replied Jennet, distracted. In truth she wasn't really listening to Alice. She gazed watchfully from the window, surveying Grace as she sauntered up the lane. Jennet was pleased to see that her friend was particularly well-dressed this afternoon. Although she wore a plain bodice and petticoats, she had removed her apron and coif and had arranged her hair tidily. She wondered now if Grace has sensed the ulterior motive in her invitation to visit, and had turned herself out accordingly.

"Is her mother not with her?" Alice asked.

"No," replied Jennet. "Goodwife Lund has too many visits to pay."

"Apart from Grace then, who else is coming to visit today?"

Alice asked, hurriedly sweeping the floor in her usual house-proud manner. She could never bear to have visitors if the cottage was anything less than spotless, or at least, as clean as could be managed when their home was attached to a farm and all its associated dirt.

Jennet sighed. "I told you earlier. Goodwife Dickenson and her son are also coming to pay a visit."

Alice cast a critical eye over the cottage. "Well, I don't think this place is up to a sufficient standard for receiving the farmer's wife from Higham. They're grander folk than us, Jennet. You should have given me more time to prepare."

"Oh, Alice!" Jennet protested. "Goodwife Dickenson is only the same as us. Their farm is much larger than ours, that is true, but the Dickensons are just ordinary folk."

"A large, successful farm like theirs means all the difference, Jennet. They've a lot better income than us; you must see that, you've visited them in Higham before."

"It's true, Jennet," Aunt Isabel interjected from her sleepy position in the corner of the room. "The Dickensons are a wealthy family these days."

Jennet nodded. It was true, the Dickensons' cottage was at least twice the size of the Holgates' home and although it was simply furnished, it was far more comfortable. She was about to concede that there was some truth in Alice's and her aunt's words, when there was a brisk knock at the door.

Alice shot Jennet a withering look. "I don't know what you're up to Jennet. Whatever it is, I hope you know what you're doing."

Jennet smiled innocently. "I'm just having some friends round to visit. I thought it better to invite them here for a little while, as one of us will need to help with the harvest later." This was true; despite the delayed spring planting, the Holgates' harvest had been plentiful and there was a lot of work to do on the farm, so much in fact that even elderly Uncle Christopher had been drafted in to help with the lighter duties. "Anyway, that'll be Grace," she added.

Grace burst in with her usual flurry of enthusiastic greetings and chatter. "Oh goodness, it is hot today! I think my cheeks must be far too rosy," she said, looking searchingly at Jennet. "Are they too rosy?"

"You look just fine," Jennet chuckled. "Please, have a seat. Can I fetch you something to drink?"

Grace nodded and sat down, but continued to fidget restlessly. "Is there anyone else coming to call today?" she asked.

"Oh yes. Goodwife Dickenson, and she's bringing her son, I think," replied Jennet casually. She glanced at Grace, looking for her reaction.

Grace smiled. "Oh how lovely! I do like Goodwife Dickenson," she said.

"And her son?" Jennet asked. Out of the corner of her eye she noticed Alice shoot her a warning glance.

"Yes, yes of course," replied Grace. Jennet noticed the hesitation in her voice. "I've known Nicholas since we were children. So, it's just the Dickensons coming to visit?" she repeated.

"Yes," Jennet replied, "just the Dickensons."

There was an awkward pause as they all waited to the arrival of the final two guests. Jennet spent those silent moments trying to avoid Alice's stare. She knew Alice realised what she was doing now, and she knew that she disapproved. Jennet's best judgement told her that she shouldn't meddle; however, she just couldn't help herself. After Grace's birthday celebrations a couple of months earlier, when she had seen the way young Nicholas Dickenson looked at Grace, she hadn't been able to resist interfering. She had tried for some weeks to engineer situations where they would both meet, so that they might spend time together and develop a mutual affection.

So far, however, Grace had been a difficult person to manipulate. She had taken Grace with her every time she had visited the Dickensons' farm, but either Nicholas had been out working with his father or, when he was in the cottage, Grace had done everything in her power to avoid talking to him. Jennet frowned. She couldn't understand it; Grace always seemed keen to see the Dickensons but she seemed hopelessly unable, perhaps even unwilling, to show any interest in their son. Despite this, Jennet persevered, certain of her conviction that Nicholas would make a loving and devoted husband for Grace. If only the flighty, giddy girl would see it.

There was a knock at the door, interrupting Jennet's thoughts. "Oh good, that'll be the Dickensons now," she said. Hopefully today Grace won't avoid Nicholas so easily, she thought.

Goodwife Dickenson was, as usual, immaculately dressed, her clothes simple but elegant, completely befitting a farmer's wife of means. Nicholas stood shyly by her side. Jennet noted that he wore his smartest, cleanest shirt and that he had tidied his hair somewhat. He was a handsome young man; very tall, with a good head of dark brown hair and hazel eyes. He was a little skinny, Jennet noted, but then he was barely a man. Obviously conscious of his great height, Nicholas hunched his shoulders awkwardly as Jennet beckoned him and his mother inside.

"Oh, Grace. It's nice to see you. I didn't know you would be visiting as well today," said Goodwife Dickenson, feigning surprise. She gave Jennet a slight, knowing smile. Jennet replied with a small, obliging nod. At least the two of them could see what a good match they would make.

Alice returned with some ale and sat down to join them. Jennet noticed now how nervous and uncomfortable her cousin looked; she really had meant her words about the Dickensons then. Goodwife Dickenson seemed to notice too, and gave Alice a warm, broad smile as she took a cup from her.

"So, how are the babies, Alice? Jennet tells me that they are both getting big now," she said.

Alice nodded and took a sip of her ale. "Yes, Goodwife Dickenson, they're growing to be very strong. They take less milk and more food now. I shouldn't think it'll be too many months before they're starting to crawl."

"Oh!" exclaimed the Goodwife. "You really will have your

hands full then, once they're on the move."

"I think we will manage just fine," replied Alice, a defensive note to her voice. "They sleep well now. We can manage anything if we have had some sleep, can't we, Jennet?" she added with a slight chuckle.

Jennet nodded and smiled in response. She glanced casually at Grace and Nicholas. Both were sitting silently, Nicholas shuffling in his seat and fiddling awkwardly with the sleeve of his shirt. Grace meanwhile sat perfectly still, staring straight ahead, an impassive look painted on her pretty face.

"Alice makes it all sound such hard work, but looking after the babies is really not so bad," Jennet said, attempting to break the silence between the pair and draw them into a conversation.

Grace let a small, deflated sound escape from her lips. "It all sounds dull to me," she said. "I don't think I will have any babies. In fact, I'm not even sure I wish to marry. It all sounds so boring," she added, looking pointedly at Nicholas. It was the first time she had even acknowledged his presence in the room, and it was certainly not the recognition he wanted. Jennet saw Nicholas's face fall, his eyes cast down, and she felt instantly sorry for him. She felt annoyed with Grace then, for surely she had noticed now how this young man looked at her, yet she had so bluntly spurned his feelings with her harsh words.

"Tell us then, Grace. If not marriage and children, what will you do with yourself?" Jennet asked, smiling in an effort to mask her irritation.

"I want excitement and adventure in my life," Grace replied, the sweetness returning to her voice now. "You know, Jennet, you make it sound like there are no other choices but marriage and childbearing, yet you have done neither yourself," she added.

Jennet's face reddened. She didn't like to have a conversation turned on her, especially when it came to the subjects of marriage or her past. The less said about both, the better. "My reasons are very different from yours, Grace," she said, trying to maintain a light tone. "Anyway, I'm too old for all that now, whereas you're young, younger than me. Don't dismiss marriage so quickly, you never know who you will fall in love with," she added, trying to give Nicholas an encouraging smile. Nicholas, however, continued to stare at the floor, crest-fallen.

Mercifully, the conversation was interrupted by a loud knock at the door. Jennet frowned. "I wasn't expecting anyone else this afternoon," she said to her guests. "I wonder who that could be."

She stood up quickly, rushing to satisfy her curiosity. She opened the door and her mouth fell open, her face immediately betraying her surprise. Standing there, filthy from a day's labour, his face and hair covered in dirt from the fields, was William Braithwaite. Jennet forced herself to catch her breath. She hadn't seen him since the night of Grace's birthday, the night when they had talked for hours, when he had enthralled her with his tales of times past and adventures yet to happen. Instinctively she touched her hand, remembering again how he had kissed it and told her he'd like to see her again. She had managed to avoid him ever since, but now, inexplicably, he was here.

"Jennet Sellers," he said after a moment's silence. "It's nice to see you again." He held her gaze for a few moments, long enough for Jennet's mind to run away again with thoughts of how lovely his eyes were, how much she liked his smile. She cleared her throat, regaining composure.

"Good morrow, William," she answered politely. "Sorry, I wasn't expecting you today." She bit her lip. What a foolish thing to say, of course he knew his visit was unannounced. "Are you here to see me?"

"Well, actually no, though it is lovely to see you," he said with an endearing grin. "I was looking for your cousin, George. I heard that you could do with some extra help with your harvest, and I came to offer my services."

"Oh," replied Jennet. She realised she sounded disappointed and immediately chastised herself. "Well, George is still out working on the farm, but if you go into the fields you should find him. I'm sure he will be glad of the help, although I can't promise he will be able to pay you much for your labour."

A loud burst of laughter erupted from within the cottage. William looked at Jennet quizzically. "I'm sorry, I didn't realise you had company," he said.

"Oh, don't worry it's only my friend Grace Lund, do you remember, the girl who was celebrating her birthday when we first met? And Goodwife Dickenson and her son Nicholas; they're here too. Just for a little while longer; Alice needs to get back in the fields soon and I will have both babies to feed when they wake from their nap."

"Goodwife Dickenson is here?" William repeated. Without any warning, he grabbed hold of Jennet's arm and pulled her towards him. He leaned over her shoulder and shut the door behind her; he was so close that Jennet could feel his breath on her neck, sending shivers down her spine. "Sorry about that, Jennet. I don't want her to see me. She wouldn't be pleased to see me here, looking for more work."

"You don't work exclusively for her, do you?" Jennet asked. "Why should she mind?"

"A good question," William replied. "Perhaps because taking work elsewhere makes me less available. She likes her labourers to be at her beck and call, especially me, since I have lodgings on her farm as well."

"Oh," replied Jennet dumbly. She found it hard to imagine Goodwife Dickenson as a tough employer, but then, the Dickensons could not have been so successful without driving a hard bargain.

"Anyway, I had better go and find your cousin and let you get back to your guests," William said, with a polite bow. Jennet appreciated the gesture; no man had ever bowed to her before. After all, there was no reason why any man should; she wasn't anyone's mistress, or even a farmer's wife like Goodwife Dickenson. In fact, she wasn't anybody at all, yet William treated her with such gentlemanly respect.

"Yes," she replied, giving him a broad smile. "Well good luck, I hope George offers you something."

"As do I. Work has been slow of late. Sometimes I've barely had much more than the Dickensons have given me. I'm hoping the harvest will change my fortunes. If I can't make a little extra at this time of year, then there is no hope of me ever reaching London," he said.

"Yes. Well, if anyone needs the help, it's George. He's got my uncle out in the fields right now, and he's an old man. Alice and I do what we can, between caring for the cottage and the babies."

"And entertaining guests," William added with a cheeky grin.

"Well…yes," Jennet stammered in response. She couldn't possibly tell William that the gathering of friends had a purpose; that she was trying to bring about happiness between two people, but that so far it had all been a hopeless failure. She felt a pang of guilt then, realising her time would have been much better spent in the fields, helping George.

"Sorry Jennet, I shouldn't tease you. I've wiped the smile from your face now, which is a pity, because it is such a lovely smile," William said, taking hold of her hand and kissing it gently. Jennet wondered if this was his parting ritual with all women, or something just between the two of them. She watched him walk away, her stomach fluttering as she realised how much she hoped that his kisses were reserved only for her.

"If I'm lucky," he said, turning back to look at her, "George will give me a few weeks' work and I'll get to see a lot more of that smile. I bid you good day, Jennet Sellers."

Jennet watched William as he walked down the lane and cut into the Holgates' fields. Once he was out of sight, she leaned her head against the weather-beaten wood of the cottage door and let out a deep breath. Today was only the second time they had met and yet…she screwed up her face, struggling to make sense of her own thoughts. This was ridiculous, she told herself, she couldn't possibly fall in love with this man, with anyone. As she had told Grace only today, she was too old for marriage. Too old, and too flawed; she was a terrible person who had done some terrible things.

Yet all this man had to do was smile and pay her compliments and in an instant she had forgotten who she was and, released from her real identity, she had begun to dream of happiness. She banged her head against the door slightly; she had to remember why she lived the way she did, why she stayed in the shadows, why she hid herself away, just like her father had hidden her and protected her for years. She didn't want anyone to really know her, to remember who she was. Above all, she didn't want to be happy, because that happiness would be another source of guilt that she would have to bear. Merely living and breathing made her feel guilty enough.

"Who was at the door?" asked Grace as soon as Jennet walked back inside.

"Just a man looking for work," she replied.

6

Under Pendle Farm, Barley
Late August 1632

"What are you looking at now?" Alice demanded to know.

Jennet spun around to see her cousin stood behind her, hands on hips, the babies both laid out on blankets on the floor in front of her. Jennet watched as little James shuffled from side to side, determined to roll over. The twins were growing up quickly; soon they would be crawling, then walking and talking. They also seemed to get bigger by the day, with chubby limbs and plump little bodies; they weighed so much that Jennet was finding it hard work to hold them now. Alice liked to hold them up like prized calves and announce that they were thriving, growing up big and strong, and that the worst weeks were behind them now. She seemed determined to hasten their development and had spent the last hour sitting behind them both in turn, holding them upright and encouraging them to sit up. James had shown some promise but Anna, who was less agile than her brother, had flopped about helplessly until she began to cry.

"I don't suppose you can rush these things," Alice had said in the end.

Jennet continued to watch James as he used his feet to turn

himself in a circle on the floor. Alice was right; he was a strong little thing, more placid in temperament than his sister but undoubtedly more determined. She wondered for a moment what sort of a man he would grow into, whether he would always have such strong characteristics or whether life's hardships would grind those traits out of him. Perhaps he would forget his childhood determination and change altogether; after all, Jennet reflected, she remembered little of her own childhood. Except the terrible parts, she thought with a shudder.

"Well?" Alice insisted. "What were you looking at?"

"Oh," replied Jennet, shaking her head slightly. "Nothing really. I was just thinking it is a very hot day. The men are working so hard in the fields, perhaps I should fetch them something to drink."

"I'm sure you'll see plenty of that William Braithwaite this evening. No need to go out of your way to see him," Alice snapped.

Jennet's cheeks reddened. It was true; William had come to the cottage almost every night for the past three weeks. It had started with an invite from George who, to show appreciation for his hard work and perhaps to compensate for paying him a meagre wage, had asked him to join the family for their evening meal. After supper, instead of accompanying George to the alehouse, William had stayed at the cottage, talking to Jennet while she performed her evening duties. The following night he returned and did the same again, and again, until he spent every evening at the Holgates' cottage. Alice had been tight-lipped about his presence, and Jennet had heard her muttering to herself on more than one occasion about certain men getting under their feet. Jennet had chuckled to herself at the irony; Alice complained frequently about George spending his evenings in the alehouse, yet she seemed to find a man doing the exact opposite equally, if not more, annoying. Why would he want to spend the evening watching us scrub pots or settle babies into their beds, Alice had demanded to know. On this Jennet had remained silent. She didn't want Alice to ask for her thoughts on the matter, because any sharing of thoughts might turn into a discussion about hopes and she did not wish to express those. She didn't want Alice to pry into her feelings, not when she could hardly make sense of them herself.

"'Tis so hot," she said quietly, half to herself. "I think I will take something out for them."

"Suit yourself," Alice huffed.

The air outside was so stifling that it made Jennet gasp. The lane was dry, dusty and sun-scorched; she could feel the heat through the thinning soles of her shoes. She tried to recall the last time it had been so hot at harvest-time in Pendle. This was an area renowned for wild winds and consistent rainfall, but the constant presence of warm sunshine was a relative rarity. As she wandered across the field to where the men were working, she reflected on the remark George had made last night concerning the weather. It was fortunate, he had said, that the intense heat had arrived only now. Any earlier, and they may have faced a ruined harvest. Despite the heat, a shiver ran up Jennet's spine at the thought of a difficult, hungry winter. She had known many in her lifetime, and always dreaded the mere prospect of it. Thanks to God for rain in July, and the safe delivery of a good harvest, she thought.

"A drink for you," she said to George as she held out the cup. George drank thirstily, draining his cup in just a few mouthfuls before handing it back.

"You're an angel sent from heaven, surely," said William as he leant on his scythe to rest. He took a cup from her and gave her a small wink. Jennet beamed.

"We're getting there, aren't we George?" he said. "'Tis hard in this heat, but we're getting there."

George mumbled in agreement and continued working. William smiled again at Jennet. "Well, best get back to it, or else the master will be cracking his whip," he said jovially, nodding in George's direction. "I'll see you in the cottage for supper, won't I?"

Jennet nodded in response, allowing her gaze to linger on him for a few moments before turning away. In the heat his thin shirt had begun to cling to the sweat on his body, and Jennet could see the contours of his strong arms, firm chest and lean stomach. His dust-coloured hair had been lightened by the sun, whilst his face had darkened in colour, a delightful red-brown which seemed to illuminate his green eyes. As she turned away she closed her eyes for a moment, committing that image of him to a drawer in a corner of her mind that she could open whenever she pleased. She shook her head then, resisting her thoughts, trying to dismiss the pleasure she felt in merely looking upon him. Sinful, lustful thoughts, she realised. How disgusted her father would be.

"See you this evening," she said over her shoulder, trying her best to sound casual, matter-of-fact. She walked hurriedly back to the house, trying to convince herself that her burning scarlet cheeks were attributable merely to the hot weather, and not a reaction to the heat which rose in her belly whenever she looked at William Braithwaite. The intense mixture of attraction and guilt, she realised, was almost too much to bear.

It was dusk before the men came home from the fields that evening, the sky awash with hues of red and yellow as the sun sunk sleepily into the horizon. Jennet had lost count of how many times she had looked out of the small cottage window to see if she could see them coming up the lane, or how many times that disapproving grunt had passed from Alice's lips each time she glanced at the pot of cold pottage which she had left on the table. The rest of the family had eaten supper at the usual time and the babies, who tended to tire quickly after dinner now, had been sleeping soundly for some time. Aunt Isabel and Uncle Christopher were also both snoring softly, unable to resist the lure of slumber brought on by the darkening skies. Alice looked up from the shirt she was mending and frowned as George burst in, William following closely behind.

"Shh! You'll wake the babies," she whispered crossly.

William smiled apologetically but George, ignoring his sister's instruction, headed straight for the pot on the table. "Is this supper?" he asked.

"Yes," replied Alice. "It's cold but it'll have to do. Why are you so late?"

"The heat slowed us down today," said George as he shovelled food into his mouth. "Once the evening came it grew cooler so we decided to carry on while it was a bit more bearable."

"George decided. I did as I was told," added William cheekily, taking the pot from George. Jennet observed how he ate with less urgency, his mouthfuls more considered and delicately taken. Noticing her watching him, William gave her a broad smile. "Want some?" he asked.

"Oh…no, thank you. We've already eaten," she stammered.

"Well," George declared, clapping his hands together, "it may be late but I daresay the alehouse doors are still open. You joining me?" he asked William in a tone which suggested he already knew the answer.

William shook his head. "No, I'd better get some rest. I'm working for the Dickensons tomorrow."

"You're not coming to help George?" Jennet asked. She sounded disappointed, she realised, but she couldn't help it. Out of the corner of her eye she saw Alice give her an inquisitive glance.

William shook his head. "No, Goodwife Dickenson says I'm needed on the farm. That's the other reason I stayed out so late to help George tonight. I won't be back for a couple of days, and by then we should be almost finished."

"Thank Christ!" declared George.

"George! Don't take the Lord's name in vain," instructed Alice.

George looked at his sister as though he was about to retort, but perhaps observing the serious frown etched upon her face, thought better of it. "I'm off to the alehouse," he said.

Alice winced as George slammed the door behind him. "Well, I'm going to bed," she said. She looked from William, to Jennet, and back again. "What will you do, William?" she asked. "Surely it's too dark to walk back to Higham now?"

William shrugged. "I suppose it is," he said, glancing out of the window. The sun had fallen below the horizon now, the remaining daylight little more than a dim red glow. "Perhaps I can get a room in the alehouse. Maybe I will go after George, have some ale with him and ask about lodgings," he offered.

Alice sighed and threw a blanket in William's direction. "You can stay here tonight. You'll have to make do with the floor though."

"Thank you," replied William gratefully. "I promise I will leave at first light. You'll hardly know I was here."

Although the light was dim in the cottage now, with just a solitary tallow candle burning in the corner of the room, Jennet could see that her cousin's face was stern. "Yes, well, just don't keep her up all night talking," Alice said, gesticulating half-heartedly in Jennet's direction. "I don't want your voices waking the babies."

"Of course."

"Right then, well good night, both of you," said Alice. Jennet could sense the hesitation as she walked away, as though she wasn't quite sure if it was proper to leave William and Jennet alone in a dark corner of the cottage.

William chuckled quietly as soon as Alice was out of earshot. "She's like your mother," he whispered.

"I know," replied Jennet, "but she means well."

"Come," said William, taking Jennet's hand. His touch made her arm tingle and her heart beat faster. "Let's go outside for a while."

Outside the night was still and clear, the sky black and filled with stars. Still holding her hand, William led Jennet over to the grass at the edge of the lane. As she sat down, Jennet noticed how, even after sunset, the ground still felt warm to the touch. The air also felt humid, the lack of breeze making it a little stifling. She would find it difficult to sleep tonight, she realised.

"I love nights like this," remarked William, breathing in deeply and looking up at the stars.

"Yes," Jennet agreed. "It's beautiful. We get so few nights like this here. Usually it is the wind and the rain that we have to contend with. It's nice to be able to sit here, enjoy the calm and gaze up at the heavens."

"The heavens," repeated William. "Is that what you see up there, Jennet? Is it heaven we are looking at?"

Jennet shrugged. It was only a remark, not an invitation to begin a theological debate. She turned away slightly; she really didn't want to have this sort of discussion. She was a Christian, of course; she believed in God, Jesus Christ, the Holy Ghost, and the rest, just as it had been told to her. She had listened to the priest's sermons in church, she believed the Bible was the word of God, and yet she felt so disconnected from it all. It was as though she knew God was there, that He created all things, and that was fine, but when it came to His presence in her life, in her affairs, He was always notably absent. If she was honest with herself, she knew that she felt God had deserted her, perhaps because of who she was and what she had done. Of course, she didn't wish to discuss any of this with William.

"I don't know," she said in the end.

"Do you doubt God, Jennet?" William asked. Clearly this was a conversation he wanted to have.

"No."

"Then, what?"

"I don't know. I don't give these sorts of things much thought."

"These things?" William repeated. His voice was tinged with a note of incredulity. "The matter of your mere existence, the fate of your immortal soul, and you don't give it much thought?"

Jennet shook her head. "I've always thought that these matters weren't for folk like me, they're for men in robes standing in pulpits to consider. Then they tell the likes of me about the word of God and I, well…"

"Nod off?"

"Yes, sometimes," she replied with a timid chuckle, trying to lighten the mood. "Sorry William. What about you, you seem to think a lot on these matters?"

"God's word is for everyone, Jennet," William replied, ignoring her question. "It's not just for men in robes to stand in pulpits and preach about. It's for everyone to know and understand."

"But I can't read," she protested. "How would I ever study the Bible?"

William sighed. "You don't have to be able to read, Jennet. You don't need churches or the sermons of ordained priests either. It's hard to explain. God's spirit alone can teach you, it can nourish and enrich you. There is so much more to understand about God than the Bible alone. By being a good and holy person, you can invite God's spirit into your life. Some say that if you achieve this, if you live without sin and in the light of God's spirit, it may even be possible to achieve heaven, right here on earth. Instead of up there," he added, gesticulating towards the starry sky.

"Is this what Master Lowther taught you?" Jennet asked. She was still wary of masters and their lessons. She recalled with a brief shudder how a master she once knew had liked to lecture her on religion, on faith. Perhaps that was another reason she felt so distant from it all now.

"Master Lowther? No," replied William, shaking his head. "It's true that he taught me many things, but my faith wasn't one of them. Before I came here, I stayed for a while in a village called Grindleton. Do you know it?"

Jennet nodded. "Yes, although I've never had cause to go there."

"When I was in Grindleton, I heard about these ideas for the first time. I was curious, so I went to Grindleton chapel. The curate there, a man called John Webster, gave a sermon like nothing I had ever heard before. This idea, this notion that any man, or indeed any woman, can know God and achieve an earthly paradise without churches, without priests, without bishops...is it not liberating?"

"I thought you said we didn't need sermons," Jennet replied.

William laughed lightly. "You're missing the point, Jennet. The point is that any one of us can preach God's word; all we have to do is live without sin and let God's spirit in to our lives. It's that simple."

"I think the priest here may say that it's blasphemy," replied Jennet quietly.

"He would certainly say that it was radical, that it didn't conform to the teachings of the Church. The Church doesn't like these ideas, and men who preach them often end up in a lot of trouble, which is why I keep them mostly to myself. But you…I trust you, and besides, I think you need to hear it."

"Why?"

William looked squarely at her and sighed. "I can never put my finger on exactly what it is about you, Jennet. It's as though…it's…you always look so… lost. See, I can't even find the right words, can I? Perhaps, one Sunday, I will take you to Grindleton and you can make up your own mind. Would you like that?"

Jennet gave William a thin smile. She could think of better ways to spend a Sunday; even a day spent with babies, Alice's endless instructions and George's silent melancholy appealed more than church. On the other hand, she thought, this John Webster might give more illuminating sermons than those she was usually subjected to, and of course, it would be a Sunday spent with William. She had to admit to herself that his apparent religious fervour hadn't made him any less appealing to her. If anything, it made him even more interesting; he really was unlike anyone else she had ever met.

Jennet turned away slightly. She had to stop feeling such an attraction for this man; it wasn't good for either of them, she told herself, it wouldn't end well. At the same time, she couldn't bring herself to disappoint him by declining his invitation to an outing which might never happen anyway. After all, the harvest would be over soon, William would go back to Higham until he left for the south, and she probably wouldn't see him again. Yes, she thought, the trip to Grindleton would probably never happen, therefore an empty promise couldn't possibly hurt anyone.

"I would like that very much," she replied.

7

Barley Village
September 1632

Jennet sighed and lifted Anna up higher on to her shoulder. The little girl wriggled, babbling angrily. She was just over six months old now and, although she couldn't form words yet, she was more than capable of expressing herself. Her movement still was not as good as her brother's but her strong will, supported by a pair of lungs capable of the loudest bellows, more than made up for this. Yes, Jennet thought, it was very apparent that this child had developed a mind of her own. It was a warm day in early September, the unusually long, hot summer having more than compensated for the extraordinary length of the previous winter, and the heat was obviously aggravating the child. She would have to take her home soon, she realised, which was a shame because the village festivities had only just started.

Jennet rocked Anna gently as she surveyed the scene around her. Everywhere she looked there were village folk bringing food and ale from their cottages to offer their neighbours, exchanging kind words with one another. Some were dancing together to the music which filled the air, kicking up the dust on the ground which hadn't seen rain for over a week. This was her first harvest festival since coming to live in Barley, and Jennet had to admit that it was quite the spectacle, the village now abuzz with the laughter of merry locals celebrating their hard work and success with one another. The jovial mood was catching, it seemed, and Jennet found that her spirits had lifted considerably, so much so that she didn't really want to leave just yet.

"Let me take her," said Alice, marching over and taking a sleepy-looking Anna into her arms.

"I was just about to take her back to the cottage," replied Jennet feebly.

"I'll take her home. James has already gone for a sleep so I'll look after them both," Alice insisted.

"Are you sure?"

Alice nodded. "Yes. Really, I don't mind. I've never been very keen on these festivals anyway. It's just an excuse to eat and drink too much, if you ask me. I'd be happier at home. I'll have Mother for company; she doesn't much like feast days either."

"Alright Alice, if you're sure."

"I'm sure. You can't miss your first harvest festival, Jennet. Stay, enjoy yourself. My father and George will be here, so you'll not want for company."

"Thank you, Alice."

Jennet found Uncle Christopher and George sitting amongst a group of other men, most of whom she recognised from the local farms. Showing them all a shy smile, Jennet sat down next to her uncle, who was nursing a small cup of ale, eyes closed, his face turned towards the sun. George gave her a brief nod of acknowledgement before continuing his conversation. The men were embroiled in a debate about the approaching end of the accounting year, when the profits from the harvest would be realised and the rents, inevitably, would have to be paid. It was a typical farming discussion; the sort of discussion into which she wouldn't be invited. Jennet took a cup of ale and sipped it slowly.

"Is that young lass you go about with not joining you today?" asked Uncle Christopher.

"Who? Grace Lund? No," replied Jennet, shaking her head. She didn't want to tell Uncle Christopher that she had barely seen Grace in the last few weeks, since she had tried, and failed, to bring her and Nicholas Dickenson together. When she had seen Grace, the young woman had been distant and a little cold, not at all like her usual spirited and cheerful self. Jennet guessed that Grace had taken umbrage at her meddling and that this accounted for her change in behaviour.

Alarmed and a little upset, Jennet had confided in Alice, who advised her to leave Grace alone for a while, to see if she would come around of her own accord. If not, then Jennet would have to accept that the friendship was lost through her own foolishness, Alice had added. Despite the glorious sunshine, Jennet felt suddenly cold and she struggled to suppress a shudder at the memory of Alice's brutal honesty.

"Oh well, not to worry," said Uncle Christopher, his eyes still firmly shut. "I daresay there will be someone else here later to keep you company," he added with a mischievous grin.

"What do you mean, Uncle?" asked Jennet.

"That young man who's been helping George...what's his name...Braithwaite?" said Uncle Christopher, emphasising the vowels in William's surname in a mocking reference to his Cumberland accent.

"William Braithwaite. What about him?" Jennet replied casually.

"He's sweet on you, is that one. Anyone can see it! Even your Aunt Isabel's noticed it. There's only one reason he comes to the cottage in the evening after he's finished his work, and it isn't because he likes Alice's cooking. He comes to see you."

Jennet's face reddened. She knew that there was truth in her uncle's words, but she didn't want to admit it to herself. She could barely cope with her own feelings, never mind entertaining thoughts about how William felt.

"Well, the harvest is finished now, so I suppose that'll be an end to it," she replied feebly.

"Well, that depends, doesn't it, Jennet? That depends on

whether you want to see him again, or not." Uncle Christopher opened his eyes now and looked at her; a long, inquisitive stare as though he was trying to decipher meaning from the expression on her face.

"It doesn't matter what I want," she answered quietly, casting her eyes downward to avoid meeting his gaze. "I can't…"

"Can't what?"

"I don't know."

Uncle Christopher sighed. The old man heaved his ancient bones out of his seat, so that he sat on its very edge, and turned to face her. He took hold of her hands, which she had clasped tensely in her lap.

"Do you care for William Braithwaite?"

Jennet continued to look down at the ground, still refusing to meet her uncle's gaze. Of course she cared for William. All that time spent with him over the last few weeks had cemented the attraction she had felt towards him the first time they met and allowed it to grow into an affection which she had never felt towards anyone before. Not only was he handsome, he was funny, interesting, daring and… unusual. Perhaps it was because he wasn't from Pendle, perhaps it was because he had tales to tell about places she had never seen and people she had never met, perhaps that was why he seemed so wonderfully different. Maybe that was all it was.

Jennet frowned as she tried to make sense of her own feelings. It was more than just his tales of Cumberland, told in that strange accent which sounded so like her own until he hit upon certain words, that made him so appealing. It was the conviction he had about where he was going, about what he wanted to do with his life; all of his hopes and dreams. He was so determined about his future, and yet he was also able to appreciate the present. He could talk endlessly not only about his past in Whitehaven, or his future in London, but also about the people and places he had seen along the way. He approached life with such enthusiasm, such a sense of adventure that she found herself completely in awe of him. Sat with her uncle, staring at the dusty ground, Jennet realised that she could never articulate exactly what attracted her to him, because it was the very essence of him that she had fallen so completely in love with. But love didn't matter. Love wasn't for the likes of her.

"Jennet," her uncle said gently, "I shouldn't pry into your feelings, I know. I just want you to find some happiness. Living with us, helping Alice, that can't last forever, you must see that. You should have a home and a family of your own."

"I can't…"

"Why not?"

Jennet looked up at her uncle now. She felt herself grow suddenly, inexplicably angry. "What if he knew the truth about me, uncle?" she asked, her voice a tense whisper.

"You were just a child."

"That's always your answer!"

"Because it's the truth. You were a poor child taken from your home, separated from your mother and kept at a grand house by an educated gentleman who put ideas in your head. None of it was your fault. You couldn't have known what you were saying…" Uncle Christopher's yellowing eyes welled up with tears. "Look at me, the silly old fool," he said, wiping his eyes. Jennet noticed his hands were shaking.

"I was old enough to understand the consequences of my words, and yet I said them anyway. Now I must live with it," she replied sombrely.

"Jennet, I beg you. Please don't let the past stop you from finding happiness. I'm an old, sentimental man, I know that. Your cousins tell me that often enough, especially Alice! The past is all I have now, for all the comfort it gives me. But you…you could have a future, if you choose to."

Jennet looked squarely into her uncle's sad, watering eyes. She hated the way he dismissed her guilt as though it were nothing, as though she could easily consign what she did to history and move forward. At the same time, she hated herself for not having the strength to heed his advice. Her guilt, she realised, had made her weak. Perhaps that was why she was so in awe of William, perhaps it was his strength that she loved above all else.

"I'm going to fetch another ale," she said.

Jennet staggered a little as she stood up to get another drink. Uncle Christopher had gone home some hours earlier, leaving her effectively without company. Grace hadn't come so she had no one to dance with, and William hadn't turned up either, so she had no one to talk to. George was still there, but he had little enough conversation to spare for her at the best of times. Jennet looked at her cousin, who was sat alone now, slumped in his chair. Poor George, she thought. If there was anyone in this world more miserable than she, then it was him. Widowed, with two young children to feed, a farm to run, and elderly parents to care for; the weight of the world did indeed rest upon his shoulders. Jennet handed him another ale, reflecting as she did so that perhaps it was better to be alone and guilt-ridden than burdened and grief-stricken.

"Someone's brew is strong," she remarked.

"Any brew is strong if you drink enough of it," George replied, taking a large gulp from his cup.

Jennet nodded in response and took a long, considered drink. She never found it very easy to talk to George; he was so quiet and reserved, and so unlike his sister Alice. She never knew how to approach him.

"I overheard your conversation with my father earlier," he said. "I think you and I have been getting the same advice."

"What do you mean?"

"Marriage."

"Oh."

Jennet took another long sip of her ale. This was not a conversation she had expected to have with George. He barely had two words for her usually, yet tonight he seemed to want to discuss matters of the heart.

"Do you wish to marry again, George?" she asked, deciding to humour him.

George smiled bitterly. "I don't think that's the right question, Jennet. I think the question is whether any woman would want me. A widower, with two young babies; I'm hardly a catch," he added, staring morosely at the floor.

"Have you met anyone…" she began. A foolish question, she realised.

George laughed; a low, self-pitying chuckle from deep in his belly. "No, Jennet. I haven't met anyone. How would I, working from dawn until dusk? The only time I relax is in the alehouse, in the company of other men."

Jennet nodded, unsure what to say. Like her, George had obviously had far too much to drink, the ale emboldening him and loosening his tongue.

"Perhaps we could help one another," he said shuffling his chair closer to her.

"What do you mean?"

"Uncle Christopher says you need a husband, and I need a wife. So, perhaps we should marry."

Jennet looked at him, incredulous. She was certain now that it was the ale talking. "George, I don't think that's the answer. For one thing, we're cousins…"

"Half-cousins, remember. We only share the same grandmother," he said pointedly. "We hardly know each other, Jennet. It's not like we grew up together, your father saw to that."

"You don't care for me…"

"I could learn to. Marriage is about more than affectionate words and loving glances. A wife runs a home, cares for the children, helps with the farm."

Jennet bristled at the cold practicality of his words. She realised what Grace had meant, all those weeks ago, when she talked of marriage in such negative terms. Jennet still felt sure that Grace had been wrong, that Nicholas's intentions were loving and tender, even if they hadn't seemed an exciting prospect to her. George's words, however, made marriage sound exactly as Grace has described: dull, boring, indifferent even. Jennet shuddered then, realising that she would rather be alone for the rest of her days than entertain a union like that.

"It's alright, Jennet, I'm teasing you," insisted George, slurring his speech slightly as he sat back in his chair. Jennet looked at him, unsure if he was being truthful, or whether he had simply read the horror on her face and decided to withdraw his candour. "Besides," he added, "you could always marry that William Braithwaite. He'd definitely have you. Never shut up about you when we were in the fields together. Kept asking me all about you."

"What did you tell him?" asked Jennet. Her heart began to pound, a terrible rush of blood coursing through her veins, making her feel sick and light-headed.

"Don't worry, your secret's safe," replied George, his face twisted into a cruel smile. "Though I daresay it won't be a secret for very long if he decides to court you."

Jennet put her head in her hands, the dizziness which had come over her a few moments ago refusing to subside. "I think I will go back to the cottage, George. I'm not feeling very well," she said, forcing herself on to her feet.

Noticing her distress, George moved forward and touched her lightly on the arm. "I'm sorry. I've upset you, cousin. My father is right; my melancholy is making me unkind. Sometimes I feel like I will never be happy again."

Jennet looked at him as squarely as she could manage, her expression filled with empathy. "I know what you mean, George..." she began.

"I miss a woman's touch, Jennet," he continued, his hand gripping her arm tighter now, pulling her towards him. "I'm so lonely," he said, as his mouth lurched towards hers, lips parted in hope.

"No!" said Jennet. Instinctively she recoiled, pushing him back; a firm shove which made him stumble drunkenly over his seat.

"Bitch!" he shouted. A few of the villagers dancing nearby

noticed the commotion; Jennet saw them frown but none approached to intervene.

"I'm going back to the cottage now, George," she said coolly. Now it was her turn to be deliberately indifferent. She didn't dare be anything else, since her sympathy had been completely misinterpreted. She understood Grace's coldness towards Nicholas now; a mechanism of self-defence against the false hopes that men seemed to find it easy to harbour.

"That's right, Jennet, run away! Run like you always have! Just don't expect to find sanctuary under my roof for much longer!" George yelled after her as she walked away.

Jennet tried to ignore his nasty words. Hot tears of humiliation and confusion spilled down her cheeks as she ran back towards the cottage. George's cottage, she said to herself, her voice shaking. After tonight, how could she ever bear to see him again, to live there again? But then, what choice did she have? She had nowhere else to go. A dreadful feeling came over her as it dawned on her how trapped she was; she had no means to get away, and no one else to turn to. As she reached the cottage door, she slumped down on the ground and wept. Her family, her real family, were all dead. All those who cared about her; gone. They were dead and it was all her fault. She clawed futilely at the sun-scorched earth as though the barren, dusty ground could somehow resurrect all those she had lost; her brother, sister, father…her mother.

"Mother," she mouthed. "Mama," she said, articulating that long-forgotten word of her childhood in a voice which was little more than a hoarse whine.

She looked to the sky then, the stars irrepressibly bright against the backdrop of their pitch-black canvas. Her mind wandered briefly over her conversation with William that night, when they sat outside gazing at the stars. He had talked with such conviction about the holy creating heaven on earth. What then, she wondered now, did the sinners create? Was it hell? Perhaps that was it; perhaps she was living in her very own hell on earth, condemned to a lonely and miserable existence, losing everyone she had ever loved. Perhaps this was her penance. She gazed upwards until her neck began to ache, as though searching the heavens for those she mourned. Then a terrible thought, a dreadful voice came into her mind. A voice she hadn't heard for so many years, not since the day he had abandoned her at her father's door. His voice. Master Nowell's voice.

"Why are you looking up there?" he asked. "They're not with God."

"I don't know!" she screamed as the stars became bright lines, painting the sky in all directions. The heavens began to whirl around above her, faster and faster until all the lines became a white glare, the brightest light she had ever seen, making her head surge with an intolerable pain. She lay down on the ground then, a moan of distress escaping from her lips. Unable to stand the agony any longer, Jennet closed her eyes and embraced a black abyss.

8

The Lunds' Cottage, Wheatley Lane
November 1632

Jennet stopped grinding the herbs and stared out of the cottage window. The first signs of winter were beginning to appear now, the brittle, brown leaves falling in abundance from the nearby trees, leaving the branches barren and desolate. Beyond the cottage the fields were still and empty, most of the beasts having been slaughtered the week after the feast of St Martin; a remnant of the old religion which now served no more significant purpose than to remind everyone of winter's beginning. Not that anyone needed reminding, she thought with a shiver. This past week it had grown suddenly very cold, the frost clinging stubbornly to the ground every morning, her breath visible in the chilly air whenever she went outside. She wrapped her shawl tighter around her shoulders as she let out a small cough.

"You're sickening for something," said Goodwife Lund as she stoked the small fire which was burning timidly in the hearth. "I'll get you a remedy for that cough. We don't want that turning into a fever," she added kindly.

"Thank you," replied Jennet, grateful once again for the Goodwife's kind gesture.

In truth, the Lunds had shown nothing but kindness towards her since she had come to stay with them just over a month earlier. Her sudden and unexplained appearance at their door had not fazed the Goodwife, who had asked very few questions about it, either at the time or since. Initially Grace had treated Jennet coolly, and Jennet worried that she was still cross about her interference in matters with Nicholas Dickenson. However, after a few days it became apparent that Grace struggled to keep a cold distance from someone now living in such close proximity, and her usual warmth quickly returned. After a couple of weeks she had completely embraced Jennet's presence in the cottage, often joking that they were now like sisters.

Despite their growing closeness Grace, who was usually so curious, didn't ask many questions about why Jennet was there and what had happened to cause her to leave the Holgates' home. Jennet suspected that Goodwife Lund had a hand in Grace's apparent restraint; perhaps she sensed that what Jennet needed above all was a sanctuary, not an inquisition. How true this was, Jennet thought as she looked out the window again. How badly she needed the Lunds' compassion at a time when she had nowhere else to turn.

The days following her argument with George at the village festival had been intolerable. Jennet recalled how she had woken up outside the cottage the morning after the festival, disorientated and suffering the ill-effects of drink, her head pounding and her stomach nauseous. She had staggered inside to be met by a few harsh words from Alice, who took a dim view of her cousin passing out drunkenly on their doorstep. As the day wore on and Jennet's headache subsided, the dreadful memory of her argument with George came back to her, piece by piece. At first she had hoped that George, in his drunkenness, hadn't meant what he had said, that it would all be forgotten. However, when George came home later that day, it was clear that he had not forgotten, a furious scowl fixed firmly on his face whenever he cast his glance in her direction.

Alice noticed immediately how coldly he treated Jennet. "Have you two fallen out?" she asked that evening, just after the babies had gone to bed.

Still feeling delicate after the previous day's events, Jennet had merely shrugged in response. In truth, she felt too weary to begin to explain, and she was wary of being too critical of George in front of Alice, feeling certain that as his sister, she would take his side.

For the next few weeks, the family looked on in confusion as George's behaviour towards Jennet grew increasingly contemptuous. Eventually the angry glances gave way to ignoring her altogether, attempting to alienate her from the family by excluding her from mealtime discussions. Initially, Jennet had borne it bravely, remaining stoic and silent in the face of George's deteriorating behaviour, Uncle Christopher's worried frowns and Alice's incessant questions about what had happened between them. She had tried to tell herself that it would get better, that eventually George would put their argument behind him. Besides, she thought, she had nowhere else to go.

Despite all her hopes, however, things did not improve. If anything, the situation grew worse, with George's venom towards her slowly infecting every aspect of the family's life. In time, Jennet grew to regret the course of dignified silence which she had chosen. She wished she had told Alice what he had done, what he had said; perhaps she would have sympathised, after all. Still she didn't really appreciate just how much George loathed her, not until one calm day in late September, when the matter came to such a terrible conclusion that she was left with no choice but to leave. Jennet had just returned from a short walk down the lane and as she walked back into the cottage, she heard raised voices.

"Jennet, don't go in there," whispered Uncle Christopher from his chair. "George and Alice are having cross words. I think it's best if you go back out for a while."

Jennet shook her head at her uncle. "They're arguing about me, aren't they?"

Uncle Christopher didn't reply, but the helpless look on his face told her that she was correct. Jennet edged closer to the door and listened.

"Alice, I don't want her raising my children," she could hear George shouting. In the background one of the babies began to cry.

"Shh, shh," she heard Alice say. "George, you're being ridiculous, what is this all about?"

"She's evil," he replied. "You must see it; you spend so much time with her!"

"George, I have no idea what you mean," Alice protested. "She's been nothing but kind and helpful. Her help got me through those dreadful first few months with the twins. I don't know what I would have done without her."

In any other situation, Alice's appreciative words would have warmed Jennet's heart. Instead, she was struck cold by what George said next.

"I didn't want to tell any of you this, but I see you leave me with no choice. You recall that she stayed out until late with me at the harvest festival? Well, after you'd all left, she plied me with ale then she tried to seduce me. She told me that she was in love with me, that she wanted to be my wife and mother of my children. When I told her that it wasn't right, that we're family, she grew angry and said she would curse my children to die a horrible death, just like their mother. Do you see now why I don't want her near them? Surely she's a witch, just like her mother and grandmother before her!"

Jennet listened, open-mouthed at what she had just heard. She hadn't realised that his anger towards her had grown into such hatred. Even now, after hearing his words, she couldn't quite believe that George hated her so much that he would tell such awful lies about her.

Alice was silent also, digesting what her brother had just said. After a moment, Jennet heard her speak quietly, her voice muted with shock. "I can't believe it," she said. "All summer long I thought all those extra trips to the fields, all those drinks and morsels to eat that she took you while you were hard at work, I thought it was all so she could see that William Braithwaite. He must have thought so too, judging by how he hung around here every evening. But all that time it was you she was hankering after."

In that moment, Jennet couldn't decide what shocked her more, the fact that George had concocted this story or the fact that Alice believed it. Alice, of all people; Alice, with whom she thought she had grown so close over these past months. She glanced at Uncle Christopher. He had heard it all too, she could see it in his eyes, which he turned away from her as soon as she met his gaze. So, he believed it too, even Uncle Christopher, the kindly old man who had always maintained her innocence over what happened when she was a child, insisting that she should forgive herself for the past. Even he believed these lies. Clenching her fists, the heat of anger rising in her belly, Jennet could take it no longer and swinging the door open, she burst into the room.

"Jennet!" Alice exclaimed. "How long have you been home?"

"Long enough," she replied curtly, trying to contain her rage.

"This isn't her home anymore," said George, still refusing to address her directly. "She needs to leave."

Jennet looked at George, who resisted her fierce gaze, then at Alice, who bit her lip, her eyes filled with regret. "I will leave. I can't stay here any longer. I can't live with people who think so ill of me. George, I pity you, your grief has made you bitter. Alice, I don't think I can express how disappointed I feel..." her voice began to waver as her anger gave way to sadness. Tears spilled down her cheeks and she brushed them quickly away.

"Oh, Jennet..." Alice began

"No," replied Jennet firmly. "No, Alice. I can't believe you thought for even a moment that such a story about me might be true. And George, to talk about my dead mother and grandmother in that way..."

"You accused them," he said pointedly. For the first time in weeks, he looked straight at her. "You told everyone they were witches, all those years ago. You told an entire court room, no less! You saw them hanged. It was you. What sort of child condemns their family to die?"

Jennet didn't say another word. She couldn't bear to be in the same room as either of them any longer. Turning her back, she ran through the door, past Uncle Christopher who had his head in his hands, and out of the cottage. Slamming the door behind her, she ran down the lane, faster and faster until the cottage was out of sight. Eventually, exhausted from running, she collapsed wearily in the fields and wept. For a time she wasn't sure why she was crying, whether her tears were for the humiliation just dealt to her by the Holgates, or whether they were for the truth in George's words. After all, his story about the harvest festival might have been a complete fabrication but when he spoke of her childhood, every word was true. She had told those awful stories about her family. She had condemned them to death. She knew that; she had to live with it every day for the rest of her life.

Lying wearily in those fields, Jennet had wanted to give up, to stay there and perish in the cold. After all, she told herself, her shoulders shaking with the effort of her own sobs, she had nowhere to go, nothing to live for now. Then, as the afternoon became evening, it grew dark and in the clear night sky, the stars began to appear. She found herself gazing upwards, remembering the starry night she spent with William a couple of months ago. It had been one of the last evenings they had spent together before the completion of the harvest. She recalled how happy she had felt, sitting outside in the company of that handsome, interesting man.

Despite her misery, a small smile appeared on her face. She remembered their conversation about God, about heaven, about salvation. Anyone could achieve salvation, that was what he had said, wasn't it? She struggled to remember exactly now, but for some reason beyond her own understanding, the memory of their discussion comforted her. At that moment she had got up off the ground and straightened her back. She wasn't ready to succumb to her own misery just yet, she decided, as she began to walk in what she hoped was the direction of Wheatley Lane and the company of the few friends she had left.

"There you are, lass," said Goodwife Lund, handing her a cup containing a sloppy, indigestible-looking concoction. "Drink it up quick; it doesn't taste nice but it'll help you feel better."

"Thank you," replied Jennet quietly.

"I plan to call on the Holgates later this week," said the Goodwife tentatively. "I haven't checked on the babies for a while. I wondered if you'd like to come?"

Jennet shook her head firmly. "No, thank you. I'll help you in any other way, Goodwife Lund, but I'm not ready to see my...that family...yet."

"Alright," replied the Goodwife with a sigh. "It saddens me to see families feuding, but I shan't pry. I just hope you all make amends one day soon. But in the meantime, you are welcome to stay here. You keep Grace busy, which is a blessing in itself," she added with a slight chuckle. "Ah! Here she comes now," she exclaimed as her daughter came in through the door, the usual spring in her step as she walked. "Where have you been?"

"Never mind that," said Grace dismissively. "Have you finished with Jennet?"

"Yes. Yes, although goodness knows what you want with her now," her mother replied.

Grace let out a small giggle and took Jennet by the hand. "Come," she said, leading her outside. "I know it's cold but it's only for a moment. I have something to tell you."

"What is it, Grace?" asked Jennet as they walked a little way down the hill, and out of Goodwife Lund's earshot. Her eyes were wide with curiosity. There was always some new excitement in Grace's life, but even by the young woman's own standards she seemed especially giddy today.

"Have I told you that I have seen a lot of Nicholas Dickenson around these parts lately?"

Jennet frowned. "You did mention it. But Grace, I thought you weren't..."

"Shh! Now, so much has happened since we last spoke about him. He's been over here with a few other men; apparently a new house is being built at Hoarstones for John Robinson and there's great interest in it...anyway, that's not important. What's important is that for the first time, I've had the chance to spend some time with Nicholas without his over-bearing mother," Grace rolled her eyes at the mention of Goodwife Dickenson. "Oh Jennet," she cooed, clasping her hands together. "I think I am now in love!"

"That's...wonderful, Grace," replied Jennet. She was unsure if she was confused, or irritated. Grace had been afforded ample opportunity to fall in love with that nice young man when Jennet had intervened during the summer. What had changed, apart from the absence of his mother at these meetings?

"Don't tell my mother, not yet," Grace instructed. "I want this to be our secret for a little while longer. I love secrets, don't you? I want to spend more time with him first. If I tell Mother, a wedding will be arranged before we know it, and...well, will you help me?"

"Will I lie for you, you mean," retorted Jennet. She realised as she spoke that her tone was a little sharp and she instantly regretted it. She saw Grace recoil slightly.

"I was thinking you could tell Mother that you're taking me to visit some friends. You wouldn't need to come with me, of course. As long as you left the cottage at the same time as me, that should be enough to convince her. That way I may be able to spend a few evenings with him, without Mother worrying," Grace explained.

Jennet narrowed her eyes. Grace was trying to make this sound so innocent, but a deception was still a deception, however much you tried to explain it away. "Grace, have you lain with him?" she asked suspiciously.

"No. No!" Grace protested, but her reddening cheeks gave the lie away.

Jennet raised her eyebrows. "You'll end up with child," she said. "Then you'll have to marry him anyway. I still don't understand why you want your...courtship...to be a secret."

"Will you help me?" asked Grace, repeating her question.

Jennet sighed. "I won't be your accomplice, Grace. You'll have to find yourself another alibi in that regard. But I won't tell your mother either. You'll have to make do with my silence."

This time it was Grace's turn to sigh. "I didn't think you'd do it," she said haughtily. "Too much of an old maid for these matters, aren't you, Jennet? But if you won't tell my mother then I'm grateful for that."

"Just be careful, Grace," Jennet warned, ignoring the insult. "I still don't understand why, if you love him, you won't just tell your mother and marry him."

Grace shrugged. "You don't really understand these things at all, do you Jennet? As I said, if you'll keep my secret, I'd be grateful."

Jennet reflected on Grace's words as she walked back into the cottage. The young woman, for all her temperament was pleasant most of the time, had a nasty tongue in her head which she was always ready to use whenever things were not going her way. Perhaps Grace was right, Jennet thought; perhaps she didn't understand matters of the heart the way other women did. It had stung when Grace had called her an old maid, but it was also true; she had turned thirty-two the previous month, and in her lifetime her only experience of romantic love had been her attraction to William Braithwaite.

As she returned to grinding herbs for Goodwife Lund, her mind meandered over thoughts of William, a watery smile resting on her face as she remembered all her favourite images of him. She thought about the first time they met in the alehouse, all those days he spent toiling in George's fields, and that evening they spent under the starlight, contemplating questions of faith. Her smile faded as it struck her how long it had been since she had seen him. Many weeks had passed since their last meeting. She wondered about him now, whether he was well, whether he was still working for the Dickensons in Higham, or if he had left Pendle altogether and she would never see him again. She wondered if he had forgotten all about her or if he, too, thought about her often, smiling as he did so. Her heart ached as she realised how much she missed him. Perhaps this is what love feels like, she thought.

"Are you crying?" asked Goodwife Lund gently, spying the solitary tear which had escaped down Jennet's cheek. "Come, come, cry and let it all out," she said, enveloping Jennet in a motherly embrace, offering the sort of comfort which Jennet had craved for so many years. Faced with such tenderness, Jennet began to sob. Unable to speak, unable to express the sorrow that she felt, she simply wept the suppressed tears of a lifetime of pain into the kind woman's arms.

9

The Dickensons' Farm, near Higham
Christmas 1632

Jennet followed closely behind Grace as she skipped happily towards the Dickensons' front door. The afternoon had grown cold and grey and Jennet shivered slightly between the gusts of wind which had picked up as they had walked up the heights, where the Dickensons' farm sat above the village of Higham. The Lunds were in good cheer, Goodwife Lund chattering happily to her husband John as they all walked along the lane. It was Christmastide after all, a time for family and festivity, as the favoured expression of the Goodwife went.

For the most part, Jennet went along with the celebratory mood, eating and drinking her fair share and fixing a pleasant smile upon her face whenever an amusing story was related or a joke was told. Inside, however, she continued to be plagued by a lingering melancholy, as though life itself sat so heavily upon her chest that at times she thought she would cease to breathe. At night she would lie awake, unable to sleep for the constant whirring of her mind. She would think about her family, those she knew when she was a child, those she condemned to die. She would think about her father, who had been dead almost a year now, and Alice, by whom she felt betrayed but who she missed nonetheless. It was ironic, really; she had spent so many years avoiding thoughts of the past and yet now, she couldn't seem to escape them. Even the arrival of Christmas hadn't managed to cheer her; the very traditions which should have served as a distraction instead offered constant reminders of Christmases past, especially those spent at White Moor with her father. How badly she missed him, she realised with a pang of sorrow. How unlikely it was that she would ever truly recover from the loss of him.

"Grace! Let your father go first," Goodwife Lund called to her errant daughter, who was racing ahead.

"Alright Mother," Grace called, stopping in her tracks obediently.

Jennet frowned at Grace. She still didn't approve of the lies Grace had told over the past few weeks, the way in which she had set about deliberately deceiving her parents so that she could spend time un-chaperoned with Nicholas Dickenson. Jennet, true to her word, had remained silent, but she had been greatly relieved when, just before Christmas, Goodwife Lund had begun to suspect that there was something between her daughter and the Dickenson boy. As Grace had predicted, the dominant topic of conversation in the cottage immediately became that of marriage, the Goodwife excitedly discussing everything from the proposal to the church service while she mixed herbs and oils. He's a good match for our Grace, she kept saying, he's from such a good family. Goodwife Dickenson, for her part, must have come to know about the budding courtship also, as two weeks ago a messenger delivered an invitation to their home on Holy Innocents' Day, three days after Christmas day, asking to bring the two families together.

"It would be nice if you two could be wed in the Spring. A quick wedding is always better, I think," Goodwife Lund had said after the messenger had gone.

Jennet recalled how Grace had answered her mother with a sullen silence, provoking a frown and an exasperated sigh from her mother, who had thrown up her arms in mock despair. Yet, judging by her excitable demeanour this afternoon, Grace was a willing bride, deeply in love. Jennet frowned again. She still couldn't understand Grace.

"Good morrow, and a merry Christmas to you all!" called Goodwife Dickenson cheerfully, swinging the door open, her arms spread wide in a welcoming gesture. "Do come in. It is dreadfully cold out here today."

Inside the cottage was cosy, a good fire burning in the hearth, which illuminated the room with its welcoming glow. Jennet breathed in deeply, momentarily unable to resist the comforting smell of Christmas fayre, the mingling scents of mulled ale and the Dickensons' best meats filling the air.

"Please, have a seat by the fire," said Goodwife Dickenson. "It is so nice to have you all here, both our families together at Christmas. I'll fetch us some mulled ale. Nicholas, you sit beside Grace," she added, gesturing insistently towards the young woman.

Nicholas, obeying his mother, sat down and grasped Grace's hand affectionately. Jennet noticed how the colour immediately rose in Grace's cheeks; the young woman looked far from relaxed now, holding herself stiffly, her shoulders square and her jaw set firmly on her pretty face. She wondered momentarily if Grace was suffering a bout of embarrassment at the display of tenderness in front of her parents, or if she was trying not to recoil. Jennet hoped it was the former explanation, but there was something about the cold look in Grace's eye…No, she thought. Grace loved Nicholas, she had said so herself.

"There we are," said Goodwife Dickenson, returning with some cups, "these will warm you all. My husband will be joining us soon; he's out attending to some business on the farm with William. You remember William don't you, Jennet?"

Jennet nodded, feeling her cheeks redden. So, he was still here, working for the Dickensons. He hadn't left Pendle yet. These past weeks, even in the depths of her despair, she had felt a small glimmer of hope whenever her thoughts turned to William. She had hoped that their paths might cross somehow, that she might get the chance to see him again. Now, confronted with this possibility, she felt light-headed; the room began to spin a little, the fire which had looked so inviting moments ago seemed now to spark uncontrollably, the shards of light dancing in her eyes. Jennet took a large gulp of her ale and swallowed hard, trying to regain composure.

"Is William joining us today?" Grace asked, her familiar broad smile now returned.

"Yes of course," replied Goodwife Dickenson. "He is almost part of the family now, although he keeps going off and finding work elsewhere. I'd always thought we paid good wages here, but it seems never to be enough for him."

"I expect it costs a lot of money to go to London," said Jennet, almost to herself. She looked up and, seeing the puzzled expression on Goodwife Dickenson's face, realised that William's plans perhaps weren't the common knowledge that she had assumed.

"London?" the Goodwife repeated.

Jennet nodded. "Well, yes. He's not from here, is he? Haven't you ever wondered why he left Whitehaven? You can't surely expect that he wishes to stay in Pendle forever..." she allowed her voice to trail off, realising as she spoke that yes, that is exactly what everyone expected him to do. Most folk were born, lived, worked and died in the same place all their lives; most folk didn't just leave their village and go elsewhere, and those who did were often viewed with fear or suspicion. For William, no doubt it had been a struggle to gain acceptance here, with his Cumberland tongue and rootless ways. He had realised that telling the likes of Goodwife Dickenson about his plans would probably be a step too far. Until now, Jennet thought, biting her lip as she realised her error.

"I shall have to ask him about this," replied Goodwife Dickenson, furrowing her brow. Jennet took another long drink of her ale, and resolved to stay silent.

"You seem to know an awful lot about his plans, Jennet?" asked Grace, refusing to let the matter lie. Her voice was sweet but there was something about her tone which was coldly inquisitive.

"Yes," replied Jennet. "He worked on the Holgates' farm during the harvest. He spent a few evenings with us and we…we talked about all manner of things, really." She tried her best to sound evasive, but inside her heart was thudding hard in her chest.

"But you no longer live with the Holgates, is that right, Jennet?" Goodwife Dickenson interjected.

Jennet nodded weakly, her heart continuing to pound. Today was supposed to be about celebrating Christmas, about Nicholas and Grace, about bringing the two families together. Yet, ever since they had arrived, it seemed that every question had been directed at her. At that moment, she wanted to disappear, to be anywhere else on earth other than in this room, talking about her conversations with William or her painful departure from the Holgates' cottage. Just when she thought she could bear it no longer, the door opened, and there was a reprieve.

"Good morrow, everyone, and a merry Christmas." It was Goodwife Dickenson's husband, John, and following closely behind him, was William.

"Ah! Just in time for the festivities to start!" declared Goodwife Dickenson, springing out of her seat to fetch them both some refreshment.

Jennet breathed a heavy sigh of relief and slumped back on her chair. How she hated feeling interrogated, and the sense of panic which the endless questions brought. How she wished that her life was uncomplicated, without confrontation or argument with others. How she wished that no one ever had cause to ask her about it. Yet, no matter how quietly she tried to live, trouble and conflict just seemed to follow her around.

"It's been a long time since our paths have crossed," said William, sitting down beside her. She noticed Goodwife Lund raise her eyebrows slightly at his approach. She ignored it; she was a grown woman, not a silly young girl like Grace. If she wished to talk to this man, or indeed any man, then she was free to do so. It wasn't like she had any family left to disgrace, she thought bitterly.

"I've been living with the Lunds these past months," she replied simply.

William must have sensed the defensive tone in her voice. "Don't want to talk about it?" he asked.

"No."

"Alright. Well, it's a pity I had no idea that you were living in Wheatley Lane. I've been working nearby at Hoarstones for some weeks now; I could have easily paid you a visit."

"Hoarstones?" she repeated. "The new house the Robinsons are building?" she remembered Grace saying something about that.

"Yes. I was apprenticed as a mason, if you remember. Nicholas has joined me some days too. He's shown a great interest in the work," he added, choosing his words carefully. Clearly William knew as well as Jennet what Nicholas had really been going to Wheatley Lane for.

Jennet glanced at Grace, who was staring at her lap, listening to her mother and Goodwife Dickenson discussing weddings in excitable, animated tones. She frowned, wondering why Grace had never seen fit to mention to her that William was working at Hoarstones. She would have recognised him from her own birthday party, if nothing else. Surely she would have remembered how he spent most of the evening talking to Jennet; she had asked enough questions about him afterwards, after all. At that moment, Grace looked up and Jennet caught her gaze; a feeble, watery, pitiable stare. Jennet looked away, unable to hold the eyes of someone so morose. It was too much like staring at her own reflection, she realised.

Later that afternoon, her stomach feeling over-filled with Christmas delights and her head heavy with the effort of jovial conversation, Jennet excused herself from the festivities to take a walk around the heights. She wandered down the lane, enjoying the beauty of the barren, frost-bitten landscape. As much as she disliked the cold, she had always loved the look of winter. She loved the way everything appeared stripped back and simplified; no leaves on the trees, no sprouting crops to nurture and coax out of the ground, no beasts marauding in the fields. There was nothing hidden, nothing complicated, about winter; it was always just as it seemed. The only drawback, she realised, was that the days were short. The light was fading already, the patchwork of grey and white above her seeming to grow darker every time she blinked. Jennet pulled her thick shawl over her hands, which were beginning to feel the effects of the dropping temperature. As she resolved to stay outside for just a little while longer, a voice behind her interrupted her thoughts.

"Jennet! What are you doing out here?"

Jennet spun around, instantly recognising William's voice. She hadn't thought he'd noticed her slip away. He had been talking merrily with John Dickenson and John Lund, who had been revelling in the festive spirit, their conversation growing increasingly raucous. It had been part of the reason that Jennet had decided to escape.

"Jennet," William called again, slightly breathless as he caught up with her. "Is it not a bit dark, not to mention cold out here for a walk?"

"I needed some air," she replied simply.

"Too much ale?"

Jennet nodded passively. If only he knew how a little Christmastime over-indulgence was the least of her worries.

"You seem different from the last time we met," he said directly. "Forgive me, but you seem a little…quiet. Sad, even. Is it your family? The ones in Barley, I mean?"

"I told you earlier that I didn't want to talk about it."

"Fair enough, you don't have to tell me anything about it. I just want to know if that is the cause of your sadness, or is it something else?"

Jennet sighed. How could she begin to tell him what had happened with George and Alice, what had caused her to leave their cottage, without revealing her terrible shame, the dreadful things she said and did when she was a child? She would have to tell him something, she realised. She had the feeling that he would not stop asking otherwise. Persistence, that was certainly another of his qualities.

"Yes, they upset me greatly. We haven't spoken since. But please, don't ask me anymore about it," she pleaded.

In the dim light she saw William nod. "Of course, you have my word. I am sorry that they have caused you pain. Family shouldn't do that," he added.

If only you knew the pain I caused my family, Jennet thought bitterly.

"Nicholas and Grace seem to be getting along well," he continued cheerfully, changing the subject. "I'm glad it's all out in the open now. I didn't approve of all that sneaking around. I suppose they will marry soon now."

"Hmm, I suppose it all depends…"

"On what?"

"I don't know. I don't know much about these matters," Jennet replied candidly.

"What matters?"

"Love. Marriage. Old maids don't know much about all that."

"Who calls you an old maid?"

"Grace," Jennet replied, a small chuckle escaping from her lips. She had no idea why she laughed. After all, it really wasn't funny, being unmarried and alone at her age.

William's face, however, remained serious. "That's a cruel thing to say."

"Grace has a sharp tongue at times. I'm sure she doesn't mean it," said Jennet, trying to be conciliatory. She didn't want William to think she was complaining.

William smiled. "You're very forgiving. But still, Grace should not be so callous. That is not how the Lord teaches us to be."

"I doubt Grace cares much for the Lord."

William sighed. "No. Perhaps she doesn't. Like many others, she probably pays mere lip service to Him every Sunday and behaves as she wishes the rest of the time."

Like me, Jennet thought, a pang of guilt resonating through her body as she was reminded of her own weak faith. She pulled at her shawl again. It was growing very cold now, the sky almost black. "We should go back to the cottage," she said.

As they turned around, William placed his hand gently on her shoulder. The gesture was gentle and protective, as though he was trying to steady her on her feet in the dark. Jennet, trying to keep her composure, did her best to ignore the tingling sensation which ran down her spine. How was it that his mere touch could have such a powerful effect?

"Do you remember I asked you about coming to Grindleton with me?" he asked.

"Yes."

"Would you still like to come? I don't plan to go for a while; I have too much work here. In the spring, perhaps. I think you would find it…"

"Interesting?"

"I was about to say comforting, and hopefully enlightening, but yes, interesting would do," William replied with a chuckle.

"Yes, I'd still like to go with you."

"Good," William said as they approached the cottage door. He turned once again to face her, taking hold of her hands lightly. "You know, Jennet, I meant it when I said Grace is cruel to call you an old maid. She's also wrong, and you're wrong if you think that you don't understand love. We're all capable of understanding all things; love, kindness and forgiveness, cruelty and hate. It's up to us to choose which path we wish to take. The Lord, he gives us this choice. Do you understand my meaning?"

Jennet nodded. "I think so."

In the dim candlelight coming from within the cottage, Jennet could see William give her a slight smile. "Good. Come on, let's go inside."

As William led the way back to the party, which was by now in full swing of drunken revelry, Jennet reflected momentarily upon his words. He was right, of course; everyone had to choose how they behaved, how they conducted themselves towards others.

However, she reflected, life was not simple and sometimes, when folk acted badly, it was because they themselves were suffering, or because they were in such strong pursuit of a noble goal that they didn't realise how their behaviour affected others. She thought of George, who had been so cruel yet his anger and resentment really stemmed from his all-consuming grief. She thought of Grace and wondered if she realised how her apparent misery perplexed those around her.

Finally, she thought about herself, momentarily pondering on her childhood behaviour. Why did she betray her family to that man, with his fine clothes, beautiful house and impeccable manners? She shuddered then, unable to bear even to remember his name. She tried to suppress her thoughts, but despite her best efforts, one notion plagued her still: what would William think of her, if he knew anything about the choices she had made in the past?

Part Two

1633

10

The Lunds' Cottage, Wheatley Lane
March 1633

Jennet took a deep breath and smiled. Inhaling the beautiful and complex fragrance of the herbs and plants as she ground and mixed them always delighted her senses. Outside, spring was on its way, the fields busy once more with labourers sewing and harrowing in readiness for a new crop, new leaves springing forth on the nearby trees, new buds on the flowering bushes. New life, thought Jennet, new possibilities.

Indeed, this year the advent of spring seemed to have infected her to her very core; for the first time in a long time, she felt renewed, perhaps even cheerful. The melancholy she had felt over the winter hadn't left her entirely; at times it still plagued her, especially at night, and she remained estranged from the Holgates who, despite Goodwife Lund's best efforts, she still resisted visiting. However, for the first time in months she found her own thoughts bearable once again, and with this reprieve she no longer felt such a terrible, crushing despair. It was as though she had managed to put the guilt she felt back in a box, safely tucked away so that, although she knew she always carried it with her, she could make sure it was invisible to others. Jennet smiled again, realising that in some small way she had reclaimed control of her life, and that in itself was a reason to feel happy.

"You are in good spirits this morning, Jennet," remarked Goodwife Lund, noting her smile. "That is nice to see."

"Yes. It must be the fine spring day. The sunshine can draw a smile to anyone's face, I think."

The Goodwife gave Jennet a sly smile. "I daresay it's more than that, lass. I daresay it has something to do with that young man who visits you, what - twice or even three times a week! Am I right?"

Jennet merely smiled in response. It was true that William's visits had given her great cause to feel happy. Work on the house at Hoarstones had been halted after Christmas due to the bad weather; however, over the past few weeks work had resumed and since then William had visited regularly, usually accepting the Goodwife's hospitality and staying with the Lunds for supper. At first his visits had reminded her of those he paid her last harvest, when he worked for George. Indeed, they took on much the same format; they would eat together, then afterwards they would sit until it was late, discussing all manner of things. The only difference was that she had no babies to put to bed now, and no Alice watching over her. To her great relief, Goodwife Lund usually made herself scarce, sometimes even joining her husband John in the alehouse so that Jennet and William were left alone in the cottage.

Well, almost alone. Grace was always there, silently hanging around in the background, listening to their conversations. At the thought of Grace, Jennet frowned. She still seemed so unhappy, so sullen and withdrawn, so unlike her usual self, and not at all like a young woman who should be looking forward to getting married. Her betrothal to Nicholas Dickenson had been quickly arranged after Christmas. The speed of it hadn't surprised Jennet; she suspected that Goodwife Lund realised what her daughter had been up to while keeping her involvement with Nicholas a secret and, fearing the arrival of an illegitimate child and the taint of scandal, hastily pressed the arrangements forward. The wedding was planned for later that spring, just after May Day. Upon announcing the date, the Goodwife had joked that perhaps the choice of date would be a good omen in bringing forth her first grandchild, for May Day was traditionally a celebration of fertility. The comment had been intended in good humour; however, it only made Grace sulk even more. It's just nerves, the Goodwife had said at the sight of her daughter's dour face. Jennet wasn't convinced. In fact, the more she thought about Grace's behaviour, the more she began to wonder if she loved Nicholas at all.

"Ah, young love. Seems like only yesterday when I…well, when John and I were courting. Sometimes I wish I was a young lass again, like you and Grace," said Goodwife Lund wistfully.

Jennet chuckled. "I'm not a young lass anymore. And William and I aren't courting."

"Of course you're still young! But time is getting on for you, Jennet. If you want William for your husband, try to tell him – don't just come out and say it, but drop hints, let him know what you're thinking. He'll do the rest, I'm sure." The Goodwife winked.

Jennet opened her mouth to reply, to protest again that there was nothing more than friendship between them, that there never would be. She changed her mind and closed her mouth again. How could she explain that she couldn't marry this man, no matter how much she cared for him? How could she explain that she wasn't good enough for him, or anyone for that matter, without telling the Goodwife the entire, terrible truth about her life, about who she was? Jennet bit her lip and resolved to remain silent.

"What are you two plotting?" Grace breezed into the room crossly and began to search about, sighing heavily.

"Oh, nothing, just giving Jennet a bit of advice. What are you looking for?" her mother asked.

"My light shawl. I'm going out. I need some air," Grace replied shortly.

"Here," her mother handed her the shawl, which had been draped casually over a stool. "You'd lose yourself given half the chance. Where are you going?"

"Does it matter?" Grace snapped. "Just out for a walk."

"Grace…" her mother began as Grace slammed the door behind her. Goodwife Lund sighed. "She's getting married soon. You'd think she'd be happy. He's a nice boy. Do you think she's changed her mind?" She looked anxious.

Jennet shrugged. She couldn't tell the Goodwife about her suspicions; Grace was her only daughter, she wouldn't hear a bad word spoken about her. "Perhaps she's just nervous. Why don't you ask her what the matter is?"

The Goodwife looked dejected. "I've tried. She says she doesn't want to talk about it, says I wouldn't understand. So she hasn't said anything to you either?"

Jennet shook her head briefly and turned her attention back to her work. No, Grace hadn't taken her into her confidence this time. A pang of guilt struck her as she realised that any time Grace had tried to talk to her about her choices, she had been met with resistance and criticism. It is little wonder then that she doesn't wish to confide in such a useless old maid, Jennet thought as she pressed the herbs hard.

Later that morning, Jennet sat down and took a gentle stretch. She had worked hard all morning and her arms and back ached; she needed a rest, if only for five minutes before she began to prepare the lunch. She was alone in the cottage now; the Goodwife had gone out to pay some visits to a few folk in need of her help, and Grace was still out walking. Grace – her misery had remained firmly on Jennet's mind, and whilst working her thoughts had been preoccupied with searching for any way she could help the girl, any way she could see to ease her suffering. Her thoughts whirled and crumbled like the concoctions she was grinding, her mind always returning to a singular persistent notion: Grace in an impossible situation. She had accepted Nicholas's proposal and no amount of hesitation or afterthought could change that. She would have to marry Nicholas now and learn to love him. Grace's problems had made her head ache as much as her body, she realised, feeling suddenly very tired. Just as she leaned back in her chair and closed her eyes for a few quiet moments, there was a loud knock at the door.

"It's open," she called casually, unable to muster the effort to raise herself from her chair. It was probably someone looking for the Goodwife anyway; she'd have to tell them to come back later.

"Jennet? It's me," called a familiar voice as the door creaked open.

Jennet's eyes flew open in an instant. "William? Sorry…I wasn't expecting you." She sat upright in her chair.

"Getting a bit of shut-eye while the rest of us are out working?" he teased.

"I'm tired. I've been up since dawn and there's…I've a lot on my mind," she confessed.

"Oh. Anything I can help with?"

Jennet gave him a faint smile. She couldn't even consider telling him of her suspicions about Grace; he was far too close to the Dickensons and besides, she had no proof of anything. "No I don't think so," she replied.

"Well, I may have an idea which will take your mind off things. Do you remember I talked to you about going to Grindleton?"

Jennet nodded. "Yes. Have you made plans?"

"Sort of." He smiled. "I've almost finished my work at the house. John Robinson sent me away early today. As tomorrow is Sunday…well, I thought we could go today, stay there tonight and go to the church tomorrow morning."

"William, I…" Jennet hesitated.

"Oh! We wouldn't be alone tonight. We will stay with some friends I have there. They're good people; they told me when I left that I would always be welcome. Say you'll come." His tone was slightly pleading.

Jennet smiled. "Alright. When do we leave?"

"How about now?"

"Now? But I've lunch to prepare and besides, there's no one

here to tell. How will the Lunds know where I've gone?"

William placed his hands lightly on her shoulders and smiled. "Don't worry about that. I saw John working in the fields when I came down the lane. I'll go and let him know, while you get yourself ready."

Jennet felt the colour rising in her cheeks at his touch. "Alright. You're used to getting your own way, aren't you?" she said, venturing to tease him a little.

"Absolutely," he smiled.

The journey to Grindleton was several hours on foot, across fields, hills and small, winding lanes. At Jennet's insistence, they took a slightly protracted route which allowed them to avoid Barley. Jennet didn't want her outing with William to be spoiled by unwelcome encounters, nor did she want to be recognised by village folk who would inevitably gossip about the Holgates' cousin wandering the countryside alone with the man with the strange accent. It was scandalous, she realised now; in her hurry to gather her things and leave the cottage, she hadn't given much thought to the fact that she was indeed a woman travelling alone with a man who was not her husband. On the other hand, apart from idle gossips, who would really care? One advantage of being alone in the world, she reflected, was that she had no one to taint with scandal, and in that respect she was free to do as she pleased. In fact, she had never felt so free before today.

William gave her a considered look. "I'll pay you for them."

"For what?"

"Your thoughts."

"I was just thinking how odd this is. When I woke up this morning I never thought I'd be in Grindleton with you by the end of the day," she said.

William laughed. "I thought I'd be working until nightfall. So I'd say today has turned out great. It's nice to spend some time with you, Jennet." His voice grew more serious. "Really, I am glad you agreed to come."

"I'm glad too. I'm looking forward to meeting your friends."

William nodded. "They're good people. His name is Richard Hargreaves; he has a wife called Bess and two children, a son also called Richard and a daughter called Jennet, oddly enough. I met them both through the church; they're very godly folk."

"Godly folk," Jennet repeated. She wasn't sure what that phrase meant. She supposed they were educated folk, the sort who liked to read the Bible for themselves so that they could talk about it. She looked down then, suddenly feeling quite inadequate.

William sensed her changed of mood. "What's the matter, Jennet? You look glum."

"I'm not...well, you know I'm not like your friends, William. I don't know the Bible all that well and I can't read and...I hope they don't think that I'm stupid."

William laughed. "They will think you're wonderful, Jennet, just as I do." A sombre look crept upon his face as he stopped walking and turned to look at her. He took hold of one of her hands. "I mean it, you know. You are wonderful. You are also in a lot of pain; you try to hide it but I can see it, always written somewhere on your face. Do you know that even when you smile your eyes are full of sorrow? Anyway, I don't know why you feel such sadness and I know you don't want to tell me but I pray to God that I might help you find some happiness, or at least some peace. Starting tomorrow, when you hear the word of God put to you in such a way...well, you'll see."

Jennet's lip trembled at the conviction in his words. "I can never tell you, William. You would never think of me in the same way again and I couldn't bear it."

"Jennet," he said, drawing her close. "I could never think badly of you. You must know what I think...how I feel..."

"Yes," she replied as a tear trickled down her cheek. "But please, don't say it."

They arrived in Grindleton just as the spring sky was growing darker, forming a majestic picture of orange and grey above their heads. At first glance, Grindleton looked just like any other village in this remote part of the world; a collection of small cottages sitting in the gentle countryside, delicate plumes of smoke trickling from their chimneys, only just visible now against the backdrop of the darkening sky. Further away, Jennet could just about make out the chapel, its modest tower standing tall, pointing upwards to the kingdom of heaven.

"Come, the Hargreaves' cottage is this way," William said, grasping her hand tightly.

He led her up a short lane, just a little away from the centre of the village. Jennet felt her heart begin to race as they approached a small cottage. William, perhaps sensing her hesitation, gave her hand a gentle squeeze of reassurance. He tapped briefly on the door and they waited for what felt like an eternity, before they heard footsteps approach from inside.

"Yes?" came a woman's voice from behind the door, which remained closed.

"Bess? It's me, it's William Braithwaite."

The door swung open wide. "William!" Bess exclaimed. "It is so wonderful to see you. What a surprise!" She threw her arms around him with a gentle, motherly affection. She glanced inquisitively at Jennet. "You have brought a...your..."

"My friend," William replied. "Bess, I'd like you to meet Jennet Sellers."

Bess gave Jennet a welcoming smile. "Please, come inside."

Inside the cottage was small and simple, but cosy; a fire burning brightly in the hearth over which hung a large pot, the delicious smell of the family's meal emanating from it. Jennet breathed in deeply, realising now how empty her stomach was after so many hours of walking. They were greeted by a tall, slim man who Jennet guessed was of a similar age to herself, and two children who were sitting placidly by his side.

The man rose from his seat to welcome her. "Richard Hargreaves," he said with a simple nod. "And these are our children, Richard and Jennet."

The children gave Jennet a shy smile. "What a lovely family you have," she said politely. "It's very nice to meet you all."

"We were about to have supper. Have you eaten?" Bess asked.

The pair shook their heads. Bess smiled at William. "Come all the way back to Grindleton for some of my pottage?" she teased.

"Of course," William said, returning her smile. "And it is Sunday tomorrow. I wanted to bring Jennet to hear the Reverend preach. Do you mind if we stay here tonight?"

"William, you are always welcome here. We told you that on the day you left," said Bess, handing them each a bowl of steaming pottage. "And your…friend is welcome, too."

Bess gave Jennet a broad smile, which Jennet returned shyly. As Bess turned away again to talk to William, Jennet found herself studying her while she ate. She was a young woman, no more than twenty-five years old, with a pretty face and bright blue eyes. Her figure was slender despite having borne two children and although she wore a coif on her head Jennet could see the evidence of beautiful dark curls falling out around her hairline. As Jennet watched her continue to fuss affectionately around William, she felt suddenly jealous; Bess was married, certainly, but she was also strikingly beautiful. Surely, no man could fail to be attracted to her, including William. Jennet lowered her head and continued to eat, feeling suddenly very plain.

"You chose a good Sunday to visit," Richard Hargreaves was saying. "There is a rumour that Roger Brierley will come to preach in the square after Sunday service."

"Really?" said William, his voice tinged with excitement.

"Richard! William, don't listen to a word he says. We hear that same rumour every week. Reverend Brierley won't come; from what I hear he's not a well man these days, all but retired from his ministry and living in Burnley," Bess explained.

William sighed. "'Tis a pity. I would have loved to hear him preach, just once."

"He was a fine preacher. I can't believe it's been ten years since he left our village," said Richard wistfully. "Even my good wife here never had the pleasure of hearing him."

Bess shook her head. "No. I was living in Giggleswick then."

William frowned. "I thought Reverend Brierley used to preach in Giggleswick, too."

"He did," Bess replied. "But I never heard him. I still lived with my father at that time, and suffice to say my father had little time for…well, God, I suppose." She gave a thin, watery smile. "Anyway, I'm sure Jennet will enjoy tomorrow's service at the chapel. Reverend Webster is excellent. Are you looking forward to it, Jennet?" she asked.

"Very much," replied Jennet, hoping that she sounded sufficiently convincing. In truth, she still found it difficult to get excited about men preaching the Gospels.

"Well, I hope his words give you much to reflect upon," Bess said pointedly, seeming to sense her lack of religious fervour.

"How old are your children?" Jennet asked, keen to change the subject. The children looked up at her inquisitively.

"Richard is six and Jennet is five." Bess beamed proudly.

"You have a lovely name, Jennet," Jennet said, addressing the little girl as she licked every last morsel of pottage from her spoon. "Just like me."

"It was Bess's choice," Richard interjected. "She wanted to name her after her mother."

"Your mother must have been very pleased," Jennet said.

"I don't know," Bess replied, her face suddenly solemn. "She died when I was very young."

Jennet bit her lip, feeling tactless. She wished they had continued to talk about dull preachers now. "I'm sorry," she said. "I lost my mother when I was a child, too."

Bess reached out and grasped Jennet's hand. "It's hard, isn't it, Jennet?" she said. "It's hard, growing up without a mother." Her voice was almost a whisper and her blue eyes, which had been so bright moments ago, were filled with sadness.

"I try not to think about her too much," replied Jennet, her tone guarded. She could feel William's eyes on her; watching, listening. She didn't want to have this conversation. She remembered how she had struggled to talk to Uncle Christopher about her mother, and he knew the terrible truth of what had happened. This woman, this stranger knew nothing about it, and that was how Jennet wanted it to remain.

"I think that's awful," replied Bess candidly. "I cannot get through a day without thinking about my mother, about how much I miss her after all these years. I was my little Jennet's age when I last saw her, yet I remember every word she said, how she told me she loved me and would keep me in her prayers...then they took her away." The young woman's voice shook with emotion.

This time it was Jennet who squeezed Bess's hand. "I'm sorry I asked about your mother," she said.

"Don't be," Bess replied defiantly. "I don't mind talking about her. I'm not ashamed of her. They said she was a witch but she wasn't, you know. She was just an ordinary woman who upset a couple of gentlemen and they decided to get rid of her. They murdered her."

Jennet gulped hard at the mention of that dreadful word. "A witch?" she repeated. She hated even saying the word; it was a word which caused so much trouble, so much pain. Slowly, an awful realisation crept over her as it dawned on her that Bess's story sounded terribly familiar. "What was your mother's name, Bess?" Her heart was pounding so hard in her chest now that she thought she might burst with sheer terror. Yet she couldn't resist asking; she had to know.

"Jennet Preston," Bess replied.

The room didn't have the chance to spin, nor did the fire have the chance to swirl and dance before her eyes. She didn't even have enough time to feel light-headed. As soon as Bess uttered that familiar name, that name from the list of names which embodied all the nightmarish recollections of her youth, Jennet merely let out a short, sharp gasp. Her last memory of that evening was William catching her as she fell from her seat, and the whole world faded immediately to black.

11

Grindleton Chapel, Grindleton
March 1633

"Jennet, are you alright?" William whispered, squeezing her hand gently as they sat down together on the hard, wooden pew.

Jennet nodded sombrely and looked forward, avoiding his gaze. In truth, she was far from fine. In her mind she kept going over and over the events of the previous night: how she had fainted, how William had coaxed her back to consciousness and sent her immediately to bed, blaming the whole episode on exhaustion from having walked so far. She remembered lying down and closing her eyes but feeling so shocked, so numb, that she was unable to pass peacefully into slumber. She had lain there most of the night, her mind racing with thoughts of the past; dreadful memories which she had buried for so long, recollections which she had tried so hard to forget.

Lying there in the still, quiet darkness, one thought kept plaguing her: Bess Hargreaves, as she was now, was Bess Preston. In her mind's eye she could see her, a little girl of no more than two, sitting on her mother's lap, chewing on a piece of soggy bread. Her mother, Jennet Preston, had been her own mother's closest friend. She remembered her sister, Alison, gossiping about kind, gentle Jennet, telling tales about how Bess was the illegitimate daughter of a gentleman named Lister. Jennet had shuddered as she recalled the expression on his face when she had repeated Alison's tales. She couldn't bear to think about how freely she had spoken to him, how careless she had been. Those stories had caused so much trouble. Those stories had cost poor Jennet Preston her life, just as they had cost her mother, grandmother, sister and brother and countless others their lives also. She must have known the consequences of her words, even as a child, and yet she had said them anyway. Why, why, why? She asked herself over and over as she tossed and turned, her chest shaking violently with the effort of her own silent tears.

"We will talk afterwards," said William, clearly unconvinced by Jennet's weak insistence that all was well. "Please, try to enjoy the service."

The congregation fell silent as Reverend Webster walked in. He was a small, slim man with sharp features; a straight nose, a square jaw, and thick, coarse brown hair appearing below his cleric's cap. Jennet was surprised to see that he was not an old man; his face, although serious, had a fresh, youthful look about it. Certainly, he was no more than twenty-five years old. Arriving at the front of the chapel, Jennet expected Reverend Webster to cast a severe eye over his congregation, as though he could obtain knowledge of sins at a mere glance. In her experience, clergymen were good at giving those sorts of looks. Jennet tried hard to avoid his gaze; the last thing she needed today was the sense that someone else was judging her. To her surprise, however, he gave his congregation a faint smile, and extended his arms in a welcoming gesture.

"May the peace of the Lord be with you," he said.

The congregation sat as Reverend Webster began to lead the first prayers. Jennet bowed her head in that familiar act of observant obedience, looking at her feet and allowing her mind to wander once again. Enjoy the service, William had said. She glanced sideways at him, noticing how his eyes were closed, his face set in a peaceful look of contemplation. She looked back down again. How she wished she could find peace in prayer, like he did. The problem was that she knew any devotion to God on her part was futile; she couldn't be forgiven, she couldn't redeem herself in his eyes. She had been damned ever since she uttered those words, those terrible words which brought death and misery to so many. She thought again of Bess, the sorrowful look on her face as she spoke about her mother. Jennet had caused her sadness; she knew it, and if William knew it too he wouldn't wish to rid her of her pain, her guilt. Perhaps he would wish her to wallow in it. Perhaps he would wish never to see her again.

Reverend Webster was delivering his sermon now. William had told her to expect a long sermon. The congregation here has an appetite for preachers, he had said, and not just in the church; afterwards they often enjoyed listening to visiting preachers in the village square. Anyone can preach the word of God, he had told her; you don't need to be educated or ordained, you just need to have let the Lord into your heart to understand the truth of his word. In truth, Jennet still grappled clumsily with William's ideas. She still could not comprehend how she was supposed to understand anyone's word if she couldn't read it for herself.

Looking towards the pulpit, Jennet tried her best to focus on the Reverend's sermon. If she was honest with herself she knew that she instinctively disliked lecturing preachers but, nevertheless, she felt duty-bound to listen. This was what William had brought her here for, after all. She narrowed her eyes, forcing herself to concentrate on what he was saying. Reverend Webster spoke about achieving heaven on earth; he was telling his attentive congregation that they didn't, indeed they shouldn't, have to wait until the next life for paradise. Jennet recalled William saying the same thing to her once, but Reverend Webster went further in his explanation. It is a sin to ask for forgiveness, he said; to achieve salvation in this life you must simply let God's light into your soul. Live in his light and you will be saved, right here, right now.

Jennet drew a sharp breath. This sermon had caught her attention now; the Reverend's words so laden with meaning, so full of hope, that even in the depths of her own despair, she could not fail to hear him. His message was so different to that which she had heard almost every Sunday for most of her life. Normally priests took great delight in lecturing their congregation on what grave sinners they were, how they must beg forgiveness from the Lord to have any slim chance of finding themselves among the saved. William was right; this church was different. She bowed her head as the congregation was again instructed to pray, and as she did, another thought struck her, like a wounding blow to the chest. It didn't matter how radical the message was, how optimistic. She knew that she could never achieve paradise, that there was no salvation even here on earth for the likes of her. She glanced sideways at William, wondering whether he thought he'd achieved his own paradise. She shook her head slightly. No, she thought, he cannot. Not while she was a part of his life, for surely all she would bring him was misery and pain.

They left the church just as the earlier sunshine began to disappear behind a thick layer of cloud. Jennet noted how much bleaker the surrounding landscape looked without the sun's bright rays to bathe it, the chapel and nearby cottages seeming duller, shabbier even. She let out a heavy sigh at the thought of the long walk home and looked up at the sky again. The clouds were growing darker and heavier by the minute. She hoped it wouldn't rain.

"Did you enjoy the service?" asked Bess, catching up with her as they walked away from the chapel.

Jennet nodded. "Yes. It was very…different to anything I've heard before." She chose her words carefully, still mindful not to offend the godly folk, as William had called them.

"Yes, it is different, isn't it? I remember the first time Richard took me to a service like that. It was like God himself had spoken to me. My life has never been the same since." She smiled.

"Are you happy?" Jennet ventured. Even as she spoke, she realised that she had no idea why she wanted to ask such an odd question but she continued nonetheless. Perhaps she was trying to ease her own conscience. Another sin committed, on top of many others. "Everything Reverend Webster said, about paradise and letting God's light in…does it work? Does it make you happy?"

Bess smiled. "Yes, it does work and yes, I am happy. I have known sadness in my life, in my past, but even so I have so much to be thankful for. I have a loving husband, two wonderful children, and a home to call my own. Life is hard, of course. We wonder every year if the harvest will fail or if sickness will come to the village and take us. These are the trials God may give us, but he also gives us so many gifts. Celebrate these gifts, revel in God's love, and live well and thankfully – there is no better heaven than that."

Jennet smiled faintly. What about those who weren't deserving of God's blessing, she thought, those who could never earn his peace; what would become of them? She didn't ask, of course; she had asked enough difficult questions already. She was glad that Bess had found happiness, but in truth, with every passing moment she found it harder to be in her company. Looking at her pretty face, her earnest smile, her bright blue eyes; it was like staring into the faces of all the ghosts she had hidden from for so long. All those tortured souls which she had singlehandedly created. She could bear it no longer, she realised. She wanted to go home, wherever that was these days.

"So…what now?" asked William, appearing behind her. Jennet noticed how again he placed his arm across her back, but not in that protective way to which she had grown accustomed. His gesture had grown more – loving, she supposed. She thought about what Goodwife Lund had said to her that morning before she had left for Grindleton. It was quite obvious now what his intentions were; indeed, he would have come out and said it if she hadn't stopped him. She wondered then what he made of her feelings, if he made anything of them at all. After all, she felt so confused that she barely understood herself.

"I think we should go home," Jennet said plainly.

William's face fell. "Did you not enjoy the service, Jennet?"

She forced herself to smile, unable to bear his disappointment. "Of course. I'm just worried that the weather is about to turn. We've a long walk home. I wouldn't want you to be stranded here and lose work tomorrow. What would John Robinson think?" she added pointedly.

"You're right," said William, his broad smile returning. "I can't pretend I'm not disappointed; when I lived here, one of my favourite Sunday pastimes was to stand in Hellfire Square and listen to the preachers. I had hoped to share that experience with you. But, as you say, we would be wise to make our way back to Wheatley Lane."

"Hellfire Square?" Jennet repeated.

William chuckled. "Yes. The square is where all the preachers who come are heard, and as you might imagine, the place has earned quite a reputation for fiery rhetoric. I shouldn't laugh; eternal damnation is no laughing matter, but the name does seem rather ridiculous."

Jennet nodded passively. Grindleton and its religious notions seemed stranger to her by the minute. "Will we go and thank the Hargreaves for letting us stay?" she suggested.

"Yes, let's," replied William, "and then home."

Halfway home it began to rain, huge droplets falling aggressively from the dark, forbidding sky. At first they continued their journey, two hunched figures marching on against the elements, increasing their pace significantly so that they might reach their destination and find shelter sooner. Jennet watched as the water poured off her sodden coif and ran into her eyes, forcing her to squint and shake her head with discomfort. After a while she began to feel chilled, her wet clothes sticking horribly to her body. She felt herself begin to shake with cold.

"There are some trees over there," William called out. "You're shivering. We should take shelter for a while, wait until this weather passes."

They headed off the lane and into the woodland, a patch of

thick trees standing idle in the midst of miles of exposed, green farmland. Underneath the trees it seemed dark but at least it was dry and offered good protection from the rain. Jennet sat down and removed her shawl, wringing the water out of it with her hands.

William stood beside her and took off his shirt, hanging it on a low branch. "Hopefully it may dry a little under here," he said.

Jennet bowed her head, averting her eyes from his bare chest. "I doubt it. There's no sunlight."

"True," he replied, sitting down beside her. "Well, I daresay I will be warmer without it."

"I will just have to make do with this until I get back to the Lunds," Jennet said, gesturing at her sodden shawl.

"Yes. At least men can remove their shirts. Just think of the scandal if you were caught under here with me, dressed only in your shift? The world is an odd place," William remarked thoughtfully. He moved closer to her, placing his arms around her shoulders in an effort to warm her. "You'd best not get a fever. Can you imagine the trouble I'll be in with Goodwife Lund if you do?"

Jennet smiled. "She's a good, kind woman."

"Yes. She's like a mother to you."

Jennet's face fell instinctively at his turn of phrase. William frowned. "Sorry Jennet, did I say something wrong?"

She shook her head. "It doesn't matter."

William turned to face her, the expression on his face solemn and insistent. Jennet tried to avoid his gaze. "It does matter, Jennet. I wish you would talk to me, I wish you would tell me what ails you."

Jennet shook her head. "I don't know where I would begin, William."

"Start with last night. What happened, why did you faint? Are you unwell? You were as white as a ghost this morning."

"No, I'm not unwell. I think it was as you said; exhaustion from all that walking."

This time it was William who shook his head. "No, Jennet. There was more to it than that. When you woke up, I could see it in the expression on your face. You looked terrified. It was as though…I don't know; I'm struggling to even find the words. I've said to you before that I always see the sadness behind your eyes, the sorrow in your smile. You carry it around with you, I know that. But last night was different; it was as though all that pain you feel was suddenly unleashed, as though you weren't in control of it anymore."

"William, I can't explain it," she began again.

"Well, I wish you would, Jennet. I don't mind admitting, you frightened me last night. You must know how deeply I care for you, but you won't let me in. It's like you don't want me to love you."

It was the first time she had heard him use the word love. It startled her slightly as it rolled off his tongue, so unexpected but so completely sincere. How badly she wanted to be able to say it back to him. How badly she wanted to tell him that she loved him.

"You shouldn't love me," was all she could say. "One day you will learn the truth about me, William. One day you will understand why you mustn't love me."

Instinctively, she stood up and grabbed her shawl. Through the trees she could see that the rain had eased a little, becoming fine and drizzly. The clouds overhead had lightened too, no longer thick and abundant, faint sunlight peeping through the cracks.

"Time to go, I think," she said simply.

As she turned to leave, William grabbed her hand and pulled her back. She gasped slightly as she found herself in his strong, warm arms. He had not yet put his shirt back on, and she noticed how hard his heart was beating in his chest. For the first time she appreciated how nervous he must have felt. She had been so wrapped up in her own problems that it hadn't occurred to her how frightening it must have been to declare his feelings, to risk rejection.

Without another word, William leant towards her face and

kissed her. It was a gentle, lingering kiss; searching but unobtrusive, as though even in this tender act he was testing her reaction. Jennet closed her eyes briefly, drawing herself closer to him. She knew how deeply she cared for him, how badly she wanted him to know that she loved him too. Yes, she was confused, and guilty, and distressed and in pain but, she realised, she was also in love. She allowed herself to respond, letting her hands wander over his chest and shoulders, feeling the peace which washed over her as she appreciated for the first time what it was like to love, and to feel loved in return.

But the tranquillity did not last long, and with her eyes still closed, a dreadful image came into her mind. She saw Bess Hargreaves, but not the smiling, happy Bess who she had left in Grindleton. This Bess was angry, staring at her with a steely look of disgust and condemnation. This was Bess Preston. Immediately Jennet broke away from William's embrace.

"I can't do this. I'm sorry, I need to go," was all she managed to say as she fled from the woodland and back on to the lane towards the sanctuary of the Lunds' cottage.

12

The Lunds' Cottage, Wheatley Lane
April 1633

"I think this will do just fine!" Goodwife Lund exclaimed, holding up a pale green petticoat. "It's a beautiful colour, matches the bodice perfectly. It was kind of Goodwife Dickenson to lend you something to wear," she added appreciatively.

Grace's straight expression remained unchanged. "I would have liked something new," she replied.

Goodwife Lund made a disapproving noise with her lips. "An expense we can ill-afford, Grace, you know that. Were it not for Goodwife Dickenson, you'd be getting married in your Sunday best. Tell you what, we'll go to the market in Colne, get you some new ribbons for your hair."

Grace responded with the stony silence which had become typical of her demeanour over the past months. Jennet looked at her inquisitively, but as usual Grace made certain to avoid her gaze. Her friend was no longer willing to share anything with her, not even her reaction to a set of new ribbons.

"Now, I think we will need to take this in a little," continued Goodwife Lund, studying the petticoat. She glanced critically at Grace. "Although not too much. Your waist has thickened, my girl, and I daresay it might a little more before your wedding day arrives," she added pointedly.

Jennet glanced back at Grace, who again remained silent, looking down at the floor. Her refusal to talk to either her mother or Jennet had not managed to divert attention from her changing shape, or the fact that she vomited frequently in the morning and following meals. It was strange, Jennet thought; everyone in the cottage had acknowledged that Grace was with child, but no one would actually say it. It was as though the pregnancy, indeed the baby, did not actually exist until Grace was married. Jennet wondered if Goodwife Lund felt some sort of conflicted shame about Grace's pregnancy; on the one hand happy that, God-willing, she would welcome her first grandchild into the world in a matter of months, but also uncomfortably conscious that Grace had conceived a child outside of wedlock.

For her part, Jennet had avoided the subject of Grace's pregnancy entirely. She assumed that, like most other topics, Grace would not wish to discuss it with her. After all, Jennet had been the one who had warned Grace about ending up with child when she had confided in her about Nicholas. The last time Grace had confided in her, Jennet thought, the familiar pang of guilt renewed. Jennet wished now that Grace would talk to her, about something, about anything. She wanted to tell her friend that all would be well, that Nicholas would be a good husband who would care for her and the baby. She wanted to reassure her that her own mother, her extremely capable mother, would be there for her during her childbed. More than anything Jennet wanted to tell her that she didn't condemn her for ending up with child, that there was no shame in her eyes. After all, she had been an illegitimate child, the product of an affair between two people who never married, passed off for years as another man's child for the sake of propriety. Yes, she might even tell her that.

The afternoon turned into a fine spring day, warm for the time of year with bright sunshine bathing the landscape in its yellow hues.

After lunch, Jennet decided that she would take a walk around Wheatley Lane; just a short walk in the immediate vicinity of the cottage since she did not venture far these days.

"Why don't you take Grace with you?" Goodwife Lund suggested. "I have no visits to pay this afternoon."

"If Grace wishes to come," Jennet replied, looking searchingly at Grace. In truth, she preferred to walk alone; it gave her time and space to mull over her thoughts. However, if it meant she might get the chance to get Grace to talk to her a little, she would be delighted.

To her surprise, Grace nodded. "Yes, I'll come. I think a walk would do me good," she added, attempting a faint smile.

The pair headed along the lane which ran down a long incline before eventually joining with the wider lane which ran towards Fence. Jennet had decided that they would take her preferred route, leaving the lane just as it met with the Fence road and heading across the fields which surrounded their small hamlet. It's the best way to enjoy the spring scenery, Jennet assured Grace. It was also the best way to avoid encountering many folk; usually the only people to be found up there were those living at Brown Brinks and Higher Blackwood.

For a while the two women did not speak, the silence hanging awkwardly in the breezeless air. Jennet searched her mind frantically for a way to begin a conversation, a way to get Grace to talk to her without feeling interrogated. In the end and in the absence of any inspiration, she decided to try a direct approach, whatever the consequences of that may be.

"Grace, are you unhappy?"

Grace looked at her with narrowed eyes. "What do you think?"

"Well I…I think you're…" Jennet stammered.

"There's no point discussing this, Jennet. It is as it will be," she said plainly, folding her arms defensively.

"Is it because you are with child?"

Grace gave a mocking splutter. "Finally, someone who speaks plainly! I did wonder how big my belly needs to grow before someone would just come out and say it."

"If it's because you're with child…please don't worry, Grace. You will be married soon, then all will be well," Jennet tried again.

Grace stopped walking. She turned, looking at Jennet squarely. The fire in her gaze made Jennet shudder. "Will it? What do you know about it anyway, Jennet?"

Jennet tried hard to resist Grace's jibe. "I know you think I'm an old maid, Grace, but I care about you. I'm just trying to understand what's wrong. You've not been yourself for months. Don't you love Nicholas anymore?"

Grace's angry look began to extinguish now, her face crumpling into an expression of anguish and despair. "Oh, Jennet," she said, throwing her arms around her friend and sobbing on to her shoulder.

"There, now. Hush," said Jennet, taken aback by this sudden display of emotion.

"I don't think I ever loved him, not truly," said Grace through her tears.

"I don't understand," said Jennet slowly. "You told me…"

"Yes! I know what I told you," Grace snapped. "I was mistaken; foolish even. And now I must bear the consequences," she added, gesturing at her rounded stomach.

Jennet frowned. "Is there someone else, Grace? Have you met someone else?"

Grace shook her head dismissively as she wiped her nose with the back of her hand. "No," she said. "I mean, there was someone and for a while I hoped…but it came to nothing."

Jennet raised her eyebrows. Indeed, there was more to Grace's sorrow than met the eye. "Who was he?" she asked. "Did he make advances towards you? Because if he did that's not very honourable…"

"No, Jennet," replied Grace, still sniffling. "To be honest, I don't think he ever noticed me. I had hoped to make him see me but…" she shrugged as she allowed her voice to trail off. Her words, however, were sufficient for Jennet to understand her meaning.

Jennet looked at her friend in stunned silence. She resisted every temptation to tell her how silly she had been, using her courtship with one man to make another jealous. If it had worked, it would have been a cruel trick to have played on Nicholas, whose feelings for Grace were beyond doubt. As it was, her ploy had failed, leaving her miserable and her betrothed deceived into believing she truly loved him. Unfortunately, Jennet thought, Grace had only herself to blame.

"I know what you're thinking – I can see it on your face," Grace said. "You think I'm a brazen harlot. Well, I have learned from my mistake but it is too late. I will do as I am expected to do. I will marry Nicholas and I will have his child; indeed, I shall probably have many more. I am young enough, after all." Her tone was cutting.

Jennet frowned. "I still don't understand. Why would you lie with Nicholas if you don't really love him? You're not his wife yet."

"You're right, Jennet, you don't understand," Grace scoffed. "Courtship comes with certain…pressures. Men ask for certain things, even quiet young men like Nicholas. Besides, I have to admit that side of things isn't so bad. It is quite the opposite, in fact." To Jennet's surprise, Grace's cheeks coloured slightly. The brazen harlot wasn't so brazen after all.

"You didn't have to…not until you were married," Jennet persisted weakly. She thought of William and his tender advances towards her. She was sure he would never dream of making any demands, as Grace called them.

Grace laughed. "Oh, Jennet, what would you know about it?"

This time it was Jennet's turn to answer with silence.

Grace arched her eyebrows triumphantly. "Exactly. You should ask yourself, Jennet, why you're unmarried at your age. I might not have got exactly what I wanted, but I am still getting a husband. You, on the other hand…well, you should ask yourself why William stopped paying you visits. He hasn't called at the cottage for weeks."

Jennet winced. It was true; she hadn't seen William since she ran away from him on that rainy Sunday on the way back from Grindleton. He hadn't come to the cottage, nor made any other attempt to seek her out. Grace's interpretation of matters was, of course, completely flawed, but that didn't stop Jennet from feeling stung by her words. Undoubtedly William had kept his distance, but not because he hadn't got what he wanted from her, but because what he had offered had been so strongly rejected.

As the pair walked back towards the Lunds' cottage at Blackwood Head, Jennet felt crest-fallen once again, cruelly reminded of how badly she had wanted William to see that she did love him in return, and how hard it had been to resist him. It was for the best, she reminded herself. As Grace had said, it is as it will be.

That evening, the sky bore witness to a beautiful sunset. Jennet stared out the window for what seemed like hours, watching the bright orange and red hues as they mingled with fine streaks of grey cloud. It struck her how exquisite the world could be; how its perfection was a demonstration of divine creation. She thought again about her visit to Grindleton, her experience in the chapel. The ideas of the Grindleton folk had seemed strange to her; nonetheless, perhaps there was some truth in them. Perhaps it was possible for people to achieve paradise here; after all, the beauty all around them could not be a more perfect backdrop. She continued to gaze wistfully out of the window as eventually, the bright colours began to fade, at first appearing to be consumed by the grey before disappearing entirely into the blackness of night. She sighed. That was the problem with beauty; it wasn't permanent, and eventually it would fade. In the end, everything faded. Perhaps that was the case with paradise too. Perhaps the best anyone could hope for was temporary displays of paradise, spread exquisitely across the sky.

"I think I will spend the day with Nicholas tomorrow. Do you mind, Mother?" she heard Grace ask. She had noticed how much more relaxed Grace seemed this evening, her familiar broad smile and conversational manner mostly restored to her. Perhaps confiding in Jennet had helped, after all.

Goodwife Lund looked up from her sewing. "Do I mind if you spend the day with the man who is soon to be your husband? Of course not, my girl! Just don't spend too much time on your feet, it's not good for...well, just don't do too much walking." Goodwife Lund stumbled over her words. Despite Grace's improved mood, she was still unwilling to talk about the pregnancy. "Jennet, will you be here to give me a hand if Grace goes out? We've a few folk to see tomorrow afternoon," Goodwife Lund asked.

"Of course Jennet will be here! It's not like she has anywhere else to go," Grace interrupted. Her expression remained cheerful but Jennet detected mockery behind those smiling eyes. She wondered momentarily if she had preferred the miserable, withdrawn Grace, then immediately chastised herself for being unkind.

"Now then, Grace," her mother said, her tone scolding. "I would very much appreciate your help tomorrow, Jennet, if you are available?" She smiled encouragingly.

Jennet nodded. "Of course."

"Right, Grace. May I suggest that you get yourself off to bed? You should be getting plenty of sleep right now," Goodwife Lund said.

Grace flashed her mother another of her big smiles. Jennet noticed that there was a challenging, almost menacing look behind her eyes. "And why is that, Mother? Why do I need more sleep than anyone else?"

Goodwife Lund gave her daughter a withering stare. "You know perfectly well why, Grace. Now, away to bed."

Grace rose from her seat and stomped crossly across the room and through the doorway towards her bed. When she was out of sight, Goodwife Lund chuckled. "And to think, that one is going to be a mother....one day," she added quickly. "I'm glad to see that she is in a better mood. Did you girls have a heart-to-heart this afternoon?"

Jennet nodded, looking down at her hands which she had folded neatly in her lap.

"Don't worry, I'm not going to ask you to break her confidence," said Goodwife Lund with a chuckle. "I'm just glad she has talked to someone. Talking to someone you trust always helps, I think."

Jennet nodded again, unsure how to respond. After all, she had never dreamed of confiding in anyone.

Goodwife Lund put down her sewing again and stretched out her legs. "I will be glad when she's married and the whole matter is settled. Not least because I've no idea how big or small to make the waist on this dress." Initially Goodwife Lund smiled at her own joke, but then her face grew serious. "Jennet, I can trust you, can't I? Can I speak plainly to you?"

Jennet drew a shallow breath, unsure of the nature of the plain speech. She nodded weakly.

"She's admitted to you that she's…with child, hasn't she?" Goodwife Lund asked.

Jennet noted the desperate, regretful look on her face. "Yes. Yes, she's told me," she replied simply.

"It worries me. I mean, aside from the fact that it is a grave sin, it creates more earthly problems, shall we say," the Goodwife said, keeping her voice low so that Grace might not hear.

Jennet frowned. "What do you mean?"

Goodwife Lund sighed. "What if Nicholas, or his family, have a change of heart and call off the wedding? Then her father and I will have another mouth to feed here, and a daughter whose marriage prospects are greatly reduced. She's behaved so recklessly. Do you think Goodwife Dickenson knows anything about her…condition? Does Nicholas know?"

Jennet shook her head. "I don't know."

Goodwife Lund threw her arms up in an exasperated gesture. "Well, I hope not. Not until after the wedding, anyway. Let's just get them both up the aisle and then we can look forward to this baby. Until then, it must be as though it doesn't exist. Grace must understand that, too. Do you think she sees that she must be discreet?" Goodwife Lund gave Jennet an anxious look.

Jennet sighed. "I don't know. I hope so." In truth, she suspected that there was a considerable difference between what Grace understood and what she chose to do.

Goodwife Lund let out another heavy, disapproving noise, shaking her head as she attended to her sewing once again. "I don't know! That girl of mine, sneaking around with Nicholas Dickenson, getting herself into trouble. I have often wondered where they were meeting, where they were...you know, away from prying eyes."

Jennet looked up thoughtfully, recalling the first time Grace spoke to her about Nicholas. She glanced at the Goodwife, resolving to remain silent. The last thing she wanted to do was admit that she had kept Grace's confidence about Nicholas; that she, in some small way, had facilitated their immoral liaisons. After all, she had known that they had been meeting at Hoarstones; Grace had told her herself in her characteristically excitable manner. Jennet furrowed her brow, trying to remember the details of that particular conversation. Nicholas had come over to Wheatley Lane with a few other men, Grace had said. He had been accompanied, yet they had managed to spend some time together. Sufficient time, it seemed, to get up to things that they shouldn't.

As Jennet took some sewing from the Goodwife, her mind continued to wander, piecing together the conversations she had had over the previous months. Grace had admitted to her earlier that she had fallen in love with someone else. In all likelihood, it had been one of the men at Hoarstones, one of Nicholas's companions; how else would she have used Nicholas's affection for her to make someone else jealous? Yes, Jennet decided, it had to be one of that group; but who? She shook her head briefly, realising that her speculation on the matter was futile. After all, Grace's plan had failed.

"It's a pity you're not seeing that William Braithwaite anymore,

Jennet," Goodwife Lund said.

Jennet nodded, hoping her silence would demonstrate her unwillingness to discuss the matter.

"Aye, it's a real shame," the Goodwife continued. "He's good friends with Nicholas. He might have known more about what Grace has been up to. He might have been someone you could have asked."

Jennet looked up from her sewing once more. William. She felt a hard pang in her chest every time someone mentioned his name. She knew that their separation was for the best, but that didn't make it any easier to bear. She attended to her sewing once again, hiding her face from the Goodwife. She didn't want to have to hear any more talk of William, or what he might know.

Then, as she continued to work, a dreadful thought occurred to her. It was the sort of idea which crept over her slowly, but once it took hold it was enough to make her heart race and her palms sweat. William had been there, at Hoarstones; he had said so himself. He had been working there while Grace and Nicholas had been using it as an illicit meeting place. Jennet flinched, dropping her needle into her lap. What if William had been the man for whom Grace had fallen? What if he had been the subject of her misguided ploy? Jennet reached down to pick up her needle, clumsily pricking her finger. She winced as she watched two or three drops of blood spill on to her apron. How terrible, she realised, to think that she and Grace might have fallen in love with the same man. Grace would have known it, too; every visit William paid to Jennet at the cottage must have wounded her like a blow to the stomach. Jennet sucked her finger, attempting to stop the bleeding. Some wounds are easily healed, she thought. Others are not.

13

St Leonards Church, Padiham
May 1633

Jennet breathed in deeply as she sat down, appreciating the earthy scent of the old rushes which had been laid on the church floor. She suppressed a yawn; she had woken very early that morning to help Goodwife Lund get Grace ready for her wedding day, a task which had proved less straightforward than it had initially appeared. Grace had risen in one of her more difficult moods, grumbling about how large she felt in her clothes; how her bodice clung unflatteringly to her stomach. Goodwife Lund, by contrast, had been a bag of nerves and excitement, flitting around the cottage, chattering constantly over every detail of the day to follow. Jennet smiled, still unable to decide what had been more challenging: handling Grace's short temper or her mother's agitated state.

Jennet looked around her and shuffled awkwardly in her seat. She had sat a few rows behind the front pew, a position which she found uncomfortable – lowly folk such as her normally sat far towards the back of a church. Today, however, there would be no one of high rank in attendance, just the families and friends of the bride and groom. She noted how busy the church had already become, a seemingly endless stream of guests filing into the church and taking their seats even though the bells had not yet begun to ring. She supposed that like her, many had made a long journey on foot to be there, and with the spring weather outside being unfavourably wet, they had hurried inside in an effort to dry themselves before the ceremony began.

Goodwife Lund, despite her excitement, had complained about the journey they had to make. Padiham was a couple of hours' away on foot, she had remarked with a sigh. It was a long journey for a bride in her best clothes. Why couldn't they be married at St Mary's, in Newchurch? It was half the distance away! In the end Grace had snapped at her, retorting that of course she must marry Nicholas on his family's terms, in their parish church. They were the Dickensons, after all. Goodwife Lund had answered her with a shrug and a thin smile; a resigned gesture which acknowledged that her daughter spoke the truth.

Jennet looked over her shoulder once again. She suppressed a gasp as she saw William walk through the heavy, wooden doors. Of course, she knew that she would see him today; he was so close to the Dickensons he was like family. Indeed, if she was honest with herself, she knew that part of her wanted to see him, to feel reassured at his continued presence in her life, even if it could only ever be a fleeting one, rooted in mutual friendships. She knew it was foolish of her to try to take any comfort in such futility and now, at the mere sight of him she felt hollow, as though the breath had been knocked completely from her body.

She watched out of the corner of her eye as he walked to a pew on the opposite side of the church. As he sat down, he looked up and caught her gaze. His expression remained unchanged; neither a smile nor a scowl crossed his face. Jennet's stomach lurched and she looked away, unable to bear the distance which his neutral stare betrayed. She looked straight ahead, drawing a few deep, considered breaths in an effort to compose herself. She found herself studying Nicholas, who by now had taken up his position at the front of the church. He looked smart in a dark blue doublet and Jennet noticed that he had grown his hair into a fashionable style, touching his collar but brushed back neatly from his face. He fidgeted awkwardly as he waited for his bride. Jennet smiled faintly, reflecting on how young he looked; indeed, how young he was, how young Grace was. Yet, after today they would be newlyweds and shortly after that, they would be parents.

The priest signalled that the congregation should stand and they all turned, en masse, to face the church doors as Grace walked in, accompanied by her father. Grace looked calm and composed, her earlier bad mood apparently gone now, a small smile on her face indicating that she was enjoying the attention. Jennet felt her eyes move instinctively to Grace's belly. Despite Goodwife Lund's best efforts with a needle, Grace's changing shape could not be hidden, a small, delicate bump apparent under her bodice and petticoats. Others in the congregation had noticed too; Jennet could hear a few ill-concealed whispers around her. She smiled encouragingly at Grace as she glided past. Gossip didn't matter now; within the hour the couple would be married and then all would be well.

The congregation sat as instructed and the priest began to lead the first prayers. Jennet looked straight ahead, studying the front pews, which were packed with members of both families. In the front row sat Goodwife Dickenson and immediately opposite her sat Goodwife Lund. Jennet suppressed a smile as she realised she could already hear Goodwife Lund sobbing. She wondered if they were simply tears of emotion at the sight of her only daughter, indeed her only child, getting married, or whether they were also tears of relief that her daughter would not be returning to her, pregnant and without a husband.

Goodwife Dickenson, by contrast, sat perfectly still, a model of composure. Jennet frowned slightly. She wondered whether Goodwife Dickenson had noticed Grace's stomach and if she had, whether it had been a surprise or whether she already knew about Grace's condition. She wondered what she thought of Grace, as a young woman, as a wife, as a daughter-in-law. Giddy was how she had once described her, but that was a while ago now, long before

Nicholas and Grace were courting, long before she had got with child. As she watched the Goodwife, she noticed how she held her head so high and so steady. She had always struck her as such a fine woman. She was a prosperous woman, of course, but there was something proper and refined about how she conducted herself. If she was aware of the taint of scandal, she would certainly never acknowledge it.

Jennet let out a light sigh. The priest had moved to give his sermon now. She prayed it wouldn't be very long; all the warm bodies packed in the church had increased the temperature somewhat and she was beginning to feel sleepy. It wouldn't be the first time she had fallen asleep during a priest's sermon, but she didn't want to do that today of all days, especially when William was in attendance. She sighed again, wondering if he was looking at her, wondering if he was giving her any thought at all. She chastised herself for her momentary self-indulgence; how cruel it was, to want the man she had rejected to remember her.

Inclining her head away from his direction, she glanced over to the other side of the church. As she surveyed those sitting there, her eyes came to rest upon a familiar face. Tucked into a corner and sat on her own was Alice, her cousin. Jennet felt her jaw clench as she recalled Alice's betrayal, how she had so easily believed George's wicked lies. Even now, after all these months, her disappointment hurt like an open wound. She turned away again quickly, determined to avoid catching Alice's eye, and clasped her hands together in readiness for prayer. She hoped that God would see fit to help her avoid any encounters with Alice today. But then, she doubted God gave her any consideration at all.

It was a long, wet journey back to Higham. As Jennet walked behind the wedding party, blinking the fine droplets of rain from her eyes, she thought about Nicholas and Grace, now beginning married life. Grace had looked happy, she thought, as she walked back down the aisle with her new husband, a small smile on her face, a daring hand placed on her swollen belly. Jennet recalled how

Goodwife Dickenson had appeared to wince at the gesture; it seemed that this proud woman would have to get used to how brazen her new daughter-in-law could be.

Jennet quickened her step as she approached the farm on the heights, glad to be invited inside and out of the rain. Presumably anticipating the attendance of a great many guests, the Dickensons had chosen to hold a feast in one of their large out-buildings. As Jennet walked in, she saw that the celebrations were already well underway, the room already filled with laughter and loud chatter. Someone handed Jennet a cup of ale and she drank it thirstily, looking around for familiar faces. In front of her, Nicholas and Grace were greeted with a round of applause as they took their positions for the first dance.

"She needs to be careful, in her condition," a woman remarked from behind Jennet.

"You mean…is she…?" another woman asked.

The first woman made a disapproving noise with her lips. "Oh yes. Can't you tell? Some lasses have no shame."

Jennet felt the colour rise in her cheeks. She turned around slowly. "And some lasses should mind their own business," she said sharply.

She could hear the pair sniggering as she walked away. She didn't care. Grace had her faults, of course; she was far from even tempered, flitting wildly from excitability to bad humour, and certainly, she had lain with a man out of wedlock and got with child. But she was also her friend, and she didn't deserve to be mocked on her wedding day. As she crossed to the other side of the room, in search of another drink and something to eat, she tried to suppress her doubts that Grace would have defended her in the same way, had their roles been reversed.

As she helped herself to the plentiful ale and cold meats, Jennet continued to watch Grace. She was still dancing, this time with other girls she knew from the village. Jennet's eyes widened as Grace shrieked with laughter; someone had spilled their beer all over the front of her clothes. Jennet sighed. Grace could never help making herself a spectacle.

"I wish Nicholas would ask her to go and sit down," said a voice behind her.

Jennet spun around to see Goodwife Dickenson standing there, her arms folded neatly in front of her, her mouth set in an expression of disapproval.

"Grace has never been very good at heeding the words of others," Jennet said, trying to remain light-hearted.

"Well, he is her husband now. She must do as he asks. But I doubt my son will ask a great deal of her, not in the early days at least. Still, she is so lively and, God forgive me...so silly. She should be more careful." The Goodwife's tone remained even, but her eyes were serious.

Jennet nodded slowly. Clearly, Goodwife Dickenson was well aware of Grace's condition. Aware, apparently accepting, but was she happy? She couldn't tell.

"I hear you and William haven't been seeing much of each other recently," Goodwife Dickenson continued, looking at Jennet pointedly. Jennet shrugged, averting her eyes to avoid her searching gaze. "William won't tell me what happened, of course. He's too good a man for that." The pointed look flashed across the Goodwife's face again.

"Forgive me, but I don't wish to talk about it either," replied Jennet, trying her best to be diplomatic. She had a great deal of respect for Goodwife Dickenson; the last thing she wished to do was offend her. Nevertheless, she couldn't bring herself to talk about William, not to anyone, and certainly not to someone so close to him.

Goodwife Dickenson frowned. "Grace's mother and I were so sure that there was something between you two. We thought that you might even marry. I'll admit that I'm disappointed – if you had made a husband of him, you might have managed to keep those rootless feet of his on the ground, kept him here with all of us. Now he seems keener than ever to leave Pendle Forest for good." Although she smiled, her voice was tinged with sadness.

Jennet's eyes widened at this news. She felt her heart begin to race, beating so hard that she thought it might lurch forth from her chest. "Is he planning to leave soon?" she asked, forcing her voice to remain even.

"I don't know, Jennet. He is always vague when I ask. I wouldn't know anything of his plans to leave, had you not told me."

Jennet felt her face redden as she recalled that day at the cottage when she had spoken of his intentions so unwittingly. "Yes, I fear I spoke out of turn that day."

Goodwife Dickenson smiled again. "Well I'm glad you did. At least now, when he does leave, it won't be a surprise." She reached out and touched Jennet gently on the arm. "I can see that you still care for him, Jennet. It's written all over your face. Whatever happened, you regret it, don't you?"

Jennet looked up, her face sombre. "It doesn't matter now. Perhaps it is best that William leaves, just as he always planned. Then we can forget each other. Excuse me, Goodwife Dickenson."

"I don't think you mean that," Goodwife Dickenson called after her, but Jennet didn't turn around. The tears were pricking in her eyes and she feared that if she turned back, her friend might see them fall.

Hours later, Jennet had buried herself in a corner of the room, slumped against the wall, an empty cup in her hand. She felt tired, the events of a long and busy day starting to take their toll on her. That familiar morose feeling had also returned; she had rediscovered it in the bottom of her umpteenth jug of ale, and now she felt it would spend the rest of the evening consuming her.

She looked around the room. She could see Goodwife Lund dancing with her husband John. She looked so merry; like her daughter, she enjoyed a party. She noticed Grace was nearby. Jennet thought that she looked weary, her face pale, her eyes heavy and dark. She was sitting now, wearing an envious expression on her face as she watched her mother and her friends dancing. Grace would find carrying a child difficult, especially as she grew heavier and rest became an increasing necessity. Jennet searched the room for Nicholas, but couldn't see him. He had disappeared with friends, no doubt. Perhaps William was with him; certainly, she couldn't see him either.

Jennet shook her head, trying to suppress thoughts of William, but no matter how hard she tried, her mind kept returning to him; his eyes, his smile, the touch of his lips on that rainy day under the trees. She looked down again at her empty cup; normally she found that an excess of ale had a numbing effect, but today it seemed to be doing the opposite. Today it made her want to dwell, to ruminate on how much she missed William's company, his conversation. How profoundly she felt the loss of him.

"Jennet? Can I talk to you?"

She looked up to see Alice standing before her. She frowned. "What do you want?"

Alice looked hurt. "I see you're still angry with me. I came over to see how you are. It's been so long since I last saw you. I presume you're still living with the Lunds?"

Jennet could feel the anger rising in her, like a wave of hot air coursing through her body. She felt her cheeks begin to burn. "Of course I'm angry," she said through gritted teeth. "What you did was unforgiveable, Alice. How could you even consider that George's words might be true?"

Alice sighed. "I know. But at the time he was so upset, I didn't know what to think…"

"You shouldn't have believed him," Jennet repeated.

"I know that now." Alice's expression was pleading. There was an awkward, lingering silence.

Jennet sighed deeply. "How are the twins?" she asked in the end. She couldn't bear the tension hanging in the air and besides, Alice seemed apologetic. Perhaps they might make amends, after all.

"They're both well. They missed you when you left. And Mother and Father are much the same – they grumble, they sleep, they eat…" Alice ventured a chuckle.

"And George?" Jennet wasn't really sure why she asked; indeed, why she wanted to know how George fared.

Alice frowned. "George is much, much worse. His mood is terrible, his appetite is poor. He works his fingers to the bone all day and he spends every evening swilling beer with his friends in the alehouse. He comes home drunk every night. It's affecting his health badly; this past winter he was so ill that I feared he might die."

"Does he admit he was…mistaken about me?" Jennet chose her words carefully.

"No," Alice said. "That's why I've never tried to see you, Jennet, since you left. George still swears by the story he told about the harvest festival. He swears you're a witch." Alice mouthed the final word, not daring to utter it so publicly.

Jennet gave Alice a solemn stare. "I suppose I should be angry with him, but I'm not. I pity him, Alice. He has never recovered from losing Ellena. If only he had met someone else, and remarried…"

"Someone like you, you mean?" Alice eyed her suspiciously.

"No!" Jennet protested. She realised that she had shouted the word; a few folk standing within earshot turned and looked at her. She lowered her voice. "I thought you said you believed me?"

Alice nodded. "I do. At least, I think I do. But these past months I have often wondered whether you had fallen in love with him, whether you told him that night at the harvest festival and made him angry. It would explain these accusations he has made about you." Alice's eyes were unusually wide and innocent.

"Oh Alice!" Jennet scoffed. "It was George who tried to kiss me, who tried to suggest that we marry! When I rejected him, he became angry. That's why he wanted me to leave, that's why he said such terrible things. I should have told you the truth months ago, but I didn't think you could handle it. He is your brother, after all."

Alice's mouth fell open. She stood there, aghast, for what felt like an eternity. Jennet began to regret her bold words, her truthfulness. It had been a mistake to be so candid. Inwardly she blamed the ale; she was as bad a drunk as George.

"George was right about you," Alice said through gritted teeth. "You are poison. What a terrible thing to say about my poor brother. He's a widower, with two young children, and you sought to take advantage of his loneliness. Then, when he rejected you, you threatened him with curses! And now, all these months later, you slander his good name to his own sister! Shame on you."

Jennet felt her face begin to crumple. "Alice, what I said is true. You have to believe me…"

"I don't have to believe anything you say, witch!" Alice bellowed.

Jennet felt every face in the room turn towards her. She sunk down against the wall, praying that it might consume her, beseeching God to take her away from this dreadful humiliation. Once again, however, God wasn't listening.

Sensing she now had an audience, Alice continued her tirade. "That's right, Jennet Sellers – or should I say, Jennet Device?" A few horrified gasps rattled around the room in recognition of that name. "Little Jennet Device, whose tales sent her whole family to the gallows for witchcraft. What an irony it is, that years later she threatened my brother with curses when he refused her seductive charms."

"It's not true, it's not true…" Jennet repeated over and over, her voice little more than a hoarse whine. Through the hot tears which stung her eyes, she could see everyone in the room staring at her, aghast. Goodwife Lund, Goodwife Dickenson, Grace, Nicholas…all of them were shocked. Then she saw one face amongst the crowd which made her wish that the ground would swallow her whole, that the devil himself might consume her, for surely hell itself was no worse fate than this. William. He had heard the whole, sorry tale. Her terrible secret was out. There was no hiding her identity anymore.

"I'm sorry," she mouthed at him, before she buried her head in her hands and wept.

14

Black Moss, near Barley
May 1633

Jennet ran her fingers through the dirt on the ground. She watched as she scooped it up and let it fall; infinite grains of earth rising and falling at her touch. She looked up through the dense trees, trying to determine what time of day it was. The shards of red and orange which lingered above her suggested that it must be getting late in the evening, that night would fall soon. Jennet shuddered. She didn't like the dark; out here, without a candle, it felt like she was lost in the middle of a great, endless abyss. It made her realise that she was vulnerable, and alone. So terribly, utterly alone.

She lay down on the ground again and sighed. She had lost track of how long she had been in the woods. It was days; perhaps two, maybe three. She closed her eyes. Time didn't matter now; she was certain she would perish out there, sooner or later. If she didn't die of exposure, then hunger and thirst would almost certainly kill her. She licked her dry lips, trying to remember when she had last had something to drink. Yes, the end wasn't far away. She welcomed death now; she looked forward to ceasing to be, to no longer having to remember who she was and what she had done. She screwed her eyes up tightly, willing herself to stop breathing, wishing to hasten her demise. If it was inevitable, then it might as well come quick. After death she would find eternal rest, or eternal torment. Only time would tell which it was, but either seemed preferable to life. After all, her life had only ever been an unending stream of grief and pain.

Jennet shook her head hard, burrowing her filthy, dirt-strewn hair even deeper into the earth. Her life; she didn't want to think about that anymore. She didn't want to remember her past, or recall how she had hidden from it. She didn't want to think about how she had lived in the shadows, how she had cowered from her own identity. Yet, out there in the woods, weak and alone, that was all she could think about. A solitary tear rolled down her cheek as she thought about how she hadn't really lived at all. She had merely existed, never allowing anyone to get too close to her, never allowing anyone to love her, in case they might discover the truth. Those dreadful tales she told as a child hadn't just killed her family; they had ruined her own life again, and again, and again. But no more. Soon, it would all be over.

"Jennet? Oh thank God, I've been looking for you."

Jennet moaned and turned on to her side, certain that she was hearing voices. Hunger and thirst could make you delirious, she knew that. She should be glad that she was hearing things. She should take it as reassurance that the end was near, that death was within her grasp. She groaned again, a low, self-pitying rasp from deep within her. She began to cough then, and once she started coughing, she realised that she couldn't stop. She started to struggle for air, and despite wishing for death over and over, she found that when confronted with the prospect of it, she panicked. At once her eyes flew wide open.

"Jennet? Can you hear me?"

The coughing continued, her chest rattling with the effort. She saw the dirt on the ground swirling and blowing in the wind created by her violent exhalations. Cough, cough, cough. She closed her eyes again. This must be the end now. This was how she was going to die, choking on phlegm and dust. It was frightening but she must endure it. It would all be over soon.

"Jennet? Jennet! Can you sit up?"

She felt someone pull her upright, detaching her from the ground which she had determined to make her home for all eternity. "Go away," she moaned between gasps. "Leave me here. Leave me alone."

"You'll die out here," the voice protested.

"I want to die," she called out in reply.

There was silence. She opened her eyes to see William sitting in front of her, his mouth open, his eyes wide with shock. "You can't mean that," he said gently, composing himself.

"I do," she replied simply, drawing her knees up to her chest. "What is there for me to live for now?"

"I've been looking for you ever since you ran away from the wedding party," said William, ignoring her question. "In the end I remembered about this place. I thought about the day we sheltered here on the way back from Grindleton...I often think about that day," he said, his voice soft and laden with candour. "Here," he said, offering her a flagon of ale and a hunk of bread. "Have this. You must need it."

Jennet wanted to refuse the jug and the food, to insist again that he should leave her alone. However, one glance at the delicious contents of his sack and her hunger and thirst got the better of her. "Thank you," she said humbly.

"I'm so relieved to have found you," William said, thinking aloud. "I was beginning to think you were gone for good."

Jennet shrugged. "I suppose you will insist that I go back, that I face everyone," she said curtly.

William smiled. "Well, that sounds like a better plan. Better than staying here until you perish, anyway. Honestly Jennet, what were you thinking? Surely nothing is ever so bad that you would wish to die because of it."

"Isn't it?" she snapped. "That's easy for you to say. You haven't witnessed your entire family being sent to the gallows on the strength of your words. You haven't had to live with their deaths on your conscience every day of your life. You haven't had to hide your identity from folk. You haven't had to pray every single time you talk to someone that they don't realise who you are. I'm tired, William. Tired of being Jennet Sellers, or Jennet Device, or whatever anyone wishes to call me. I wish I had gone to the gallows with my family. That would have been justice."

"You were just a child," William said quietly. His face had grown serious now, his brow furrowed, deep in thought.

Jennet sighed. "So you know the whole story?"

William nodded. "Yes, although not from Alice. She left the party just after you did – I think she was shocked by what she'd done. I asked Goodwife Dickenson and she told me about your family," William paused, drawing a considered breath. He sat down beside her and took hold of her hand; that familiar gesture which, under any other circumstances, would have made Jennet's heart melt.

"Forgive me," he said, "I know you're weak and tired, but I want to hear it from you. Is it all true?"

Jennet felt herself shrink, her shoulders hunched, her eyes cast down. She bit her lip, struggling to find the right words. "I don't know where to begin."

"Start at the beginning," William said gently. "Wherever you think that is. Start there."

Jennet took a deep breath, trying to ignore how hard her heart was beating in her chest. "I was born in a cottage called Malkin Tower, on the hillside near Blacko. My mother was Elizabeth Device. I had a brother, James, and a sister, Alison. My father was…well, my mother had a relationship with a man called Richard Sellers. He was my father. James and Alison's father was John Device. He was dead by the time I was born."

William nodded. "I remember you saying your father had died, and that was why you had gone to live with the Holgates. I presume that was Richard Sellers?"

"Yes. I went to live with my father after the rest of my family died."

"Alright. So your family were all accused of witchcraft?"

Jennet nodded. "Yes. My grandmother, Elizabeth Southerns, also lived with us at Malkin Tower. In fact, I seem to remember that Malkin Tower was actually her home, and we all lived with her, if you see what I mean. She was very elderly. She had a reputation for…" Jennet searched for the right words, "I think she would have called it cunning knowledge. She knew how to heal sick animals, deliver babies, use herbs to make remedies for all sorts of things which ailed people."

"Like Goodwife Lund?"

"Yes, but…it was more than that. She also knew how to…"

"To curse? To bewitch?"

Jennet frowned. "Yes. She was very clever about how she used her abilities. I remember her saying how easy it was for folk to accuse a cunning woman of witchcraft. She made sure that folk saw her as a healer." Jennet sighed heavily. "Unfortunately, my sister Alison wasn't so clever."

Sensing where the story was going, William squeezed her hand. "What happened to Alison?"

"When I was eleven years old, my sister met a pedlar near Colne. She asked him for some pins; when he refused, she cursed him. Moments later he fell down lame. Alison was accused of witchcraft and arrested." Jennet threw her arms up in despair. "Alison was convinced her curse had caused the pedlar's sudden illness. She was summoned before the magistrate, Master Nowell of Read Hall, and she confessed to it all. She must have told Master Nowell about my grandmother then, because days later she was also arrested." Jennet bit her lip hard, fighting the tears which were stinging in the corners of her eyes.

Seeing her distress, William put his arm firmly around her shoulders. "I'm sorry, Jennet. You don't have to go on."

"No, it's alright," said Jennet, collecting herself. "It's just that I've never told the story like this before, from start to finish. It is hard, saying it aloud. But you asked me to tell you in my own words, so I will." She paused, taking another deep breath. "After my grandmother was arrested, things just seemed to spiral out of control. Folk just kept accusing each other, and there were more and more arrests. Eventually my mother and brother were also arrested. I was taken with them, for questioning."

"You were only a child," William said. "You must have been terrified."

Jennet shook her head. "I wish I had been; then I might have kept my mouth shut. Master Nowell, the magistrate, was really kind to me. I remember walking into his big, grand house and feeling so tiny, so overwhelmed. I'd never met anyone like Master Nowell before. He was so knowledgeable, so refined. He talked to me, told me a lot of stories about himself, about what he liked, what he thought and what he believed. He asked me a lot of questions about my family, too." Jennet shuddered. "That was where it all went wrong. I told him too much about us."

"How long were you at Read Hall?" William asked.

Jennet narrowed her eyes, trying to remember. "It felt like a long time. I was there from my mother's arrest at Easter, until the trial in the summer."

To her surprise, she felt William become tense. "That was a long time," he said through gritted teeth. "A very long time for a powerful man to fill a little girl's head with ideas."

"No," Jennet protested. "I never told him anything that wasn't true. When I said I had overheard my mother cursing folk like the Robinson brothers, it was true. When I recited charms to him, it was because those were actual words that my grandmother used. When I told them how my brother wished Mistress Towneley dead after she accused him of stealing her turves, it was also because it was true. The point is, I should have told him nothing, perhaps then all their deaths might have been avoided."

William sighed. "It sounds like this man Nowell was hell-bent on finding witches. I don't think what you might have said, or not said, would have made any difference to the outcome."

"Perhaps not," Jennet replied. "But getting up in court and testifying against my family almost certainly made the difference between them living and dying."

William's eyes seemed to grow darker in the fading light. "Yes, that's the part of the story which Goodwife Dickenson could recall. Apparently it was the talk of the villages at the time, the little girl who had been the Assizes' star witness."

"I wasn't that little, really," Jennet pondered. "I mean, I was small for my age, I suppose. But I was almost twelve by the time the trial started. I have often thought that I was old enough to know better."

"Jennet, you must stop blaming yourself…"

"No," she shouted. Her voice echoed in the silence of the descending night. "I've spent all these years asking myself why I did it, why I betrayed them all. In truth, I still don't know. I think that, after several months of living with Master Nowell, I had come to believe my own family's guilt. He had this way of explaining what they had done that was…I don't know, different to how I had ever understood our way of life. Like I said, he was clever. But that doesn't excuse what I did. It is my fault that they are dead, and I have to live with it. Now do you see why I would rather die?"

Her outburst was met with a long, lingering silence. It was getting very dark now; in the fading light Jennet could barely make out William's face. She wondered what he was thinking; was he shocked, disappointed even? How did he feel, now that he knew that the woman with whom he had fallen in love was actually a murderer and a coward?

"Thank you for telling me," he said quietly. "It must have been hard for you to speak about what happened."

"I've never told anyone the whole story like that," Jennet replied. In truth, the recitation of all those awful events had made her feel quite light-headed, her head seeming to pound as though her thudding heart had relocated itself within it.

"I still think you lay too much blame on yourself. But I do understand why you have trouble living with what happened. I understand why you have behaved the way you have, why you have always been so…guarded. A lot of what you have said and done makes sense to me now." William's tone was reflective, thoughtful.

"Why did you come to find me, William? After what you heard, after what Goodwife Dickenson had told you...most folk wouldn't want anything to do with me."

"Because I love you, Jennet," he replied simply. "And knowing about this doesn't change that. You know I love you, I told you so that day under these very trees." In the shadow of the rising moon she saw him gesticulate upwards.

"But why would you love someone who...who did as I have done?" Jennet protested.

William sighed. "You acted out of childish innocence, out of naivety. Master Nowell persuaded you that your family had done wrong, you said so yourself. It is he who we should condemn, not you. You need to forgive yourself, Jennet. You need to find a way to live your life in the best and most Christian way you can. Then you will find peace."

Jennet frowned, recalling Reverend Webster's sermon, that day in Grindleton. "I need to live in God's light?" she asked, repeating the priest's words.

William chuckled. "So you were listening in church. Yes, that's right. If you embrace the spirit of God you will live without sin. I will take you to Grindleton again; I think attending the Reverend's services will help."

Jennet hesitated. "I need to tell you something about Grindleton, about why I became unwell while we were there. It's about your friend, Bess Hargreaves. I realised that I knew her as a child. She was the daughter of one of my mother's friends. Her name was Jennet Preston; she was executed in York a few weeks before my family was sent to the gallows. I said some things which...I believe were used against her."

"I see," replied William. "Little wonder you fainted when you realised who she was. It must have been a shock to see her."

"Not as much of a shock as it would be for her if she realised who I was," Jennet answered. "I'm sorry, William, I don't think I could face Grindleton again. See, I told you I am a coward," she added glumly.

William sighed heavily. "Jennet, you are no coward. It seems to me that you have faced more than your share of pain and sorrow. I once said to you that I could see the sadness in your eyes. Now I understand why."

Jennet drew herself closer to him, feeling comforted by his touch. She still couldn't understand how he could be so calm, so accepting of what she had said. No one had ever shown her such compassion before. She looked up; night had fallen now, the stars twinkling gently above, the swaying shadows of the trees visible in the brightness of the moonlight.

"What do we do now?" she asked.

"We stay here tonight," he said firmly. "The country isn't safe to be wandering about at night. At first light we will go back to Higham, to see Goodwife Dickenson."

"Goodwife Dickenson?"

"Yes. She's a reasonable woman, I think. I will ask if we can both stay with her, for now."

Jennet frowned. "I don't understand. What about Goodwife Lund?"

William let out a heavy sigh. "I don't think Goodwife Lund will want you to go back there. She was distraught when she realised who you were." William drew a deep breath. "You need to remember, a lot of folk still believe that there are witches roaming these parts. Some believe those with…abilities like Goodwife Lund are as good as witches, too. I'm afraid she won't want to be associated too closely with anyone whose family was tainted by accusations of witchcraft, even if it was a long time ago."

"Why do you think Goodwife Dickenson will feel any differently?"

"I don't. All we can do is hope, and have faith. Besides, she is fond of me. I hope I can appeal to her good nature."

"Why are you doing all this for me?" she asked again.

"I told you. I love you. And you love me, I know that now."

"You do?"

"Yes. I had my doubts for a while, after you ran away from me that day under these trees. But as soon as I heard what Alice said, it all made sense. It wasn't really me that you were running from, was it?"

"No, it wasn't."

"Jennet, I plan to leave Pendle soon, to continue my journey south. My work at Hoarstones is nearly finished, and I've told Goodwife Dickenson of my intention to leave shortly afterwards." He paused briefly. "I would like you to go with me, as my wife – if you will agree," he added.

"Your wife?" Jennet gasped.

"Yes. I want to get you far away from here. In truth, I think it might be the only way you will ever feel free of your past. We can go to London together; we can start a new life. I will get a job in the Law. We can get a nice house and who knows, if we are blessed we might have a family of our own." His voice was wistful now. "So, will you marry me?" he asked.

"Yes," she replied, almost giddy. For the first time in months, perhaps years, she heard happiness resonating in her own voice.

William kissed her then; a passionate, lingering kiss. "I love you, Jennet Sellers," he said as they settled down to sleep under the stars.

15

The Dickensons' Farm, near Higham
May 1633

"Come, Jennet. We're nearly there," William said, gently urging her on up the hill on the heights. He grabbed her hand and held it tightly as she staggered wearily behind him. The events of the past few days had begun to take their toll on her. She rubbed her face with her other dirty, dusty hand, unable to recollect when she had ever felt so exhausted.

She had awoken early, just after dawn, to the sound of the spring birds singing cheerfully in the branches above her. At first she had felt enlivened, recalling with a smile William's proposal under the stars. He loved her. He wanted to marry her. Her mind ran over the details once, twice, a thousand times, until she felt quite dizzy. They would move to London. They would start a new life together. She would begin anew, not as Jennet Device or Jennet Sellers, but as Jennet Braithwaite. Goodwife Jennet Braithwaite, wife of William. She smiled again, reciting the words over and over in her mind.

However, as she lay on the ground, listening to William's soft breathing next to her, feeling the warmth of his arms contrast with the cool morning breeze, that familiar feeling of dread crept back over her. She remembered that William had said he would take her to see Goodwife Dickenson today. She gulped hard, realising that Grace and Nicholas would likely be there too. She would have to face them all. She felt a lump rise in her throat as her mind ran over all the possibilities that this meeting held. Would Goodwife Dickenson welcome her, or would she turn her away, condemning her for what she had done? What would Grace say, now that she knew the truth?

She shuddered, wishing that she did not have to find out. She wished that they could leave straight away, that they could disappear together and never look back. But they couldn't; William had work to finish before he could be paid and they badly needed the money for their travels. And until they could leave, they needed somewhere to live. Jennet had prayed then, for the first time in a very long time. She prayed that Goodwife Dickenson would show sympathy and charity, that she would take them in. She prayed that she might be as forgiving and accepting as William had been towards her. But even as she prayed, that familiar churning, nauseating feeling continued in the pit of her stomach. In truth, she doubted that anyone could be as kind as William.

Now, as she looked up the hill where the cottage and outbuildings which made up the Dickensons' farm rested, she realised that it was time to find out. She drew a deep breath, urging her pounding heart to grow steady, telling her face not to betray her fear. Right now, she needed to be brave. William gave her hand a firm squeeze of reassurance.

"Come, let's get this over with."

They walked up to the familiar door of the Dickensons' cottage. William knocked firmly. After a few minutes, the door swung open.

"William? We wondered what had become of you! You could have just come in," said Goodwife Dickenson. She looked from William to Jennet, and back again. "I see you found her," she said shortly.

"Yes," replied William simply. "Sorry for bringing you to the door – I didn't like to just walk in after being away for a couple of days." His tone was guarded and, Jennet thought, a little over-polite. Clearly he was as nervous as she was.

"This is your home," the Goodwife insisted.

"Yes. That's what I would like to talk to you about," William replied.

Goodwife Dickenson glanced at Jennet again, her eyebrows raised. "Then you had best come in," she said, beckoning them inside.

William found Jennet a chair and urged her to sit. "May I fetch Jennet something to drink?" he asked. "She is very weak."

Goodwife Dickenson nodded, a slow careful movement of her head, as though she was unsure what to make of the situation unfolding before her. "Fetch her some bread, too. Or pottage, there's some in the pot."

William returned with a small cup of ale and some bread, which Jennet accepted gratefully. She teased the bread apart nervously with her fingers, waiting for William to speak.

William cleared his throat. "Goodwife Dickenson, I hope that I come to you as a valued labourer and a good friend. As you know, I plan to continue my journey to London once the work at Hoarstones is finished. I've asked Jennet if she will come with me, and she has said yes. I…"

"She's going with you?" Goodwife Dickenson interrupted him, her tone incredulous. Jennet bowed her head, sensing already that this conversation was not going well.

"Yes, she will come with me," William repeated, "as my wife." Jennet noticed his posture stiffen; he stood tall, unrelenting but, Jennet realised, very defensive.

"William," Goodwife Dickenson said, deliberately softening her tone, "I don't understand. How can you wish to marry her? You heard what she did, who she is. We all did! I know you went to find her, but I thought, well, you're a Christian man, I know enough about you to know that. But marrying her…that's a different commitment altogether."

Jennet looked up then, feeling the anger rising inside her. She didn't like how Goodwife Dickenson spoke as though she wasn't even in the room, as though she didn't matter at all. She bit her lip to prevent herself from speaking. After all, nothing she could say would make this situation any easier to bear.

"Because I love her!" William burst out. "It does not matter to me what happened in Jennet's past. I love her. I believe I have loved her since I first set eyes on her in that alehouse in Fence." The conviction in his words made his cheeks redden and his eyes seem wild.

"I see," said Goodwife Dickenson quietly, careful to maintain her characteristic reserve and pleasant manner. "So, have you come to tell me that you're leaving now?"

"No," replied William with a sigh. "I have come to ask if we may both stay here with you, just until my work is finished. We shall not be a burden and we will pay our keep. Jennet will give you whatever help you need and I will labour on the farm, just as I always have."

"William, I…" Goodwife Dickenson began hesitantly.

She was interrupted by the abrupt opening of the cottage door. Jennet turned around to see Nicholas and Grace standing there, wearing matching puzzled expressions. Jennet noticed how much larger Grace's belly looked; it had only been a few days since she had last seen her, yet she seemed to have bloomed already. Jennet noticed how she rested a proud hand on her growing stomach, and how Nicholas hovered attentively behind her. Undoubtedly Grace would have command of him until the baby was born, if not forever. She saw William give Nicholas a brief nod of acknowledgment, which Nicholas returned discreetly, clearly keen that his wife should not see him.

"What are you doing here?" Grace asked curtly, folding her arms and looking expectantly at William.

Jennet opened her mouth to speak. "Grace…" her voice was a mere feeble croak. Grace continued to avoid her gaze.

"William was just telling me how he plans to marry Jennet, and take her with him to London," Goodwife Dickenson explained.

"He has asked if they may both stay here until he finishes the job at Hoarstones."

Grace's mouth fell open. "She can't stay here! You heard what she did! What if she hurts the baby?" again that protective hand found its way on to her stomach.

Jennet saw Goodwife Dickenson flinch. "The baby?" she repeated.

"Yes. You heard her own cousin denounce her as a witch," now Grace turned the full force of her venomous gaze upon Jennet, her mouth twisted angrily, her eyes filled with hatred. "She deliberately hid who she really was from all of us – hiding behind false names and vague stories…I can't believe she has been living in my family's cottage all this time." Her voice was filled with terror.

"Hush lass, getting upset won't help the baby," said Goodwife Dickenson gently. "Nicholas, take Grace and fetch her something to drink. Try to calm her down," she instructed.

Jennet watched as Nicholas obediently led Grace away. She looked at William, noticing how weary and strained he looked. She realised that this was the first time she had ever seen him at a loss as to what to do; usually he was confident, so certain in his actions. Now, he looked hopeless, crushed.

"Alas, I think you have your answer," Goodwife Dickenson said evenly, looking William directly in the eye.

"You can't surely believe any of this is true." William's eyes were pleading. "Jennet has harmed no one."

"Really?" asked Goodwife Dickenson. This time she looked straight at Jennet. "So you didn't give evidence against your own family and countless others for being witches, evidence which sent them all to the gallows? You're not Jennet Device?"

"Sellers was my father's name," Jennet replied quietly. "I didn't deceive anyone so that I could bring them harm. I only wish to live quietly and in peace."

"You see," said William. "Is it any wonder she uses her father's name? She was a child, for goodness sake, a child! As Jesus said, he that is without sin among you, let him cast the first stone at her."

Goodwife Dickenson fixed a thoughtful gaze upon Jennet. "I keep looking at you and thinking, how did I not realise? When we first met and you said you were a Holgate cousin…but then, they are such a large family and your surname meant nothing to me. Of course, now I think on it I remember hearing talk all those years ago that Jennet Device was a bastard but still, it never occurred to me that it was you. It was a clever ploy, using his name."

"I used it because it is my name," Jennet said, teeth clenched. "My father took me in and he raised me. He loved me despite what I had done. He loved me unconditionally."

"Like this man here," said Goodwife Dickenson, nodding towards William. "I just hope he does not live to regret it."

William's face reddened. "Honestly Frances, I thought better of you than this."

Jennet flinched. She had never heard him use Goodwife Dickenson's first name before. It hung in the air impertinently. Goodwife Dickenson glared at William; a cold, hard stare from which most men would shrink back. But not William; he continued to stand firm, his posture straight, his expression indignant. Jennet had to admire his bravery.

"I do not like to be deceived, William. I welcomed this young woman into my home, into my life, as did Goodwife Lund and Grace and you. You might be so blinkered that you can see past her deception, but I cannot."

"You cannot possibly think that she's a witch!" William's voice was almost a bellow now.

Goodwife Dickenson sighed. "It doesn't matter whether I think she is a witch or not. What matters is that she lied about who she is. What else might she be lying about?"

"I have been completely honest with you, Goodwife Dickenson," Jennet replied solemnly.

"Well that might be the case, Jennet, but you cannot stay here. You saw how Grace reacted to your presence. I have a grand-child to think about now. I'm sorry both of you, but I must ask you to leave."

William moved towards Jennet, offering her a supportive arm and a small, grim smile. "Goodbye Goodwife Dickenson," he said, his voice filled with cold formality. "I thank you for your past kindness towards me. I doubt we will meet again, so I wish you and your family every blessing."

Goodwife Dickenson nodded obligingly. "And to you, William. I won't lie; I have grown very fond of you. I hope that the choice you have made is the right one."

William squeezed Jennet's hand. "I have every faith that it is."

They left the Dickensons' cottage in a deflated silence and started to walk back down the lane, hand in hand. The weather, which had been pleasant earlier, was beginning to change, dark clouds moving across the sky, driven by the wind which had begun to whistle angrily across the hilltops. Jennet pulled her shawl tighter around herself and adjusted her coif. She looked up at William, whose eyes were cast downward, a frown fixed on his handsome face. He was deep in thought, she realised. He was trying to work out what they should do next.

"It'll be fine," he said, noticing her inquisitive glance. He forced a smile. "I will think of something."

"I have caused you so much trouble already. Perhaps Goodwife Dickenson is right. Perhaps this is not the right decision for you. Perhaps I am not right for you," she said quietly.

"Jennet," he said, looking at her squarely. "After today I am more determined than ever to take you away from all of this. Trust me, I will find us somewhere to live."

As they continued down the lane, they saw two figures approaching. Jennet squinted through the rain which had now begun to fall, to see that it was Nicholas and Grace. She hadn't realised that they had left the cottage again while she and William had been talking to Goodwife Dickenson. Obviously, Nicholas's solution to Grace's disquiet had been to take her out of the way completely. As they drew nearer she sighed heavily, anticipating a confrontation. After all, she knew enough about Grace to realise that she wouldn't be able to resist one more dramatic scene.

"I hope Mother sent you packing," Grace called spitefully as she drew nearer. Jennet noticed her use of the word 'Mother' in reference to Goodwife Dickenson; clearly she had settled comfortably into her new role in the Dickenson household.

"Grace, there's no need to say anything more," said William, exasperated. "Jennet and I will be on our way. Nicholas, take your wife home." He added with a grim smile at his friend. He took Jennet's arm, gently urging her to turn away from the conversation.

"How could you?" Grace called after them. "All those months you lived with us, helping my mother, breaking bread at our table, and all that time you were lying about who you were. And how could you threaten your poor cousin with curses? After all he has been through, hasn't he suffered enough? You're an evil woman, Jennet Sellers!" she bellowed.

Jennet turned around slowly to face Grace. As she met her gaze, she noticed how her green eyes glistened with hatred and fury, how her usually pretty mouth was twisted into an expression of utter contempt. Jennet drew a sharp breath; she had assumed until now that Grace's anger towards her was at least partly feigned, that she behaved this way because it afforded her other people's attention, perhaps even sympathy for being the unwitting victim of a witch's deception. Now, upon seeing her expression, she began to wonder if in fact Grace really believed that she was a witch.

"Grace, I…" her voice faltered. She wanted so badly to repeat her denial, to tell her that George had lied, to explain the reasons why she had kept her identity a secret. However, as she looked at Grace's cold, unkind expression, she realised that her words were futile. Grace had made up her mind, and nothing, no amount of explanation, would ever change that.

"Grace, I wish you and the baby well," she said in the end and turned quickly away.

"Don't you talk about my baby!" Grace yelled after her, before grasping her stomach and falling to the ground. "Ow, ow!" she cried. "She's hurt my baby! The witch has hurt my baby!"

Jennet turned back in horror to see Nicholas trying to lift his writhing wife off the ground, his face wild with an expression of sheer panic. "Oh God," she said to William. "I swear I didn't, I swear it wasn't me."

"I know that," replied William evenly. "She's worked herself into a bit of a state. She needs to calm down or she will harm the baby. Come, there's nothing more you can do here. It would be best if we just go."

The rain grew heavier as they continued down the lane, hard, heavy droplets relentlessly pounding the earth, creating puddles which soaked her skirts within minutes. They had no shelter from this, she realised miserably, nowhere that they could seek sanctuary, nowhere that they could call home. Struck by the hopelessness of their situation, Jennet began to cry; hot tears which contrasted with the coolness of the raindrops as they struck her cheeks.

Instinctively, William wrapped his arms around her. "Now, come," he said. "I swear this is the last time I will ever see you cry."

"William, where will we go? We have nothing, nobody," she sobbed.

"We have each other, Jennet, and whilst ever that is true, nothing else matters."

"But where will we live, what will we eat?"

William placed his finger gently on her lips. "As our Lord said, do not worry about your life, what you will eat or drink. Seek first our Lord's kingdom and his righteousness, and all these things will be given to you as well. Do not worry about tomorrow, for tomorrow will worry about itself. As I keep saying, Jennet, have faith and accept His spirit. All will be well, you'll see."

As the rain continued to fall around them, Jennet buried her head in William's chest, as though from his touch she might absorb the reassurance which she struggled to take from his words. She admired the strength of his faith, of course, but she found that when confronted with it, it served only to remind her of the weakness of her own.

"I hope you're right," she said quietly.

16

Hoarstones, near Wheatley Lane
Late May 1633

Jennet sighed deeply as she took hold of her brush and swept. Sweep, sweep, sweep; sometimes she felt as though that was all she did, all day long. The hard earth floor in this building was so filthy, so engrained with years of animal dirt that no amount of sweeping ever seemed to improve it. But then, this place was never meant to house people. It was a small barn, an outbuilding, meant to house piles of straw, or pigs in the cold winter months. Yet right now, and for the foreseeable future, it was their home.

Jennet leant heavily on her brush as she looked around her barn. William bemoaned her calling it a barn, but it was true; it wasn't a cottage, and she wasn't prepared to pretend that it was. But it was a place to live, and one for which she was grateful. The idea of living in the barn had come to William all of a sudden, as they sheltered miserably from the driving rain under trees below Higham heights, just hours after being turned away by Goodwife Dickenson. She remembered how he had snapped his fingers, his eyes bright with relief, and declared that he knew exactly where they should live. She recalled the journey to Wheatley Lane,

William marching determinedly ahead, whilst she lagged wearily behind him. Once there, William had sought out Edmund Robinson, a mason with whom he worked and had become quite friendly. Edmund, William had explained, was the cousin of John Robinson, whose house they were erecting at Hoarstones. He was a good man; he would be able to help them.

Jennet remembered how she had nodded dumbly, too tired to share his enthusiasm. Standing in front of Edmund Robinson's cottage at Little Blackwood, she had looked wistfully up the hill to where Goodwife Lund's cottage lay on Blackwood Head. It had been almost evening, the night drawing in quickly on account of the heavy rainclouds which continued to fill the sky. She recalled the amber glow of candlelight flickering invitingly in the Lunds' small windows. How hard it was to believe she had lived there just a few days earlier; it felt like an eternity had passed since Grace's wedding.

"I thought you were living with the Dickensons, over in Higham?" Edmund Robinson had asked. "And who's this?" he had added, looking at Jennet with his brow deeply furrowed, emphasising the creases on his already heavily lined face. Jennet had to strain her neck to look up at him; he was unnaturally tall, powerfully built just as any mason should be, but with small, sly eyes set deeply into his face. She lowered her gaze, chastising herself for judging this man's appearance so harshly. He was a good man, William had said so.

"I was – it's a long story, but suffice to say we've nowhere else to go," William had replied. "I'd like to stay and finish my work here, but without somewhere to live…" he allowed his voice to trail off, but his plea was clear enough.

"I see," said Edmund. "Well, I don't see any reason why you can't live in the outbuilding, although whether it's fit for people to live in is quite another matter." His eyes slid sideways as he returned his stare to Jennet. "Is she going to stay there with you?"

"Yes," replied William. "We are to be married," he added, grasping her hand.

"I see," said Edmund again. "William, you're a good worker and, from what I know of you, a Christian man. If you want to stay in the barn then it's yours – for a modest rent, of course. You can keep an eye on the house at night, too, which will ease my cousin's mind. I know he worries about thieves and, well, you know these are dangerous parts."

"Thank you," William replied gratefully. "And the rent – should I speak to John? He could take it straight from my wage."

Edmund shook his head. "No need for that," he said, lowering his voice. "We will keep that part of the arrangement just between us. John's a busy man, after all. Just pay your rent directly to me," he added.

"Alright," said William evenly. "Well thank you again, Edmund. Thanks to you we won't have to sleep under trees tonight."

"You might find after a couple of nights in there that you'd prefer the trees!" Edmund called after them. "That place needs a bit of work. Not worth fixing it up though; John wants to knock it down once his house is finished."

Anxious to arrive before nightfall, the pair had made a swift journey about half a mile along the lane to where the barn at Hoarstones sat. Still leaning on her brush, Jennet closed her eyes, recalling the first time she saw it. Even in the dim light, its derelict condition had been apparent. Its large wooden door had almost rotted away to nothing and its windows, although mercifully small, were exposed holes in the walls. The roof was mostly intact, except in one corner where it had obviously suffered considerable damage at some point in its history.

"At least we won't choke on the smoke from our fire," said William cheerfully, nodding towards the large hole in the thatch.

Inside, William took a candle from his sack. In the dim candlelight, the pair surveyed the grim scene before them. The floor of the barn was covered with remnants of old, dried animal excrement, and the walls, although built from strong local stone, were dampened from years of exposure to rainfall from the leaking roof. The only furnishing was a pile of stinking old straw and a couple of broken stools.

Jennet sighed heavily. "Edmund Robinson was right. I do prefer living under the trees. I can't believe he expects you to pay rent."

William shook his head disbelievingly. "Neither can I. He will want to keep it quiet, too; I'm sure the landlord wouldn't be delighted if he heard his tenants were sub-letting. I expect Edmund plans to keep the money for himself, without telling John. Alas, I will oblige him. It's only for a little while and let's face it, we don't have any other choice." He shook his head. "I'm afraid I was a little too trusting of Edmund. I don't think he's quite, well...I thought he would have been more charitable."

Jennet gave him a tired smile. She didn't want to tell him that she didn't like the look of that man, that she didn't trust him one bit. After all, he had given them a roof over their head, however disgusting it might be.

"You like to see the good in everyone, me included." She slumped down on to the filthy ground, feeling suddenly exhausted. "You wouldn't be living in this barn if it wasn't for me. It's barely fit for animals, never mind us." She wanted so badly to lay her head on the straw and sleep, but the smell emanating from it made her retch.

William chuckled. "If it was good enough for Christ our Saviour, then it's good enough for us. Besides, starting tomorrow we will tidy the place up, make it more comfortable. It'll do during the summer months; the house should be finished by the autumn so we can leave before the winter arrives."

Jennet nodded. "And tonight?"

"Tonight we will have the ground, and each other."

Jennet smiled, listening to those words over and over in her mind as she continued to sweep. She thought about that first night they had spent in the barn, how they had spread out her shawl in an effort to shield themselves from the filth on the floor, and how they had slept there on the cold, hard earth, wrapped in each other's arms. She remembered waking the following morning and although her neck was stiff and her hips pained her, she felt such happiness, such hope, her clarity of thought restored by peaceful slumber. It was as though she had woken up on the first day of a new life, and that realisation had given her a sense of freedom which she had never experienced before, a sense which had stayed with her ever since. For the first time in her life she felt as though it might be possible to escape from her past, to start anew, to be reborn.

Of course, she thought, she owed it all to William. All the admiration, all the love she felt for him before he brought her to the barn had been multiplied at least tenfold since they had been living together. True to his word, he had worked tirelessly to make their home more comfortable, fixing the door, crafting small shutters for the windows, fixing the stools and even making a table. He had collected pots and utensils from generous friends and acquaintances so that Jennet could cook over their fire and brew ale, and had acquired fresh straw for them to sleep on. When he wasn't working on their barn, he was working at the Robinsons' house a little further along the lane, sometimes from dawn to dusk, earning enough money so that he could take her away to London to seek a new beginning together, just the two of them.

William did all this for her, yet seemed to expect nothing in return. Jennet frowned, recalling how uneasy she had begun to feel after a few nights spent sleeping next to him in the barn. She remembered how she had lain there on the soft, new straw, listening to him snoring gently beside her, thinking about something Grace had once told her about men and their expectations. Courtship comes with pressures, Grace had told her. Men ask for certain things. Those words had played over and over again in Jennet's mind. She and William were far beyond courtship. They lived together now, and she had agreed to marry him; indeed, their arrangement was such that they effectively lived as husband and wife, albeit without a priest's blessing. William had left her in no doubt of his love for her; he was tender and attentive, never failing to kiss her and hold her in his arms as they fell asleep each night. Yet he had never indicated that he expected her to lie with him, his affection always loving but restrained.

In the end, on one calm spring evening a couple of weeks earlier, she had decided to broach the subject with him as they sat by the fire, eating the watery pottage which Jennet had cobbled together. The taste of her own bland food and impotent ale served to remind her each day that William was not getting a wife blessed with domestic skill either. She wondered if he minded, or if this was just something else that he didn't expect from her.

"William, do I make you happy?" she had asked as she played idly with the food in her bowl.

"Yes," replied William between hungry mouthfuls. "Why do you ask? Are you not happy?"

"Yes, yes of course," she had insisted.

"Then what makes you think I am not?"

She gestured towards her bowl. "My food isn't great. You could find a wife with better skill…"

William put his empty bowl on the ground. "Your food is fine, I have no complaints." He frowned, studying her expression. "There's more to this than your cooking skills, I can tell. Come Jennet, tell me. If we are to be married we shouldn't have secrets. I daresay there've been enough of those. Let's have no more," he added gently.

Jennet sighed deeply. "It's just, well, when we go to bed at night, you don't…" she struggled to find the right words. She could feel the colour rising in her cheeks and inwardly she chastised herself for being a silly old maid. What must William think? They were going to be married and she couldn't even talk about what should happen in bed.

"Oh." William put down his jug of ale and looked at her thoughtfully. "We're not married, Jennet. Not yet." To her surprise, she saw his cheeks begin to redden. "I'm sorry, I didn't realise that you wanted to…"

"No, no!" she protested. She began to panic a little, her heart beating faster. This conversation was not going well. "It's not that.

I mean, of course I do, but…I'm sorry, I'm not explaining myself very well, am I?" She laughed nervously.

William smiled. "No, you're not," he said patiently.

Jennet took a deep, considered breath. "It's just that Grace once told me that a man expects things, you know, during courtship. She said that Nicholas put her under considerable pressure to, well, I think you know what I mean. To lie with him."

To her surprise, William began to laugh. "Sorry," he said in response to the frown on her face. "Really, I am sorry. I'm laughing because I was worried. For a moment there I thought that I was letting you down somehow. Now I understand."

"Do you?" asked Jennet, confused.

William nodded. "Yes, I think so. Listen, Grace was partly right in what she said to you. There are some men who expect certain things from girls they are courting, and Nicholas undoubtedly was one of those men. You wouldn't have thought it for someone so reserved but…anyway, Grace was more than willing to yield, shall we say. I saw them sneaking off together on many occasions. Truly, it's no wonder she ended up with child before they were wed. However," he continued after a moment's pause, "I am not one of those men. I'm a religious man as you know, Jennet. I believe we should be married before we lie together."

"I see," she said simply. "I have to say, I'm relieved."

William frowned. "Are you? Why?"

"Because I was beginning to think it was me; that you didn't want to…"

"Jennet," William said firmly, taking hold of her hands. "Please understand that it is because of my faith that I show restraint. It is not, nor will ever be because I don't desire you. I find that living with you, that seeing you each day has deepened the love I feel for you. I love you more than I ever thought I was capable of loving anyone. Please believe that."

Jennet smiled again to herself as she finished sweeping. She was glad she had asked him, that she had allowed him to put her mind at ease. He was right; they should have no more secrets from each other.

She looked out of one of her small windows. It had been a pleasant day, summer almost upon them, the air mild and the surrounding trees plentiful with leaves and birds who sang from when the sun rose until it fell. If William had one complaint, it was that she did not venture away from their barn often enough. When he first remarked upon it she had protested, insisting that her life was full, busy, that she went outside almost every day, and to market at least once a week, since they had no land upon which to grow food or keep pigs. William had chuckled at that remark. It is good practice for London, he had said; in the city there are markets on every street. His comment had been intended lightly; however, it made Jennet pause for thought. How different London must be from Pendle, what a strange and interesting new world they were going to. How excited and nervous she felt.

William was right in one sense; since moving to the barn Jennet had all but given up on mixing with other local folk. She had always had a habit of keeping to herself, socialising little and trusting even less and this continued to be her guiding instinct, helped by the isolated situation of her new home. She had received a few visitors, of course; no doubt they had heard that Jennet Device had moved into a wreck of a barn and, curious, they had come to see for themselves. Edmund Robinson's wife had paid several visits, sometimes bringing vegetables from their land or fresh milk from their animals. Jennet recalled how Goodwife Robinson had studied her so carefully, her eyes filled with such caution that Jennet had cause to wonder if the offerings were not given as gifts at all, but as attempts to pacify the local witch.

On one occasion Goodwife Robinson had brought her son, also called Edmund. Jennet remembered him as the small, skinny boy with the knowing eyes and noisy tongue who she had encountered on her first visit to Wheatley Lane. Was that really only a year ago? It seemed longer. On seeing the boy Jennet had shuddered, reminded of that dreadful day when Ellena had died, a day which in hindsight seemed to have set so many other terrible events in motion. Had Ellena not died, George might never have made those horrible accusations which had caused her life to unravel so quickly. Had Ellena not died, she might still be living with the Holgates, helping them to care for the twins, listening to Uncle Christopher's endless complaints. Had Ellena not died, she might never have met William. This thought stopped her in her tracks. How odd life was; all that tragedy had occurred yet in a strange way it had led to her greatest happiness. She had smiled at the little boy then, a smile which he had returned broadly, as though he might be some sort of good omen for happy times yet to come.

Apart from the Robinsons' polite and guarded visits, however, her life was undoubtedly a solitary one. When William had challenged her, for the umpteenth time, to make an effort and make some new friends, she had simply shrugged and told him that she didn't see the point, since they would be gone in just a few months. In truth, she couldn't bear the thought of trying to create new bonds here. She was sure that most folk thought she was a witch, and those who didn't surely thought her a liar and a coward. She had come to realise that she was happier with her own company; for the first time in years she was learning to live with herself and the mistakes she had made. For the first time in years she felt happy, as though her lifelong wounds were finally beginning to heal. All she needed was William and their little barn, and their hopes and dreams for their future in London. What she certainly didn't need was other folk, their harsh words and judgmental expressions. In fact, that was the last thing she needed.

17

Wheatley Lane
Midsummer's Eve 1633

Jennet watched the fire as it burned intensely, bright shards of orange and yellow dancing upwards before her eyes. All around her, men and women from the village were making merry, dancing and singing, eating and drinking. Midsummer was a time of festivity, when in many villages folk would come together and light a bonfire in celebration of the summer, of long days, green fields and crops in full swell before the time of fruiting and harvest. Like many other feasts, the eve of St John the Baptist, to call it by its other name, was not celebrated without controversy, with some calling it popery for its reverence to a saint. Nonetheless it was a popular feast around these parts, second only to Christmas in its importance.

As Jennet gazed at the flames, she reflected upon how little she had seen of these festivals in her lifetime. Her father had always kept her away from most popular gatherings, and the Midsummer fires were no exception. Superstitious nonsense, he had called it. He had a point, of course; for many, Midsummer was a mystical time when fire had magical properties, when mere flames could ward off evil spirits. After his experience with Jennet's mother, his aversion to magic was understandable, as was his desire to keep his daughter away from it.

Jennet bit her lip as she thought about her father. He had always tried to protect her, ever since she was a little girl, abandoned on his doorstep. She felt certain that he would have approved of William; his kindness and selflessness towards her would have appealed to him. However, she suspected he would have been less impressed with their plans to go to London. Damn foolishness, he probably would have called it, to leave their beautiful northern wilderness for the south, and a city no less! Cities were full of strange folk, unfamiliar places, odd customs. Cities were dirty, crowded and dangerous. Why would you choose life in London over life in the Pendle countryside?

In her mind she ran through her counter-arguments. In London she could be anonymous, she could start afresh. In London, no one would need to know about her past. In London she could find security, as William's wife, as no one important from nowhere special. Here, no one could keep her safe, not even William. Her thin veil of anonymity had been torn from her and with it, any chance of leading a quiet, happy life. Here she would forever be Jennet Device, the child of witches, the wicked girl who condemned her family to die. Here she would always be reviled and suspected. Here her identity was a noose around her neck, connecting her to the gallows which loomed like a spectre, threatening any peace she might find.

She took a considered sip of the ale which she cradled in her hand. She kept her head bowed slightly, shoulders hunched in her shawl, coif pulled well towards her face. She didn't wish to be noticed tonight, or indeed, on any night. Until she could leave, the only chance she had of protecting herself was to allow people to forget about her. She could never restore her anonymity; that was gone forever, thanks to Alice, but she could find safety in seclusion, if she shut herself away from the world in her little barn.

William, however, continued to have other ideas. Indeed, it was due to his insistence that she was there tonight at all. "We should go to the Midsummer fire," he had said as they ate their evening meal a few nights earlier. "Plenty of the men I work with will be there. They'd find it odd if we weren't."

Jennet had raised her eyebrows at him as she stirred her food thoughtfully. "I'm surprised at you," she had said, "I thought you would find these traditions ungodly."

"Yes, well I suppose I do," he replied, laughing. "But I also think it's important we go. Besides," he added, a cheeky grin spreading across his face, "it's said to be a time of friendship and reconciliation, as well as magic. I daresay such things wouldn't hurt you right now. I don't like to see you alone."

"I'm not alone," she had insisted. "I have you."

William had frowned at her then, a deep, lingering furrowing of his brow. "I work all day. You spend too much time in your own company, it is not healthy. I worry about you. I worry what this solitude will do to you."

His concern had made her feel guilty and reluctantly she had agreed to come. She tipped the remaining contents of her cup into her mouth and looked around. She could see William, laughing with his friends from Hoarstones. She noticed that he stood next to Edmund Robinson, a sly look fixed on the tall man's face as he shared the joke that another man was telling. She narrowed her eyes; she still didn't like that man, she found him conniving, ruthless, the sort who would do anything for his own personal gain. William was always quick to see the good in people but when it came to Edmund Robinson, she was sure there was no good to be found. Edmund caught her gaze, a slow smile spreading across his face as he looked her up and down. She shuddered; she disliked the way he looked at her – never at her eyes, always elsewhere. The pit of her stomach churned with her disgust and she turned away.

"Jennet, is that you?" came a voice from behind her.

Jennet spun around to see Goodwife Lund standing there. Upon recognising Jennet the Goodwife opened her arms wide, a broad smile on her face. "Jennet! It is good to see you."

Reluctantly, Jennet accepted the affectionate gesture,

momentarily enjoying the familiar motherly embrace which Goodwife Lund's big warm arms afforded. "Goodwife Lund," she said. "Are you well?"

"Yes, yes," she said, almost dismissively. "And you? I hear you are to be married."

"Yes," she replied simply. "William has asked me to be his wife. We are leaving soon, for London."

"Yes, so I have heard. I believe you're living in an old barn near the new house at Hoarstones?" Goodwife Lund looked around, a brief flicker of apprehension crossing her friendly face. "Come, lass, walk with me. We don't want prying eyes and ears."

They walked a few yards together, an awkward silence lingering between them.

"I hope you understand why I have not been to see you," Goodwife Lund said in the end, her earnest eyes dancing with the firelight emanating from the torches lit all around them.

Jennet nodded. "William told me that I have caused you a lot of grief. For that I am sorry."

"Oh, lass," Goodwife Lund wrapped her arms around her once again. "I can't lie; I was very upset when I found out who you really are. Not because it bothers me, but because you felt you had to lie. Although now that I have had time to reflect upon it, I do understand why you hid your identity from folk," she added.

"You do?" Jennet asked, surprised.

"Yes. It does not take much in this world for a woman to be accused of witchcraft; of all the people here, I should know that. A few badly-mixed herbs, a few ill-chosen words and suddenly you stand accused of cursing someone. It has always been my greatest fear."

Jennet frowned. "I thought you'd be angry with me."

Goodwife Lund sighed. "No, lass, I'm not angry. I was shocked at first, but never angry."

Jennet shook her head. "I don't understand. You've not come to find me; you've not spoken a word to me since Grace's wedding..."

"I know." Goodwife Lund cast her eyes down. "And for that I feel some shame. But you have to understand, folk were calling you a witch and well, you know what sort of trade I ply…"

"You were worried folk would think you guilty by association?"

Goodwife Lund nodded, a look of regret flashing across her plump face. "Yes. I'm sorry."

Jennet put up her hand in protest. "Don't be," she said gently. "It is no worse than what I did, hiding who I was. We all do things to protect ourselves. But if you're so worried about being associated with me, why are you speaking to me tonight?"

Goodwife Lund shrugged. "It's Midsummer – when is there a better time to make amends? Besides, everyone here is drunk! They won't remember a thing by tomorrow morning."

Jennet chuckled lightly and looked around. It was true - the ale had been flowing freely for hours and would continue to flow for some time yet. In the middle of the village, the bonfire still burned brightly and the music grew ever louder in competition with the inebriated laughter of the village's inhabitants. "How is Grace?" she asked.

Goodwife Lund grimaced. "Not well, I believe, although I have seen little of her since she wed."

"Really?" Jennet asked, surprised. "She is your daughter, why won't she see you?"

"I don't know," Goodwife Lund said with a shrug. "She doesn't invite me to visit, and when I try to call on her unannounced she refuses to see me, sends a message via Nicholas saying that she's unwell, or tired."

"That's a shame," said Jennet. "You must be worried."

Goodwife Lund nodded. "Yes. I hear she does not fare well as she gets nearer to her time. I want to be able to help her, but she won't let me." Her voice was tinged with anguish.

Jennet shook her head. "I'd try to speak to her, but I fear I would make matters worse."

Goodwife Lund drew a considered breath. "I daresay that's true. She was very distraught to discover who you are."

Yes, Jennet thought, and she believes that I'm a witch too. She shuddered as she recalled how Grace had screamed at her as she left the Dickensons' farm. "That witch has hurt my baby," she had cried. Those words were ringing in her ears now. Did Grace really believe that she could have done that to her unborn child?

Goodwife Lund gave Jennet an affectionate smile. "I have missed having you with us, Jennet. I know you'll be leaving soon so…I just want you to know that I wish you well. I wish you both well."

"Thank you, that means a lot to me," said Jennet, embracing her friend.

"It's good to see you both together," said William, walking up behind them. Jennet noticed that he was a little unsteady on his feet and wondered how much ale he had drunk. She frowned. It wasn't like him to drink too much. "Sorry, I hope I'm not interrupting," he added.

"No, not at all." Goodwife Lund gave Jennet's shoulder a slight squeeze. "Take care of yourself, lass."

"See, what did I tell you about reconciliation?" William asked as they watched Goodwife Lund walk away. His breath was pungent with the stench of ale.

"You're drunk," said Jennet. "I think we should go home now, before you're unable to walk at all."

William laughed as he wrapped his arms around her. "Giving me orders already, wife?" he said teasingly.

"I'm not your wife. Not yet."

He pressed his nose softly against her neck, making her spine tingle. "I can't wait until you're my wife," he whispered, his breath caressing her skin. "I was thinking about it tonight. We should marry before we leave for London."

Jennet looked at him, eyes wide. "Do you mean it?"

William nodded. "I had thought we'd wait until we got to London. There are many different churches in London, we could easily find a congregation…you know, like the one in Grindleton. But the longer we wait, the harder it grows to wait," he looked at her meaningfully. "What do you think?"

"Yes!" she cried, embracing him.

"What's all this? Sharing some happy news?"

Jennet turned to see Edmund Robinson standing there, a wide grin fixed on his face. She noted how he swayed from side to side; clearly, he was suffering the ill-effects of the evening's ale consumption. His eyelids drooped heavily as he spoke. "So, is there something to celebrate? Will I fetch more ale?"

"Edmund!" William declared happily. "Yes, please join us. Tonight I am a happy man - Jennet is going to marry me."

"I thought you both had already agreed to marry?" Edmund asked, a look of suspicion flickering briefly across his haggard face.

"We had, but we've just agreed to bring the date forward a little," William explained.

"Oh! I see," replied Edmund, letting out a wicked chuckle. "Been finding ways to keep warm in that old barn, have we?" He looked at Jennet. "Don't look so serious. You're not the first lass to get wed before you start showing."

Jennet looked at him, open-mouthed. "No, you misunderstand," she protested. "I am not with child."

Edmund Robinson waved his hands at her in a defensive gesture. "Look, lass, who am I to judge?" His smile turned into a sneer. "I daresay you've done worse things in your time."

"I beg your pardon?" It was William who grew defensive now.

"Oh, I know who she is," Edmund replied, pointing at Jennet. "I remember your grandmother, you know. And your mother, too. Roaming hither and thither, offering charms and casting spells." He drew close to her, so close that she could feel his rancid breath against her cheek. "Jennet Device, eh? Where have you been hiding all these years? Folk thought you were gone, or dead. Seeing you, it's like seeing a ghost."

"Edmund, I ask you as a friend; step away from Jennet, please." William's tone was even but Jennet could tell he fought hard to maintain control of himself.

"Do the names James and John Robinson mean anything to

you, Jennet?" Edmund continued, ignoring William's plea.

Jennet shook her head and cast her eyes down. It was a lie, of course; she knew exactly who Edmund spoke of.

"Well, they should. They were members of my family, murdered by your mother. You should remember their names, Jennet, you said them in court. You told everyone that it was your mother who killed them. How can you not remember that?" He leered at her mockingly.

"Enough now, Edmund," William insisted. "Just leave her be. Come, Jennet, I think it's time for us to go," he said, taking her arm.

"It's no wonder you're running away to London!" Edmund called after them. "The guilty always run!"

The pair hurried down the lane, so fast that within minutes they were amongst the trees, Wheatley Lane little more than a warm glow behind them. Abruptly Jennet stopped; she was breathless, retching, her heart pounding and her stomach lurching. In that moment, every conceivable emotion seemed to course through her body; fear, anger, humiliation. Her legs gave way and she staggered helplessly to the ground, William going down behind her, his arms placed rigidly around her shoulders as though they might form a sort of armour, shielding her from insult and abuse. Too late for that, she thought, Edmund Robinson's cruel words stinging her as they replayed in her mind.

"Oh my love, I am sorry," William breathed, his mouth pressed against her ear.

Jennet let out an involuntary wail. "Now do you see why I wish to hide myself away?" she cried.

"Yes my darling, yes I do," William whispered. "I am sorry. It is my fault that you came tonight. If it hadn't been for me, you would never have had to endure that."

His apologies fell on deaf ears. Jennet could not hear him over the sound of her own sobs; big, heavy, wet tears of sorrow and grief. All the pain she felt, all the anguish which she carried with her now burst to the surface, made raw once again by the venom of Edmund Robinson's drunken tirade.

"You should have left me, William. That day, when you found me in the woods. You should have left me there to die. I am no good for you. I am no good for anyone. All I ever bring is misery and suffering."

"No!" William protested. "Never say that! I could not live without you."

He spun her around, kissing her gently on her mouth. He allowed his lips to linger, their warmth and tenderness causing Jennet to respond. She closed her eyes, letting his loving touch soothe her, as though his passion might be able to cleanse her wounds, as though it could expel her misery. As his kisses grew firmer and more urgent, she felt a sort of heat rise within her. Her eyes flickered open briefly as she recognised the strength of her own desire; stronger than any anger, mightier than any pain. Her spine tingled with delight as William moved his lips down her cheek, on to her ear, and down her neck. She moaned lightly as he laid her down on the ground, his hands searching under her skirts, his lips moving to the swell of her breasts.

"I want you," he breathed, "but we must stop this. It would be a sin."

It was a feeble protest and he continued to kiss and caress her. In the end, it was Jennet who took charge, pushing him away. "Then we should stop. I don't want the first time we lie together to be a sin for you."

William cleared his throat, regaining composure. "It would be a sin for both of us."

Jennet nodded. "Perhaps, but I believe I lack your commitment to God. I also fear that considering my past sins, enjoying the pleasures of the flesh while unwed is unlikely to be my defining, damning act on the day of judgement." She tried to laugh but could hear only sadness in her voice.

"Your past sins are not your own, Jennet; they were the work of others." William's tone regained its measured seriousness. "I am sorry. I was weak. If you hadn't stopped me I would…"

"It doesn't matter."

"I'm afraid my haste to marry you isn't entirely honourable."

"I know. That doesn't matter either."

In the moonlight Jennet could see his familiar, handsome smile return to his face; that broad, honest smile which she had fallen so hopelessly in love with. She smiled back; a shy smile, but one which acknowledged a moment of affection and understanding passing between them. It was the sort of tender moment which seemed to make the harsh words of Edmund Robinson pale into insignificance, and the rest of the world seem distant and inconsequential. She closed her eyes briefly, wishing that she could always feel so cocooned from the hard realities of life as she did right there and then. But, like all good things, that moment would have to come to an end.

"Come," said William, getting to his feet and offering her his hand. "I think it's time we went home."

And with his words, their moment passed.

18

St Mary's Church, Newchurch-in-Pendle
September 1633

It was a crisp day in the early autumn, a lukewarm sun shining amongst wisps of white cloud, a gentle breeze teasing yellow leaves which had already fallen on to the ground. Jennet walked arm-in-arm with William as they made their journey from Hoarstones to Newchurch-in-Pendle. She smiled slightly to herself, feeling grateful for the favourable weather. She had risen early, leaving William to sleep while she went to wash in the river and to dress in the fresh shift, bodice and petticoats Goodwife Lund had given to her the previous week. She had been surprised by the Goodwife's visit to her home and was reluctant to accept the gifts. However, Goodwife Lund had insisted. They're just some things Grace had left behind, Goodwife Lund had told her; they might as well be put to good use. After all, she had added, she doubted Grace would come back for them now. Jennet had noted the anguished expression on her friend's face and instinctively embraced her, silently wishing that Grace could see the pain she caused her mother.

"I hope you're not having second thoughts," William remarked, noticing the serious look on her face.

Jennet smiled. "No, not at all," she said. "I was just thinking about Goodwife Lund."

"It was good of her to agree to be a witness today. We couldn't be married without sufficient witnesses, or church attendances, or banns." He rolled his eyes then flashed her one of his broadest smiles.

Jennet gave a sigh of mock-exasperation. "William Braithwaite, you are impatient and you have little regard for custom, do you know that? The minister only asks what is required of him."

William's smile faded. "I would dispute that. Do you know that in London you can go to the Fleet Prison and be married by a minister for a little coin? Yet this minister wanted me to sit through his sermons week in, week out, so that he may count me among his flock. And why the requirement for two witnesses? A popish rule, surely."

Jennet let out an amused chuckle. Seeing the serious expression on William's face, she clapped her hand over her mouth to suppress it. "I'm sorry. He's just cautious, I'm sure. You're not from his parish, whilst I'm..." she hesitated, "I'm hardly a regular in his pews on a Sunday."

William's smile returned. "Well I don't suppose it matters now. The minister has agreed to marry us, and thanks to his diligence I can consider myself once again to be well-versed in the doctrine of the English church. But most importantly, we will be married by the end of today." He kissed the side of her head. "And I can't wait until you're my wife."

Jennet gave him an affectionate squeeze, enjoying the sentiment but always confused by his views on faith. She knew that she had a simple understanding of these matters, but still she could not understand why the 'English church', as he called it, offended him so greatly – did its ministers not preach the teachings of Jesus Christ and the word of God as written in the Bible? Was the church in Grindleton not also part of the English church? She felt unsure. She hoped that when they went to London they would find a congregation which suited him. Perhaps in time she would come to a better understanding of his beliefs, and of her own, although the idea of spending a lot of time in church still did not excite her.

They arrived at the church as the sun rose higher into the sky, indicating the approach of midday. At the church gates they were greeted by Goodwife Lund, who was pacing impatiently, a young, skinny man stood by her side.

"Oh good, you're here! I was beginning to worry," she said. "I presume this is your other witness?" she nodded in the direction of the young man, who shuffled awkwardly on his feet.

"Yes," replied William. "This is James. We work together." He gave his friend a nod of acknowledgement.

"Right, well, you should both go inside and see the minister," Goodwife Lund instructed. "Jennet and I will follow you in a few moments." She gave Jennet a reassuring smile. Jennet felt glad that her old friend was taking charge.

"Thank you," she said to Goodwife Lund as they watched the two men head into the church. "It means a lot to me that you're here today."

"It's the least I could do for you, lass," she replied simply. "How do you feel? Nervous?"

"A little," Jennet let out a small chuckle. "But happy."

"I see you've left your hair uncovered," Goodwife Lund observed. "It is nice to see you dressed as a maid – it makes you seem younger."

Jennet nodded at the compliment, her hands self-consciously drawn to her long dark hair. "Thank you. It seemed a shame to cover it. It is the last time I will wear it loose, after all."

"I wouldn't be so certain of that," Goodwife Lund replied, wrinkling her nose. "London has some strange customs. You might find plenty of undressed heads down there. Even here you can find women who have abandoned their coifs – I've often seen Goodwife Dickenson without one. But you're right to leave it loose today; tomorrow you will be a maid no more," she added with a grin and a wink.

Jennet's cheeks reddened at the remark as she took the Goodwife's arm and walked towards the church, her stomach leaping all the way.

Inside, the air was cool, the atmosphere still; her footsteps, although softened by rushes, seemed to echo in the silence. She had only ever been in this church when it was full of people waiting for worship on a Sunday morning. Now, in its emptiness, with just the four of them and a minister within it, the church seemed eerie. She shuddered, a cold draft wafting its way up her back as the heavy wooden door slammed shut behind them. She looked up the church towards the altar, where she could see William standing, waiting for her, illuminated by the streaks of sunlight which had begun to shine through the windows. At least the light inside was not dim; the minister had even taken care to light a handful of candles.

"Are you ready?" Goodwife Lund whispered.

Jennet nodded. "I think so."

"Good. I will take my seat then."

Jennet began to walk down the aisle towards her betrothed. A pang of sadness struck her as she reflected that, for many other women, this walk would be accompanied by their father. Weeks ago, William had asked her if she wanted someone to give her away; one of the older men he laboured with, perhaps, or Goodwife Lund's husband, John. She had given it some thought but in the end had decided that, in the absence of her father, she would rather walk alone. As she walked down the aisle now, it occurred to her that her decision, although sentimentally made, had been a fitting one. She could not be given away, in the traditional sense, as she had no one left to offer her; a fact which was sad, but also liberating. Her lack of family meant that she could give herself away, choosing her own husband, her own path in life. Walking down the aisle alone was a demonstration of the independence she had gained through the tragedy of circumstance.

"Are you alright?" William mouthed as she approached the

altar.

She nodded and took hold of his hand, looking up into his bright green eyes which seemed to shine with happy anticipation. Her stomach fluttered as she prepared to make her vows, to commit herself to this handsome, unusual, some might say radical, man. This man, who wanted to marry plain old Jennet Sellers with her dark brown hair and pallid complexion. This man, who seemed not to care that she could not read, that she did not know what her opinions were on God. This man, who gladly forgave the fact that the only interesting thing about her was something so terrible that she had tried her best to conceal it from him. She did not deserve this man, yet by his insistence, she would have him for her husband anyway.

"We don't have to marry in church, you know," she had said to him, several nights ago as they lay together, enjoying the restrained embraces which had become part of their evening routine.

Her statement had caused William to pause. "What do you mean?" he asked.

"Do you not have handfasting in Cumberland?"

Her question made William laugh out loud. "Oh, Jennet! I thought you were being serious."

"I am."

In the darkness, she sensed him frown. "Yes, there are people who marry through handfasting ceremonies all over England. But you know, even if you marry through troth-plight, you're still supposed to have a church wedding soon afterwards. And you're not supposed to lie together until you do," he added meaningfully.

"Oh," she replied simply. "I just thought it might be a solution. I can tell that you tire of waiting."

William had wrapped his arms tightly around her then. "I know that I am being impatient. I can't deny that I find it hard to wait. But we must; if we are to marry then it should be done properly by a minister, before God, not by making promises to each other in front of a handful of folk from the village."

"Are we not always before God?" she had asked innocently.

Her question had gone unanswered. Undoubtedly they stood before God now, in front of His altar, facing one another, a virulent mixture of nerves and excitement hanging in the air like dandelion seeds in the summer.

"Dearly beloved, we have come together in the presence of God to witness and bless the joining together of this man and this woman in Holy Matrimony," the minister began.

Jennet returned her gaze to William, who looked at her intently, a serene expression fixed upon his face. It didn't matter to him now that this wasn't Grindleton, that it wasn't some radical curate leading the ceremony. He no longer cared about the obstacles placed in their way; the banns, the cost of a licence, the long walks to St Marys every Sunday morning when in truth they both would have gladly stayed in bed together.

In that moment it struck Jennet that she had never seen William happier, and that his happiness was because of her. She smiled at him as he took hold of her hand; the bringer of suffering and death had become the bringer of joy. How complete her transformation was. Perhaps it was possible to create your own heaven. Perhaps that was what they were doing today.

Her smile broadened as she listened to him making his vows to her. When it came to her turn, she did not hesitate. This surprised her; she had spent so much of her life crippled by guilt and sadness, hiding herself away, avoiding life. Marrying William was the biggest decision she had ever made and she had been sure that, however much she loved him, when it came to committing herself to him she would stumble, crumbling and cowering just as she always did. Instead, she embraced the words, reciting them excitedly, as though they were not an end in themselves but a beginning; the beginning of a new life, the beginning of happiness and peace.

"Those whom God has joined, let no one put asunder," the minister said. He bade them both to kneel and began his blessing of their marriage, likening the bond between Christ and his church to their union, urging them to love, honour and cherish one another. Jennet winced a little at his insistence that they should live in true godliness; she had felt so far from God for so many years that she doubted this was something she could ever aspire to. Perhaps she would learn, in time. No doubt, William would try to teach her.

Just as the minister was about the say the final 'Amen', the ceremony was interrupted by the sound of the church door opening, its old hinges making a loud creaking noise. Jennet's heart began to pound and she closed her eyes momentarily, praying that it wasn't George, or Alice, or even Edmund Robinson, come to spoil her day. She turned around slowly, her mouth falling open at the sight of Goodwife Dickenson standing at the rear of the church. The Goodwife panted heavily, trying to catch her breath. Immediately, Jennet noticed that she was not her usual, immaculate self. Her coif was ill-set upon her head, so badly so that much of her grey hair now fell beneath it. Her face shone with beads of sweat. Clearly, she had come in a hurry.

"I'm sorry," she said, still breathing heavily, addressing the puzzled faces standing before her. "I wouldn't have burst in like that if it wasn't necessary. I've come to fetch Goodwife Lund. It's Grace – she's in childbed and we need your help."

"Childbed?" Goodwife Lund repeated. "But it isn't her time yet. Are you sure?"

"Yes, I'm sure," Goodwife Dickenson snapped, losing all her usual composure. "Come, I fear we haven't much time."

Goodwife Lund looked helplessly at Jennet, who gestured to her to go. Her plump face pale and her eyes wide with fear, she followed Goodwife Dickenson out of the church, the door slamming shut behind them.

"I hope Grace will be alright," said Jennet, half to William, half to herself. "I hope she'll let her poor mother near her. What a terrible time Goodwife Lund has had."

"Come, wife," he said, taking hold of her hand. "Let us say a prayer for her before we leave. Let's ask God to deliver Grace and her child safely from childbed. We cannot do more than that;

Grace is in God's hands, just like us all."

"Amen," replied the minister with a grim smile.

They left the church and walked home together, hand in hand. The fine autumn day which they had enjoyed earlier had begun to dissipate, dark clouds looming overhead as they walked down the lane. Instinctively they picked up their pace as the first few cold, heavy droplets fell from the sky. It reminded Jennet of the first time William had kissed her, under the trees, sheltering from the pouring rain. She remembered how she ran away from him like a frightened child. She smiled; there was no fear now, only joy. In fact, if the ground hadn't felt so soggy underfoot she would have skipped home with delight.

They arrived back at their barn in the late afternoon, just as the light began to fade. They were both soaked to the skin, the rain having poured down on them for at least half the journey. Nonetheless they were in good spirits, William lifting Jennet into his arms and carrying her through the little doorway, placing her gently on to their straw bed.

"I will light a fire," he said, kissing her tenderly on the lips.

"I hope you're not sorry it's just the two of us," Jennet said as she removed her sodden bodice and petticoat.

"What do you mean?" he replied, returning to sit beside her.

"At the very least, most folk will go to the alehouse after their wedding. Some folk hold a feast for the entire village. I hope you're not disappointed that it is just you and I tonight," she said meekly.

"Jennet, you are the only person I want to be with, now and always. Besides, we were right to keep our wedding just to ourselves and a couple of others - we wouldn't have wanted unwelcome attention," he added meaningfully.

"That's true," agreed Jennet. The fire had begun to warm the room now and she started to remove her soggy shift.

"What are you doing?" William asked.

"I'm taking this off. It's wet."

He gave her a mischievous grin. "Jennet, we got married today.

As your husband and on our wedding night, I insist that it is I who gets to take off your wet shift."

"Alright," she replied, feeling suddenly self-conscious as she raised her arms, allowing him to tease the damp fabric away from her skin. Although they had lived together for some time, she had never allowed him to see her naked before. William had never asked either, perhaps feeling that her bare flesh was too much of a temptation.

Now, with the blessing of a priest there were no more barriers, yet inexplicably she felt anxious. William seemed to notice. "Is something the matter?"

It's just…I…" she gestured helplessly.

William smiled. "I know. I'm nervous too. Here, help me take off my clothes; we will be the same then. Perhaps we should have stopped at the alehouse, after all. A few jugs of ale would have given us both some courage."

"Like that night on the way home from the Midsummer fire," she remarked as she fiddled clumsily with his unfamiliar items of clothing.

"I had too much courage that night!" he said, laughing. "There," he said finally, lying her down on the straw. Looking at her intently, he ran his fingers across her forehead, down her cheek and on to her breasts. Jennet shivered with delight. "You're beautiful," he said as he began to kiss her neck, her shoulders; every part of her.

"I love you," Jennet said simply as she closed her eyes, enjoying his touch, basking in his affection. This was what it was like to love, and to be loved. Right here, in this moment, their two bodies locked together, glistening in the heat of the fire; this was love, this was heaven.

"I love you, Jennet Braithwaite," William replied.

19

Hoarstones, near Wheatley Lane
All Saints Day 1633

William closed the barn door firmly behind him, startling Jennet, who spun around in alarm. He was home several hours earlier than expected, and for a moment she thought he was an intruder. He clapped his hands together excitedly and gave her a beaming smile. "Well, the house is finished!" he declared. "A few weeks later than I had hoped, but still – John has said he will pay us in the next few days." He grasped her hands excitedly. "Just think, Jennet, this time next week we could be...well, I don't know where! But further south than here. One step closer to London."

"I can't believe it," she replied, sitting down on her stool. She had been feeling unwell lately and needed to steady herself. "I can't believe that we are really going to go. I thought this day would never come, and yet..." she paused, hesitating over her words.

William looked at her squarely. "You're not having second thoughts, are you?"

"No, not at all." She smiled. "But I think I will miss this place."

"What, this rotten, squalid barn?" he said in mock-disbelief.

"Our first home together," she said simply. She looked around at its humble walls, its basic furnishings, rickety stools and a straw bed. "This place has been my sanctuary."

"Hmm," replied William thoughtfully. "It is true that you seldom leave it. All the more reason to leave, my good wife; you have become too attached."

He grinned mischievously and took hold of her in his arms, burying his nose in the side of her neck. Jennet closed her eyes as he began to kiss her, pushing the neck of her shift aside as he moved on to her collarbone. This was usually how it began. She began to anticipate his next move, waiting for him to lift her up and carry her over to their bed, where he would undress her and they would lie together before eating their evening meal.

William freely admitted that no amount of hunger and thirst following a hard day's toil could compete with the desire he felt as soon as he held her in his arms. Sometimes, after supper, they would lie together again and afterwards, as they dozed in front of the lowly embers of their extinguishing fire, Jennet would lie with her head against William's chest, listening to the steady rhythm of his heart, praying that they would never tire of each other.

To her surprise, William interrupted their embrace. "I think we should celebrate," he declared.

"Oh?" she replied, trying to conceal the disappointment in her voice that he had not taken her to bed.

William nodded. "Let's go to the alehouse together."

"Can't we just celebrate here, just the two of us?" she asked. She sat down again, that feeling of light-headedness returning suddenly. She hadn't mentioned it to William. No doubt he would tell her that it was due to a lack of fresh air; that it proved his point that she should get away from the barn more often.

William looked at her, his head slightly over to one side, as though he was trying to get the measure of her. "A lot of the other lads are going to The Horse and Gate, just for a few ales, to celebrate a job well done. You remember the place, surely? It's where we first met."

Jennet hesitated. "I'm not sure, William. After what happened with Edmund Robinson..."

William smiled and placed his hands gently on her shoulders. "It's just a quiet drink with a few of my friends, Jennet. It isn't a big village feast; in fact, it isn't in this village at all! I think Fence will be a safe enough distance away from Edmund Robinson, for tonight at least."

Jennet sighed heavily. "Alright," she agreed, feeling irritated with herself. She may have learnt many things in these first few weeks of marriage, but she still hadn't learnt how to say no to William.

They ate an early supper then made the short journey on foot to the nearby village of Fence. Despite her reluctance to go, once outside Jennet found that she enjoyed the walk. William had come home so early that it was not yet dark, although the late autumn daylight was dim and grey, thanks to the heavy clouds permeating the sky. As she walked, Jennet breathed in heavily, enjoying the plethora of fragrances lingering in the damp, still air; the soggy leaves underfoot, the smoke from nearby cottages, even the smell of those animals which still remained in the fields. She couldn't recall a time when she had noticed different scents so keenly. Perhaps this new appreciation was due to the amount of time she had spent cooped up in her barn. Perhaps William was right; perhaps she did need to get outside more.

"You're quiet," William remarked. "What are you thinking about?"

Jennet shook her head. One thing she had discovered about herself over these early weeks of marriage was that increasingly she felt unwilling to share every single thought she had with her husband. At first she had given them over freely, and William would always be interested, no matter how superficial they might be. He loved to talk to her about anything, everything. He could talk for hours. He could talk until she felt exhausted by talking and began to crave silence.

After a while, Jennet had started to keep some things to herself. It wasn't that she resisted telling William something in particular;

indeed, sometimes she would keep her own counsel on even the most mundane of details, like how she preferred the smell of wet wood to burning wood, or how she thought last night's pottage had been better than the one she had made that afternoon. Often she would chastise herself for holding back from him; he was a kind, attentive husband who loved her dearly, and she had promised to return his love, body and soul, before a priest. But sometimes, with all the talking and sharing, it was hard to remember where she ended and he began.

"Oh dear, are you upset with me?" he asked.

"No, why?"

"You've not answered my question."

"Don't you ever like to just be quiet for a while?" Jennet asked him.

"Only when I'm before God," he answered.

She stopped walking and turned to face him. "Are we not always before God?" she gestured wildly with her arms. "Did God not create everything around us? Is he not here, right now?"

William smiled. "Jennet, you're beginning to sound like a bit of a pagan. You'll be aligning stones on top of Pendle hill next."

Jennet shot him a serious look. "You were the one who said we don't need church to find God's spirit. Well, where else would his spirit be, if it cannot be found in the earth He created?"

William put his arm lovingly around her shoulders. "You know, Jennet, it is wonderful to hear you say such things."

Jennet frowned. "Why?"

"Because when I first met you, you seemed indifferent to God, if not completely without faith. It's such a relief to me that you have begun to give these matters more thought." He hugged her closer to him. "Oh my love, I can't wait until I get you to London. We shall find a good congregation and what's more, I will teach you to read. Then we may study the Bible together."

"Yes," she replied simply. She didn't have the heart to tell him that the thought of reading the Bible still did not excite her. That was something else which she would just keep to herself.

The alehouse was busy, the atmosphere alive with the sound of chatter and raucous laughter. They were greeted by William's friends, the usual set of young men with whom he socialised. She saw the tall, skinny man, James, who had acted as a witness at their wedding. She gave him an obliging nod. She realised that despite recognising all the faces in front of her, she had never taken the time to get to know any of them. William was right; she did shut herself away from folk. She sighed lightly as William handed her a cup of ale. She didn't suppose it mattered now. They would be leaving soon, going far away, far enough for her to become anonymous again. Perhaps then she would have the confidence to socialise more.

She fixed a small smile on her face as she tried to concentrate on the merry conversation going on around her. Labouring talk, mostly; stories from their time together at Hoarstones, gossip from the surrounding villages and, of course, the occasional bawdy joke. She began to feel awkward, the only woman in a group of men, unable to relate to any of their discussions. She wished then that William hadn't insisted on her coming. She would have been much happier if he had gone by himself and left her at home in her quiet, empty barn. The room was so hot and so full of noise. She could feel herself becoming flustered, that dizzy feeling returning once again. She rested her hands on the wooden table, trying to steady herself.

"Jennet, are you alright?" William placed a supportive hand at her back. She looked up at him, concern etched on his face.

"I feel a little light-headed, that's all. It's nothing, just the heat in here, I'm sure."

"Here," he said, offering her a stool. "You should sit."

Obediently, Jennet sat down and placed her head in her hands. She took a few deep breaths. "Thank you," she said, after a moment. "I feel better now."

William smiled at her. "Good, I'm glad. Have you seen that Goodwife Lund is here tonight?"

Jennet looked up. "No. Is she with John, her husband?"

William nodded. "Yes. And Nicholas, too. I haven't seen Grace, though."

"I would imagine she's at home, nursing her baby. I wonder how she is, how they both are." Jennet's stomach lurched as she recalled Grace's words the last time they saw each other, how she had called her a witch and accused her of hurting her unborn child.

"Well, here's your chance to find out," replied William, nodding in the direction of Goodwife Lund, who was walking over to greet them.

"Jennet!" Goodwife Lund embraced her affectionately. "I'm sorry I haven't visited since your wedding. We've been so busy with the new baby!" She beamed with pride.

"How is Grace and her…I'm sorry, I don't even know if she had a boy or a girl."

Goodwife Lund nodded. "A boy. They named him Nicholas after his father. He's well. He cries a lot but I've told her, some babies are like that. He'll grow out of it, I'm sure."

Jennet smiled. "Yes. I remember what the twins were like." Her voice was tinged with a note of regret as she recalled how long it had been since she had last seen little James and Anna. "And Grace, how does she fare?"

"She has recovered well from the birth. She's young, of course, and healthy. She's tired, but that's to be expected." Goodwife Lund hesitated, a pained expression crossing her face. "She's come with Nicholas, his mother and the baby to stay with us for a few days. It's the first time she's been back to Wheatley Lane since she married and I have to say, it's good to have her home." Goodwife Lund beamed once more. "Anyway Jennet, I daresay it'll be your turn next, now that you're a married woman. In fact," she added, looking Jennet up and down, "I think it'll be your turn sooner than you think." She winked mischievously.

Feeling suddenly self-conscious, Jennet placed her hands across her belly. "I don't think so. No, not yet."

"I can always spot the signs, you know. I knew Grace was with child probably before she did." Goodwife Lund screwed up her face. "Of course, I didn't breathe a word about it – she was unwed then. Anyway, I must leave you, Jennet. We will need to go home. I don't like to leave Grace for too long."

"Is Goodwife Dickenson not with her?" Jennet asked.

"Yes, of course" replied Goodwife Lund. "But even so…I must get back." Again a look of anguish flashed across her face.

Jennet nodded and bid her friend farewell. Her heart raced as she watched her leave, her thoughts running over the Goodwife's words. She was with child, the Goodwife had said. How did she know that? How could she tell just by looking at her? Jennet touched her belly again lightly with her fingertips. It was her body, yet she hadn't noticed any signs of a baby within; although, in truth, Jennet wasn't sure exactly what those signs would be. How should she know if she was with child? She tried to remember when she had last bled. She couldn't recall, but that didn't mean anything; after all, it wasn't something which happened very often.

The dizzy feeling which had been plaguing her returned, accompanied by a churning sensation in the pit of her stomach. Her cheeks burned; the room was so hot, too hot. It was so stifling, she could hardly breathe. She had to get outside, get some air. As she ran towards the door, William caught hold of her hand, pulling her back to him.

"No!" she protested. "I need some air. I'm going for a walk. You stay here."

It was the first time that she had spoken to him so firmly. William looked taken aback.

"Alright," he said after a moment. "But take care out there. You never know who is wandering about."

Outside, she slumped down on to the damp earth and took a few deep breaths, the cold evening air shocking her lungs and steadying her heart. Slowly, her mind stopped racing, and the dizziness began to subside. Calm prevailed now, although it was not accompanied by clarity; her thoughts seemed clouded, muffled even, as though her mind was struggling to absorb the evening's revelations. Grace had given birth to a healthy boy. Despite her accusations towards Jennet, no harm had come to either mother or baby. Yet Goodwife Lund seemed reluctant to talk about her daughter's health. Why? Then Goodwife Lund had suggested that she was carrying William's child. Did her cunning friend really have some insight, or was she just guessing?

Jennet sighed deeply. She had never thought that she would be a mother and now, when confronted with the possibility, she felt frightened. She put her head in her hands, recalling Ellena's lifeless body lain on the floor as screaming babies were torn from her belly. Childbed was a dangerous business; if she was fortunate enough to survive it, what sort of mother would she make? And what about William - would he be happy at the prospect of fatherhood? Would they still be able to go to London? She didn't know.

Jennet stood up and looked around her. Night-time was arriving now, the endless black falling fast beyond the dim lights of the village. At that moment, she had meant to go back inside, to join her husband and his friends. She had meant to heed his warning and take care. She had not meant to go wandering. Yet, despite all this, she found herself walking in the direction of her home; her steps quick, her mind deep in thought.

She arrived back at the barn a little while later, shrouded in darkness. Indeed, it was a miracle that she had found her way home at all and now, still alone in the dark, she felt unnerved. She hurried inside and lit a small candle, feeling comforted by its warm glow. She removed her clothes, stripping down to only her shift, and sat down on her bed. Gently, she placed both hands on her belly and sat very still, waiting for something, anything, which might suggest that a small life was growing within. After a few moments, she sighed heavily. No sign, no movement. Nothing. Perhaps Goodwife Lund was wrong, after all. Perhaps she wasn't going to be a mother, not now, not ever. Perhaps her chance at motherhood had passed her by years ago. After all, she had celebrated her thirty-third birthday last month. Surely now she was too old to bear a child.

Her thoughts were interrupted by an odd scratching sound at the door. Alarmed by the noise and conscious that she was alone and half-dressed, Jennet called out: "William, is that you?"

The scratching continued in reply, followed by a weak thudding sound. Someone was trying to get in. "Who is it?" Jennet called, her voice trembling now. "Whoever you are, you are not welcome. My husband will be home soon."

The person at the door laughed now. "Your husband!" they shrieked. "My husband, you mean." It was a strained, high-pitched cackle, but Jennet could tell that it was a woman's voice.

"What do you mean; your husband?" Jennet's indignation emboldened her. Without another thought she flung open the barn door and gasped, her mouth falling open in disbelief.

There, standing in front of her, her dishevelled hair peeking untidily from beneath a dirty coif, was Grace. Jennet looked her up and down, aghast. Immediately she was struck by her face, which seemed not to hold its usual pretty features; her cheeks looked sunken, whilst her eyes seemed big and white, especially in contrast to the dirt smeared all over her face. Strapped to Grace's chest in a shawl, Jennet spied a sleeping infant.

Grace noticed Jennet look at the baby. "I've brought my son to see you," she said with a smile.

"At this time of day, alone, and in the cold and dark?" Jennet asked, incredulous. She beckoned Grace to come inside and closed the door behind her, shutting out the wintery chill once more.

Grace scowled. "Yes," she snapped. "I know what I'm doing with him, you know. He's my baby. Everyone thinks that I can't take care of him, but I can. I know what I'm doing," she repeated.

"I'm sure you're a good mother," replied Jennet smoothly, trying to be conciliatory. "Please, sit," she added, gesturing to one of her old stools. "It is nice to see you."

They sat for a few moments in silence. Jennet stared at Grace. She couldn't help it; she seemed to have changed so greatly, and not for the better. Indeed, this woman sitting before her, with her filthy appearance and wild eyes, could not be more different to the buoyant, immaculate young woman she used to know. Jennet wondered now if this was exactly what Goodwife Lund had not wished to discuss, why she had moved the discussion on to speculating about Jennet's condition so swiftly. It was far easier to talk about being with child than to talk about your only daughter losing her mind.

Grace began to giggle excitedly, shuffling about on her stool. "You didn't win, you know. Your spells didn't work. I've come to show you how fine and handsome he is, just like his father."

"Grace," Jennet began, smoothing her shift with her hands while she considered her words carefully. "I am not what you think I am. I am not a witch. I did not, and I could not, attempt to harm you or your son."

"Liar!" Grace shouted. Her baby started to cry. "You tried, but you failed. I almost died in childbed, you know. It was so long and so painful, and if it hadn't been for my mother's healing ways, we would both have perished. Your curse on me failed, although I know your magic is still strong in other ways."

"I don't have any magic!" Jennet protested.

"Yes, you do!" insisted Grace through gritted teeth. Her baby continued to cry and she cradled him tightly in her arms. "How else would you have taken William from me?"

Jennet felt the heat of anger begin to rise in her belly. "I didn't take William from you, Grace," she said evenly, trying to remain calm. "He was never yours to take. If William was the man you told me about, the one you hoped would fall in love with you…well, you told me yourself that it came to nothing."

"Oh, Jennet," Grace said mockingly, a strange smile fixed on her face. "You really don't know anything, do you? You really are a fool. William was in love with me, until you cast your rotten spell on him. He was mine. I know this to be true, because this is his child."

"No," Jennet said, that light-headed feeling returning once

more. "It cannot be. It is Nicholas's child. You lay with him many times before you wed, you told me so yourself."

"This is William's child," Grace repeated. "Look at him; he looks just like his father."

"No!" Jennet shouted. The dizziness she had been experiencing suddenly gave way to a burning nausea, deep in the pit of her stomach. She put her hand over her mouth to prevent herself from vomiting.

The front door burst open and Goodwife Lund walked in, followed by Goodwife Dickenson. "Grace! Whatever's the matter with you? We've been looking everywhere for you," said her mother, her voice laden with panic.

"Mother…" Grace wailed. She appeared to crumple into her mother's arms, the fury of a few moments ago giving way to sorrow and anguish.

"I'm sorry we came into your home like that, Jennet. It's just that we heard shouting and…well, we feared what she might do. As you can see, Grace is unwell," Goodwife Lund said, her voice unusually quiet.

Jennet glanced at Goodwife Dickenson, who was hovering helplessly in the doorway. She caught Jennet's eye briefly, then looked away. "Come, let's get Grace home," she said. "I still don't know how you managed to leave the cottage without me knowing."

"Never mind that now," said Goodwife Lund. "No harm done is there, Jennet?

Jennet shook her head, her mouth still open in disbelief as she watched them all leave, one woman on each side of Grace, as though she had not the strength to carry herself home.

She closed the door behind them and leant against it, letting out a slow, considered breath. She could not believe what had just happened, the things that Grace had said. Surely, Grace had lost all sanity, to believe that she had bewitched William and tried to bewitch Grace and her child. Moreover, to believe that William was the child's father…how could that possibly be? Grace had gone mad; there could be no other rational explanation.

A sharp pain shot through Jennet's belly, seeming to take the breath from her body. Stunned, she sat back down on her stool. The light-headedness returned too, leaving her feeling disorientated, as well as in agony as strong waves of pain seemed to surge through her lower abdomen. She took a few deep breaths and tried not to panic. Where was William when she needed him? Why had he not come home to look for her? She looked up at the small window of her barn; distracted by her conversation with Grace, she had neglected to close the shutters. For a moment she thought she could see a face, a small pale face, like that of a little boy, peering through the window at her. She stood up, moving closer and narrowing her eyes so that she could see better in the dim light. In the blink of an eye, the face was gone.

Jennet cried out as pain seared through her body once again. It was followed now by a strange warming sensation, like hot water running down her leg. Her head felt light once more and she stumbled over, falling clumsily on to the floor. She was losing consciousness now, she realised, her eyes heavy, the pain overwhelming her and sending her to slumber.

The last thing she saw was a pool of blood which had formed on the floor, like wet rose petals scattered on the dry earth. Instinctively she breathed in deeply, but she realised that there was no pleasant, floral fragrance around her. Instead, there was a smell she knew all too well, a smell she had experienced once before, a smell she dreaded. It was the smell that had lingered in the air on that awful day, all those years ago, when she watched her mother, brother and sister as they were hanged. Yes, Jennet thought as she closed her eyes one last time, it was the smell of death.

20

Hoarstones, near Wheatley Lane
Late November 1633

Jennet looked out of the barn window and shivered. Outside, everything looked so frozen, so desolate. She stared hard at the surrounding trees for a long time, as though studying every speck of glistening ice which had attached itself to the bare branches. In truth, she wasn't really concentrating on anything; her gaze was vacant, her thoughts elsewhere. It had been like this for weeks now. Each day, she was there in body, but in mind she was decidedly absent. She told herself to stop, to come out of this strange, involuntary stasis and yet, no matter how hard she tried, she couldn't prevent herself from feeling...

She looked away from the trees now, moving her eyes to her cold earth floor. How did she feel? For the first time in her life, she didn't know. In her thirty-three years of life she had known many emotions – sorrow, guilt, happiness, love. She had always been readily able to identify how she felt, even if dealing with her feelings had been a different matter entirely. Now she wasn't sure; in fact, she was beginning to believe that she no longer felt anything at all, that the trauma she had suffered had been so great it had rendered her incapable of emotion. Yes, she felt nothing; she was numb now.

"Here's supper," said William as he walked through the door, clutching a dead rabbit. Jennet glanced pitiably at the small creature. She didn't like William going out and hunting for their food – it was poaching, she had told him, and he could end up in a lot of trouble if he was caught. Of course, he hadn't listened to her. Killing a few rabbits isn't the same as taking someone's sheep or pig, he had insisted, and besides, who's to say who a wild rabbit belongs to? The masters will say, Jennet told him. The local gentlemen own the land and claim to own everything on it, and he ought to know that. That had been her last word on the matter. After all, she knew that they had to eat, and that they needed to be careful now that they had no income. A poached meal was better than no meal at all. Not that she was very hungry. She never seemed to be hungry these days.

"I think we're stuck here for the winter," William continued as he sat down and began to skin the rabbit. "The weather is really beginning to turn. There's talk of snow in the village."

"Hmm," replied Jennet absently. She returned to the window, retreating once again into her empty gaze.

"I will need to try to find some work. Not easy to do this time of year, but I must try. Otherwise, all the money I put aside for our journey south will be wasted on rent for this place." He grunted slightly. "This one's tough. Might not be the tastiest we've had."

"Hmm," said Jennet again. She continued to stare, not caring about money, or London, or rabbits.

"Well, I think it is wise for us to remain here until the spring. By then, the weather will be more favourable and I hope you will be feeling better, that is, well enough to travel." William eyed her cautiously. "I should get this on the fire, I think. Will you join me for supper?"

"I'm not hungry."

"Oh Jennet, will you come away from that window and sit by the fire? At least do that for me, please?" He walked over to her and placed his hands coaxingly on her shoulders.

"William, please…" she began, but her protest was weak. Obligingly she joined him in front of the fire, the warm flames inviting, the rabbit cooking nicely.

"Do you want me to send for Goodwife Lund tomorrow?" He looked at her helplessly. "You seem so…low-spirited. Perhaps she has a remedy to help."

Jennet looked away. "There's nothing Goodwife Lund could offer which would make me feel any better. Our child is gone, William. The child we didn't even know I was carrying until it was too late." A solitary tear rolled down her cheek.

"I know," he replied, drawing her closer to him. "And I'm sorry. I wish I had been with you that night."

Jennet rested her head against William's shoulder and looked back towards the window. Her eyes moved to the floor, where the large, red bloodstain still remained. William had scrubbed at that floor for weeks, but to no avail. The mark would stay there, serving as a constant reminder of that night; the agony, the fear, and the profound sense of emptiness which had been with her ever since.

"I think I will ask Goodwife Lund to visit," William said finally. "If anyone can cheer you up, it's her."

Jennet attempted a smile as she sat down by the fire. "Alright," she said. "I don't suppose it can do any harm."

Two days passed before Goodwife Lund came to visit her. As William had predicted, the weather had worsened, the violent winter storms arriving with unprecedented frequency. William braved the elements every day, walking miles to hunt for food and to look for work. Even through the mist of her own despair, Jennet admired him; his spirits unshaken, his faith always firmly intact. She wished that she had his strength and determination. She wished that she was not so stricken by this hopeless malaise.

She passed the time standing by the window, staring out as countless hailstorms battered their barn, the wind whipping through the hole in the roof and extinguishing every fire she attempted to light. Sometimes she would seek solace in her straw bed, pulling her blankets around herself in an attempt to find some warmth. No matter what she did, she could not find any comfort, caught in a dreadful mix of restlessness and despondency.

Her mind constantly returned to thoughts of that night, and regardless of where she stood, her eyes always seemed to look towards the bloodstain and the window. Sometimes she would glare at that window, willing herself to see the little face she had seen that night, wishing that she could make sense of it. Who was there? Who had seen her, and yet had not come to her aid? She closed her eyes, remembering. A little, pale face, like that of a boy...but which boy? Indeed, was it a boy at all? Or was it the devil himself, come to mock her? She had shuddered then. She recalled thinking once that if it was possible to have heaven on earth, then surely hell could just as easily be created. And here she was now, alone in the depths of a bleak winter, plagued by her memories, tormented by the cold, lost to her own sorrow. Here she was, trapped in a hell of her own making.

"How are you feeling?" Goodwife Lund asked as soon as she arrived, ushered in by an icy wind.

"Better," Jennet lied, wearing a tight smile.

"Well you don't look it." Goodwife Lund was never easily fooled. "You're very pale. And you don't look like you're getting enough sleep, either."

Jennet shook her head. "I'm fine," she insisted. "How's Grace?" she asked, keen to change the subject.

Her friend flinched. "Much as she was the last time you saw her, I'm afraid. Her mind is very disturbed. She sleeps little, and frets constantly about that little boy, even though he's the healthiest baby I've ever seen."

"Is she still at home with you?"

Goodwife Lund shook her head. "No. Goodwife Dickenson took her back to Higham a few weeks ago. That's where she should be, I suppose, with her husband and his family." A look of anguish flashed across the Goodwife's face.

"Have you been to visit her?"

"Yes, whenever I can, although she has little to say to me. I don't know if she will ever come back to her senses." Her lip quivered and she breathed in deeply, suppressing her tears.

Jennet sat silently, her posture stiff, her hands placed tensely in her lap. She wished she could offer her friend some reassurance; she wished she could put her arms around her shoulders and tell her it would be alright. But she couldn't. How could she offer anyone else any comfort when she could find no solace herself? Her eyes wandered back towards the window again, her mind back towards that awful night and the pallid face which bore witness to her suffering.

"I'm sorry Grace came to see you that night," Goodwife Lund said suddenly. "She seems to blame you...I don't know why. She has nothing to blame you for – her baby is well, she has a good husband and his family are kind to her."

"As you said, her mind is disturbed," replied Jennet, not wishing to share Grace's delusions about William being the father of her child. She hadn't told anyone what Grace had said that night, not even William. There was no point; it couldn't possibly be true. Magic, spells, curses, fictitious love; it was all a figment of Grace's very confused imagination.

"Did she upset you that night? I worry that she caused you to lose the child," said Goodwife Lund. "The thought of her being somehow responsible plagues me, Jennet."

Jennet gave a grim smile. "Grace's visit was upsetting. To see her in such a state was hard, as it is for everyone who loves her. But I had been feeling unwell for most of that day. I don't think Grace coming to the house like that caused me to..." she found she couldn't say the words. "I don't think it happened because of Grace."

Goodwife Lund reached out and touched her hand affectionately. "Oh, lass. You've had such a terrible time. I am sorry. But there's time yet for you to have a baby."

Jennet blinked hard, fighting back the tears which pricked in the corners of her eyes. "I don't think I could bear to be with child again. I couldn't bear the…I couldn't face it happening again."

"But you could go on to have a healthy child. That would make you both so happy."

"But I can't know that for certain! No one can," Jennet burst out. "I sometimes wonder if what happened is some sort of punishment…"

"For what?"

Jennet gave her friend a meaningful glance. "For what I did in the past. Perhaps I am cursed."

"Oh come, Jennet, you're starting to sound like Grace. You mustn't think like that – it was all a very long time ago. You were just a child." Goodwife Lund patted her hand again.

"Now you sound like William."

"He's a good man, sensible too. Have you talked to him about how you feel?"

Jennet shook her head. "No. In truth, I find it hard to talk to him. I know I should – it's just…"

"Just what?"

Jennet sighed. "I don't know."

"He will understand, you know."

"Yes, he will. But I'm not sure I really want him to."

Goodwife Lund frowned. "Why not? He must see how sad you are."

Jennet considered her words. "He knows that I am downcast, yes, but that is all. William has such strength, such faith and conviction. I worry that if I told him how I feel, that I feel cursed, perhaps even damned, that I might compromise him somehow. William has always sought heaven in this life, whereas I…I have never felt very close to God, especially now." She coughed, choking back the lump which was growing again in her throat.

Goodwife Lund looked at her, her eyes wide at the gravity of Jennet's words. After a moment she regained composure, and gave her a tender smile. "You've spent too much time alone in here, lass. Too much time spent alone with your thoughts isn't good for anyone. You must come to us for Christmas. Both of you must come."

"Thank you," replied Jennet bleakly.

Night had fallen by the time William came home. Goodwife Lund had left in the middle of the afternoon, leaving Jennet alone in her bitterly cold barn to ruminate on their conversation. She found that her friend's visit had not given her the comfort which William had hoped for. Instead, she felt tense, panicked even, her words echoing endlessly around her head. She shouldn't have told her about her fear of being with child again. She shouldn't have told her how wretched she felt; she shouldn't have made those comments about being damned. It was unfair, she realised, to burden someone who already had enough problems of her own.

Eventually, feeling exhausted, she collapsed on to her straw bed and pulled her blanket over her head. She lay there for what seemed like hours, hiding from the world, not caring to light a fire or close the shutters, while the growing darkness enveloped her. The endless black; that was all she could see nowadays.

"Jennet, where are you?" William called as he walked through the door.

She groaned, shuffling uncomfortably on the straw. "I'm here."

William grumbled a little as he groped around in the dark, bumping into every conceivable obstacle as he found his way to their bed. "Sorry I'm so late home," he said as he lay down beside her. "I haven't brought any supper, either. It's not been a very successful day, I'm afraid."

She sensed a disheartened note in William's voice. Talk to him, Goodwife Lund had said. She drew a long breath, mustering some determination from deep within herself.

"You didn't find any work?" she asked.

William sighed. "No. No one needs anyone to labour this time of year, no fields to tend, nothing to plant. Any animals folk have, they've already slaughtered. And no one builds anything in the wintertime. It's like everyone just, well, goes to sleep until spring. Everyone just huddles together in their homes, praying that they have enough food to see them through."

"When I lived with my father, I found winter a comforting time. I used to love watching the snow fall outside as I sat beside a roaring fire," Jennet said, her voice wistful for a moment. It was funny how being struck by this momentary recollection of a happy time seemed to lighten her mood. No doubt the feeling was temporary, but she relished it nonetheless.

"And now?" William asked, encouraged by her cheerier tone. "Do you still find comfort in winter?"

She let out a weary breath. "I rarely manage to keep a fire going for long enough to cook our food, never mind to warm my feet and hands. I can't remember the last time I didn't feel cold."

"I'm sorry I've let you down so badly," William said. The sadness in his voice made her jolt, and she turned to face him.

"No, you haven't," she insisted, caressing his cheek. She noticed it was unusually rough and dry, inflamed by winter's chill. "It's my fault that we're stuck here, not yours. We'd have left this place by now if it wasn't for me."

"Jennet, you can't help what happened. It's no one's fault. It's the will of…" he stopped short of finishing his sentence, perhaps sensing his mistake.

"It's the will of whom, William? The will of God?" Jennet asked, her voice raised in anger. "Then it is a punishment, surely. A God who chooses to do this to someone can only mean to punish."

"I don't pretend to know what God has planned for us, Jennet. I don't pretend to understand why such suffering happens. Perhaps God means to challenge us, to provoke us into living holier lives? I don't know. But you need to accept what has happened and make peace with it; only then will you feel better." He wrapped his arms tightly around her, and placed a tender kiss on her forehead. "I pray to God that you will feel better."

"Perhaps when spring comes," said Jennet thoughtfully. "Perhaps when I see the trees and plants renewed, perhaps when I feel the warmth of the spring sun again. Perhaps then I too might feel restored."

"I hope so," William replied. "In the meantime, we both need to persevere. I need to find work and you need to start eating better – you've grown very thin over these past weeks."

Jennet let out a small laugh. "So have you! Man cannot live on rabbit alone," she said mockingly.

"Ah! A moment of sharp wit from one so sorrowful – this I am glad to hear," William retorted. He paused, allowing the joviality between them to linger in the cold night air. Jennet could sense how they both clung to this rare and precious moment, realising how it reminded them of happier times.

"Speaking of hearing things," he said eventually, "I heard some strange talk when I was out in the village today."

"What do you mean?"

"Two men I saw in Wheatley Lane, stopped me as I was coming home. 'Do you know there are witches abroad?' said one, then the other starts rambling about greyhounds and horses turning into people and vice versa, and a grand witches' feast with all manner of food coming down from the roof…"

"A witches' feast?" repeated Jennet. "You mean, a Sabbath?" She suppressed a shudder; these stories sounded too familiar.

"Yes. None of it made any sense, but apparently some little boy in the village saw it all. It all sounded like the ludicrous tales of drunken men, if you ask me."

"These men, did they say who the witches were?"

In the darkness, she sensed William shake his head. "No. As I say, just stories."

"Yes, just stories," she repeated.

As she closed her eyes and began to drift towards slumber, she felt an old, buried sense of dread resurfacing from the pit of her stomach. Folk liked to tell stories, she reflected; they liked to marvel at the fantastic, at the unbelievable, at the supernatural. The problem with stories was that when folk began to believe them, when real people's names became associated with them, they could take on a life of their own. At some point, stories stopped being just stories and became dangerous, perhaps even deadly.

She fell asleep shivering, partly because of the cold and partly because she remembered all too well how fine the line was between an entertaining fiction and a terrible tragedy.

21

The Lunds' Cottage, Wheatley Lane
Christmas 1633

Jennet breathed in deeply, enjoying the delicious smell of roasting meat which was drifting out of the Lunds' cosy cottage. Goodwife Lund always provided some good fayre, especially at Christmastide. As she drew nearer her stomach growled hungrily, reminding her that it had been weeks since she had tasted such good, nutritious food. She had tried, with William's encouragement, to recover her appetite and to eat a little better. Despite her best efforts, however, she remained frail and painfully thin, only managing a few mouthfuls of food throughout the day. At each meal William would sigh, pointing at the food left in her bowl as he mopped his bowl with a piece of bread. She would grow defensive then, claiming that her cooking was not very good, that she did not find her own food appetising.

If she was honest with herself, however, Jennet knew that most of the time, she simply did not feel hungry. She smiled faintly as her stomach grumbled once more. It was heartening to feel her hunger pangs return. Perhaps this was a subtle sign that she was beginning to get better.

"Smells delicious, doesn't it?" said William, seeming to read her thoughts.

"Yes," she agreed. "Goodwife Lund is an excellent cook. I've been looking forward to today."

"Have you?" Jennet noted the surprise in his voice. "I'm really glad to hear you say that."

"Come, let's hurry inside. It's freezing out here. I think it may snow again." She gave him a broad smile and knocked on the cottage door.

After a few moments, the door swung open and they were greeted by Goodwife Lund who embraced them both merrily. "Come in," she beckoned them, "and a merry Christmas to you both."

"Yes, merry Christmas," Jennet repeated cheerily. As she spoke, she realised how much she meant those words, how much she wished to be happy once again.

Inside, the little cottage was bustling with the Lunds' friends and family. Jennet looked around, realising that she did not recognise many faces among them. William, however, seemed to know quite a number of people there. He squeezed her hand and gave her a quick kiss on the cheek; it was his way of asking if she would be alright without him. Jennet gave him a brief nod and smiled as she watched him walk over to a group of men who were sat together in the corner. William was always so effortlessly sociable.

"Isn't Grace here?" she asked Goodwife Lund, who had returned to attending to the meats roasting on her roaring fire. She hoped that her friend did not detect the note of apprehension in her voice.

"No, she hasn't visited this Christmas," she replied simply. "We've been to Higham to see her and the baby, but at the moment…well, we think it best if she doesn't travel far."

Jennet nodded. "I understand. I hope she begins to feel better soon." It was a feeble wish, but she did not know what else to say.

"As do I, Jennet," said Goodwife Lund quietly. She looked around her to see who else might be listening. Clearly, she did not want her other guests to overhear their discussion. "I'm not sure how much more of this Nicholas and his family can take. If she carries on in this way, she will end up coming home to us permanently."

Jennet's eyes widened. "You mean that she will have to leave her husband?"

Goodwife Lund nodded. "Folk are beginning to say that she is mad, and no man wants a mad wife. He loves her now, but for how long?" Jennet noticed the strained, weary look on her friend's face as she spoke. Grace might not live with her, but nonetheless her condition was taking its toll on her mother.

"Folk shouldn't be talking about her like that," said Jennet, her tone scolding. "Surely it's none of their business. How do they know what Grace is going through? They don't know her."

"Spoken like a true friend who knows and loves her." Goodwife Lund smiled and patted Jennet's hand. "You are a good lass." She glanced warily around the room again. "We will talk later, in private. In the meantime, go and find that handsome husband of yours and please, eat, drink and be merry! Lord knows, you deserve it!"

Jennet smiled at her friend's familiar, jovial tone. Goodwife Lund was not someone whose natural good humour could be easily suppressed. And thank God for it, she thought.

As the evening wore on, the atmosphere in the Lunds' cottage grew more excitable, and more raucous. Jennet made merry with everyone else, indulging herself in the pleasures of good food and plentiful ale. For the first time in many weeks, she felt happy, laughing loudly at jokes and even accepting William's invitation to dance without any inhibitions whatsoever. She wasn't sure what had caused her spirits to lift, whether it was the time of year, the perseverance of her loving husband, or simply the comfort of a cosy cottage filled with friendly folk and a warm fire. Whatever it was, she relished it, willing this contented, light-hearted feeling to stay with her always. She felt as though a heavy black cloud had been lifted from her, allowing her to see clearly, allowing her to look to the future. Once again, she began to look forward to what was to come, to the exciting journey she would soon embark on, and to hers and William's new life in London.

"It's wonderful to see you looking so happy tonight," William said as they danced. "For a while I thought I'd never see your beautiful smile again."

Jennet smiled shyly at the compliment as she twirled around in his arms. "I am enjoying myself," she agreed.

"I can tell," he said, drawing her close to him. "I have missed you; it felt as though you had left me, and I worried that you might never return. I can't begin to tell you how glad I am. I was hoping that tonight, when we go home, you might let me take you to our bed, just like I used to…" His words were cryptic but Jennet could not fail to see the look in his eyes; cautious hope mixed with burning desire.

She hesitated. "I'm not sure, William, I don't know if I can…" She felt a wave of panic creep in, infecting her happy, relaxed state. She still didn't feel able to tell him that she feared becoming with child again, that she didn't think she could bear another loss like the one she had just endured. The weight of her own sorrow might have begun to lift from her shoulders, but that didn't mean she was ready to take another chance, to expose herself to more suffering and grief. She felt annoyed then. Why did William have to ask this of her now, when she had just remembered how to enjoy herself?

"I'm sorry," he said, seeming to sense the gravity of his request. "I shouldn't have said that. Of course I will wait until you are ready. As I said, I have missed you." His eyes looked sad now.

"Let's see what happens when we go home," she relented. She knew it was wrong to give him false hope, but at the same time, she couldn't bear to see him sorrowful. She picked up another cup of ale. A few more of those, and perhaps then she would have enough courage. She shook her head slightly at herself; what sort of woman needed to be inebriated with drink to go to bed with her husband? Perhaps she was fooling herself. Perhaps she was far from recovered, after all.

They stayed at the Lunds' cottage until late, dancing, drinking and enjoying themselves so much that time seemed to pass by at an extraordinary rate. Noticing the other guests begin to leave, Jennet picked up a brush and began to help Goodwife Lund to clean up. She saw William give her an inquisitive look, as though to ask her what she was doing, and to remind her that she no longer lived there. She answered him with a wide-eyed stare. Of course she should help her friend to tidy; the place was a mess of empty mugs and half-eaten fayre.

She had other reasons to linger as well. Tonight she had felt like a different, happier version of herself, somehow liberated by merriment and celebration. Normally when she attended social gatherings such as this she felt uncomfortable, wishing the time away, willing herself to be back at home. By contrast, tonight she had revelled in the company of others. She did not want the evening to end, and now that it was drawing to a close, she dreaded going back to her cold, quiet barn. She feared that such familiar surroundings would cause the sad, withdrawn Jennet to return. Her contented state was a fragile one, she knew that. She was sure that one glance at the blood stain on the barn floor would be all it took to reduce her to an anxious, tearful wreck once again. She also worried about being alone with William; she had encouraged him, she knew that, too. Yes, she thought as she swept; she could think of a hundred reasons to stay, and very few reasons to leave.

"It's been wonderful to see you smiling again, Jennet," Goodwife Lund remarked as she began to gather up the discarded food. "Are you feeling much better?"

"Yes." Jennet nodded. She looked up briefly, mindful that William was in earshot. "I think I am almost recovered." A half-truth, she knew, but kindly meant. After all, Goodwife Lund had enough worries of her own.

"I can't believe the number of folk who've left their mugs behind," Goodwife Lund tutted. "Now I shall have to find out who all these belong to."

"At least almost all of the food was eaten," Jennet replied, pointing to the small pile of abandoned bones and gristle which her friend had collected. "I would just keep the mugs – let the owners come to you to claim them."

"Good idea, lass." Goodwife Lund's smile swiftly disintegrated into a heavy sigh. "I'm too old and tired for all this tidying up. Thank goodness you stayed to help me."

Jennet looked pointedly at William, who was sat nursing a cup of ale, tapping his fingers impatiently on the side of the mug. "It's my pleasure."

With another sigh, Goodwife Lund abandoned her cleaning and heaved her rotund frame onto a wooden stool. "Just a few minutes' rest," she said, picking up a mug of ale and taking several long, thirsty gulps. "Sorry I cut our conversation short earlier," she added, wiping her mouth with her apron. "I don't want the whole village knowing my business, especially when it comes to my poor daughter." The familiar saddened look returned to her face.

"Do you really think she will come home to you?" asked Jennet. She stopped sweeping and leaned hard on her brush.

"Yes. Unfortunately, I think the Dickensons won't tolerate her for much longer. Goodwife Dickenson is patient and discreet when it comes to Grace's condition, as you saw for yourself that night..." Goodwife Lund's voice trailed off, her face colouring up a little as she remembered what else had happened that night. "I'm sorry, Jennet," she added after a moment.

Jennet forced a grim smile on to her lips. "It's alright," she said. "Please, go on."

Goodwife Lund drew a deep breath. "My worry is Nicholas. He has told me himself that he thinks she's mad and doesn't see why he has to put up with her. Honestly, Jennet, he's like a petulant child about the whole thing! He says that if she can't be a proper wife to him, then she shouldn't be his wife at all. He's even suggested that their little boy isn't his son, that he might be some other man's, someone who she met and fell in love with before him. Apparently, she told him so herself." Goodwife Lund frowned. "I don't know who she could mean."

Jennet's cheeks flushed as she remembered what Grace had said about William.

"Who knows," she shrugged. "She's unwell. Perhaps she doesn't know what she's saying." There was no point in repeating Grace's lie. She glanced sideways at William. He was staring at his hands, disinterested in their conversation.

Goodwife Lund threw up her arms in despair. "I keep hoping and praying that Grace will get better, that things will improve for her, and for us. It just seems to be one misfortune after another at the moment; first with Grace, and now there's all this nonsense going around the village about us…"

"What nonsense?" Jennet asked. She noticed William look up. He was paying attention now.

"Surely you've heard the stories that little rogue Edmund Robinson is telling?"

Jennet scoffed. "Little! Edmund Robinson is a giant compared to you and me."

"Not the father; the son." Goodwife Lund shook her head. "Scandalous stories, and not a bit of truth in them, but you know what stories are like, how they can get out of hand…" she gave Jennet a meaningful look.

Jennet immediately shed the wry smile she had been wearing on her face. "What are these stories?" she asked.

"Oh! Some utter rubbish about us being witches, how we can turn into animals and how we have big witches' Sabbaths at Hoarstones." She shook her head again, but this time her dismissive gesture was accompanied by a look of fear in her eyes.

Jennet glanced at William again, who was looking at them both, perturbed. "Us?" she repeated. "Who does he mean by 'us'?"

"He says it's me, Goodwife Dickenson, and…" she hesitated.

"And?" Jennet prompted.

"And you, Jennet," she said sadly.

Jennet dropped the broom she had been leaning on. She

searched quickly for a stool to sit on. Her legs felt so weak, she feared they might give way beneath her. She sat down carefully, and placed her head in her hands. She struggled for a moment to digest what her friend had just told her. She sat there for what felt like an eternity in a dumbfounded silence.

"Jennet, are you alright?" William asked gently.

She looked up. "Did you know?" she asked him. "That day a few weeks ago, when you came home repeating those stories you'd heard, did you lie to me when you said you didn't know who the supposed witches were?"

William looked at her, aghast. "No, Jennet! I swear on the Holy Bible, I did not know. As I told you, the men were drunk; their stories were little more than a garbled string of strange fantasies. They didn't attribute any names to them."

"I can't believe this is happening…" Jennet began, her voice wavering as the tears began to fall.

Instinctively, Goodwife Lund came and placed an arm around her shoulder. "Now come, lass. They're just the idle tales of a silly little boy. I'm sure no harm will come from it." Despite her words of reassurance, Goodwife Lund sounded less than convinced.

"Goodwife Lund is right, Jennet," William interjected. "Try not to worry about it. Surely the boy's stories won't be believed."

Jennet gave her husband a long, withering stare. "You mean, like my stories weren't believed?" she said.

"Oh Jennet, this isn't the same, that was years ago…" he began.

"Pendle hasn't changed that much, William. Many of the folk here still believe that witches live among us, casting spells and cursing people. Look how people reacted when they found out who I was – look how even those who once called themselves my family have used my name against me," she added, thinking bitterly of Alice.

"Yes," William agreed, "Alice publicly denounced you as a witch months ago, and yet no constable has come to arrest you. Perhaps this too will blow over."

Jennet shook her head. "No, William. I'm sorry, I wish I could agree with you, but this is different."

She began to sob again, unable to convey her meaning to him through her tears. William had a better and deeper understanding of most things, but not of this. In this, sadly she was the expert. She knew the strength of the fantastic, frightening story; she knew of its ability to grip the grotesque imagination of the powerful, to set them against ordinary people in their mission to root out evil. She knew how one little tale would grow, becoming increasingly terrible, more impressively supernatural, encompassing more and more people as accusations and counter-accusations flowed freely before the constables, the sheriffs, the magistrates.

Jennet knew that stories such as the ones told by Edmund Robinson could only have one possible ending: suffering and tragedy. She knew this because she had once been such a storyteller. Now, all these years later, she was poised to play a different role. If she hadn't felt so frightened and so upset by Goodwife Lund's revelations, she would have chuckled at the irony.

"Jennet may be right," Goodwife Lund said quietly. "What the boy has said is being repeated all over – it's bound to reach the ears of the Law sooner or later. His tales aren't easy to refute either – the events he has spoken of supposedly took place at the house at Hoarstones and at your little barn, and he says he's the only witness. If this makes it as far as a magistrate, there's no one who can speak in our favour."

Jennet wiped her eyes. "The boy – Edmund Robinson – says that he witnessed a Sabbath at my barn?"

Goodwife Lund nodded. "Yes. He's told folk that we took him there, and that when he tried to escape you, Goodwife Dickenson and I pursued him."

Jennet frowned. "Has he said when these events supposedly took place?"

"On All Saints Day just passed."

Jennet gasped. "It was his face that I saw at the window," she whispered.

"What did you say, Jennet?" William asked.

"I think that little Edmund Robinson was watching through my window that night when Grace visited. I think he saw you and Goodwife Dickenson take her away, and I think he saw me collapse afterwards."

This time it was William's turn to furrow his brow. "But that doesn't make any sense," he said. "All that proves is that you were all together on that night, and that the rest of his tale is a fabrication."

Jennet nodded. "Yes. Undoubtedly, he's a child with a vivid imagination. Children like to tell stories. The problem comes when adults believe them."

"We just have to hope that young Edmund's story is too wild to be taken seriously," said Goodwife Lund, attempting to lighten the mood. However, Jennet could still see the look of disquiet in her eyes.

William took hold of Jennet's hands, kneeling down to her so that his eyes looked directly into hers. "What do you want to do, Jennet?"

Jennet sighed. "I don't think there's much we can do. We can't leave yet – it's the middle of winter, and in any case I'm not strong enough to travel miles on foot. All we can do is wait until the weather improves and leave at the earliest opportunity, just as we had planned to."

"Alright," said William. "But the first hint of this becoming a real danger to you, and we must flee. You too, Goodwife. You and John should think about what you will do, if it comes to it."

Goodwife Lund smiled bravely. "William, I have lived here all my days and it is here I shall remain, no matter what happens."

William embraced Jennet tightly. "Don't worry, my love," he whispered in her ear. "I will keep you safe."

"I know," she replied, glad that her husband couldn't see the distress which she knew was etched on her face. She couldn't begin to explain what it felt like to be trapped in the midst of something like this. She couldn't tell him how it rendered anyone involved in it completely powerless. She couldn't make him understand how storytellers and subjects alike became vulnerable to the whims of the rich and the mighty of the land as they played God with people's lives, deciding who to believe and who to condemn.

She couldn't make William see that when it came to stories of witchcraft, no one could ever be safe.

Part Three

1634

22

Kildwick, Cravenshire
Late February 1634

"Come now, Jennet, we're going to be late!" William called.

Jennet frantically adjusted her coif and ran from the room, down the rickety wooden staircase and into the alehouse. The innkeeper was waiting for them, tapping his foot impatiently.

"You said you'd be out before now," he said, glaring at her. Jennet felt her face redden.

"I'm sorry, Goodman. My wife and I must have slept too long. Do we owe you anything more for the room?"

Jennet noticed the emphasis William placed on their marital status; he was keen to stress that they were a respectable couple, not a pair of elopers or vagabonds. She made an effort to smile pleasantly at the man, who shook his head at them both. "No, nothing owed."

"Good," she said, still maintaining her smile. "We thank you for your hospitality, but we must hurry to church. Come, William," she added, taking him by the hand.

"Godly folk, always the same – no wonder they can't keep to time, what with all that Bible reading," she heard the man mutter as they walked away. She ignored him; she wasn't about to let some grumpy old innkeeper ruin her day.

They had arrived in Kildwick the previous evening and had found lodgings at the village's only inn. After a hearty supper they had retired to their room and, undoubtedly exhausted by the long journey, they had fallen soundly asleep within a few moments. As they walked along the lane leading to the church, Jennet thought about how comfortable the simple truckle bed had seemed after so many months of sleeping on straw. It was little wonder that they had both overslept.

"Perhaps we are not so late after all," she observed, noticing other worshippers walking in the same direction.

"Let's hurry anyway. Afterwards, I'd like to speak to Reverend Webster if I can. This will be the last time that I will hear him preach – he probably won't remember me but nonetheless I want to thank him, to say goodbye."

William quickened his pace as they hurried towards the church. Jennet knew how much he had been looking forward to today. He had suggested coming to Kildwick a few days earlier, after learning that Reverend Webster had recently become the church's curate. Jennet recalled how he had come back to their barn and excitedly told her the news, asking her if she'd like to go to Kildwick to see the Reverend preach.

"It's several hours' journey on foot," he had said, "over the county border in Cravenshire. Think of it as good practice for our long journey soon to come," he had added with a cheeky smile.

Jennet had smiled and agreed without hesitation. After all, it had been at her insistence that they had not returned to Grindleton. Although she knew that William would have dearly liked to say goodbye to his friends there, she could not muster the courage to face Bess Hargreaves. It would have been cruel to stand in William's way a second time and besides, the more she thought about it, the more the idea of going to Kildwick appealed to her. She still didn't share William's religious fervour, but she liked the idea of putting a safe distance between herself and Pendle, at least for a few days. As William had so persuasively put it, they were practising for the real event, for their final departure.

As they approached the church, Jennet breathed in deeply, enjoying the fresh, crisp air as it flooded up her nostrils. Spring was in the air already, she could smell it; the sweet scent of life made anew hung from the buds which were beginning to appear on the trees. It had seemed a long, cold winter. January had been an endless stream of violent storms, with strong winds and every form of frozen precipitation falling heavily from the sky. Jennet had spent week upon week trapped in the confines of her freezing, draughty barn, trying to hide from the relentless onslaught of horrid weather in a building which was ill-equipped to provide either shelter or comfort. At least for the most-part, William had been there too, unable to find work or hunt for food in the frozen, desolate wilderness outside. So there they had huddled together, for weeks on end, surviving on scarce rations of pottage.

The weather hadn't been the only thing they had hidden from. After Goodwife Lund's revelations at Christmastide, both of them had been set on edge, looking over their shoulders for signs of trouble, fearing the constable's knock at the door. At first, Jennet had been certain that her arrest was imminent, and she had reacted angrily, railing against the silly little boy to William and sometimes, just to herself.

"I wish we could leave now!" she would yell. "I don't want to give the father of that horrible little boy another penny in rent!" William would have to calm her then, reminding her that they were stuck for the winter, that if they left now they would surely perish.

"The roof over our heads and the meagre food in our bellies is the only thing keeping us alive," he would remind her. "We must thank God for all blessings, no matter how hard they might be to see sometimes."

As the weeks passed, nothing happened – there were no frantic visits from Goodwife Lund bringing more bad news, or visits from men of the Law. By mid-February the wind and snow had started to subside, and Jennet had begun to pray that the boy's tales had been just another storm she had weathered, that his moment had passed, that it had all blown over. With the arrival of spring imminent, she began to look forward to the future, the better weather bringing with it a new optimism, new opportunities. A new life away from Pendle. A new beginning, away from danger.

"When we get home, I shall have to call on Goodwife Lund. I haven't seen her since Christmas," Jennet remarked.

"Yes," William agreed. "You won't get many more chances. If this weather holds I think we should leave as soon as possible." He looked at her. "If you think you're ready, of course. The winter was hard, and I fear you've not yet recovered your strength completely."

"I managed the journey here without any difficulty," Jennet insisted. "I agree – let's leave as soon as we can."

"Alright. I have one job left to finish, but it shouldn't take more than a couple of days."

Ironically, the winter storms had provided William with some work and over the past few weeks he had been steadily repairing walls and buildings for local folk. Jennet had been relieved to see them get some badly-needed additional income at last. She knew how much they would need it on the long road ahead.

"Come," William said quietly as they walked through the heavy wooden church doors. "Let's find a pew."

The church was small inside and very busy, and they managed to find only a small space in the middle pews. A middle-aged plump woman gave Jennet an obliging nod as she shuffled along the wooden bench to accommodate them. She bore a striking resemblance to Goodwife Lund, reminding Jennet again that she must make an effort to see her friend. Jennet thanked the woman with a friendly smile, and looked around. Most of the congregation sat in a state of quiet contemplation, some with their heads bowed in prayer, waiting for the service to start. She looked at William, who had closed his eyes, his lips moving slightly as he communed directly with God. Sensing her eyes upon him, he reached over and squeezed her hand.

She saw Reverend Webster emerge from the vestry, enrobed

entirely in black, his face sombre. He began with the usual prayers, and Jennet tried her best to feign some serious observance and to prevent herself from looking around the church. She couldn't help it; she had an odd fascination with the expressions on people's faces when they were caught up in prayer. Was it fascination, or was it envy, she wondered. After all, she couldn't recall when she had ever been able to close her eyes, to concentrate solely on speaking to God. She had never had the commitment for that sort of prayer; her prayers had often been fleeting, sometimes desperate, and probably always in vain. She stared at her hands as she folded them repeatedly in her lap. She hadn't the will to pray like William; she didn't have his strength of faith.

"What is the meaning of this?" she heard Reverend Webster say, his firm tone cutting through the quiet atmosphere like a knife.

Instinctively Jennet jolted, sitting upright in her seat and looking towards the altar, where Reverend Webster had been standing. All around her, the congregation murmured and shuffled, trying to locate the source of the disruption. Jennet's eyes followed the curate as he made his way towards the back of the church. Slowly, she turned her head and gasped. There, sitting near the door on a tall stool, was little Edmund Robinson. The boy cast a menacing gaze around the room. Jennet gulped hard.

"It's the boy who discovered witches," she heard someone whisper.

She grasped William's hand and held it tightly. "William…" she began, but he merely looked at her and shook his head, his brow knitted together in an expression of anger.

"What is the meaning of this?" Reverend Webster said again.

Jennet saw a man stand up and approach the curate. He was a tall, stocky man, his sand-coloured hair flecked with grey, his cheeks a ruddy colour. "Who's that?" she whispered to William.

"James Robinson, Edmund's brother and little Edmund's uncle," replied William, his tone unusually curt.

"Beg your pardon, Reverend," James Robinson began, "but with your permission, the boy here has something important, you might even say terrible, to report to your congregation."

"This is very unusual," remarked Reverend Webster. "What is this terrible business of which your boy wishes to speak?"

"He's my nephew, Reverend. And the business concerns witches. You see, Reverend, the boy here is a witch-finder," James explained, puffing his chest out proudly.

Upon hearing those words, Jennet lowered her gaze, pulling her coif further over her head in an attempt to avoid recognition.

"Stop," whispered William. "You will draw attention to yourself."

"There's one here already, Reverend," the boy called out. "I can see her in your congregation. Her name's Jennet Device and she's a witch."

Little Edmund pointed towards Jennet. Jennet felt the gaze of every person in the church follow the child's finger before coming to rest upon her. She looked down again, shoulders hunched with the weight of every single pair of eyes in the room boring into her. She could feel their fascination, their fear, their contempt. She gulped hard as her face grew warm. In that moment, she wished that the ground would open up and swallow her whole.

"Boy, this is a house of God. We don't try witches here. I'm sorry, but I won't permit you to come in here and fling wild accusations like this." Reverend Webster's voice was loud, firm and authoritative.

"Suit yourself, Reverend," said James rudely. "Come Edmund, there's plenty more folk round here who will want to hear your story."

James lifted the boy from the stool and walked out of the church, allowing the door to slam shut behind him. Jennet startled at the noise, then slowly turned back to face the altar. She could still feel everyone's eyes upon her, probably wondering who this woman was that the little boy had so confidently accused. Probably wondering what she had done to merit such an accusation. Or perhaps, even in a place so far away as Kildwick, remembering exactly who Jennet Device was and what sort of family she came from.

"I'm sorry for the interruption," Reverend Webster said, walking to his pulpit. "I know none of us appreciate it when the peace and sanctity of God's house is disturbed."

He moved seamlessly into delivering his sermon, preaching a complex message about the Laws of Moses and whether or not subjection to them was necessary to be saved. After a while, Jennet realised that although she was hearing the Reverend speak, she wasn't truly listening. His message was something about which Jennet knew little and cared even less; it was this sort of theological pondering which gave her such little appetite for religion in the first place.

However, that wasn't the only reason she couldn't focus on his words, why her mind was elsewhere. She was in shock, she realised, her mind reeling from the events of the past few minutes. She had felt so happy, so relaxed upon walking into the church that day. She had fooled herself into believing that Kildwick represented a safe haven from Pendle, no matter how temporary. She had made herself believe that Edmund Robinson, his stories, her name, and her past could not reach her there, and yet they had, in the most public and humiliating way possible. As she sat there, pretending to listen, one single thought ran over and over again through her mind: how far would she have to go to escape from herself?

After the service, most of the congregation made their way swiftly out of the church. No doubt they wanted to gossip about the events which had just unfolded, Jennet thought. No doubt they wanted to discuss the woman who Edmund Robinson had named a witch. She was relieved when, instead of following the crowd, William took her by the hand and led her towards the front of the church. At least she wouldn't have to face a bloodthirsty mob outside just yet. Together they approached the altar where the curate still stood, clutching his Bible as he blew out the candles.

"Reverend Webster?" William said.

"Yes?" The curate's expression was serious but Jennet sensed that there was warmth behind it. He looked at them both expectantly.

"My name is William Braithwaite. I doubt you will remember me, although we have met before. I have heard you preach on many occasions, although I fear not as many as I would have liked," William paused, gesturing towards Jennet, who lingered nervously behind him. "My wife and I are soon to leave this area and go south, eventually to London. I doubt I will hear you preach again, so I just wanted to thank you – your words have inspired me to a better, holier path."

Reverend Webster gave William a small smile. "That is kind, although I should point out that it is the word of God I preach – I am merely a simple messenger, showing His flock the way to the light."

"Yes, of course, but nonetheless, thank you."

The curate drew a deep breath. "I'm only sorry that our service today was marred by that awful business with the boy and his uncle." He shook his head in disbelief. "To talk of such things as witches in a church...I had heard this sort of thing has been going on over the border in Lancashire, but now that I've seen it for myself, well, it makes me wonder what the world is coming to."

Jennet heard William sigh. She stepped forward anxiously, unable to believe her ears.

"Forgive me, Reverend, did you say that this has happened before?"

The curate nodded. "As I say – not here, until today, but I believe the story of the boy who finds witches originated in the Pendle area." He cast a studious gaze at Jennet and frowned. "Are you not the woman the boy pointed at?"

Jennet felt the colour rise in her cheeks once again. "Yes, it...I mean..." she stammered.

"It was my wife that the boy pointed out, but none of what he says is true," said William, placing his hand lightly on Jennet's shoulder. "It is a terrible injustice, what that boy and his family are doing, and all for profit, I might add."

Jennet frowned. What did William mean by profit? What did he know about what the Robinsons were doing? She clenched her jaw as every muscle in her body tensed in indignation. What had William not told her?

Reverend Webster pursed his lips disapprovingly. "I intend to get to the bottom of this matter myself. I will seek out the boy and his family, and interview him. Surely someone must try to ascertain what truth, if any, can be found in the boy's stories," he paused, giving William a firm stare as he opened his mouth to protest. "And if, as you say, these stories are lies, a work of mere fantasy, then it is indeed a most un-Christian thing to do."

William nodded. "Thank you, Reverend. I hope that after interviewing the boy you will be satisfied that his tales are completely without foundation." He extended his hand to the curate, who gladly accepted it.

"I wish you both the best of luck," he said.

Jennet struggled to contain her fury as they left the church. Outside the lane was quiet, the congregation having dispersed now; clearly even those who had hoped for a second glance at the 'witch' had given up and gone home. She walked along, arms folded, mouth set in a tight expression. She couldn't even bring herself to look at her husband, the man she trusted, the man she thought would never keep anything from her. The man she loved above all others, above anything else in the world, had lied to her.

Day after day, week after week, every time he returned to the barn after a job or a hunting expedition, she had asked him if there was any news, any hint of what the Robinsons planned to do with little Edmund's story. On every occasion, William had insisted that he had heard nothing, that no news was good news, that indeed, the story seemed to be a spent force, forgotten with the coming of spring. He had told her this, yet in one brief conversation with a curate he had shown the depths of his deception. If he had lied about this, what else had he lied about?

William quickly tired of her stony silence. "I'm sorry I didn't tell you," he said.

Jennet spun around. "How could you keep that from me?" she said, spitting her words.

William sighed. "Please, my love, try to understand. I only wished to protect you. You were starting to feel better – I couldn't bear to burden you all over again."

"How long have you known?"

"A couple of weeks. From what folk have been saying, I believe that these church visits the Robinsons are conducting only started about a month ago."

Jennet narrowed her eyes at him. "And what are people saying? What did you mean when you said they are doing this for profit?"

"I think we should sit awhile." William took her hand and led her to the grass at the side of the lane. He took a deep breath as he sat down beside her, looking her intently in the eye.

"It seems that to begin with, young Edmund and his family were content for the boy to tell his story to anyone in the village who'd listen, as you know. Then, after a while, Edmund's father starting charging folk to hear the boy talk about his experiences, inviting them over to his house or taking the boy down to the local alehouses; anywhere he could find an audience. Over the past few weeks, they've been visiting churches, presenting the boy as a witch-finder, just as you saw." William frowned. "I'm not sure what profit they're getting from that – you can't exactly charge folk to go into church. However, I'm guessing that by coming out as far as places like Kildwick, the family are trying to increase the boy's notoriety, and Edmund senior will no doubt smell a profit in that."

Jennet gasped. "This is getting out of hand, William."

"I know, my love. That was why I insisted earlier that we should leave for London as soon as we can." He gave her a sorrowful glance. "Are you angry with me?"

Jennet's face was solemn. "Yes, I'm sorry William, but I am. I understand your reasons, but I also recall that you once said we shouldn't have any more secrets from each other – do you remember? Yet, here you are, keeping a secret from me. It makes me wonder what other secrets you are keeping."

William chuckled. "Jennet, what on earth do you mean?"

Her expression remained serious. "That night Grace turned up at our barn, the night I lost our baby." She took a deep breath. "She told me that you are her baby's father. I told myself it couldn't possibly be true, but now I am wondering…well, Grace was with child before you and I were together…"

"Jennet, Grace is mad – you cannot possibly believe a word she says," William's protest was strong but she could see the hurt lingering behind his eyes. She bit her lip, regretting her words. She had been right months ago; it was a mistake to repeat Grace's lie.

"So you didn't know that she was – perhaps still is – in love with you?" she asked him.

William shook his head. "No, Jennet. I swear on God's holy word, I had no idea. I have only ever wanted you, ever since the first time I met you. Please, you must believe me." His eyes were pleading.

"I'm sorry," she said. "Of course I believe you. I don't know why I said that about Grace. I'm just so angry, and frightened, and…"

Her words were interrupted by William's kiss, planted firmly and spontaneously upon her lips. She closed her eyes for a moment; it had been a while since she had enjoyed him kissing her like that.

"I know," he said as their lips parted. "I'm worried too, but more than anything, I'm angry. God, I don't remember ever being so angry about something!" she saw him clench his fist. "You are innocent. Why would anyone want to hurt you in this way?"

Jennet shrugged. "Folk like a good story. They like a witch-hunt, too. The Robinsons know that. I don't suppose it matters to them who gets hurt. And I suppose that in my case, they reckon I deserve everything I get." She smiled sadly.

"Well, we're not beaten yet," William replied, his voice tinged with a renewed stoicism. "Come, let's go home, we need to get ready to leave."

"When?"

"Tomorrow. Forget the job," he added, gesturing casually with his hand. "As you said, this is getting out of control. We should leave immediately." He lifted her on to her feet. "I still worry about you having the strength to travel. You're as light as a feather," he observed.

"I'll be fine," she insisted. "Let's just get away from Pendle for good."

They spent much of the journey home walking in silence. Jennet stared ahead down the lane, deep in thought. It was a pleasant day, the clouds high and light, meaning that she could see far into the distance, across the rolling landscape, towards Pendle. It was the only place in the world that she had ever known, the only place she had called home. Even after her family had all gone, even when she found herself alone, Pendle still offered her comfort, it was still home. But no longer. Now when she thought of Pendle, she thought only of danger. She no longer felt herself bound to it. Indeed, she realised as they walked, all she wanted now was to get as far away from Pendle as possible.

23

Hoarstones, near Wheatley Lane
Late February 1634

Jennet exhaled slowly as she closed her modest sack for the last time. She had taken far longer to pack it than its meagre contents merited. She felt tired, she realised; the journey back from Kildwick yesterday had taken its toll on her. They had arrived back at supper time, and after a small meal had both collapsed into bed, exhausted. Jennet had slept deeply, not waking until the winter sun had risen. She felt glad of the peaceful slumber, undisturbed by dreams, and had woken feeling calm, albeit still weary. William was right; she hadn't quite recovered her strength. She would have to take care on the long road ahead.

She lifted her sack on to her back, trying it out for comfort. It wasn't heavy, but then it was only a small collection of useful items; a flagon and a couple of mugs, an extra shawl, a spare shift. There were no trinkets in her bag, no sentimental possessions either. As she packed, she had reflected on how little she had acquired over her lifetime, how every personal possession she had amounted to the contents of a tiny bag.

She smiled. At one time, such a thought would have made her feel sad but now, as she readied herself for her final departure from

Pendle, she felt strangely liberated by it. Her heart, like her bag, felt light; soon she would be free from danger, free from fear. Soon she would be freed of herself. No more abominable Jennet Device. No more meek and cowardly Jennet Sellers. In London she would simply be Jennet, wife of William, a woman whose name is not synonymous with curses and spells, bewitchment or the Devil. A woman whose name means nothing to anyone. Yes, she thought as she got to her feet, in London she would be truly anonymous at last.

"Are you almost ready?" William asked.

Jennet nodded. "I think so."

"I've given everything we borrowed from folk to James. He's a good lad; he'll see that they get back to their rightful owners. I wanted to return everything myself, but I don't want to draw too much attention to ourselves." He looked at her meaningfully. "If we are discreet, Edmund Robinson won't even realise we're gone until I fail to turn up with the rent. By then, we should be many miles away."

Jennet smiled. "I've still to see Goodwife Lund. I can't go without saying goodbye to her first."

"Yes, of course. She has been a good friend to you. We will go together, then leave straight from her cottage."

Jennet winced at the finality in his voice. "Sounds like a good idea."

William looked at her quizzically. "Are you alright, Jennet?"

"Yes, I am fine," she said, although she could hear the doubt resonating in her answer even as she spoke it. She lowered her gaze. Moments ago she had felt so keen on this new adventure, yet now she hesitated. "I suppose it just struck me that after today I probably won't see Goodwife Lund ever again."

William put his arms around her, holding her tightly. "I know, my love," he said simply.

Jennet rested her head against his shoulder. "I will miss her," she said, an involuntary tear escaping down her cheek.

"I know," he said again. "Today will be a hard day, but we will face it together. I will always be here for you. I don't want you to worry about anything, not about leaving this place or about the journey ahead. I will keep you safe. I promise."

Jennet lifted her chin and kissed him firmly on the lips. William looked surprised; it wasn't like her to make such an assertive gesture of affection. "You're a good man," she said with a smile. "I don't deserve you."

He laughed quietly. "Of course you do," he replied. "Now come on, let's go and say our farewells."

It felt strange leaving the barn for the final time. As William shut the rickety old door they looked at one another for a moment, holding each other's gaze with sadness in their eyes, acknowledging in their silence that this was the passing of a short era. The barn, for all its inadequacy as a home, had been their home nonetheless, a place which had sheltered them, a place where until recently they had felt safe. Now, with the door closed firmly behind them, they had no choice but to look forward to a future which was both exciting and uncertain.

They walked briskly along the lane to Goodwife Lund's cottage at Blackwood Head. The air outside was still cool and damp, the ground still tinged with morning dew. Above them the clouds had broken, allowing them to feel the warmth of the sun which hinted at the spring soon to come. Jennet said a quick prayer, asking God to preserve this weather for them on the long road ahead.

Goodwife Lund must have seen them approach, for she swung the door open enthusiastically to greet them. "Jennet! William! It is good to see you both." She frowned. "Has it not been a long winter? Surely it was Christmas when we last spoke!"

Jennet nodded. "Yes," she replied. "It has been a while. How have you been?"

Goodwife Lund waved her hand dismissively. "Oh, I am just as you always find me. Please," she beckoned, "come inside, both of you."

Jennet walked in through the little door. Inside the cottage was cosy, the pleasant fragrance of ground herbs mingling with the scent of the Goodwife's cooking. Instinctively, Jennet breathed in deeply, allowing the familiar aromas to drift up her nostrils one last time. She used to find comfort in those smells; now she found that they left her with a hollow, sinking feeling in the pit of her stomach.

"I was just making some pottage," she remarked. "Can I fetch either of you something to eat, or to drink?"

Jennet shook her head and sat down, clasping her hands together in her lap. She didn't know what to say to her friend, she realised; she didn't know how to tell her that this would be the last time they would meet. She looked at Goodwife Lund, her eyes heavy with sadness. She knew that for her safety, she needed to leave. She knew that there was no possibility of the Lunds coming too; Goodwife Lund had been clear about that. She knew there was no other choice, yet when it came to this final, difficult moment she felt herself faltering, unable to say goodbye.

Goodwife Lund drew a deep breath, giving them both a pained look. "You're leaving, aren't you?" she asked, taking a seat beside them.

"Yes," William said quietly. "I don't think we can wait any longer. We must go now."

Goodwife Lund sighed. "I daresay you're right," she replied. "All this talk about us being witches is getting a bit too much, isn't it?" Her tone was jolly, but Jennet could tell it was forced. Goodwife Lund knew as well as she did how serious the situation had become.

"Won't you think about leaving too?" Jennet asked, her voice pleading. "It has become too dangerous for all of us."

"It's out of the question." Goodwife Lund furrowed her brow. "I've never left Pendle for a single day of my life. Where would I go? And what about Grace? I can't just abandon her."

"She could go with you," Jennet replied quietly. "Her, Nicholas and the baby. You could all start afresh."

"Jennet, Grace would not survive the journey. Her mind is

weak, and now Goodwife Dickenson tells me that her body ails her too. No, Wheatley Lane is my home and it is here I shall remain." She gave them both a reassuring smile. "But you two – well, you're young and fit. You should go, get yourself far away from here, far away from danger."

Jennet flung herself into her friend's arms. "I will miss you. You have been like a mother to me."

Goodwife Lund chuckled. "I will miss you too. You are a good lass, I have always said so." She cleared her throat and tapped her hand on her knee. "Now, will you not have some pottage before you leave? I can't send you on such a long journey on an empty stomach, and I bet neither of you have eaten." She gave them both a knowing look.

Jennet and William both grinned. It was true; it was past lunchtime and they hadn't had so much as a bit of bread between them.

"We're much obliged to you, Goodwife," said William. "I know I've never got to know you like Jennet, but nevertheless, you have been kind to us both. I only hope we meet people as good as you when we reach London."

Goodwife Lund wrinkled her nose a little. "Well, folk are different down there. I'm not sure what you'll find, but whatever happens I wish you both health and happiness," she added diplomatically, handing them each a bowl of steaming pottage.

"I tend to find that there's good and bad wherever I go," William replied. "I doubt London will be much different."

"Ah Jennet, I forget you are travelling with an expert in these matters!" Goodwife Lund teased.

Jennet smiled meekly at them both. "I am in safe hands," she said, slowly spooning up her pottage.

Their conversation was interrupted by a hard knock at the door. Immediately they all stopped speaking, their three heads turning in unison. A heavy silence filled the air. After a moment the visitor knocked again, this time louder, more impatient.

"I wasn't expecting anyone this afternoon," said Goodwife

Lund, a note of trepidation in her voice.

"Perhaps it's someone who needs help," replied Jennet. "When I lived here, folk used to call round at all hours to ask for remedies."

"That's true," Goodwife Lund replied with a nervous chuckle, "although I've not had so many visitors lately. Well, I suppose I should see who's there."

She opened the door slowly. Jennet could see the reluctance in her movements. She wondered if her friend reacted like this every time someone came to her door, convinced that it was the constable's knock. She shook her head slightly; it was no way to live, in constant fear of the gallows, and yet still her friend refused to leave. She peered round, trying to see who was there.

"Who are you?" she heard Goodwife Lund ask, her usual friendliness displaced by a brusque tone.

Without answering, two men forced their way past her and walked inside. Jennet dropped her spoon and looked at them, open-mouthed. They were both tall, heavy set men, with untidy hair and grubby-looking clothes.

Jennet shuffled backwards slightly on her stool. "We don't have anything," she said defensively.

One of the men laughed. "We're not here to rob you!" he said. "We're looking for Jennet Lund."

Goodwife Lund curled her lip at them in disgust. "I am Jennet Lund," she said. "Who's asking? And who do you think you are, coming into my home like this? If you've come for a remedy, I've a good mind to send you out of here right this minute!"

The same man laughed again. "We're not here for one of your potions either. We come on the business of two local gentlemen, Masters Shuttleworth and Starkie. You need to come with us to Gawthorpe Hall."

"Gawthorpe Hall?" Goodwife Lund repeated dumbly.

Jennet looked helplessly at William. She knew what these men were here for. She had seen all this before; she had watched her whole family as they were taken away in much the same manner, by men working for the wealthy, powerful gentleman who lived at Read Hall. Master Nowell - Jennet whispered his name, recalling his face, his eyes, his beard, his fine clothes. She remembered his library; that ornate, wooden room filled with books, where they would sit and talk for hours. She remembered how interested he had been in her life and her stories, how he had smiled at her and told her she was clever.

She closed her eyes for a moment, allowing the memories which she had buried for so many years to flow freely through her mind. She remembered how Master Nowell's men had come to Malkin Tower three times, each time assuring the person they sought that they would not be gone for long, that their master only wanted to ask a few questions. She recalled her mother's hysteria when the same men had returned for the final time. By then, there had been just herself, her brother and mother left; her sister and grandmother had already been arrested and incarcerated. In her mind's eye she could see her mother wailing uncontrollably, telling the men that they were liars.

"We will never come back here!" she had yelled, and she had been right. The family had never returned to Malkin Tower. They had all perished at the gallows in Lancaster, all except for little Jennet, the survivor, the traitor, who was abandoned by Master Nowell at her father's door. Malkin Tower, their beloved home, was left to crumble.

"Goodman," William said, making an effort to be polite. "Can you please explain what all this is about?" His expression was typically calm and neutral, but Jennet could see the panic in his eyes.

"And who are you?" the man asked, furrowing his brow.

William cleared his throat. "William Braithwaite," he replied. "And this is my wife, Jennet Braithwaite."

"Braithwaite," the man repeated. "Henry, are we looking for any Braithwaites?" he asked his companion.

The man named Henry shook his head. "No, I don't think so. Mind you, there's so many of them, I keep forgetting who we're looking for!" He turned and looked at Jennet, studying her. Jennet tried to avert her eyes from his searching gaze. "We are looking for another Jennet though, and if my memory, poor as it is, serves me correctly, this Jennet looks much like the one the boy described."

The first man sighed. "Come on then Jennet Braithwaite, I suppose you should come with us as well."

William stepped in front of Jennet. "You will not take Goodwife Lund or my wife anywhere unless I get an answer from you. What do you want?" He spoke firmly.

The man narrowed his eyes at William. "I wouldn't get in the way of our master's instructions. Tell him, Henry. Tell him what happens to men who get in the way."

The man named Henry drew a small knife and pointed it at William. "Move aside," he instructed.

William stood there, steadfast in his refusal to move, his eyes narrowed and lips set in a look of contempt which Jennet had never seen him wear on his face before.

"William…" she whispered pleadingly.

"What are you worried about anyway?" said the other man. "She might not be the Jennet we're looking for. She might be back home and in your bed by supper time." Both men laughed raucously.

William continued to shield her. "You have not explained what you want and until you do, my wife is going nowhere."

"There are accusations of witchcraft," the man named Henry blurted out, exasperated by William's persistence. "Our masters are just trying to clear up the matter, in accordance with the law of this land. Now, are you going to move?" He raised his knife once again. A tense silence followed.

In the end, it was Goodwife Lund who intervened. "Come William, this isn't worth making trouble over. I think Jennet and I should go and answer the gentlemen's questions, shouldn't we, Jennet? We've done nothing wrong. The gentlemen will soon see that, I'm sure."

Jennet stepped forward and touched her husband's arm.

"William, you'll end up being arrested too if you carry on like this," she said gently.

He turned to face her. "I think I'd almost prefer that," he said with a sad smile. "At least then I could stay with you." He breathed in deeply as a tear rolled down his cheek.

"Oh, my love…" she began, wiping away his tears.

"You know how this works, Jennet," he said quietly. "You know what happens here. You told me yourself how this ends. Are you not afraid?"

"I've been afraid of this moment for my entire life," she answered. "I think I always knew that this would be my fate. At least now that I am confronted it, in a way that means I can stop fearing it."

"I'm terrified that I will never see you again. We had such wonderful plans…" he began, his voice made uneven by suppressed sobs.

"Whatever happens, I will always love you," she said. "We will see each other again, I promise." She smiled and held his tear-strewn face in her hands, kissing him tenderly on the lips.

"I will wait for you," he said. Jennet tried to ignore the desperation in his voice. She could not crumple now, she realised; she had to remain strong, for William and for Goodwife Lund.

"I am ready," she said, stepping in front of William and surrendering to the two men. The man named Henry took her by the arm and led her out of the cottage, where his horse was waiting. The other man followed with Goodwife Lund who wore a dazed expression, as though she couldn't quite believe what was happening.

"Jennet, I love you!" she heard William call, his voice a strained, awful wail which made her heart ache. As they rode away, she fixed her eyes on the horizon, holding on to her captor for dear life as the horse galloped faster and faster. She couldn't bring herself to look back at her husband. She couldn't bear to see the pain on his face, to have that final, dreadful image of him etched on her memory forever. She couldn't stand to see what his love for her had reduced him to, a grieving wreck of a man who would forever wait for a woman who would never come home.

"That was a brave performance you gave back there," Henry called over his shoulder. "You must be a little bit frightened though, surely. The likes of you will have never met a gentleman before, or been in a house as grand as Gawthorpe Hall. One glimpse of the place and you'll be confessing to all sorts, begging for a reprieve. I guarantee it." He gave a cruel laugh.

"Not this time," she muttered.

24

Gawthorpe Hall, near Padiham
Late February 1634

"We're here," the man named Henry called to her, his voice muffled by the force of the wind. The pleasant weather had dissipated after they left Wheatley Lane, the sky now filled with heavy black rain clouds, the once calm air growing blustery. The sun had gone too, making the day seem much colder. Jennet shivered as an icy chill travelled through her bones.

"Just look at that – splendid, isn't it?"

Jennet squinted, her eyes made dry by the cold air which had been soaring relentlessly in her face. In front of her stood a magnificent building, a giant structure of beige-brown stonework, interspersed with many large glass windows. In its centre was a tower-like feature, standing so tall that as far as Jennet was concerned, it might as well reach for the heavens. She gasped. As a child Read Hall had been impressive; a tall building, with its three sides all surrounding a grand courtyard. She closed her eyes for a moment, remembering the summer afternoons she spent there, basking in the heat of the sun, twirling around and around in that fine dress he had given her...

She opened her eyes again, shaking off the memory. If Read

Hall had been grand then Gawthorpe Hall, it seemed, was even grander. She wondered then who Gawthorpe Hall belonged to. Surely behind such an awe-inspiring house there was a rich man. A clever man. An important man. A man just like Master Nowell.

"Bet you're not feeling so brave now," Henry sneered as they drew nearer. "Remember, Master Shuttleworth is a gentleman, so mind your manners."

"Does Gawthorpe Hall belong to Master Shuttleworth?" Jennet asked, choosing to ignore his condescension.

"Of course it does!" replied Henry mockingly. "Folk like you never cease to amaze me. So ignorant."

Jennet bit her tongue, resisting the temptation to point out that this man, in his plain, grubby doublet and with his rough manners, was not vastly different from her. How she would have liked to tell him that she had once held the favour of a gentleman, how she had learned the hard way that rich folk find it easy to use ordinary people for their own ends, only to discard them once they had outlived their usefulness. She wanted so badly to ask this man if, after he had rounded up all these so-called witches for Master Shuttleworth, he thought that he would continue in this gentleman's employment or if he would be put aside. She pressed her lips together tightly, knowing that such impertinence towards her captor was unwise.

The horse stopped abruptly as they reached the entrance to Gawthorpe Hall. Henry dismounted first.

"Get down," he instructed her gruffly.

Her attempts to get off the horse were clumsy; she had never ridden before and was unfamiliar with the practice. After watching her struggle for several moments, arms folded, eyes glazed with a vague amusement, Henry sighed heavily and lifted her down.

"At least you don't weigh much," he remarked. "The river's over there, you know. I daresay Master Shuttleworth might consider dunking you – if he does, my money's on you floating. You're as light as a feather." He smiled sardonically.

Jennet frowned at him but said nothing in reply. She watched as the other man's horse arrived with Goodwife Lund rooted to the back of it, her face filled with fear, her hands clinging on for dear life. Like Jennet, the Goodwife struggled to dismount, grappling fearfully with her balance as her arms and legs appeared to move about involuntarily. When the man approached to assist her she lost her footing completely, tumbling over and sending them both falling to the ground.

"Why do I always get the fat ones?" she heard him grumble to Henry as he dusted himself off. "At least yours is quite pretty."

"Aye," Henry replied. "But I reckon that husband of hers would slit my throat in my sleep if I so much as touched her."

"That's never stopped you before," retorted the other man, nudging his friend in the ribs. Both men burst into wicked laughter. Jennet shuddered and turned away, closing her ears to their despicable conversation.

"Jennet, I'm frightened," whispered Goodwife Lund as she adjusted her coif.

Jennet forced a smile to her lips. "Try not to worry – if they see you're scared, they will use it against you. And don't say anything, unless it is to protest your innocence."

"Oh lass, I am glad that I am with you," Goodwife Lund replied, clutching her hand.

The men led the two women inside. Jennet drew a sharp breath as they were confronted with the entrance hall, a grand area with a high, elaborately decorated ceiling, the walls covered with fine wood panelling, beautifully carved. She reflected that the entrance hall was at least twice the size of her barn, and a good deal taller. The man who brought her here had been right; it was an exquisite place, a grand display of wealth and power and…Jennet paused for a moment. Fear. For all its splendour, somewhere like this could only ever inspire fear in the likes of her.

They were taken through a seemingly endless succession of corridors, all richly decorated, portraits hanging on every wall. With every footstep, Jennet felt her heart beat faster, the blood coursing through her veins with such ferocity that she felt light-headed. She struggled to keep her composure, sweat running profusely down her spine. As she walked, she found herself wishing that William was there with her, that she could run into his arms, hold him tight and never let him go. She tried to suppress the dreadful thought that she would probably never feel the warmth of his touch again.

Finally they arrived at a large room. Like much of the house its walls were laden with dark wood panelling, its ceiling decorated with an intricate and beautiful frieze. In it was a grand collection of furniture, mostly tables and chairs, all of which were finely carved. At its heart sat a large fireplace, a fire roaring and crackling loudly within it. Jennet shuffled uncomfortably in her shawl, finding the heat in the room unbearable.

"This is the drawing room," said Henry, as though he might be giving his captives a tour of the house. "We will wait in here. Our masters should be along shortly."

Jennet glanced at Goodwife Lund, who returned her gaze with an anxious stare.

"Please, don't worry," Jennet tried to reassure her once again, taking hold of her hand and giving it a gentle squeeze. In truth she didn't know if she could keep up the pretence of serenity for much longer. Her hands felt cold but clammy, and she was conscious of the beads of moisture which were forming on her brow.

After what felt like an eternity, the heavy wooden door opened and two men walked in. They were both exquisitely well-dressed, their doublets and breeches made of the finest material. She noticed that one of the men wore a cape, his cheeks a little ruddy and his long hair slightly dishevelled, as though he had just arrived on horseback. The man caught Jennet's gaze and she instinctively cast her eyes downwards, looking at his boots, which again were of the highest quality, tall and turned over at the tops, perfect for riding.

"These must be the two Jennets," said the other man, stroking his pointed, greying beard in a gesture of contemplation as he studied the two women, his eyes moving slowly back and forth between them.

"Hope so, sir. We're not sure about one of 'em," said Henry.

The man gave a small frown before touching his beard again. "I'm sure we'll soon know whether she's the right Jennet or not, Henry," he replied, waving his hand in a dismissive gesture towards his faithful servants, who both gave slight bows before duly leaving the room.

"Do you know who we are and why you're here?" the man asked, turning his attention back to his prisoners.

"No, sir," replied Jennet, while Goodwife Lund simply shook her head in response.

The man gave a light sigh. "Please, have a seat," he gestured towards two of the rooms' many chairs. "My name is Master Shuttleworth, and this is Master Starkie," he said, taking a seat directly across from them both. "We are both Justices of the Peace. That means we may question you and establish whether either of you have broken the law of this land. Do you know what crimes you stand accused of?"

Out of the corner of her eye, Jennet saw Goodwife Lund glance towards her. Jennet shook her head vigorously.

"No sir, we do not," she replied.

"Your honour," Master Starkie interjected. "You should address us both as 'your honour'."

Jennet gave Master Starkie a cold stare. "No, your honour," she repeated. "We do not know what crimes we are accused of. We are both sure that we have committed no crime."

Master Shuttleworth gave her an amused smile. "You must be Jennet Sellers. Or is it Jennet Device? I have to say, our witness couldn't decide."

"As my husband told your men, I am Jennet Braithwaite. I do not have any other name."

"Oh, but you did!" replied Master Shuttleworth with a chuckle. "Jennet Device – oh yes, I remember the stories well. Master Nowell was an acquaintance of mine, of course."

"And a relation of mine," added Master Starkie. "May God rest his soul."

Jennet flinched at Master Starkie's words. She knew that, in all likelihood, Master Nowell was dead; he had been around sixty when she encountered him twenty-two years ago. However, to hear confirmation of his passing startled her, although in truth she didn't really understand why. William had been right, after all; Master Nowell had undoubtedly used her, manipulating her childish naivety for his own purposes. Yet when she remembered him, all she could think about was how he smiled at her, his eyes bright with interest, the encouraging nods and compliments in response to everything she said.

Master Shuttleworth gave her a long, considered stare. "It's quite odd seeing you standing here, a grown woman. When I hear your name, the image it conjures is usually that of a little girl, standing on a table at the Assizes, condemning her entire family to die."

"Yes," Master Starkie agreed. "How do you live with it, I wonder? Someone with less strength would have thrown themselves into the river long ago. But not you, Jennet Device – Sellers, Braithwaite, whatever you call yourself. You strike me as a survivor." He smiled at her cruelly.

"Yet here you are, accused of the same crimes as those committed by your mother, grandmother, sister and brother before you. The family trade, of course," Master Shuttleworth mused, sitting back and folding his fingers together, his elbows rooted firmly on the arms of his chair.

"Your honour, I have committed no crime," Jennet insisted, her face growing warm with indignation.

"Really?" asked Master Starkie. "So you deny that you killed Isabel Nutter?" his narrowed eyes shifted their gaze to Goodwife Lund. "And you, Jennet Lund, do you deny killing James Higgins and countless cows and horses through wicked and bewitching practices?"

"Your honour," Goodwife Lund replied, dissolving into tears. "I swear to you, I am a good woman, I have not done these things you say. Please, I have a daughter and a husband who need me.

Please, believe me, please…" She begged, burying her head in her hands as she wept inconsolably.

"We are innocent, your honours," Jennet replied, giving them both a steadfast look. "We have done nothing wrong. I have never heard of an Isabel Nutter; I have never met her, therefore I don't see how I could have caused her death."

"Ah!" Master Starkie exclaimed. "Witches and your riddles – you are all the same! I remember that man Hartley and his riddles, when all along it was he who had caused mine and my sister's bedevilment." His face grew dark, his eyes wide, his stare menacing.

"John," said Master Shuttleworth gently. "That was many years ago now."

"Yes but it plagues me," Master Starkie insisted. "Such is the damage that these cunning people cause. Edmund Hartley has been dead for many years yet his magic haunts me still. We must rid the world of this menace." He clenched his fists angrily.

Master Shuttleworth gave his colleague a wary look before proceeding with his line of questioning. "So you would both deny your involvement in a witches' Sabbath, which took place near a house named Hoarstones on All Saints' Day last? You would deny that you have been seen just weeks ago making pictures from clay of those you wish to harm; that you stick thorns into these pictures in order to bring about illness or even death?"

Goodwife Lund nodded weakly and looked at Jennet.

"Yes," replied Jennet firmly.

Master Shuttleworth gave a short laugh. "You're well-versed in denial, Jennet Device. You learnt your lesson during your time with Master Nowell, I suspect. I think it's likely that we will go round in these circles all day, won't we?"

Jennet answered his question with a hard stare.

"Of course," he said, glancing at his fingernails. "It doesn't matter how strenuously you deny these accusations – we have a witness who will willingly attest to both your satanic practices. And not just you two, either. There are many more witches in these parts, and myself and Master Starkie have made it our mission to find them and submit them to justice."

Goodwife Lund looked flustered. "Who – who else have you arrested?" Jennet could tell what she was thinking – did they have Grace?

Master Starkie chuckled nastily. "Oh, there have been a few sent on to Lancaster before you," he said. "Though one name above all others should be familiar to you – a certain Frances Dickenson."

Goodwife Lund gasped. "No! No! Oh Grace, how will you manage?" she called out.

"Goodwife Lund, hold your tongue," Jennet hissed. The worst thing anyone could do in this situation was to start mentioning other names. Gentlemen like Master Starkie and Master Shuttleworth would seize upon a new name, any name, no matter what the innocent connection might be. She knew from bitter experience that this was how accusations spread to others.

Master Starkie frowned. "Who is Grace?"

"She is Goodwife Lund's daughter, your honour," Jennet replied. "Goodwife Lund fears for her as she has recently had a baby and she is very ill. Goodwife Dickenson was caring for her," she explained grudgingly.

"It's her mind, your honours; it troubles her greatly," Goodwife Lund added.

Jennet gave her a warning glance, urging her to keep quiet.

Master Starkie waved his hand dismissively. "Well, madness is not proof of innocence." He looked at his colleague. "Richard, what was the name of that woman – you remember, surely? The one who…"

Master Shuttleworth looked at him sharply. "Margaret Johnson," he replied. "Well," he said, clapping his hands together, "I am satisfied that we have two of Pendle's most dangerous witches in our custody. You will remain here until you can be dispatched to Lancaster to await trial." Jennet flinched at his cold, procedural tone.

Immediately the door to the room opened and the men who

had brought them to Gawthorpe Hall walked back in. Clearly they had been listening outside, both of their faces wearing smiles of tantalised amusement.

"Henry, Robert," Master Shuttleworth addressed them, "please escort these two women downstairs and lock them up for the night."

Henry gave his master an obliging nod. "Come," he said abruptly. Jennet shuddered as he placed a firm hand on her arm, drawing himself so close to her that she could feel his breath on her neck. "Looks like you'll be staying at my master's pleasure for a while. I might get chance to pay you a visit yet," he whispered.

Jennet closed her eyes briefly and said a quick prayer, beseeching God to not let such an awful, leering man near her. A single tear rolled down her cheek as she wished again that William was there to protect her, to stand in front of her and shield her from this brute and his clever masters. As she was led out of the room she stifled a sob. More than anything, she realised, she wished that she could feel the loving reassurance of being enveloped in his strong arms just one last time.

They were taken downstairs and along a seemingly never-ending series of narrow corridors. Eventually, they arrived at a small room; a dark, cramped space with a tiny, high window offering the only source of natural light. The room was sparsely furnished, containing little more than two piles of straw and two pots, one in each corner. As the men ushered them inside Jennet noticed how cold the air felt, an unrelenting damp chill penetrating through her clothes. She breathed in and wrinkled her nose in disgust at the lingering smell of sweat and excrement. Clearly, the room had been occupied by many other prisoners before their arrival.

"Home for tonight," said Henry gleefully. "I'll be back to check on you in a while. Might even bring you something to eat if I'm feeling generous."

He winked at Jennet, giving her a broad smile which showed off a mouth of filthy, rotting teeth. Jennet's stomach lurched.

The men left the room, slamming the door shut behind them
and turning a key in its lock. Jennet looked at Goodwife Lund, who
sighed deeply as she sat down on the straw and buried her head in
her hands. For a few moments a heavy silence lingered in the air as
Jennet stood there, dumbstruck, watching her friend's shoulders
shake with the effort of her silent sobs.

"I can't believe this is happening," she said in the end, lifting
her head and looking helplessly at Jennet, her green eyes wide with
fear. "What will become of us?"

"I'm sorry that you have been dragged into this," said Jennet,
evading her friend's question. She didn't have the heart to tell her
how bleak their prospects were, how unlikely it was that either of
them would survive this. She sat down beside her, placing a
comforting arm around her shoulder. "I am so sorry," she said
again.

"Oh lass," said Goodwife Lund, wiping her eyes. "What have
you to be sorry for?"

Jennet looked at her, her eyes heavy with remorse. "After you
found out who I was, your first instinct was to stay away from me.
You were right; you should have kept your distance. If you had,
you might have been safe. It's because of me that you're caught up
in this now."

Goodwife Lund let out a sad chuckle and tapped her lightly on
the hand. "No lass, you're wrong there. I have a certain reputation,
as you know, much like your grandmother did. I'm an easy person
to pick on and anyway, it sounds like these gentlemen have cast
their net fairly wide in their search for so-called witches. How many
of us do you think there are?"

Jennet shrugged. "I don't know, but I'm certain that they won't
stop until they think they've found every last one. That's what
happens with these things, you see, they just grow and grow
and…" her words faltered as she gestured wildly with her hands.

Goodwife Lund nodded. "That Master Shuttleworth seems a
cold, serious type. I don't know what to make of Master Starkie!
Did you see how wild his face became when he started talking

about Edmund Hartley? Mind you, I'm not surprised, that was a terrible business for him and his sister…"

"You know what he was referring to?" Jennet asked, surprised.

Goodwife Lund gave her a cautious glance. "Aye lass," she said, lowering her voice. "I was just a young girl at the time, mind you. Folk said that he and his sister were possessed by the devil. They had the most terrible and frightening fits; it was the talk of villages for miles around. The man Hartley was employed to cure them but in the end old Master Starkie, he was this Master Starkie's father, decided that it was he who had bewitched them and Hartley was sent to the gallows at Lancaster." She gulped hard. "Just like us. That's how we're going to end up, isn't it?"

Jennet frowned. "I don't remember any of this," she said, again ignoring her friend's question. "What year did this happen?"

Goodwife Lund rolled her eyes upwards for a moment. "Must have been about 1595, and I think Hartley was hanged a couple of years later. Poor man, may God rest his soul."

"No wonder I don't remember. I wasn't born until 1600," said Jennet. "I'm surprised. I didn't think Master Starkie looked that old."

Goodwife Lund let out a wry chuckle. "Good living. The wealthy don't age so badly as the rest of us." Her face darkened again as she gripped Jennet's hand tightly. "Oh lass, I'm frightened."

Jennet gave her friend a grim smile. "I know," she said. "But trust me, the worst thing you can do is show your fear. If you show that you're afraid, they know that they've won. You must show them nothing. You must tell them nothing."

"But they said it didn't matter what we said," the Goodwife protested. "They've got a witness – that Robinson boy, I imagine."

"No doubt," Jennet replied, biting her lip hard. Another witch trial. Another child witness. History was repeating itself all over again.

"I'm glad I'm with you, lass. If anyone knows how to get us out of this mess, it's you."

Jennet nodded glumly as she lay down on the straw. Yes, she thought, she had experience of these matters; of that there was no doubt. Despite her knowledge, however, she couldn't see any way out of their current predicament, any glimmer of hope which might ease their way to freedom. Turning to face the wall she closed her eyes, recalling those long-buried memories of herself, the star witness, basking in the court's attention as she gleefully uttered the evidence which had condemned her entire family to die. She wondered what little Edmund Robinson was thinking right now; was he enjoying the attention as much as she had? Did he feel any guilt at how his stories had taken on a life of their own? Everything she had told Master Nowell had been true, and yet still she struggled to live with it – how would young Edmund cope with the knowledge of his lies for the rest of his days?

She sighed deeply. No, there was no way out of this. Indeed, as she fell into an exhausted slumber, she realised that all she could sense in front of her was a final wounding humiliation, followed by suffering and finally, death.

25

Gawthorpe Hall, near Padiham
Early March 1634

"Come on," Henry said roughly, shaking Jennet and Goodwife Lund from their sleep. "It's time to go."

"Go where?" said Goodwife Lund, but her question went unanswered.

Jennet grasped her friend's hand tightly as they were led from the small, locked room which had been their gaol for several days and nights. Outside, the sun had barely risen, mere hints of its orange hue languishing sleepily on the horizon. The two women were led to the side of the great house, where they were loaded into a small cart attached to a rather weary-looking horse. In the front sat their other gaoler, Robert, his mouth fixed in a protracted yawn.

"Too early for me," he remarked to Henry. "It's your turn to do this next time."

"Next time?" asked Henry. "I hope these two are the last of them."

For one moment, just before the horse began to trot, Jennet caught Henry's eye. She couldn't resist giving him a cold, hard stare, the sort which suggested disgust and condemnation. He was unperturbed, however, merely putting his finger to his lips before giving her a small, mocking wave. She frowned. She wasn't going to speak to him; she had nothing to say. She had neither parting words nor questions. She knew exactly where she was being taken. She closed her eyes, remembering how as a little girl she had watched from a small window at the top of Read Hall as her mother and brother had been taken away in a little cart such as this.

"At least he didn't come near you, lass," Goodwife Lund whispered as the cart drew away. "I was worried that he might have, you know, tried something."

Jennet nodded. "Perhaps he thought I'd put a curse on him if he did."

She gave her friend a small, wry smile. At one time she would have laughed, she realised, but now terror had overcome her, dampening her spirits, superseding any other feelings. She gazed behind her for a long time, watching Gawthorpe Hall as the grand house became an impressive, dark silhouette in the distance. For the first time in her life, she reflected, she found it far easier to look backward than to look forward.

The horse was nimbler on its feet than she had first judged, and the journey to Lancaster seemed to pass quickly, no doubt assisted by the favourable condition of the roads, which were mostly dry. After several hours of travelling with only a handful of brief stops, she spied her first glimpse of the town as they approached it in the late afternoon light. It had been many years since she had last been there but she found it to be mostly unchanged, row upon row of small dwellings seemingly stacked on top of one another up the hill, building like a crescendo towards the dark, forbidding castle in the centre.

As they approached Lancaster Castle, Jennet couldn't resist a shudder. The last time she had walked through those heavy gates it had been as a naïve, energetic child, there to give the evidence which would send her family to the gallows. Now she was the prisoner, going in there to await her fate. Perhaps this was justice, after all; not the kind envisaged by the likes of Masters

Shuttleworth and Starkie, but the sort which God handed out to ensure that all wrongs were somehow made right. She sighed heavily, realising that she had long suspected that it was only through her own death that she could ever hope to atone for the things she had done.

The man named Robert led them from the cart and delivered them to the gatekeeper's quarters, where a stern-looking old man met them, casting a beady, suspicious eye over them both.

"Jennet Device?" he said to her.

"Braithwaite," she corrected him. "My name is Jennet Braithwaite."

"Says Device here," he replied, pointing to a large book, well-thumbed and filled with scrawled handwriting. "Awaiting trial for witchcraft?"

She nodded glumly.

"Then Device it is. That's the name I've been given. Jennet Device and Jennet Lund." He gave them both a withering stare. "The guard will take you to the Well Tower. That's where we're keeping the witches. No doubt you've some friends in there," he added, flashing them a nasty smile.

The two women were ushered away by a tall, solid man with an impatient manner and a set of large keys jangling noisily at his waist. They were led a short distance to a small doorway, beyond which lay a narrow set of stairs. Behind her, Jennet heard Goodwife Lund groan with fear. Jennet looked down but could see nothing except a dark, miserable abyss. If the air hadn't felt so cold, she would have sworn she was walking straight down to hell.

"Go on," said the guard, gruffly. "Down you go."

They walked down the stairs slowly, their careful steps filled with trepidation. Frightened of falling, Jennet grasped at the stone wall. She recoiled, realising it was wet. She could hear the sound of water dripping, reminding her of her little barn at Hoarstones, the damp walls here reminiscent of her crumbling home on a rainy winter's day. She bit her lip, suppressing the tears which stung in her eyes. How she longed to be back there now.

As she descended further into the Well Tower, she heard new sounds; groans and murmurs, the pitiable noise of other human beings enduring intolerable misery. New scents wafted up her nose; ghastly fragrances, like the smell of damp mixed with the smell of death. She reached the bottom of the stairs and squinted, trying to see into the room before her. In the darkness, she could make out only shadows of the unfortunate souls already inhabiting this dreadful place. And there she was, here to join them.

"Go on," said the gruff guard. "Get in there."

The guard lit a candle and prodded them towards a corner of the room, where two sets of empty shackles lay waiting.

"Sit down," he instructed. Jennet gulped as the metal clanked against the hard, stone floor. "There, that'll do," he said as he fastened them in place. "Don't want any of your witches' mischief down here."

If she hadn't been subdued by the prospect of wearing chains around her ankles, Jennet would have told the foolish man that if they had been witches, a few flimsy pieces of metal would have hardly kept their devilish powers at bay.

The guard left the dungeon and shut the door, taking the candle with him and returning them all to the darkness. Jennet put her head in her hands, feeling suddenly exhausted. She sat quietly for a moment, listening to the sounds of the other bodies around her, shuffling and coughing somewhere in the black. Next to her, she could hear Goodwife Lund sobbing softly.

"I can't believe they've just left us down here. We will die, surely we will die," she heard her friend whisper.

For the first time since their arrest, Jennet didn't hurry to offer her any comfort. She no longer had the ability, she realised. Despite her best efforts, her own fear had taken its toll on her, overwhelming her now as she looked out into the black nothingness before her. She tried not to think about how her family too must have languished in there, awaiting trial all those years ago. She tried not to think about how they must have suffered, about how they must have spent every day in the endless dark, feeling the cold, damp air infecting their bones, breathing in the nauseating stench. She tried not to think about them now; such thoughts were intolerable.

"So, they've finally brought you in," someone said. The voice was hoarse but familiar.

"Goodwife Dickenson?" Jennet called out.

She winced, remembering how she had been turned out of the Goodwife's house all those months ago. She had been unable to show her any mercy, unable to see past her lies; she had said so herself. Jennet recalled the last time she had seen her, that evening on All Saint's Day, when Grace came to her cottage. She remembered the cold, indifferent look Goodwife Dickenson had given her; how she had barely acknowledged her despite bursting into her home. A hollow pain coursed through Jennet's stomach as she remembered everything she had lost that night.

"Yes, I am here," said Goodwife Dickenson, her voice glum.

"Master Starkie said you had been arrested," Goodwife Lund said in a whisper.

"Yes," she said again. "On some ridiculous charge – apparently I bewitched a man named Edmund Stevenson." Her tone was haughty and irritated but beneath it, Jennet sensed sadness and deep regret.

"And what of Grace?" Goodwife Lund asked.

"Well, she isn't here. They didn't come for her, only for me," said Goodwife Dickenson, her tone cutting. "I had to leave her with Nicholas and John. I had no choice."

"But how will she fare? Without me, without you…"

"Jennet," Goodwife Dickenson addressed Goodwife Lund, her voice quiet and restrained, "there's nothing we can do for her now. I'd be more concerned about our prospects and I have to say, those look fairly bleak. That Robinson boy and his father have stitched us up well and truly." The bitter note returned to her voice once again.

"I'm sorry you've been arrested," Jennet muttered. "I can't help thinking that if you and Goodwife Lund hadn't befriended me, then you'd have never got caught up in all of this."

"Oh, Jennet, this isn't your fault…" Goodwife Lund protested.

"No," said Goodwife Dickenson firmly. "I'm sorry, but I can't be as forgiving as you, I'm afraid. Jennet has to accept some responsibility for all of this. We invited her into our homes, our lives, without knowing who she really was. Indeed, she hid it from us. So yes, her reputation, as it were, is part of the reason we are here today."

Jennet swallowed hard, her mouth and throat feeling suddenly very dry. Goodwife Dickenson's words were harsh, but of course, they were also true. She had concealed her identity from them, enjoying their friendship without letting them into the secret of who she really was. It has only been through Alice's spiteful actions that they had discovered the truth. The web of lies and half-truths she had woven had only ever had selfish ends; the only person she had ever sought to protect was herself. Her heart began to race, making her head pound as the blood coursed through it. She deserved everything that was coming to her. She deserved this trial, this death. She had earned it, but they hadn't. These two women were only here because of her. Although her stomach was empty, she felt suddenly sick.

Goodwife Dickenson took a deep breath. "However," she continued, "I fear that my association with Jennet is not the whole reason that I am here."

"Frances, what do you mean?" Goodwife Lund asked.

"A short while ago, my husband John refused to give Edmund Robinson credit to purchase a cow. He hadn't the means to pay, you see, and we knew it. So, quite sensibly I would contest, we declined to sell to him. It was a business decision and nothing more, but Edmund took offence. I'd say that these tales his boy has been spreading have proved a good way for Edmund to have revenge on his enemies."

"I see," said Goodwife Lund quietly. "Well Edmund has certainly never liked me, or my potions, as he likes to call them. He's an ignorant lump of a man."

Goodwife Dickenson laughed dryly. "Yes he is. But unfortunately for us, he's not stupid. If this trial goes his way, he will have got rid of every woman he's ever disliked. Who knows, perhaps he's even accused a few men along the way, too. Though I thank God he has left my dear husband and son alone."

Jennet flinched at Goodwife Dickenson's mention of her loved ones. Since her incarceration at Gawthorpe Hall, Jennet had struggled to think about William. It was as though her mind couldn't come to terms with the idea of never seeing him again, so instead it stubbornly refused to dwell on thoughts of him at all. The agony which she felt in her chest at even the merest notion of him was enough to knock the breath from her body; an empty, hollow ache which seemed to infect her very soul. This was the difficult part of being in love, she realised; the dreadful feeling of profound emptiness which comes from the loss of someone you care for so deeply. What pained her even more was that she knew William would be feeling exactly the same way.

Goodwife Lund's stomach groaned. "Oh I am so very hungry," she complained.

"You'll soon lose your appetite," Goodwife Dickenson replied. "They seldom feed us, and when they do the food tastes awful. Rotten, just like everything else in here," she added.

Jennet said nothing more to either of the women, choosing instead to lie down with her head rested uncomfortably on the damp stone floor. After all, there wasn't anything else to do now, except lie there and wait for the inevitable to happen.

Despite her best efforts, her thoughts drifted once again to her mother. It occurred to Jennet that this is what it must have been like for her all those years ago, laid on the floor of that stinking, pitch black room day after endless day, sitting up only to take a small drink or a morsel of food when fleetingly offered by the guards. She wondered if, after a while, her mother had begun to welcome death, even to pray for it. After all, Jennet thought, surely death was preferable to this living hell, trapped in the dark, half-starved, the smell of decay lingering constantly in the nostrils.

Surely anything was better than this existence.

26

Lancaster Assizes, Lancaster Castle, Lancaster
April 1634

"Come on, hurry up!" barked the guard.

Jennet shuffled behind the line of men and women as they were marched towards the court room, their hands bound. Progress was slow, but then none of the prisoners were in good health after so many weeks of incarceration in filthy surroundings, deprived of good food. Jennet had grown even thinner, her waist so small that she struggled to keep her petticoats up over her shift. One of the guards had shone a candle in her face, cruelly remarking upon her sunken cheekbones and large eyes, which now seemed to protrude from her wasted face.

"'Tis a shame," he had said. "You were pretty when you first came in here."

Jennet's stomach churned with a vile mixture of desperate hunger and anxiety. For a moment she felt light-headed and lost her balance, almost falling on the woman in front of her.

"Sorry," she said as she turned and stared at her. She immediately looked away, unable to face the fear in the woman's eyes.

There were many people standing trial over the coming days. As she could have predicted, Masters Shuttleworth and Starkie had cast their net wide in the hunt for witches. Each day the gaol of Lancaster Castle had received yet more prisoners until it had been burgeoning with bodies. As the room filled up the conditions within it deteriorated further, the lice, the fleas and the smell of rot infesting everything in sight. Jennet's stomach churned again at the thought of the vomit-inducing stench she had lived with for so long. She screwed up her eyes, trying to remember how many weeks she had been there. In truth she had lost all concept of time now; one day spent in a dark, cramped space rolled seamlessly into another.

That morning they had all been summoned from the cesspit which held them. After so many weeks in darkness, Jennet had been unable to bear the daylight, screwing her face up as it pained her eyes and made her feel dizzy. Eventually, as her eyes became more accustomed, she allowed herself to enjoy these few precious moments of light and fresh air. It pained her to think that this was probably the last time she would enjoy life's simple luxuries. It pained her to think of anything now.

They approached the courtroom. Jennet instantly recognised the wide, heavy wooden door beyond which lay her fate and the fate of so many other souls. She remembered how the door had been flung open for her once before, how she had been greeted by a room filled with gasps of wonder and bewilderment as she, the child witness, was introduced to the judges. Her soul heavy with guilt, she remembered how much she had enjoyed her days in court, how she had basked in all those eyes upon her, hanging on every word she said. Even her mother's cries of protest, her bellows of horror had not been enough to silence her. She shuddered as she was led inside; she would not relish the proceedings today.

The prisoners were seated on a long wooden bench and told that they should rise only when instructed. They would be tried one at a time, they were told, and they must not speak unless asked to answer a question. All around her, Jennet could sense people talking and pointing, telling each other what each witch had allegedly done. She tried to close her ears to their gossip. The toxic mixture of marvelling and condemning voices would only poison her mind when what she needed right now was a clean spirit and clarity of thought. After weeks spent in the dark and with an aching, empty belly, however, it was difficult to muster either. She pulled her filthy shawl tighter over her shoulders and wrung her hands together nervously; like the rest of her, they were cold but clammy.

All murmuring in the courtroom ceased as the doors opened and two official-looking men walked in, both wearing fine red robes and stern expressions. Jennet shuddered again one of them glanced at the line of prisoners awaiting their fate; it was a cold, procedural look, devoid of any sympathy for the set of poor creatures in front of him.

"All rise in court for Sir George Vernon and Sir Francis Crawley!"

Jennet stood up obediently, taking a few deep breaths in an effort to steady herself. She forced herself to look at the floor, not daring to look at the judges, or the jury, or indeed any of the multitude of incredulous spectators waiting with bated breath for proceedings to commence. She knew that if she looked around the room now, if she allowed herself to absorb its details, to provoke her old memories, then she would surely begin to lose her mind. She knew that to have any slim chance of surviving this ordeal, she had to keep her wits about her.

"This court calls Margaret Johnson to answer the charges laid before her," said one of the judges.

Jennet looked up, recognising the name as one mentioned by Masters Shuttleworth and Starkie. A tiny old woman stepped forward from the line. She was a decrepit sight, her shrivelled body hunched over uncomfortably at the shoulders, her face heavily lined. Jennet's heart sank. This woman was at least sixty years old, maybe more, and so frail and delicate. If they could try this little, ancient woman and find her guilty, what hope was there for anyone else?

"Margaret Johnson," the same judge addressed her. "You are accused murdering by witchcraft one Henry Heap, and of wasting the body of Jennet Shackleton by the same means. How do you answer these crimes?"

"I didn't kill anyone," Margaret protested, her voice as feeble as her body. "But I can swear to you that I am a witch."

Everyone in the courtroom gasped at her admission. Apparently oblivious to her awe-struck audience, Margaret proceeded to tell the judges a series of tales about how she had sold herself to a devil named Mamilian, a powerful creature capable of commanding the weather and causing instant death to a person. It was he, she said, who did the killing. She also confessed to attending a number of witches' Sabbaths, including one at Hoarstones.

Jennet sat, open-mouthed, listening to the woman's confessions in horror. It was quite clear to her that her stories were a complete fabrication, the ramblings of an old woman who had apparently lost her mind. She remembered that Master Starkie had inferred that the woman was mad.

She glanced at the judges, who seemed quite absorbed in the old woman's tales, asking her questions and prompting her for more detail. Margaret Johnson, meanwhile, continued to talk herself towards the gallows. Jennet wanted so badly to stand up and tell them all to stop, to tell them that they were foolish and unkind to indulge this poor and confused woman. Of course, she didn't dare; any words from her would only prejudice the judges further against her when her turn came. Instead she bit her tongue hard, forcing herself to remain seated.

One by one, each of the accused was called to stand before the judges. Jennet's heart sank as she witnessed Goodwife Lund's tearful responses to the charges against her, followed by Goodwife Dickenson's stoic, unflinching silence as she was accused of crimes she could never have committed.

As time went on, the accusations seemed to become even more ludicrous, such as those levelled at one woman named Mary

Spencer, who was on trial for bewitching a bucket. Jennet watched in sympathy as Mary, a pretty young woman of no more than twenty-five, listened nervously while it was explained how she used her powers to move a pail full of water fourteen yards up a hill. By the end of her examination, young Mary was in tears, telling the judges that she would pray for forgiveness for Nicholas Cunliffe, the spiteful man who had seemingly seen fit to accuse poor Mary of this ridiculous crime.

"This court calls Jennet Device to answer the charges laid before her."

Finally, after what seemed like hours, it was her turn to face the judges' examination. For some reason, they had saved her until the very last, almost as though someone, somewhere, wished to add further torment to her ordeal. Her heart pounding hard in her chest, reluctantly she took the stand.

"Jennet Device," one of the judges began, "you stand accused of bewitching to death Isabel Nutter. How do you answer this charge?"

Jennet gave the judge a hard stare. "As I have never met anyone by the name of Isabel Nutter, I plead that I am not guilty of this crime."

"So you deny that you are in fact a witch?" the other judge asked, his tone mocking. "You deny that you were present at a witches' Sabbath at Hoarstones on All Saints' Day last?"

"My home was at Hoarstones, your honour," she replied. "So I was present at that place every day. But I swear to you, no witches' Sabbath took place." She looked around the courtroom then, feeling the heat of anger rising within her. "Where is your witness who swears these things to be the truth? I have not yet seen him brought forward."

The judge's eyes widened with horror. "Impertinent creature!" he cried. "It is not your place to ask questions. Any more outbursts like that and I will hold you in contempt of this court."

Jennet clenched her fists, digging her nails into her palms. She wanted to shout and scream at these two wealthy men with their fine robes and clever words. For all their authority, for all their learning, they were still foolish enough to believe the fanciful stories of a little boy. She cast her eyes down, certain now that she would be condemned to hang.

The judge continued to read through the list of charges against her in greater and more horrific depth than she had ever heard. Young Edmund's deposition spoke of how she and Goodwives Dickenson and Lund had kidnapped him and taken him to their wicked feast. The boy had given Masters Shuttleworth and Starkie a list of names in attendance at this so-called Sabbath; many were names of people on trial today. She gulped hard as the stories continued; tales of their ability to change into animals, of seeing them make clay pictures of people in order to inflict injury or death.

"How do you answer these charges?" the judge asked.

Jennet shook her head. "All lies," she replied.

The judge seemed to grow exasperated. By now, most of those who had gone before her had either been reduced to tears, had fallen into a defeated silence, or had incriminated themselves.

"Masters Shuttleworth and Starkie have noted that you have the marks of a witch," he said with a sigh. "Two marks between your legs, in your private areas," he added for clarification. A few in the courtroom sniggered.

She looked up, her eyebrows raised in an expression of surprise. This was evidence she had not heard before. Where had this accusation come from? Certainly, no physician had been called to Gawthorpe Hall to examine her or Goodwife Lund. She recalled how weary the two men, Robert and Henry, had seemed on the morning they left Gawthorpe Hall, how they had seemed keen to see their witch-hunting duties come to an end. In their haste to dispatch them to Lancaster, had one of them overlooked one of their duties? If so, their oversight was now her opportunity, she realised, looking the judge squarely in the eye.

"I don't see how they could know that, your honour. My private parts have not been examined." Without meaning to, she emphasised those words. She couldn't resist feeling a little gleeful as she noticed the judge's cheeks redden. There were a few more amused chuckles around the court. If she hadn't been on trial for her life, she would have laughed herself.

The judges looked at each other for a moment, clearly perturbed. One banged his hammer.

"The court will adjourn," he said. "The jury will return with its verdicts on all the cases heard today."

The accused were ushered out of the courtroom and back towards the Well Tower. As she walked, Jennet felt nauseous, her emotions swinging wildly between hope and despair. She knew that she had cast doubt on Edmund Robinson's aspersions; she had seen it written all over the judges' confused faces. Masters Shuttleworth and Starkie had overlooked one small detail and that was all it had taken to call into question the authenticity of the rest of the evidence given. At the same time, however, she couldn't be sure that the little bit of doubt she had introduced would be enough to overturn the mountain of accusations which faced them all. After all, she thought bitterly, folk loved a public hanging as much as they loved a witch trial.

It was only a short while before the court reconvened. Jennet felt dizzy as she walked back into the courtroom, the day's events finally beginning to take their toll on her. She wondered why the jury had reached such swift verdicts. Were they about the throw all these cases out of the court, to expose the so-called evidence for the spiteful, preposterous nonsense that it was? Or were they so convinced of all the accused persons' guilt that no deliberation had been required at all?

"Good men of the jury; have you reached your verdicts?" one judge asked.

"We have, your honour," a juror replied.

There was a long pause. Jennet took a sharp breath and held it there, waiting anxiously for the juror to speak. The courtroom was silent, the tension hanging in the air like a thick fog on a winter's morning. Then, one by one, the judge read through the long list of names and, one by one, the juror answered that they were guilty.

Finally, Jennet exhaled, placing her head in her hands and weeping as she heard her name – guilty. That was it; it was all over now. She would return to the Well Tower and wait to hang. At least in some strange way, she knew that this was justice. An eye for an eye, as the Bible said. The accuser, the infamous child witness of one witch trial, was now the condemned in another.

"This is wrong!" someone called from the crowd. "This isn't justice! Have you no mercy? Have you no shame? All these poor souls before you are innocent, can you not see that?"

The voice was loud and angry. It was also familiar.

"William?" Jennet mouthed weakly, her eyes darting back and forth wildly, trying to find him in the crowded room.

"Silence!" the judge barked. "Whoever you are, if you are not quiet I will have you removed from this court."

But William could not be dissuaded. "Jennet, Jennet!" he cried. "I will get you out of here, my love. I swear, even if it takes me every day of the rest of my life, I will not stop fighting for you." He stood up then, his arms outstretched to her, half-pleading, half-loving.

"Oh my love," she mouthed back.

She looked at him longingly, absorbing every detail of him once again. His face was strained and weary-looking, but it was still as handsome as she remembered. She smiled at him. During the past few weeks, as she sat in the Well Tower, lingering in the depths of her own despair, she had often found it too painful to think of him, to remember how she hadn't been able to look back at him as she was taken away. When her mind did wander to thoughts of William, it had been to chastise herself for all those times she should have lain with him and hadn't, all those moments she should have told him that she loved him but didn't. Getting to see him this one last time seemed like a gift. There was the face she would remember as she went to the gallows. There was the memory she would cling to as the life was choked from her body.

She looked on helplessly as two guards manhandled him out of the court. "I love you, Jennet!" he called one last time as he was taken away.

"I love you too," she replied, her voice barely a whisper as she tried to suppress her tears.

"As the court has heard, the defendants have all been found guilty," one of the judges pressed on, undeterred by William's outburst. "However, as judges we are responsible for passing sentence."

He paused for a moment, trying to find the correct words. Instinctively, Jennet held her breath again. Something about the way he spoke was unusual; at her family's trial she could quite clearly recall the judge passing swift sentences, barking cruelly at the condemned, almost gleefully telling them that they were to hang. Something was different here, the judge's tone more careful, more considered. For someone awaiting their fate, it was also excruciating.

"In this instance," the judge continued, "we have decided to refer the matter to His Majesty's Privy Council for their learned opinion. Sentencing is therefore delayed until such a time as that opinion is received. Those convicted today will remain imprisoned here until then."

Jennet looked at them both, stunned. She had been right; she had said enough during her examination to make them doubt the evidence. She had not been able to convince the jury, of course, but these two educated gentlemen had sensed that something was amiss; she was sure of it. Perhaps they weren't such fools after all.

All of the prisoners were removed from the court and walked back towards the Well Tower once again. Jennet's heart sank as she walked down those steep, damp steps and back into the endless black.

"I don't understand, lass, what does all this mean?" Goodwife Lund croaked hoarsely as they were chained to the floor once again.

"It means that we might yet live," Jennet answered.

"Yes, but down here, in this horrible place? For how long?" Goodwife Lund asked.

Jennet merely sighed, too exhausted to reply. Goodwife Lund was right: although there was a glimmer of hope, in order to realise it they would have to endure many more weeks, perhaps even months, surviving in this dreadful hole. She took a deep breath, allowing the room's rancid scent to infest her nostrils once again. She might as well get re-accustomed to it, she realised. She was going to be in there for a while.

27

The Well Tower, Lancaster Castle
Mid June 1634

Jennet stared at the wall, watching the water run down in small, wriggling trickles, roaming into every nook and crack and back out again, down towards the floor. Whenever the guards left a lit torch hung up over the steps, casting a dim but sufficient light into the room, Jennet had gazed at that wall. There wasn't much alternative; after all, she had no desire to look at her fellow inmates' faces, their hopeless expressions too chilling a reflection of her own state of mind. The wall was a safer option; the wall could be studied, but could not return a stare. Walls could not judge, walls could not peer into the soul.

She often wondered where all the water came from. It couldn't be rainwater, as it was present all of the time, so it had to have another, more constant source. She mused that perhaps the building's name, the Well Tower, was more than coincidentally apt, that there was indeed a well contained somewhere within it. But then, that didn't explain why the walls were always so wet, for surely a well would be beneath them, not all around them.

"Why do the walls run with water?" she had asked a guard in the end.

"I wouldn't drink it, if I were you," he had replied, handing her a bowl of runny-looking pottage. "It isn't just water, you know. They say the walls of this room run with the sweat of the corpses buried nearby."

After hearing that remark, she hadn't touched the wall again. She supposed that whatever the water was, and wherever it came from, she should be grateful for the distraction it provided. She could sit for hours, mesmerised by the multitude of different paths the droplets took. No matter which way to water ran, however, it always ended up at the bottom, as though its decline was somehow inevitable. Decline; the word stuck in her throat, a solid lump which raised tears to her eyes. She swallowed hard, trying to overcome it.

She looked away from the wall, towards the empty shackles beside her, towards the space where her friend had been. Stuck in this God-forsaken place, she had come to realise that people weren't much different to the trickles of water. They could take whatever path they chose, yet in the end, it was all for nothing. In the end, every person would die; every person would descend into the earth and disappear, just like the water running down the wall. She blinked back tears as she looked at the empty space beside her once again. She wondered what they had done with the Goodwife's body, now that she was dead.

Goodwife Lund's illness had begun benignly enough; she complained of a sore head, and developed a mild cough. Jennet had thought nothing of it at first, since none of them were in good health and many had developed illnesses of their own. Even when she became feverish Jennet had still not fretted, concentrating instead on comforting the poor woman as she wept bitterly for want of one of her own remedies. It was only when the rash appeared, several days after the other symptoms had manifested, that Jennet began to realise that her friend was seriously ill. Gaol fever, she had heard one of the guards say, his tone grim.

At the same time, some of the other inmates had begun to display similar symptoms. The guards made themselves scarce then, feeding the prisoners even less frequently, leaving those who were well to attend to the sick. Sitting there, listening to the moans and wails of the dying, clutching her friend's hands, it had occurred to Jennet for the first time that there were fates worse than hanging. She had always been so terrified of the noose and yet now, listening to Goodwife Lund's delirious cries, breathing in the stench of rotting flesh emanating from her gangrenous sores, she realised that the gallows would have been a mercy. For the first time, she wished that the judges had sent them straight there instead of leaving them all to fester in this purgatory.

"Jennet, I am a witch. I am a witch, aren't I?" Goodwife Lund had said to her a few days ago as she sat by her side. Her breathing had become laboured and her mind, ravaged by fever, was confused.

"Hush now," Jennet had replied. "Of course you're not. It's all nonsense, remember?"

"Why am I here? If I'm not a witch, why…" she screwed up her face, pain overcoming her.

"You are a good woman. You are a good friend," Jennet insisted.

"I'm frightened, Jennet. When I'm gone…if you survive this, please look after Grace. She needs…she is not well…" Goodwife Lund's breathing grew louder and more strained.

Jennet squeezed her friend's hand. It was so hot now that it felt as though it was on fire. "I will, I promise," she said.

She turned away briefly, not wishing Goodwife Lund to see her tears. When she turned back, her friend had gone.

After Goodwife Lund, several other prisoners followed. Jennet always knew when someone had died down there, as a few guards would arrive together, clutching a coarse brown sack into which they would place the body before carrying it back up the stairs. Jennet couldn't help wondering whether the corpses would be buried nearby, whether soon it would be the sweat of their fellow prisoners which ran down the walls. At one time, such thoughts would have made her shudder, but not now. Now Jennet envied the dead; they had escaped, they were no longer stuck in this torment. William would say that they had gone to a better place, to be by God's side. Jennet shook her head; she wasn't so sure about that anymore.

"At least she's at peace now," said Goodwife Dickenson, nodding towards the empty space. "God was merciful, in the end."

"Was he?" Jennet asked. "She suffered a good deal, for a number of days. If he was truly merciful, he would have made it quick."

In the dim light, she saw Goodwife Dickenson shrug. "His ways are certainly mysterious."

Jennet bit her tongue. Such comments from the faithful always irritated her. William had made similar remarks; whenever he could not explain or condone God's actions, he simply attributed them to divine mystery. She bit her tongue harder, almost drawing blood. She was thinking about William again. She did not want to think about her husband right now.

"I daresay we shall all follow her, soon enough," Goodwife Dickenson continued, her tone characteristically matter-of-fact. "Gaol fever is catching, you know."

"I wonder if that's what killed my grandmother," said Jennet, thinking aloud.

Her grandmother had died in prison there before her trial could take place. In the darkness of the Well Tower, Jennet's thoughts had often turned to her. Sometimes, in the dead of night when all was quiet, she thought she could see her image sitting in the corner, looking at her, studying her. She would close her eyes then and dream, a stream of vivid recollections from her childhood running unabated through her mind.

In her dreams she would see not only her grandmother, but also her mother, her sister and her brother, their images so clear that she felt as though she could touch them. In her dreams, they were always angry, chastising her for the things she had done, for the way she had betrayed them. After a while she would wake sweating, her entire body shaking as her mind clung to a single picture of them, surrounding her, their collective disappointment hanging in their eyes.

"I imagine that your grandmother died of a lot less than that," replied Goodwife Dickenson. "She was an old woman, after all. But I suppose we will never know."

"No," Jennet replied, "I don't suppose we will."

Later that day the silence was interrupted by the sound of the door above them opening, accompanied by a number of loud voices. Jennet had been dozing, the now familiar fleet of long-buried memories running through her mind. At once her eyes flew open, and she looked to her side. She saw that Goodwife Dickenson still languished there and she breathed a sigh of relief. At least she was still alive. Goodwife Dickenson caught her gaze and gave her a sad look. Jennet averted her eyes once again. Her heart was pounding, and she realised how deeply she feared being left alone.

"They're down here, my Lord," she heard someone say. She could hear footsteps drawing closer, followed by the sound of coughing.

"Oh, God in your mercy, what a dreadful smell!" another voice said. "I cannot speak to them down there. You will have to bring them up to me."

"What, all of them, my Lord? Some of them are sick, you see, and…"

"Bring all those who can walk."

"Yes, my Lord."

Jennet squinted as a candle was shone in her eyes, a man's face peering inquisitively into hers. "This one looks alright," he said, unfastening the chains from around her ankles. "Come on, up you get," he said sharply.

Jennet glanced anxiously at Goodwife Dickenson as she was also freed from her shackles and escorted up the stairs. As she rose higher, Jennet could feel the warm air of early summer breezing in through the door. She breathed in deeply, enjoying the refreshing sensation of clean air in her nostrils.

As she reached the top, she found that the light outside was so bright that she could barely keep her eyes open, her eyes struggling to grow accustomed to it after so many weeks locked away in the darkness. She felt disorientated as they were led away from the Well Tower and towards another tall building on the other side of the castle. As she walked past, she glanced at the gatehouse. Her heart sank as she saw that the strong, forbidding gates were closed and heavily guarded. Clearly the gatekeeper was taking no chances when there were unshackled witches on the loose.

The guards ushered them all into a small room. Jennet looked around her as the other prisoners crowded in, familiar putrid smells emanating from their filthy clothing. The room felt cramped, but at least it enjoyed some daylight. Jennet edged towards one of the little windows, enjoying the bright sunshine as it flooded in. She wished she could break the glass on that window, jump through it and run. A solitary tear ran down her cheek as she thought of running into William's arms, the two of them going far away together, so far that she would never have to see the inside of the Well Tower ever again. Her stomach ached as she recalled their plans to go to London; such dreams seemed painfully distant now.

"This is all of them, my Lord," one of the guards said, bowing lightly as an old, distinguished-looking man walked in.

Jennet could see right away that he was a clergyman of considerable rank. He wore a fine cassock and gown with balloon sleeves and on his head was a stiff cap which, along with his long, thick beard, gave him a severe look. His deep brown eyes peered out from his lined face, looking critically at those standing before him.

"My name is Dr John Bridgeman, Bishop of Chester. I have been sent here by His Majesty's Privy Councillors to obtain information from you so that they may consider the case against you. You are required to cooperate fully with me." He paused, glancing sharply at the mystified faces before him. "You have all been found guilty of the most heinous crime, that of witchcraft. The trial at the past Assizes was conducted in accordance with the law of this land. However, the law also allows judges to seek further counsel before passing sentence. I am charged with ensuring that such further counsel can be given." He looked around the room once again and frowned. "Is this really all of them?" he asked.

The guard standing beside him nodded. "Yes, my Lord. A few have died and some are sick."

"I see." Jennet thought she caught a glimpse of pity in the old bishop's eyes. "I have a list of names here, offenders whom the Privy Council wish me to question."

The guard glanced at the list. "Those three are dead, my Lord, and that one's very sick. The fever has struck down there, and it's catching."

"That leaves three – Frances Dickenson, Mary Spencer and Margaret Johnson." The bishop sighed. "This really won't do, the Privy Councillors won't be happy to hear of this…"

"What about that one as well, my Lord?" the guard asked. Jennet drew a sharp breath, realising the man's finger was pointed in her direction. "Got links to the big witch trial back in twelve, has that one," he added, giving her a sardonic smile.

The bishop furrowed his brow deeply as he studied her. Jennet felt her face grow warm, her heart thudding hard in her chest.

"What's her name?" he asked the guard.

"Jennet Device," he announced. "Ever hear of Old Demdike? Well, that's the grand-daughter."

Jennet gritted her teeth hard, feeling angry. She wished her gaolers would stop calling her Jennet Device. She had not been Jennet Device for years; she was Jennet Braithwaite, wife of William. Hot tears ran down her face as she thought of her husband, alone without her, wondering if she was alive or dead. She should be with him, not locked up here, convicted of crimes she didn't commit under a name she no longer answered to. Surely she had paid for her past sins now. Surely she had been punished enough.

"Yes, alright," replied the bishop, brushing his hand at the guard dismissively. "Jennet Device, you may join the other three for questioning. As for the rest of you – guards, let them remain here and wait, and bring them all something to eat and drink."

The guards nodded reluctantly. Jennet and the others chosen for questioning were separated from the group and told to stand behind the bishop. She glanced at Goodwife Dickenson, who frowned anxiously at the sight of her tear-stained face but said nothing. Jennet cast her eyes down, longing for the motherly comfort of Goodwife Lund.

"Lord have mercy on these poor wretches," she heard the bishop mutter as they were led away.

They were taken to the medieval keep, a strong building of old, heavy stone which sat at the heart of the castle. They were led through the chapel on the ground floor and up a set of seemingly endless stone stairs. As they climbed higher, Jennet began to struggle, her legs weakening several times, causing her to stumble. She breathed a sigh of relief when, eventually, they reached the top floor. They were ushered into a sparsely furnished room by a guard and ordered to sit on an uncomfortable-looking wooden bench. Jennet glanced towards the small window, catching a glimpse of the town below them. Sometimes, in there, it was hard to remember that there was a world outside, continuing regardless.

"A fine old building," the bishop remarked as he took a seat in front of them. "Now," he began, clasping his hands together, "I have here a list of the charges laid against you at the trial in the spring. I'm going to ask each of you about them, and I want you to answer them honestly – do you understand?"

The four women nodded. "Yes, my Lord," Mary Spencer said meekly.

"Good," the bishop gave them a reassuring smile. "Now, Mary, we will begin with you. You were accused of bewitching a bucket. I have say that is an unusual charge, how did you answer it?"

"Not guilty, my Lord," Mary replied.

The bishop gave the young woman a thoughtful look. "I see.

So, if you are not guilty, how then would you explain this accusation?"

Mary shook her head. "I do not understand, my Lord."

"Why would someone accuse you of bewitching a bucket if you didn't do it?"

"It was Nicholas Cunliffe, my Lord. He accused me. I used to play a game with my bucket, you see, rolling it down the hill. All buckets roll downhill don't they, my Lord? There's no magic in that. But Nicholas, he told Masters Shuttleworth and Starkie that this proved I was a witch. I swear to you, my Lord, I am no witch," Mary grew breathless with the effort of her hurried explanation.

"Alright, Mary," the bishop said calmly. "In your opinion, why did Nicholas say these things about you?"

Mary's face reddened. "In truth, I think he is in love with me. In fact, I know that he is, or was, in love with me. I know because he told me, my Lord, but I said that I did not love him…" Mary's voice broke off and her lip trembled. "I wish now that I had not rejected him – because of me, my father is dead and my mother is sick with the fever." She began to sob loudly.

The bishop looked at her with kindness in his eyes. He stretched out his arm. For a moment Jennet thought he was about to comfort Mary; however, he withdrew and gave a small cough.

"Thank you, Mary," he said gently. "Was it Nicholas Cunliffe who also accused your parents of witchcraft?"

Mary nodded sadly. "Yes, my Lord."

Over the course of the afternoon, the bishop continued to question them, taking each of their charges in turn and asking them to answer the accusations. It was so unlike the hurried, procedural questioning conducted in the courtroom; instead, the bishop took his time, asking them probing questions, but also inviting them to explain why they thought they had been accused by their friends and neighbours. Jennet had been unable to resist smiling at his bewildered expression as he listened to Margaret Johnson's ramblings. Clearly, incarceration had done nothing to subdue the old woman's madness.

As the sun dropped lower in the sky and evening beckoned, it occurred to Jennet that the bishop was listening to their side of the story, that he might even be genuinely impartial and willing to give them the benefit of doubt. If only the justices of the peace and the judges at the Assizes had adopted the same approach, she thought. If they had taken the time to really listen to the accused men and women, then perhaps all of this would have become nothing more than the foolish tales of imaginative boys and jilted men.

"Jennet Device," he said, finally turning to address her. "You were charged with bewitching Isabel Nutter and participating in a witches' Sabbath. How did you answer these accusations?"

"I am not guilty, my Lord. I don't know an Isabel Nutter, so I cannot explain why I was accused of her murder. As for the supposed Sabbath, I might know a little of where that particular tale sprang from."

"Oh yes?" asked the bishop, clearly intrigued.

Jennet proceeded to tell him how Edmund Robinson's story had grown from the tall tale of a little boy into a witch-hunting enterprise under the guidance of his father. She told him how the boy was taken around the county to perform for audiences, hungry for tales of murder and witchcraft. She explained how his stories grew and grew, taking on a life of their own, becoming unstoppable, becoming dangerous.

"One thing is true," she concluded. "Little Edmund Robinson was at my barn near Hoarstones on All Saints' Day. He peered through my window and watched Goodwife Lund and Goodwife Dickenson visit. They came to take Grace Lund home as she had called upon me but was unwell." She bit her lip, suppressing her tears. "After that, I think the little boy watched as I collapsed. I was with child at the time but that night, I lost my child." Out of the corner of her eye she saw Goodwife Dickenson's mouth fall open. She hadn't known.

"You were with child." the bishop repeated, his tone musing, "The boy, he did not come in, he did not fetch help?"

Jennet shook her head. "No, my Lord. He ran away."

"I see. Frances Dickenson, are Jennet's words true? Were you at this barn near Hoarstones on the evening described?"

Goodwife Dickenson nodded. "Yes, my Lord. I did not know Jennet was with child or that she had lost her child. I am sorry to hear it. That must have brought Jennet and her husband William great sadness. I was there as Jennet has said, and no witches' Sabbath took place, only the meeting of friends." She gave Jennet a tight smile.

"Thank you, Frances. And the charge laid before you, that you bewitched and murdered Edmund Stevenson…?"

"It's a lie," replied Goodwife Dickenson emphatically. "Edmund Robinson senior, the boy's father, even offered to drop the charges if my husband John paid him forty shillings. That shows you how true it is. He only accused me in the first place because we refused to sell him a cow. We didn't trust him to pay, you see." Goodwife Dickenson's tone was bitter.

"Thank you," the bishop said again. He glanced out of the window at the fading light. "I have kept you all in here long enough. I will ask the guards to bring you some food before returning you to the Well Tower."

Jennet's heart started to pound at the mention of that dreaded prison. As the bishop rose to his feet, she began to panic, cold sweat pouring from every part of her. She looked at Goodwife Dickenson who returned her gaze, her hands clasped tensely in front of her, her eyes pleading.

"My Lord, please forgive me for asking, but what will happen to us now?" She had to ask; she couldn't bear the thought of returning to that cesspit without knowing.

The bishop gave a weary sigh. "Tomorrow all four of you will be taken away from here for further questioning and examination. After that, it is in the hands of His Majesty and the Privy Council." He turned towards the door.

"Away?" Jennet asked. "To where?"

The bishop sighed again. For a moment, Jennet recoiled, fearing she had overstepped the mark. Clearly, the bishop was tired after so many hours of interviewing prisoners.

To her relief, he turned around and faced her question. "To London, of course. Privy Councillors will not come to you; you must go to them. Tomorrow, you will go to London."

The women's mouths fell open in shock, all except for Margaret, who was too busy mumbling to herself.

"London," Jennet repeated quietly, "London."

The place of all her hopes and dreams, the final destination for her new life with William: London. Instead, now it would be the place upon which her fate, and the fate of all the others, so desperately depended. As she accepted some dry bread from one of the guards she stifled a sob, trying to suppress the sadness she felt at the bitter irony which was not lost on her.

"Is this punishment enough yet?" she muttered, although in truth she had no idea who she was asking anymore. If God had ever existed, surely he had deserted her now.

28

Greenwich, south-east of London
Late June 1634

Jennet opened her eyes wearily as the cart jolted over a hole in the road. It was impossible to sleep on this never-ending journey, day after tedious day spent in a dusty old cart, night after night in a succession of noisy inns or uncomfortable barns when no inn could be found. Even in the quietest moments she could always hear the soft sounds of Margaret Johnson's incessant murmuring, or Mary Spencer's muffled sobbing. It was impossible to get any sleep, but then what else was there to do but try to sleep?

At first she had spent hours looking out on to the English countryside. She had been captivated by it. Before embarking on this journey, she had never thought about how other parts of England might differ so greatly from her own home. She had never appreciated how England was such a land of contrasts, of hills so high that they seemed to meet the clouds, of plains so flat that you could enjoy uninterrupted views for miles. She had never understood how big England was, how vast and in some parts, how empty. These realisations made her long to have made this journey with William, to have enjoyed these discoveries together. After a while, such longing made her weary. As they travelled further and further she grew more and more tired, and less able to take an interest in her surroundings.

The journey had taken around two weeks, although as far as Jennet was concerned it might as well have been an eternity. Each day they made a little slow progress southwards, and each night their escorts found somewhere, sometimes anywhere, for them to lay their heads. At each county border they stopped and waited for the next set of men to arrive and take custody of them. It was the County Relief system, a guard had explained to them, whereby each county constable was responsible for seeing them delivered to the next county. "It saves one lot of poor souls having to do that whole journey with you," he had remarked. Jennet had frowned at him. At times the journey was so intolerable she almost wished she was back in the Well Tower.

"It could be worse," the man had added, seeing her scowl. "At least the roads are dry. You should see the state they get into when the rain comes. It would take twice as long to get you all to London then."

Since then, Jennet had wished for the good weather to hold. She had not prayed; she no longer prayed, since she was now convinced that no one was listening to her. Often she would watch Goodwife Dickenson, eyes closed and hands clasped together, muttering prayers with her lips raised towards heaven. It reminded her of William and how he had always shown such devotion through prayer. Her faith had never been strong enough for that, she realised. Now it was almost non-existent, just another void in her life to be filled by regret, guilt and hopelessness.

"Almost there!" one of the guards shouted from in front.

Jennet and Goodwife Dickenson exchanged nervous glances. "It's grown noisy out there," Goodwife Dickenson muttered. "I daren't look."

Jennet listened. It was true; outside she could hear the bustle of busy streets, the shouts of innkeepers and merchants, the chatter of townspeople as they went about their business. As they continued on, the sounds grew louder until Jennet was certain they were in the very midst of it all. Was this London? Unable to curtail her curiosity any longer, she peeked out of the cart. Through the small hole she could see many faces shining in the bright sunshine, coming in and out of a myriad of buildings all lined up next to one another, in front of which stood a multitude of street sellers trying to trade their goods. She sniffed the air, a strange, unfamiliar smell lingering in it. As they passed through the crowded street the place seemed to open up once again to trees and lush green grass. She gasped as she spied a grand, white house sitting upon it. It was the finest, largest building she had ever seen; bigger than Read Hall, bigger even than Gawthorpe Hall. Was this where the King lived?

A few moments later, the cart came to an abrupt halt. "Are we here?" asked Goodwife Dickenson anxiously.

"I don't know." Jennet peered outside again to see a tall, tidy looking building, the sunlight reflecting brightly from its large windows. In front of it sat a number of grubby men, their faces glistening with sweat, enjoying a flagon of ale and a moment's rest in the summer heat. "I think it's an inn. Why have they brought us here?"

"Come on, out you come," called one of the guards in an unfamiliar, southern tongue.

Everything felt so different here; the buildings, the people, even the air seemed different. Jennet breathed in deeply, still trying to identify the strange smell which kept flooding up her nostrils.

"Where are we?" she asked.

The guard grunted. "Welcome to Greenwich," he said. "Lord knows how long you unfortunates will be here, but in the meantime you will be staying here at the Ship Tavern. To be honest, I thought they'd have sent you all straight to one of London's gaols, but it's not for me to question these things." He gave a light shrug.

"The sheep?" Jennet repeated, still trying to understand the man's accent. "Is that what I can smell?"

The guard roared with laughter. "No! S-h-i-p." He pronounced the word slowly, as though she was an imbecile. "As for the smell, well that's fish, isn't it?" He sniffed the air. "And perhaps a little salt from the Thames. The Thames is the river – it's just over there. Don't you have fish in the north?"

Jennet shook her head dumbly. She couldn't remember the last time she'd eaten meat at all and after months of watery pottage for sustenance, her stomach growled at the thought of it. For a moment, Jennet cast her mind back to cosy Christmastide evenings spent at Goodwife Lund's cottage, sitting beside a warm fire, tucking in to delicious meats. A lump grew in her throat as she thought about her kind and warm-hearted friend. She tried to suppress the image of her now, her pale corpse lying in a deep, cold ditch. She chastised herself for remembering her in that way. Perhaps she too was losing her mind, just like Margaret Johnson.

"Hmm," the guard mused, looking warily at her, "I've heard the north is a strange place."

"A friend of mine once said the same thing about London," she muttered sadly, thinking again of Goodwife Lund.

"Sorry, what was that?"

"Nothing."

"The north is full of wild folk who still cleave to the old religion, so I've been told," the guard continued. "Mind you, there's plenty of popery in London too…"

"I have no interest in any of that," Jennet remarked, her words cutting into his idle chatter like a knife.

The guard gave her a withering stare. "I daresay you don't. After all, you're a witch, aren't you?" His tone was irritatingly mocking. "Come on then, in we go."

Inside the tavern felt cool, a welcome chill brushing over Jennet's arms now that she was out of the summer sun. The tavern was a pleasantly decorated place, the walls covered with wooden panelling, the hard floors even and recently swept. It was nothing like the exquisite decor at Gawthorpe Hall, but it was smart nonetheless. The guard exchanged a brief nod with the innkeeper and proceeded to lead the four women up several flights of stairs, to a couple of rooms at the very top of the building.

"Two in each," he said, his manner rougher now. Jennet bit her lip, regretting her earlier insolence towards him.

Jennet opted for a room with Goodwife Dickenson, leaving poor young Mary to fend for herself with Margaret. She shook her head at the old woman; the heat seemed to have made her even more deranged and her nonsensical rambling had become unbearable.

Inside the room was plain and sparsely furnished, containing little more than two small truckle beds and a crumbling chest of drawers. The room felt warmer than the tavern downstairs, the heat of the afternoon sun cascading through the window. The bustle of the streets below could still be heard, although the noise seemed more distant now. Compared with the Well Tower, however, the Ship Tavern seemed like luxury. Jennet fell down on to her little bed, her eyes heavy. She was sure that she could sleep for years.

"Get some rest," instructed the guard. "We'll fetch something for you to eat a bit later on. And – just in case you were thinking about it – no funny business. I will be standing outside."

Goodwife Dickenson gave him an anxious look. "Why are we here? Why are we being kept in this place?"

The guard shrugged. "I only take orders, I don't give them." He looked around the room. "I wouldn't ask too many questions, if I were you. Not many convicted witches get put up in a nice little tavern, do they? But then, I suppose you four aren't your average witches."

Jennet sat bolt upright on the bed and frowned at him. "What do you mean?" she asked.

The guard gave her a sardonic smile. "You're the talk of the city. I've heard that someone's even writing a play about you all. You've caused quite a stir."

"Do you know how long we will be kept here?" Goodwife Dickenson persisted with her questions, a worried frown etched on her gaunt face.

"No," the guard answered. "As I said – I don't give the orders.

Now, rest. You've got a busy evening ahead of you."

Jennet furrowed her brow deeper. "What do you mean?" she said again.

He gave her a mischievous grin. "You'll see," was all he said as he closed the door behind him.

Jennet lay back down on the bed, sighing heavily as she closed her eyes. Although she was tired, she couldn't help feeling unsettled. She knew that she should be grateful for the comfortable surroundings, yet she sensed that something was amiss. They were prisoners; should they not be in gaol? And what was planned for them this evening?

"I hate this place already," said Goodwife Dickenson, breaking the silence.

"Why?" Jennet asked sleepily. "It's better than being left to rot in a gaol somewhere, surely?"

Goodwife Dickenson looked at her for a moment before throwing her arms up in exasperation. "I don't understand you, Jennet! Does none of this upset you?"

Jennet's eyes flew open. She sat up and looked squarely at her. "Of course it does. Like you, I have committed no crime. Like you, I have been torn away from my husband, who I miss more and more each day. Like you, I had to watch my friend suffer a painful death in that miserable pit they call a prison. And like you, I have had to travel hundreds of miles just to satisfy the curiosity of a group of powerful men who wish to gawp at a set of so-called witches."

For a few moments Goodwife Dickenson was silent, no doubt sensing her anger.

"How can you even consider sleeping?" she asked in the end.

"Because I am tired," Jennet replied, lying back down and shutting her eyes once more. "And because this bed is very, very comfortable."

The sun had begun to set by the time the guards came to wake them, its steady descent announced by the fiery streaks of red emblazoned across the summer sky. They were handed some bread and a bit of meat; the cheapest cuts from the local market, no doubt, but the best food that Jennet had tasted for months. She ate hungrily, her appetite fuelled by an afternoon of peaceful slumber.

"Time to go," said the guard, as she shoved the final morsel of bread into her mouth.

"Go where?" she asked.

"Ah!" exclaimed the guard, tapping the side of his nose. "Now that would spoil the surprise, wouldn't it?"

Outside they met with Mary and Margaret, who had already been escorted downstairs by another guard. Jennet looked at Mary, who gave her a weak smile, her face grey with exhaustion. No doubt Margaret had afforded her little peace during the course of the afternoon. Jennet glanced at the old woman who, for once, was quiet, staring vacantly across the road.

"Do you know where they're taking us, Jennet?" Mary whispered in a soft voice. Jennet was surprised; Mary had seldom spoken on the long journey here. Evidently, the young woman was as anxious as the rest of them.

Jennet shook her head regretfully. "No," she whispered back.

They were loaded back into the cart with some urgency and swiftly driven away. As the cart moved at a steady pace through the streets, Jennet peered out, catching sight of that grand building once more. In the fading light it looked magical, the red and orange hues of the evening sky casting wondrous shadows across its white walls.

"What are you looking at?" asked Goodwife Dickenson, her tone irritable.

"I'm not sure," Jennet replied, turning away from the view outside and facing her fellow prisoners once again. "A house, I think. Whatever it is, it's beautiful."

"I don't know what's the matter with you, Jennet," she scolded. "Here we are, imprisoned and hundreds of miles from home, and you're gawping at grand houses. What would William say, I wonder?"

Jennet gave Goodwife Dickenson a hard look but said nothing in reply. The heat of suppressed tears burned in her eyes as she thought about her husband far away in the north. It was cruel of Goodwife Dickenson to mention him like that. She must have realised how much Jennet missed him, how she longed to lay her eyes upon his handsome smile once more, how she wished more than anything that she could lie with him on their straw bed and talk to him late into the night. She breathed in deeply, stifling a sob. At times she used to tire of talking to William. How ungrateful she had been; how she wished she was at home with him now, answering his hundreds of questions.

Goodwife Dickenson stared at her unapologetically and Jennet looked away. She wrung her hands together as she imagined William beside her now, looking out on to that big white house. She felt certain that he would have admired it, just as she had. She felt sure that, even in these dire circumstances, William would have sought out and relished the beauty present around him, that he would have enjoyed the narrow cobbled streets, the flat green countryside, the odd smell of the river. God's work, he would have called it; the miracle of God's creation. She clasped her hands tighter as she realised again that she struggled to attribute anything to divine influence anymore.

A little while later, Jennet felt the cart draw to a halt. She hadn't looked outside again since Goodwife Dickenson had chastised her, and as the motion of the cart ceased she felt herself begin to panic. Where were they now? She listened carefully, not daring to look out. She could hear the sound of people chattering, interludes of raucous laughter and, a little beyond that, the pleasant medleys of music drifting through the evening sky. Wherever they were, it sounded lively.

"Time to go," said one of the guards abruptly. Jennet was disappointed to see that it was the same man who had watched over them at the Ship Tavern earlier. She disliked his manner, and the way he liked to tease them.

"Go where?" Jennet asked as she climbed out of the cart. "Where are we?"

The guard spread his arms in a mocking gesture. "Welcome to Southwark," he said.

Jennet cast her eyes around her. Everywhere she looked were buildings crammed tightly together, their lanterns outside lit in anticipation of the coming dark. The streets were busy with people coming in and out of the many alehouses, enjoying an evening's revelry. Others were walking together in groups, talking merrily. Jennet looked up. At the centre of this busy scene was a tall, circular building, the sound of music and laughter coming from it.

"Is this not London?" Mary asked innocently, a bewildered look fixed on her face.

"Almost," replied the guard. "London's over the other side of the river."

"I don't understand," said Goodwife Dickenson. "Why are we here?"

"To earn your keep," the guard answered her, a hint of exasperation in his voice now. "A comfortable bed in the Ship doesn't come cheap. Come on, your audience awaits you."

They were led towards the tall building, outside of which a modest stage had been built, a makeshift wooden sign set in front of it.

"What is this place?" Jennet asked.

"The Globe Theatre," the guard replied. "And tonight, you four are part of the show. Well, the spectacle outside at any rate. Now, climb up on to that stage."

Jennet breathed heavily as she clambered up as instructed. She was still weary, and making even this small exertion took considerable effort. She stretched out her hand to help Goodwife Dickenson who was struggling behind her. Goodwife Dickenson gave her a strange, cold look, but reluctantly accepted her assistance.

The four women stood together in a line, all very still apart from Margaret, who fidgeted relentlessly. Jennet wondered if the poor old woman was even aware of what was happening. Jennet gazed straight in front of her, her heart thumping hard in her chest. She tried hard to distance herself from what they were being ordered to do. A spectacle, the guard had called them. Standing there together on that stage, they were certainly that. Jennet gulped hard, feeling self-conscious, exposed.

"Come and see the infamous Lancashire Witches!" the guard began to yell.

Jennet felt her face redden as the first handful of curious spectators made their approach. She glanced at Goodwife Dickenson, who had her eyes closed, too proud even now to look upon the baying mob. She felt Mary edge closer to her, swaying unsteadily. She grasped hold of the young woman's hand.

"Hold your nerve," she whispered.

"Come and see the notorious witches and murderers, come all the way from the wild north!" the guard continued to call. "Behold this rare spectacle for one night only! One night only, I tell you! Show your appreciation and show it well," he added, shaking a bucket which contained a bit of coin. A few folk added a contribution to the collection.

"Look at that one," a woman shouted in that strange southern tongue, pointing at Margaret. "She looks half mad! You sure you got witches there? She looks like she should be in Bedlam!"

Jennet cautiously moved her eyes over the growing crowd. A number of them had come from the nearby alehouses, swaying drunkenly as they gawped at the four women. Others were clearly gentlefolk, perhaps out enjoying an evening of theatre when the guard's bellowing had caught their attention. Some of the women were dressed very finely, with expensive lace attached to their bodices and huge balloon sleeves cut off at the elbow, their hair fashionably loose around the ears. Goodwife Lund had been right; there wasn't a single coif to be found amongst them. She bristled slightly at the memory of her friend, her sadness still too raw to confront.

"What did this one do?" shouted a man, a long, shaky finger

extended towards Mary. Jennet felt Mary take a step backwards.

"Witchcraft!" shouted the guard. "They're all witches, every last one of them!"

The man looked at Mary again, his head leaning over to one side. "She looks too sweet to be a witch." He moved nearer, attempting to clamber up on the stage. "Come here, sweetheart. I'll find your witch's marks!" The man staggered closer, almost grasping hold of Mary who cried out, her face turning a deep shade of scarlet. The poor young woman fell to her knees and buried her head in her skirts.

"Get down from here, or I will have you arrested!" ordered the guard, pushing the man back. "These witches are here at His Majesty's pleasure." A few gasps came from the crowd. "That's right," added the guard, nodding, "His Majesty King Charles. So don't touch them!"

Jennet helped Mary to her feet. She was whimpering, her whole body shaking.

"I can't endure much more of this, Jennet," she whispered. "I wish I was dead, just like my father and probably my mother too. I wish I was with them, at peace."

"Hush," said Jennet. "You don't mean that." She embraced the young woman, trying her best to comfort her as though she was a child.

"Alright, alright, that's enough," said the guard roughly, separating them.

Jennet looked at him disdainfully. "How much longer must we stand here?" she demanded.

The guard looked at her, but didn't answer. Instead, he continued yelling at the crowd, enticing passers-by to have a look and to shout, to mock, and to insult the four women. The spectacle went on for what felt like an eternity, until night had fallen and the guard's bucket had been filled with coin. By the time they were loaded back into the cart Jennet felt numb, her mind and body so exhausted by the ordeal that she no longer felt capable of feeling anything anymore.

As the cart began to move once more, she remembered again what William had taught her, that people could create their own heaven, or their own hell, here on earth. In her life, she realised, she had experienced little glimmers of both. Lying on her straw bed with William, listening to the rain battering her derelict old barn while she enjoyed his touch, had been heaven. The Well Tower, containing so much darkness, putridity, disease and death, had been hell.

A tear slid down her cheek as she remembered the high hopes she and William had harboured for a new life in London, how they had wished to create their own paradise in this city. Instead, she had been brought to London as a prisoner and a new kind of hell had been created for her, an insidious sort of hell, where beneath the comfortable truckle bed and nice food lurked a new set of horrors: humiliation, degradation, mental torture. Mary was right to admit that she didn't think she could endure it. As the cart rattled along the road back to the Ship, Jennet realised that if she was honest with herself, she wasn't sure how much more she could bear either.

29

The Ship Tavern, Greenwich
2nd July 1634

Jennet opened her eyes wearily as the morning sun streamed into the room. It was early, before breakfast time, but the streets below were already bustling. Jennet couldn't recall this place ever being quiet; even as she drifted off to sleep at night she could hear the sound of footsteps, of people chattering outside. As time went on she began to crave the silent comforts of home, the peace that could be found in the Pendle countryside. She had never appreciated her home so much as she did now; now that she might never see it again.

She glanced sideways towards Goodwife Dickenson's little bed, where she still lay sleeping. Jennet sighed. Since their arrival in Greenwich, she had tried to be a comfort to the woman, to keep her spirits light and to cheer her. They had been friends once, after all. Yet despite her best efforts, Goodwife Dickenson remained cold and subdued, and above all, angry. Sometimes the woman seemed so filled with quiet fury that Jennet would withdraw, falling silent for fear of provoking her further. It wasn't clear who Goodwife Dickenson was so angry with, whether it was the Robinsons for accusing her, the court for condemning her, or the

Privy Council for having her dispatched to this God-be-damned place, as she called it.

Jennet often wondered if she still blamed her as well. She remembered her words in the Well Tower clearly enough; Jennet's reputation was part of the reason they were all there. It was part of the reason that they had all been condemned, and it was part of the reason why Goodwife Lund was now dead. Jennet swallowed hard, trying to suppress the thought, fighting against the guilt which always threatened to consume her.

"Is it morning already?" mumbled Goodwife Dickenson, her eyes still shut tight.

"I'm afraid so," replied Jennet, trying her best to sound cheerful. "Although they've not yet come to rouse us." She frowned. Usually the guards had come to wake them by now.

"Well in that case, I'm going back to sleep," Goodwife Dickenson said.

Jennet raised her eyebrows at the note of childish petulance in the woman's voice. As the days wore on, Goodwife Dickenson's mask of reserved propriety seemed to slip more and more. She no longer stood up quite so straight; she no longer cared that her face was clean or her hair was tidy. Perhaps these were the signs of her mind unravelling, just like Margaret's rambling and Mary's tearful outbursts. For a moment, Jennet wondered how she seemed to the others, whether she gave them any cause for concern, or whether they were now too absorbed in their own troubled thoughts to give her any consideration at all.

"Do you sleep well?" against her better judgement, Jennet decided to try to talk to her.

Goodwife Dickenson groaned. "I would rather be asleep than awake these days," she said. "When I sleep I dream about home, about my husband and my boy. My beloved boy Nicholas. And my beautiful grandson, of course - may God keep him safe from his mother."

Jennet winced at the bitterness in her voice. "I'm sure Grace wouldn't hurt the baby," she protested weakly.

"Lord knows what she would do," Goodwife Dickenson scoffed. "She'd do anything to get what she wants, the little harlot. She only got herself with child so that she could trap my son into marriage. Am I wrong?"

Jennet didn't respond. She knew there was nothing she could say which would be conciliatory; in fact, she was fairly certain that any answer she gave would have served only to widen the rift between them. Nicholas was also responsible for getting Grace with child, but to point that out would have been tactless at best. And she couldn't even imagine telling Goodwife Dickenson that Nicholas, her precious boy, was Grace's second choice, and that in fact Grace was in love with William. Jennet bit her lip, wishing she had never tried to strike up a conversation. An awkward silence descended for a few moments.

"Do you sleep well, Jennet?" Goodwife Dickenson asked, turning around in her bed to face her. She attempted a tight smile, which Jennet returned gratefully. Perhaps it had been worthwhile to try to talk to her, after all.

Jennet nodded. "Mostly," she replied. "Although I wish I dreamed of home as much as you do."

Goodwife Dickenson frowned. "What do you dream about?"

Jennet shook her head. "It doesn't matter."

She looked away, not wishing to discuss it. In truth, the realisation of the horrors created by her own subconscious terrified her. Her waking hours resembled Goodwife Dickenson's dreams, pre-occupied with thoughts of home, with hankerings for the Pendle countryside and her barn and the warmth of William's touch. Her sleeping hours, however, were a different matter entirely. Instead of indulging in happy memories, she was plagued by a dreadful nightmare. It had started on the first night they spent at the Ship, and had recurred every single night since. At the thought of it, Jennet shivered.

It always happened in the same way. She was always alone, sat in a filthy little cart, being bumped along a road. She was always taken to the same place; the gardens of Read Hall. They looked exactly as they had when she was a child, wonderfully sculpted and glowing in the summer sun, and in her dream she could feel herself smiling at the sight of them. However, her smile never lasted long. Once there, she was sent up on a high wooden stage, denounced as a witch and stripped naked. She would stand there then, shivering, while a faceless crowd mocked and taunted her.

After a while Master Nowell would appear. "Time to go, Jennet," he would say, a kindly, almost doting smile etched on his face as he pointed towards the gallows which seemed to have come from nowhere.

"Go where?" she would ask, but as she spoke she could feel the tightening of the noose around her neck, the sensation of the floor beneath her disappearing and her legs dangling helplessly in the air.

What frightened her most about this dream was not the horror of the spectacle itself, but the fact that she never woke from it. Instead, she continued to sleep as she felt herself choking and struggling for breath; she continued to sleep as she felt herself dying. Eventually she would see everything fade away and she would drift in a silent, black abyss for hours. By the time she did wake it was always morning, the sun streaming in through the window, reminding her that she was still alive. She shuddered. Goodwife Dickenson managed to dream of home, yet all she could dream about was death. Perhaps this was a sign that she too was losing her mind.

The door flew open, startling them both from their beds and on to their feet. The guard walked in, giving them both a broad grin. Jennet narrowed her eyes at him.

"Good morning," he said cheerfully. "Or not," he added, noticing Jennet's scowl.

"Where are we going today?" Goodwife Dickenson asked wearily. "More performances for profit, I suppose."

They had spent every day since their arrival in Greenwich being carted around and shown off to curious audiences. It had become part of the routine now, not that the regularity of the experience made it any easier to bear. In fact, Jennet reflected, it was little wonder that she was suffering from such terrible nightmares.

The guard smirked. "It's not profit, it's the money needed to keep you lot in this palace." He gave them a dramatic gesture with his arms. "But you will be pleased to know that no performances are planned for today."

"So we just stay here?" Jennet asked.

"Not quite. You've another appointment, shall we say. There's a physician who wants to see you. Privy Council's orders, I believe."

Jennet furrowed her brow at him. She hated the way this man talked in riddles. "A physician? Who? Where?"

The guard drew a deep breath. "Can't say who because I don't know. But I've orders to take you all to the Fleet."

"The Fleet Prison?" Jennet gasped in horror.

The guard gave a teasing chuckle. "Ah! You know it, then? Not such a stupid northerner, after all."

Jennet nodded grimly, remembering William's tale about how folk could be married there for a little coin. She had thought little of his story at the time, excited as she was by her own forthcoming wedding. She wondered now what would drive anyone to want to marry in a gaol.

"Why are we being taken there?" Goodwife Dickenson asked.

The guard threw up his arms in exasperation. "Well, you are prisoners, aren't you? That's where you should go! I daresay it's where you'll remain from now on, as well. We haven't made nearly as much as we'd hoped from showing you all off around London."

The two women looked at each other, their mouths wide open in disbelief. "You're a liar," Jennet said quietly. "That bucket has been filled with coin every day. You must have kept some of the profit for yourself."

The guard's face turned a perfect shade of scarlet. He walked towards her, getting so close that she could feel the warmth of his breath on her cheek. Even at this early hour, he smelled of ale and sweat. "I'd keep your mouth shut, if I were you," he said through gritted teeth. "Accusations like that could cause a lot of trouble. I'm warning you."

Jennet gave him a hard stare. "I'm already condemned for witchcraft," she replied. "I am likely to die for it. What could you possibly do to someone who is already brought so low?"

The guard narrowed his eyes, shifting his gaze from Jennet to Goodwife Dickenson and back again. Jennet held her breath, awaiting his retort, but none came.

"Time to go," was all he said.

The journey took a couple of hours on another bright summer's day. The heat in the cart was oppressive, making them all sweat profusely. Jennet licked her lips, which were dry like her mouth; the guards had not given them anything to eat or drink before rounding them up to leave and after a while her temples began to throb from her thirst. She sat quietly, her head bowed. She didn't bother having a look outside as they passed through Greenwich, then Southwark; these places had all become horribly familiar to her now. Even that palatial white house which she had so often gazed at no longer held any interest for her. At only one point, when they ground to a halt on the busy London Bridge, did she take a brief look out, peering down towards the river flowing below them. She dreamt for a moment of jumping from the cart and flinging herself into the water. She wondered how far away the tide would carry her lifeless body. She wondered if drowning was preferable to hanging.

The heat must have made her weary, as when they arrived she was fast asleep. When the cart stopped for the final time, she began to rouse, moving to that strange, delirious state between waking and sleeping where her mind couldn't recall exactly where she was. For the briefest of seconds, she thought she was back at home in her barn, waiting for William to return from a day's work. For the most fleeting of moments she thought she held a baby in her arms; her child, William's child, the child that never was.

"Jennet," she heard Mary say softly. "Wake up. I think we're here."

She knew then that she was dreaming, but she didn't want to let the dream go. Reluctantly she opened her eyes, her arms suddenly light and empty, her heart suddenly sore and hollow. Every awful detail of where she was and why she was there came flooding back to her. She put her aching head in her hands as her tears began to fall. She didn't want the other women to see her cry.

"Out you all come," said the guard.

As she climbed out of the cart, Jennet screwed up her bleary eyes in the bright sunlight, struggling at first to focus upon her surroundings. The heat of the midday sun bore down relentlessly, making her wince at the pain in her head. Shielding her eyes with her hands, she looked up at the towering, solid building in front of her. It was obvious that this was a prison, and a very old one at that; its weathered grey stone walls looked as though they had stood for many hundreds of years. She had never seen such a big building; it seemed to stretch up into the air for miles. She gulped hard as she remembered the Well Tower at Lancaster Castle, a place which was tiny by comparison. If the Well Tower was a gaol, then this place was an impenetrable fortress. Her stomach churned with dread. Once she walked into this place, she felt certain that she would never leave it.

The guard led them over to the prison gates. There they were met by the gatekeeper, a burly old man with a straggly forked beard which he stroked with amusement as he studied his four new arrivals.

"Device, Dickenson, Johnson and Spencer," he read out their names from his list. "Well, well," he said, looking at them all with his dark, watchful eyes, "the infamous Lancashire witches have come to the Fleet."

"Not nearly infamous enough," the guard grumbled. "We didn't make half as much coin as we expected from showing them to the crowds." He shot Jennet a warning glance. "But it'll be enough to pay their keep in here, I expect."

The gatekeeper grunted. "Just as well, or they'll end up like them over there," he said, gesturing towards one of the lower barred windows from which a sea of hands kept appearing, desperately begging passers-by for scraps of food.

"Lord have mercy," Jennet heard Goodwife Dickenson mutter.

They were led inside and through a myriad of long, narrow corridors past a great number of gaol cells. The smell in there was so terrible that Jennet tried her best not to breathe; the stench of vomit, excrement and filth that wafted from each dungeon was so overpowering that it made her feel faint. Jennet tried not to look at the inmates contained within, their pitiable faces too much to bear. Instead she looked straight ahead, walking steadily behind the guard as they continued their endless march through this hellish place. Eventually, the guard stopped walking. He turned and gestured towards a small, empty room.

"In there," he instructed them, that familiar devilish smile returning to his face.

Obediently, they walked inside. It was another small, stinking room just like so many they had passed. The air in the room felt hot, even though the stone walls were cold to the touch. They were still on the ground floor of this place, and Jennet could hear the bustle of the busy street outside. How terrible it must be to be imprisoned here, she thought; so close to freedom that you can reach through the barred windows and touch it.

"What are we doing here?" she asked.

The guard gave her a sardonic grin. "You're to wait for the physician. He will be here soon, I'm sure." He turned towards the door.

"You're leaving us?"

"That's my orders – lock you in and leave you to wait. I suppose this is goodbye," he added mockingly.

"Good riddance, more like," Goodwife Dickenson murmured. Jennet raised her eyebrows at the woman's uncharacteristic retort.

The guard's face grew red with anger. He turned quickly, reaching out and grabbing Goodwife Dickenson by the neck. The woman let out a surprised yelp as she was pushed up against the wall.

"Sour old goat," he said through clenched teeth. "I've a mind to teach you a lesson."

Jennet looked on in horror as he began to loosen his breeches. Goodwife Dickenson whimpered helplessly, her head turned away, her eyes screwed shut in denial. The sight of this fine, proud woman being demeaned in this way was too much for Jennet to bear. Before she knew what she was doing, she had launched herself at the guard, jumping on to his back.

"No! No!" she yelled over and over again.

In his surprise, the guard lost his balance, falling to the ground with a loud thud. Despite this, Jennet kept going, landing heavy blows on his back, clawing at him, digging her nails hard into his skin, so hard that she could see him begin to bleed below his shirt. All the anger, all the fury she had felt over the past weeks bubbled to the surface. She could no longer control how she felt. She could no longer control what she did. At that moment, she realised, she had lost her sanity.

The guard seemed to regain his senses and, with an almighty shove, he pushed her away from him. She flew across the room, pain searing up her spine as she landed hard on her back. She tried to move but she couldn't. Dusting himself off and flexing his considerable arms, the guard walked over to her. Jennet winced with discomfort as she drew a sharp breath. Around her, she sensed Goodwife Dickenson, Mary and even Margaret make themselves scarce. The guard got down on his knees and drew himself close, so close that his nose was almost touching hers. Jennet flattened herself against the ground, wishing it would swallow her whole.

"Go on then," she said, mustering all the courage she could find. "What are you waiting for?"

"I wouldn't lay a hand on you," he replied, his voice so low it was almost a whisper. "You think I didn't ask about who I was charged with watching? I know who you are. I know what you did, now and all those years ago." He moved backwards slightly, his eyes roaming all around her face, as though taking in every detail of her. "There is something Godless about you. There is a darkness right behind your eyes. I wouldn't touch you."

He stood up and, without a backwards glance, walked towards the door, opening it and allowing it to slam shut behind him. As he turned the key in the lock, Jennet began to weep, hot tears of terror, of humiliation, of relief pouring unabated down her cheeks.

Goodwife Dickenson walked over to her. For a moment she stood, looking down on her, that familiar stony look set on her face. Jennet recoiled again, wondering what harsh words the woman had for her. Then, to her surprise, Goodwife Dickenson extended a hand.

"Come," she said simply, helping her up.

Through heavy sobs, Jennet gratefully accepted the help. As she clambered to her feet, Goodwife Dickenson's hard look melted away and she too began to cry. Instinctively, the two women embraced each other, weeping into each other's arms, their tears giving expression to their terror and their sorrow, but also for the first time, their common understanding and their solidarity.

"Thank you," Goodwife Dickenson whispered through her tears.

Jennet gave her a watery smile. "All these months together and yet this is the first time that I have seen you cry."

Goodwife Dickenson bit her lip. "I've been too afraid to cry."

"And now?" Jennet asked. "Are you not still afraid, Goodwife Dickenson?"

Goodwife Dickenson shook her head. "I think I am beyond fear now. I think my heart is numb and that I shall never feel anything again."

Jennet nodded, holding her friend tightly once more. "I know," was all she could manage in reply.

The door flew open with a sudden bang, startling the women apart. All four prisoners gasped in unison as a man with grey hair, black robes and a heavy brown bag walked briskly inside. Following obediently behind him were two prim-looking women in dark petticoats, crisp white coifs placed upon their immaculate heads. The man cast a critical gaze around the room before his inquiring eyes came to rest upon them.

"I'm Doctor William Harvey," he said, "physician to His Majesty King Charles. I'm here to examine you."

Jennet blinked several times in disbelief. The guard really had told a set of half-truths. This wasn't any physician; this was the King's doctor, the highest medical authority in the land. This man attended to royalty, and yet here he was now, sent to…do what, exactly? Examine them – what did that mean? And who were these women who accompanied him? Jennet swallowed hard, her dry throat painful with the effort. She looked at Goodwife Dickenson, who returned her stare, her eyes wide. Perhaps they weren't beyond fear, after all.

30

The Fleet Prison, London
4th July 1634

Jennet winced with discomfort as she moved on the hard, cold floor. It had been another long night in the Fleet, her sleep constantly disturbed by the coughs and moans of the other prisoners, the chatter of the guards, the noise from the street outside. As the hours had passed, the gaol had grown cool and Jennet had found herself shivering for the first time since her arrival in London. She had pulled her little shawl tighter around herself and wished then that she was back at the Ship, tucked up in that warm truckle bed. She sighed. Perhaps the guard had been telling the truth, perhaps there had not been enough money to keep them there. She had hated those dreadful performances she and the others had been forced to make, but now she would endure a hundred of them if it meant she could get away from this hellish place.

She let out a small groan as she sat up. Her back felt as though it was on fire as she forced it to bear the weight of her shoulders. She was only thirty-three, yet too decrepit now to be able to tolerate sleeping on the ground. She looked down at herself. She was thinner than ever; months of poor sustenance had taken its toll on her, her clothes hanging loose on her body, hiding the bones which protruded unattractively through the skin below.

She recalled with a shudder how the physician had gasped at the sight of her as the women had stripped her naked at her examination two days earlier.

"This one is under-fed," he had remarked as he cast his clinical eye over her body, before instructing her to lie down on the floor.

Jennet shuddered again as she tucked her hands between her knees. No matter how hard she tried, she struggled to suppress the memory of her examination, the way she had been poked and prodded, the way that no area of her body had been off-limits to the physician's cold stare. Even her privy parts had been scrutinised; she remembered how her face had burned with humiliation at the feeling of the women's cold hands checking between her legs. By the time they had finished with her, she didn't feel like a woman anymore; she felt like cattle being readied for market. It was this feeling which had remained with her ever since; the feeling that trapped in this filthy, stinking place, her clothes turning to rags and her skin covered in dust, she was less than a person now. She looked around the gaol cell at her fellow inmates, wondering if they felt the same.

"Are you alright, Jennet?" asked Mary kindly. The young woman had wept a great deal over the past few days, so much that her eyes bore permanent red rims around them.

Jennet shook her head. "I can't stop thinking about that physician examining us," she whispered.

Mary glanced at Goodwife Dickenson and Margaret, both of whom were still sleeping. "Me neither," she whispered back, her lip quivering again. "It was awful. I cried all the way through it, which seemed to annoy the doctor. The women who helped him told me to be quiet, but that just made me cry even more. Jennet – he looked everywhere. I mean, really - everywhere," she emphasised, her eyes wide.

"Yes I know, it was the same for me," Jennet replied. She had been taken first for her examination. When she returned she had been unable to look at the others, as though her eyes might betray the horrors awaiting them. Now, she looked squarely at Mary; a sad look, a look of mutual understanding. "They looked everywhere with me, too."

Mary shivered. "Did you see how Margaret behaved when she came back?"

Jennet glanced at the sleeping old woman, curled up peacefully on the floor. She nodded. "I don't think Margaret is of a sound mind, Mary," she said gently.

"She cannot be," Mary replied. "Who laughs after going through that? It was as though all of this amuses her, as though she couldn't care less whether she lives or dies." Mary lowered her voice again. "Sometimes I wonder if she really is a witch, Jennet. Sometimes I look at her and I think I can see the devil staring back at me."

Jennet frowned. "None of us are truly witches, Mary, you know that."

"But Margaret confessed. Every time she has been asked, she has confessed."

"As I said, Margaret is sick in her mind. She is old and confused; she doesn't know what she is saying."

Mary bit her lip, her wide eyes thoughtful. "I suppose you may be right," she said in the end. She glanced over her shoulder towards the corner of the room where Goodwife Dickenson lay. "And what about her? What about Frances?"

Jennet shook her head. "She hasn't spoken a word to anyone for two days."

"Not even you?"

"No. Not a word to anyone. She is a proud woman; I fear it's all too much for her." She glanced sadly at her friend, her once neat frame lying sprawled carelessly on the floor, a broken shell of a woman now.

Mary nodded slowly. "She sleeps so much. She sleeps almost all of the time."

"Yes," Jennet replied. "I think she would rather be asleep than awake. I think when she's asleep she's somewhere else, somewhere far away from here."

Mary lowered her gaze. "I think we'd all rather be somewhere else. I'd rather be dead, Jennet. I wish to die every day now. Is that terrible?"

Jennet shook her head. "No. I don't think it's for any of us to say what's terrible anymore. As soon as you think you know what horror is, something even worse happens."

"Do you wish to die too?"

Jennet shrugged. "I'm not sure that there's any peace for me in death either. I don't think I wish to be anything anymore."

Mary furrowed her brow, wrinkling her little round nose as though she didn't quite grasp Jennet's meaning. As she opened her mouth to speak, they heard the clatter of keys, the sound of the lock turning. Instinctively, Jennet reached out and grabbed Mary's hand as the door to the gaol cell slowly creaked open.

A guard walked in. There were so many guards here that it was never the same one who visited twice. This one was young and quite stocky, with hair the colour of sand and piercing blue eyes. He would be handsome, thought Jennet, if it wasn't for the sneer set across his mouth. All the guards looked like that in here, as though an unkind face and a vindictive temperament were requirements of the job.

"Still sleeping at this time, eh?" he remarked, inclining his head towards the two slumbering bodies still lying on the floor. Jennet winced as he kicked Goodwife Dickenson. She made an awful, high-pitched squeal as she woke, like the sound pigs make when they're agitated. Jennet cast her eyes down, unable to bear to watch as Goodwife Dickenson climbed pitifully on to her feet. It was funny; Mary said that she wanted to die so often that, in truth, Jennet doubted that she really meant it. Goodwife Dickenson had never once declared to have given up on life, yet one glimpse at her hollow, distant expression was all it took to convince her that this woman would welcome death now.

"Come on," the guard said gruffly. "There's someone who

wants to see you."

"Who?" Jennet asked. She recoiled, fearing for a moment that it was another examination.

"Damned if I know," snapped the guard, grabbing hold of her arm. "Come on, let's go. And don't even think about trying anything – the only way out of the Fleet is by pardon or the noose."

He marched the women through the murky corridors of the Fleet. They walked at a painfully slow pace behind him, and a couple of times the guard turned round and told them to move more quickly. Despite his warning tone, none of them wished to hurry; ever since they were first arrested all those months ago, whenever someone had wished to see them it had been to interrogate them, to strip them naked and examine them, to take them hundreds of miles from their homes just to stare at them. It was little wonder that they moved at a snail's pace, every step filled with trepidation. Besides, after so many months of incarceration they were weak, their muscles wasted from inactivity and malnutrition. Walking briskly was no longer an option.

After several minutes they arrived at a comfortable-looking room, sparsely but smartly furnished with a desk and several chairs. Within the room sat a man with an air of officialdom and importance about him, wearing a cleric's cap and the robes of a man of the cloth. Jennet glanced briefly at his face, glimpsing his sharp features; a large nose and comparatively tiny mouth set on a face which would have been heart-shaped face were it not for an elongated chin. The man caught Jennet's eye and immediately she looked away. She no longer dared to stare authority directly in the face.

"Please, sit," the man said, venturing an encouraging smile as he gestured towards the seats in front of him. "My name is William Juxton, the Bishop of London. Please, do not be afraid."

Behind her, Jennet heard the guard draw a sharp breath. "Need me to stay, my Lord?" he asked.

The bishop shook his head and waved his hand casually. "No,

that'll be all."

Despite his dismissal, the guard continued to hover. He placed an unwelcome hand on Jennet's shoulder. "You sure, my Lord? Only, this one attacked one of the council's men the other day. Have a care, these are feral creatures. Lord knows what they'd do to you, given the chance."

The bishop gave the guard an amused smile. "I'm sure once these women have heard what I have to say, they won't feel inclined to attack me."

"Alright, my Lord. Well, I will be just outside. If they make any sudden moves, shout and I will hear you."

Jennet listened to the heavy thuds of the guard's boots as he left the room. For a few moments the bishop was silent, his head inclined thoughtfully to one side, studying them all. Jennet wondered then how they must appear to him, this fine gentleman of the church, this bishop. How he must ponder at their ragged clothes, their filthy faces, their strange accents and rough manners.

"I trust you are all being fed and well cared for," the bishop began. The women did not respond but sat there dumbly, unsure whether this was a question or a statement of fact which was not to be challenged. Surely the bishop could see how pale and gaunt they all were; surely he could see that they were not well looked after.

"I have come here at the behest of the Privy Council, with orders from Archbishop Laud." The bishop frowned at their blank expressions. "Do you know who that is?"

Jennet shook her head. "No, my Lord."

"Archbishop Laud is the Archbishop of Canterbury, the leading bishop of our great Church of England. He, like a number of other prominent men, is a member of His Majesty's most loyal Privy Council." He frowned again at their baffled faces. "My Lord in heaven, how ignorant you northerners are."

"Forgive us, my Lord. We are simple women," said Mary, giving the bishop a sweet smile. Jennet blinked, taken aback by Mary's sudden forthright manner. She wondered for a moment if it had been that smile which Nicholas Cunliffe had found so wickedly beguiling.

"Of course you are." The bishop smiled tightly. "Anyway – to the purpose of my visit; I've come to bring you news about your case." He drew a sharp breath. "It would seem that some – irregularities, shall we say – have been identified."

Jennet frowned. "What sort of irregularities, my Lord?" she asked.

"Well," the bishop began, "Doctor Harvey has reported his findings to the Privy Council. It would seem that his examinations did not find any witch's marks upon any of your persons. It would seem, therefore, that these allegations are unfounded. It would also seem that the northern authorities overlooked the need to find evidence to support these allegations before permitting them as evidence in your trial." He shifted uncomfortably in his seat, choosing his words carefully.

Jennet gave the bishop a measured look. The humiliating examination had been worthwhile, after all. "At the trial in Lancaster, I did tell the judges that I had never been examined."

The bishop looked at her thoughtfully. "Yes. Well, they must have been in some doubt; otherwise they would not have referred the decision on sentencing to the Privy Council. You were right to speak up."

Jennet showed him a bleak smile. "I fear it was too little, too late, my Lord."

The bishop leaned forward. "There's more. My esteemed colleague, the Bishop Bridgeman of Chester, was not satisfied with the strength of the testimony against you. He reported his concerns to the Privy Council a number of weeks ago, and was asked to conduct further investigations."

"What do you mean, my Lord? What further investigations? We were sent straight to London." Jennet replied.

The bishop nodded. "Yes, and whilst you have been here, the Bishop of Chester has made his enquiries, conducting interviews, trying to piece together the truth of what happened. In the course of his investigation, he interviewed a young boy named Edmund

Robinson. I believe this young man was the originator of many of the accusations put forward to the Assizes…"

"All lies." Jennet could not resist interjecting.

To her surprise, the bishop nodded again. "Well, it would seem so. Young Robinson has, after much questioning, retracted all of his allegations. Indeed, he has admitted that he fabricated the whole thing, and that he colluded with his father to profit from his deceitful venture." The bishop shook his head disapprovingly. "A most un-Christian thing to do."

Jennet gasped. She glanced at the other women. Mary's mouth had fallen open in surprise; however, she was the only other person to show a reaction. As usual, Margaret was away in a world of her own, whilst Goodwife Dickenson stood there dumbly, her expression blank. Jennet sighed. Even these startling revelations could not bring her back to herself.

"I hope you've arrested Edmund Robinson – the older one. The other one is just a boy, of course," said Mary, her tone resolute.

The bishop raised his eyebrow at her. "Indeed. Edmund Robinson senior is currently imprisoned in London at His Majesty's pleasure."

Jennet glanced at Mary, noticing how the colour had risen once again in her cheeks, a glow of optimism emanating from her eyes.

As ever, Jennet felt less hopeful. "Forgive me, my Lord, but a great many of us were tried in Lancaster in the spring, and not all of us were accused by Edmund Robinson. What will become of us all now?"

The bishop stroked his chin for a moment. "Now that is a more difficult question to answer," he said. "At this stage, I am not sure; it will be for the King and his Privy Council to make the final decision on the matter. All I have been asked to do is to advise you of these developments – to advise you, and to fulfil one other important order."

Jennet frowned. "What order is that?"

The bishop drew a deep breath. "You must not be alarmed.

311

You must understand that this is a great honour being bestowed upon you; indeed, probably the greatest honour for any person in this land. His Majesty has decreed that you must come before him – all of you."

Jennet gasped. Beside her she sensed Goodwife Dickenson bristle. It was still possible to provoke a response from her, after all.

"His Majesty? His Majesty King Charles?" Mary asked, her voice filled with incredulity.

"Yes, the King. We should make haste – the King wishes to see you this afternoon, and it is not wise to keep him waiting. Guards!" he yelled.

Almost immediately, two guards burst into the room. "Something the matter, my Lord?" one asked, giving the women a stern look.

"No, nothing is amiss. Can you see to it that a carriage is readied for the prisoners? Quickly, and with the fastest horse you can find."

The guard furrowed his brow. "A carriage?" he repeated. "I don't understand my Lord, are the prisoners going somewhere?"

The bishop nodded. "Yes," he replied. "They are to travel on His Majesty's orders to Whitehall."

The guard still looked confused but gave the bishop an obliging nod. "Yes of course, my Lord."

"I think I'm going to faint," whispered Mary. She took hold of Jennet's hand and gripped it tightly. "Why are we to see the King? What does he want with the likes of us?"

"I don't know, Mary," Jennet replied. "But I don't think we've any choice in the matter. Hold yourself together – I know you can," she added pointedly.

"I'm scared, Jennet."

Jennet put her arm around the young woman's dainty shoulders. "I know," she said. "Me too." She glanced at Goodwife Dickenson, whose vacant stare had returned, her eyes watery and distant. "But it can't be any worse than staying here."

"I'd rather die than stay here," Mary said.

Jennet looked at Goodwife Dickenson again, noticing that beyond the glazed expression, there was a glimmer of agreement with that sentiment. It was in her eyes, which were filled with such hopeless grief that to stare into them too long caused a contagious sadness. If they didn't get out of there soon, she realised, at least one of them would die and not by the noose. The greatest danger to them all now was despair.

31

The Palace of Whitehall, London
4th July 1634

The carriage thundered through the streets of London, accompanied by the rhythm of the impatient clatter of hooves. The summer weather remained warm and pleasant as they travelled the couple of miles across the city to Whitehall, their carriage basking in the yellow glow of the mid-afternoon sun. Jennet had never travelled in a carriage before, she realised; its proper seats and ample windows would have been a novelty if she had felt herself able to relish them.

Instead she sat there, her head bowed, her heart pounding in her chest, her mind racing over every piece of information that the bishop had imparted to them. None of the evidence given against them in Lancaster had been proven; on the contrary, it had been found to be lacking at best, and at worst, a complete fabrication. She clenched her fists hard, so hard that her long, unkempt nails dug painfully into her hands. She felt so angry with Masters Shuttleworth and Starkie, and the two judges at the Assizes. They had been so quick to believe that they were all witches. They had been so quick to see them condemned. Indeed, if it hadn't been for that tiny morsel of doubt which had crept over the judges as they prepared to pass sentence, then in all likelihood she would have already been hanged, along with all of the others.

Jennet felt her entire body tense as her mind returned continuously to one name: Edmund Robinson. The boy, the deceitful child, who had admitted that he had lied, and that his father had seized upon his lies for profit. It had been nothing more than a money-making scheme, and an opportunity for Edmund's spiteful father to rid himself of those he disliked. It has been just as William had suspected all those months ago.

Jennet sighed heavily. William. The thought of his name immediately conjured the image of his kind smile, his bright and shining eyes. She folded her arms tightly across her chest, closing her eyes and wishing that she could feel the strength in his lean arms as he enveloped her gently in his embrace, the feeling of his lips as he whispered sweet words in her ear. Her heart lurched into her mouth as she realised she could no longer recall the sound of his voice. Her eyes flew open. They had been apart for so long now. Soon she would forget his face. Soon she wouldn't be able to remember any part of him. Soon it would be as though he had never existed, as though he had never walked into her life and given her such hope, such renewed purpose; such love.

"Stop the carriage! I'm going to be sick!" she cried out.

The bishop tapped hard on the roof. Almost immediately the horses whinnied and the carriage drew to an abrupt halt. Without a moment's hesitation, the bishop flung the door open and pushed Jennet out of the carriage. Her feet, which were still shackled, gave way beneath her and she landed on the ground with a thud. Pain seared through her frail bones as she fell down hard on her knees, but even the shock and discomfort couldn't prevent her from retching. She sat on the ground for what felt like an eternity, wave after violent wave of nausea passing through her as she made the most abominable heaving noises. No matter how hard she retched, however, no sickness came. It was as though her tiny, wasted body knew that it couldn't afford to expel the little food it had received. It was as though her body had given up and even vomiting was beyond its capability now.

"Are you quite finished?" said the bishop sternly.

Jennet nodded, wiping her saliva-covered mouth with the back of her hand. "I'm sorry, my Lord."

The bishop gave her a pitying look. "It can't be helped, I suppose. But please, do not vomit in the presence of His Majesty."

"Yes, of course, my Lord," she replied grimly.

She sat on the ground for a few moments, taking some deep, considered breaths in an effort to collect herself. She looked about her, absorbing her surroundings for the first time. She had been so overcome by her sudden sickness that she hadn't noticed they were travelling through a pleasant green field, a straight road lined with neatly sculpted trees running through it. Until now every glimpse she had caught of this city had been all dust, all foul stench, all crowded streets and dwellings built so close to each other that it was hard to determine where one house ended and another began. It was comforting to see some countryside, to see something which reminded her of home. She breathed in deeply again, enjoying the clean, odourless air.

The bishop climbed out of the carriage and spoke to the guard who was steering the horses. Jennet closed her eyes as she listened to their brief exchange. The bishop seemed irritated that they had travelled this way, insisting that they had doubled back on themselves rather than taking a direct route to Whitehall. The guard protested; this way would draw less attention to them, he said. The last thing they needed was a baying mob gathering as the women were taken to see the King. His cautionary words made Jennet gulp hard, her anxiety sticking in her throat like a knife.

"Are you ready now?" the bishop asked, standing over her. He tapped his foot impatiently.

Jennet opened her eyes, nodding obediently. She got back on to her feet slowly, her legs still threatening to buckle under her as she climbed back into the carriage.

"What were you doing?" Mary asked in a hushed voice as Jennet sat back down beside her.

"The field out there," she replied. "It made me think of home."

"It's St James's Park," the bishop snorted. "I can't imagine that St James's Park could even vaguely resemble the north!" He chuckled, an amused smile fixed on his face.

"Perhaps not, my Lord," she replied, trying not to bristle at his mockery. Beside her, she felt Mary reach over and grasp her hand. They exchanged a knowing glance; they both knew where they would rather be, and it certainly wasn't this sprawling, stinking city.

Moments later, the horses slowed and the carriage came to a gradual standstill. They all climbed out of the carriage, the bishop leading, his formidable enrobed shadow cast long across the ground as the later afternoon approached. Jennet looked up, squinting against the bright sunlight as she tried to absorb her surroundings. Behind her, she saw that they had passed through a tall gatehouse, one of the grandest structures she had ever seen, with four towers at its top, ornate stonework all around it. She drew a sharp breath; if the entrance to this place looked like a castle itself, what was the rest of Whitehall like?

A few immaculately-dressed ladies gasped and whispered as they walked past. Jennet could not help but stare back at them, their fine satin skirts shimmering in the sun, their hair perfectly curled at the sides. She looked down at herself, her petticoats dirty and nibbled by rats, her matted hair stinking beneath her filthy coif. What a spectacle she must have seemed. She rubbed her face hard, hoping that the beads of sweat upon her brow might remove some of the dirt engrained in her skin. She could not believe that anyone wished her to appear before her King in this state.

The bishop hurried them towards an entrance at the side of a tall, rectangular building fashioned in a pale stone. Jennet supposed this was why they called this place Whitehall; every façade around her had a blanched quality to it, the white surfaces reflecting the sunlight and dazzling her. As she walked into the shade, she felt relieved; she was unsure how much more bright splendour her eyes could bear.

"This way," said the bishop as he swiftly nodded them through several heavily guarded doors and into the main body of the palace.

Despite the bishop's impatient tone, Jennet walked slowly, unable to stop herself from gawping at the palace's interior. Just like outside, everything was white, with high, curved ceilings which were beautifully and intricately carved. The grand hallway through which they walked was sparsely furnished with cushioned benches, upon which more well-dressed courtiers sat; mostly men now, some clutching handfuls of papers. They fell silent as the four women were led past them, some of them casting disparaging glances, as though the poor, filthy creatures before them were unwelcome vermin in this most splendid palace.

"Where is the King?" Mary whispered anxiously.

Jennet shook her head. "I don't know," she replied. She realised that her voice was shaking. She had never been so awestruck in all of her life. She had never been anywhere like this before; even Read Hall, even Gawthorpe Hall paled in comparison to this place. She grimaced, realising that she had been so foolishly impressed by the little palaces of the local gentlemen, so blinded by their apparent authority that it had been easy to forget that there was someone far more powerful than they. She was about to walk before the most powerful man in the land, a man who could condemn her to die with a click of his fingers, but also a man who could pardon her just as quickly. She swallowed hard, not daring even to hope.

"Do you think Frances and Margaret understand what's happening?" Mary whispered again.

Jennet glanced at the other two women. Goodwife Dickenson's expression was no longer quite so vacant, but it was twisted into a look of painful resignation. Margaret's lips, meanwhile, moved incessantly, her eyes darting wildly, making her appear agitated and confused. Jennet sighed. If the King hoped to get any sense from her today, she feared that he would be out of luck.

"I'm not sure," she replied.

The bishop led them to another set of guarded doors. Jennet watched as he leaned towards one of the guards, whispering a few words to him, the guard whispering back in response. She strained to listen but could not hear what was said. The bishop spun around, turning to face them. Jennet noticed the severe expression on his face, his eyes narrowed, his lips pursed. He waved a long, thin finger at them, as though they might be naughty children.

"When you walk through these doors, you will be in the presence of His Majesty, King Charles. When you see him, you must lower your gaze and curtsey. Thereafter, you must only speak when you are invited to speak – if you are invited to speak at all. Otherwise, remain silent. Do you understand?"

"Yes, my Lord." Mary said quietly.

Jennet simply nodded. She noticed Goodwife Dickenson standing next to her, staring at the floor. She wondered if she had heard anything the bishop had said.

The guards opened the doors and the bishop beckoned them inside with a firm nod of his head. Jennet gasped as she looked around the large, white room in front of her. Like the hallway, the ceiling was high and curved, but even more magnificently carved. From it hung large, draped green curtains which were pulled closed, dividing the room. For a moment, Jennet wondered what lay behind them. At the sides of the room stood pillars of coloured marble, and on the walls hung a great many fine paintings; most of them portraits, interspersed with the occasional hunting scene. Jennet returned her gaze straight ahead, resisting the temptation to study the faces contained within the pictures.

In the middle of the room, sat on a single chair upholstered with berry-red cushions, was the King. As instructed, Jennet curtseyed deeply, casting her eyes to the floor as she dropped her gaze.

"Your Majesty," said the bishop, his voice dripping with polite deference as he bowed. "Please, forgive the intrusion. As instructed, I have brought before you the four women from Pendle." He rose slowly, wincing as he forced his ageing frame to straighten. He gestured subtly with his hands, indicating that they should now stand up also.

The King frowned as he stroked his pointed beard. As Jennet rose, she noticed his gaze fall upon her, his dark eyes looking her up and down, his expression coldly inquisitive.

"These are the women we discussed with the Privy Council?" the King directed his question to the bishop. Jennet observed his unusual accent; a rolling emphasis of some sounds detectable amongst the crisp oration which she now identified as the speech of London's rich and powerful. She recalled being told once that the King had been born in Scotland. Clearly, he had not altogether lost his Scottish accent.

The bishop nodded. "Yes, Your Grace. If you recall, their case was referred to the Privy Council for examination prior to sentencing."

"And what were the findings?"

"The case against them is very weak, Your Majesty. The evidence was poorly constructed and one of the main witnesses –a boy of ten – has admitted that he lied to the authorities."

The King made a disapproving noise with his lips. "I see."

He rose from his seat and approached them. Jennet noticed that he wasn't particularly tall, and although his doublet had a short waist, it did little to lengthen the appearance of his legs. As he walked towards her, it struck Jennet that he was also a person, just like her. She realised that she had expected to find herself standing before a richly bejewelled, extravagantly enrobed Messiah, not a rather short man dressed in fine but quite plain clothing, almost head to toe in dark colours except for the bright white lace collar around his neck. Jennet lowered her gaze again, making an effort to emphasise her respect and humility. After all, the only slim chance she had of ever seeing William or her home again was to appeal to the King's mercy.

The King walked slowly all around them, his boots clicking rhythmically against the hard floor. "What is that dreadful smell?" he asked the bishop, wrinkling his large, straight nose in disgust.

"They've been kept at the Fleet, Your Majesty. Conditions there are not very comfortable, especially in this hot weather." The bishop chose his words carefully.

The King took a few steps away from them. "I see," he said again. "Perhaps it is just as well that the Queen could not be here this afternoon – she was as curious as I to see these women for herself. Alas, she is checking on the works to her palace in Greenwich."

"Ah yes, Your Majesty, I rode past the white house just last week. It is magnificent," the bishop gushed.

Jennet's interest piqued at their casual conversation. She wondered if the palace they were discussing was the grand white building she had stared at so many times on the way to and from those countless humiliating public displays. If it was, then it was no wonder that it had impressed her; it was a home fit for a Queen.

"Indeed," replied the King, restoring a formal tone with his singular response. "Now, to return to the matter at hand," he paused then, ushering in a lingering silence.

Jennet kept her head bowed but could feel his eyes pass between each of them. She drew some shallow breaths, trying to steady her nerves. Still she could not understand what the King wanted with simple women like them. Surely, the prosecution of a few northern witches was a trifling matter for the most powerful man in the land?

"Do you wish to question them, Your Majesty?" the bishop asked.

Jennet sensed the King shake his head, his long dark hair swishing at his shoulders.

"Not as such. I may converse with them, perhaps - if that is at all possible," he added haughtily.

"I cannot guarantee you will get much from some of them," the bishop replied, "although that one has always seemed quite talkative."

Jennet glanced up long enough to see the bishop extend a long finger towards her. Her heart began to race as she felt the weight of the King's gaze upon her once again.

"You," he said. "What is your name?"

"Jennet Braithwaite," she replied, keeping her eyes cast down. She bit her lip; or was it Device, or Sellers? She couldn't even remember the name they used for her anymore.

"Pardon?" the King replied. "William," he said, addressing the bishop, "I can't understand this woman. Can you?"

"She is mumbling, Your Majesty, and I find it takes a while for the ears to grow accustomed to the rough northern tongue."

"Indeed."

The King walked back towards Jennet, reaching out his arm and lifting her chin. Reluctantly, she raised her eyes to look at his face. She saw that his eyes were filled with curiosity, and his mouth was upturned slightly in an expression of vague amusement. Next to her, she thought she heard Mary let out a small gasp.

"That's better," he said. "I think that if we are to talk, I will need to see your lips move. Now, can you tell me your name?"

"Jennet Braithwaite, Your Majesty." She enunciated her words carefully. She saw the bishop frown at the surname, but he made no further remark.

"Jennet – my Lord the Bishop of London has advised that the case against you is weak and now doubtful. What have you to say to these findings?"

"As the bishop has said, Your Majesty, the little boy who accused me has admitted that he lied."

The King turned back to the bishop. "William, were all these women accused by the same little boy?"

The bishop drew a hesitant breath and shook his head. "No, Your Majesty. However, it is not just the little boy's evidence which has been found wanting. Your Majesty's esteemed physician, Doctor Harvey, has examined the women himself and found no evidence of the witch's marks they were all alleged to bear. I would not wish to bore Your Majesty with the finer details as this has been a very complex case to unravel, but…"

The King waved his hand dismissively. "Yes, yes. In your opinion, William, and in the opinion of those who have examined these women and their case, are these women guilty of witchcraft?"

The bishop shook his head. "No, Your Majesty. In my opinion, there is not enough good, solid evidence to support the conviction made at the Lent Assizes."

On hearing the bishop's words, Jennet felt her legs grow weak, threatening to give way beneath her. Next to her, she heard Mary begin to weep quietly, her shoulders shaking with the effort of trying to suppress her sobs. For the first time in a very long time, she suspected that Mary's tears were those of relief rather than sadness. She glanced at Goodwife Dickenson. Her friend had raised her head now, regaining at least a hint of that dignified posture she used to hold. Although her expression betrayed little emotion, Jennet could see a handful of tears rolling down her cheeks.

"However," the bishop continued, "as Your Majesty is aware, the Privy Council has not yet met to reach its final decision on the matter."

The King turned back to face the women, giving them all a final, considered look. "There is no need for that," he replied. "The council has more important business to attend to. William, see that these women are issued with a King's pardon and sent back to Lancashire."

Jennet's shaking legs finally gave way and she collapsed on to the floor, tears of joy streaming down her pale, sunken face. She would go home. She would see William again; she would see his kind, loving smile, she would feel the warmth of his touch, she would be soothed by the sound of his voice as she fell asleep beside him each night. She would fulfil her promise to Goodwife Lund and help to care for Grace. She would go back and stay in Pendle; she wouldn't leave it for another day for the rest of her life. No more plans to leave, no more dreams of faraway places and a better life. The best life, she realised, was the one she had all along, in her crumbling barn with the man she loved. She needed nothing more than that now.

Part Four

1636

32

The Well Tower, Lancaster Castle
Two Years Later
November 1636

Jennet shivered and wrapped the inadequate shawl tighter around her shoulders, as though she might be able to extract some warmth from such a thin rag. It was hopeless: the winter outside was so terribly cold and in here, in this dreadful place, the ice seemed to seep through the thick dungeon walls, the frost biting relentlessly at the prisoners' limbs, making them shiver uncontrollably and groan pitiably in their sleep. It was incredible how such strong, heavy stones could keep these wretched souls detained inside, deterring even the vainest hope of escape, but couldn't prevent at least a little of winter's chill from breaking through.

Jennet looked down and examined her legs which were partially exposed, her skirts growing ever shorter as the material rotted around her calves. She saw that her ankles were covered in small red sores, caused no doubt by the relentless cold and the discomfort of the hard stone floor upon which she slept. She pulled at her skirts, teasing them down over her weeping flesh. Out of sight, out of mind, she thought to herself, an inexplicable chuckle escaping momentarily from her chest, followed swiftly by that heaving, racking cough to which she had grown so accustomed.

Her mind: these days, she swore she was slowly going mad. It was bad enough in the summer, when she still had the energy to talk to herself. Back then, she had frequently caught herself mumbling incessantly and had realised, to her alarm, that most of the time she had no idea what she was muttering about. Now, months later, the lack of proper food combined with the want of warmth had begun to wear her down, sapping all of her will, making her body ache and her soul tired. She no longer talked to herself. She couldn't; she needed all her remaining energy to breathe, because those heavy, rattling breaths were the only difference between this life and the one waiting for her below, in the eternal fires of damnation. Perhaps that was why she laughed, she realised; there was a degree of irony in knowing that she would die shivering, only to burn forever thereafter.

There were only five of them left now; all silent, some sleeping, though never restfully. When she had first arrived back from London towards the end of that long, hot summer, the Well Tower had still been full, although a considerable number of them had perished in the first bout of gaol fever. Jennet winced as she recalled how Mary had been inconsolable upon learning of the death of her mother. The poor young woman had wept for days, her pained, excruciating cries echoing through the gaol day and night until the sound of her grief became almost intolerable. She glanced at Mary now; a thin, cowering figure, hunched over in the corner. Like her, she was one of the remaining five. Like her, she hadn't spoken a word for weeks.

Jennet remembered the jubilation of the other prisoners as they were told of the King's pardon. She recalled how they had talked excitedly amongst themselves, sharing their hopes for the future, their happiness at the prospect of seeing their families again, their relief that this dreadful nightmare would soon be over.

"If we're all to be pardoned, why have you four been brought back here?" some had asked.

Jennet had merely shrugged. "I suppose they have to do things properly," she replied. "I suppose we all have to be formally pardoned and released."

Recalling her words now, she sighed. She had been so naïve.

Of course, their elation had been short-lived. Not long after she and the other women had arrived back in Lancaster, the prison warden had come down into the gaol to speak to all of them. It had been over two years but she could still recall that day clearly, his grey, grim face emerging from the shadows as he shone his bright torch down on them all.

"As most of you have heard, the King has issued a pardon to all those from Pendle convicted of witchcraft at the Lent Assizes," he had begun.

A few muffled cheers echoed around the gaol, their murmurs of delight mixing with relieved sobs and the surprised grunts of those who had been more sceptical.

"However," he continued after a moment, "a prisoner cannot be released until all of their debts are paid."

Immediately there were cries of indignation. "What do you mean? What debts?" someone shouted.

The warden raised his voice angrily. "Do you think we keep you for free in here? All of you owe for your food and lodging; some owe a lot more than that."

"Lodging?" someone yelled. "This place isn't fit to house my animals."

"You can't ask for much for food," someone else said. "You've barely fed us a proper meal in months."

"That is the law of this land," replied the warden. "Prisoners in England pay for their own keep. Whether you're guilty or pardoned, none of you are exempt from paying."

The voices of consternation continued. "But how are we supposed to pay? We've been locked up in here for months; none of us have any money!"

In the dim light, Jennet saw the warden give a smooth gesture with his hands, urging calm. "We will get word to your families, friends, even your neighbours," he said, his tone more diplomatic now. "Hopefully those who love you will come forward and pay your way out of here."

"I shan't hold my breath," Jennet heard someone mutter. "It's thanks to our neighbours that some of us are in here in the first place."

Jennet lay down on the hard floor as she descended into fits of coughing once more, her aching chest heaving with the effort of it. As the coughing subsided and her breathing regained its slow, shaky rhythm, she thought again about that day. A single tear rolled down her cheek and on to the dusty floor as she recalled her horror upon learning of the size of her debt. Months of food and lodging in the Well Tower, followed by transport to London had not come cheap. She owed a fortune; more than she could ever afford to pay. At that moment she had begun to despair. The warden would send word to William but it would do no good. They were poor; they would never have the means to secure her release.

Slowly, she closed her eyes and began to drift off. She found that thinking, remembering, made her tired now. She tried to succumb to slumber but found that her mind continued to reel. So many people had gone now, their families finding the funds to pay their debts and take them home. She recalled the day Goodwife Dickenson had left, just weeks after they returned to Lancaster. Without warning, her friend had been unshackled and led away, her slender frame so weakened by incarceration that she had to be carried up the steps by two guards.

"Please, look after Grace!" Jennet had called after her.

But Goodwife Dickenson never looked back. She never said goodbye.

Jennet rolled restlessly on the ground as she continued to drift, languishing in the confusing state between awake and sleeping. So many people were dead; Goodwife Lund – had it really been over two years since she had last seen her dear friend? Margaret Johnson, the mad old woman who had also travelled to London; she too had perished. Jennet recalled how she had found her death ironic, the incessant rambler passing away quietly in her sleep.

Mary's mother and father, too, were both gone – poor Mary, an orphan now, with no hope of ever escaping this place. She used to cry every night. Now she didn't cry at all.

By contrast, Jennet cried often. Although her silent sobs produced the most violent coughing fits, she found that she couldn't help it. At first she would cry for William, for the love she still felt for him even though she now struggled to remember how he looked, how he sounded, how the touch of his hand felt. She would cry for the life they had never had together, for the laughter they had never enjoyed, for the children they had never had. She would cry so much that her heart would ache, as though in the long, cold night it was freezing, growing brittle, and breaking bit by bit.

After William, she would cry for all those she had lost, for Goodwife Lund, for the baby she had briefly carried, for her father, for her mother, for the rest of her family. She thought about her Device family often now. It was funny; when she tried to recall William's face the image grew ever more blurry, yet the faces of her family whom she had not seen since she was a child grew ever clearer, ever bolder in her mind.

In her restless slumber, images of childhood recollections would come to her; playing with her sister Alison in the woods, helping her mother feed the dogs, helping her grandmother prepare an evening meal. She would weep tears of sadness that they never got to see her grow up, that she was never able to enjoy having them around her, that she was always so alone. She tried not to remember that they too languished in this prison cell; that they died at the gallows not far away from here. She tried not to think about who was responsible for their deaths, who still had their blood on her hands. She knew that her frail mind couldn't cope with those thoughts.

Struggling to breathe, Jennet sat up again, looking round at the shadows of her fellow inmates. She suspected that she would be the next to die now, that the end was not far away for her. As much as she suffered in there, the thought of death still terrified her. She was certain now that all this was her punishment for the things she had done, for the suffering she had caused all those years ago. There was no other explanation; to have been brought so close to freedom and yet to have had it snatched from her grasp could only be divine retribution. She had been wrong to doubt God; of course he existed, of course he was righting her wrongs through her continued suffering. She knew also that the punishment would not end with death; that it would continue in hell. She chuckled to herself again. William had been right; you could create your own heaven or your own hell. This place was hell on earth, but it was the hell below which really frightened her.

She glanced again at Mary, who still sat motionless, staring into an abyss. In the company of four other pitiful souls, at least she wasn't alone. She feared solitude more than anything now, perhaps even more than death. No one spoke anymore, all were trapped within themselves by their own despair, but nonetheless the presence of other people offered her a tiny morsel of comfort. By contrast, solitude was a frightening prospect: without company she would be forced to confront the multitude of nightmares which plagued her restless mind, she would be haunted by all those ghosts that she didn't ever want to see. She would have no choice but to replay those dreaded scenes from her past over and over again in her mind. She would be forced once again to feel the shame, guilt and remorse that had chided her so often. Perhaps worst of all, she would have to face the question which had tormented her for most of her life: why did I betray them?

Epilogue

Aboard the Dilligent
July 1638

William hung his head over the side as the ship lurched back and forth on the rough sea. He vomited, not for the first time that day, the salt of the dry, well-preserved meat he had eaten for lunch sticking in the back of his throat. Wiping his mouth with his hand, he looked towards the horizon. Sea; endless sea. They had been at sea for weeks now, and it would be many more weeks before they would see land again. This was the right thing to do, he told himself. No looking back now. Behind him it was all pain and suffering and death. He didn't want to be a part of that anymore. No, he had to look forwards, to this new land, this godly land, a land filled with new people and new opportunities. He would find work; he would make a life for himself – just as she had told him to. He would make her proud of him. He clutched the piece of cloth in which he had wrapped a lock of her hair. It was all he had left of her now.

He recalled the day she was released from Lancaster gaol. He had struggled to hide his shock when he saw her grey, sunken face, her hollow eyes, her shrivelled frame. It was hard to believe that this was his Jennet; she looked like a woman twice her age. She was so weak that she could hardly stand, and he remembered lifting her up and carrying her to the cart. She was as light as a feather, there was almost nothing left of her.

"At least I'm going home to die," she had said as he placed her in the cart and wrapped a multitude of blankets around her.

"Of course you're not going to die," he had said. "You're with me again now. You're going to be fine."

A tear rolled down his cheek at his recollection of his words. How wrong he had been.

He had ridden quickly; the roads, although frozen, were mercifully dry, making the journey easier. He planned to take her straight home, to the Lunds' cottage in Wheatley Lane. Home; by then, he called it home. He had been living there ever since the day she was taken away to Lancaster with Goodwife Lund. He recalled how stricken with grief and shock he and John Lund had been, both reeling at the sudden and dramatic disappearance of their wives. At first he had intended only to stay for a few days, but as time wore on he realised that for the first time in his life, he could not bear solitude. As he and John became company for one another, he decided to remain there in solidarity with a fellow man who, he knew, felt the gnawing ache of pain and loss as keenly as he did.

It had been a strained existence. William remembered the day that John had learnt that his wife was dead, how he had wept quietly for hours. Every day after that William had woken and his first thought had been, is today the day that I will learn that she is dead? Is today the day that she will go to the gallows? Is today the day that she will die, starved of sleep and food, in that dreadful place? As the weeks had turned to months he had begun to feel drained with the worry, worn down by the uncertainty as to whether he would ever see her alive again.

Then one day, a hot, sticky day in August 1634, a messenger had arrived. She had been pardoned by the King, he had explained. She could be released from prison just as soon as her debts were paid. William recalled how he had wept when the messenger told him how much money was owed. It was more money than he had ever had in his life, and the amount grew by the day. They took her to London, the messenger said. They took her to see the King. Kings and cities don't come cheap. William had gasped at that revelation. She had been one of the women who had gone and obtained the pardon. She had been to London, the city of their hopes and dreams, and he had known nothing about it.

As the messenger left, he had rallied, a renewed sense of determination coming over him. He would work his fingers to the bone, earning every scrap of coin that he could to secure her release. He would see her out of prison. He had wished then that she could read, so that he could have written to her and told her. He would have told her to hang on, to have faith. He would have told her that he was coming for her.

When he saw her that day, staggering out of Lancaster gaol, he knew that he was too late. It had taken him more than two years to raise the money to pay her way out of gaol. It had been over two years before he had been able to make the journey to Lancaster with enough coin in a purse to pay the warden. He closed his eyes briefly, recalling the day; a cold, bleak December day, an icy wind hurtling through the air, stinging his face as he rode his horse to Lancaster, pulling a cart laden with blankets. Thank goodness for the blankets; if he hadn't taken those, in all likelihood she would have perished on the road home.

He grasped tighter at the lock of hair in his hand as he remembered arriving back in Wheatley Lane, the frost on the ground crunching underfoot as he carried her through the Lund's cottage door. By then, she had become delirious and feverish, her eyes rolling back in her head as she slipped in and out of conscious. He remembered taking her inside and setting her down gently on his bed. He had looked at her then, her body still, her face pale, her eyes shut tight. If it hadn't been for the laboured, rattling sound of her breathing, he would have sworn she was already dead.

He had remained at her side for many days, watching faithfully as she slept, offering her small sips to drink whenever she stirred.

In truth, he didn't know what else could be done. Her body, he realised, was broken; these past years of neglect had weakened her and now she was succumbing to fever. All he could do was hope; all he could do was pray to God for a miracle.

One evening, about a week after he had brought her home, she woke again. He had been dozing at her side, and he recalled how the sound of her voice had startled him. For a moment his heart had leapt; she had come back to him, she had recovered. He had sat up, his heart sinking again as he looked down at her grey face, her dry, cracked lips, her eyes which were still struggling to focus. She was weakening; she was growing worse and there was nothing he could do.

"Where am I?" she asked, her voice an uneven rasp.

"The Lunds' cottage," he told her. "I have been living here, while you've been…away."

"Is Goodwife Lund here?"

William shook his head sadly. "No, Jennet. She's not with us anymore. Don't you remember?"

Jennet had given him a weak smile. "I will see her soon."

He had crouched down at her side then, grasping her hands with a sense of desperation. Her hands were like the ice outside; white and frozen. "Please don't talk like that. I have brought you back to me."

She didn't seem to hear him. "Grace…where is Grace?" she mumbled.

"She's at home with Nicholas, with their boy. He grows taller and stronger by the day."

The lie had stuck in the back of his throat. He hadn't had the heart to tell her that Grace was dead, that she had drowned herself in the summer of 1634 after learning of her mother's death. The poor young woman had never recovered her sanity and Goodwife Lund's demise, it seemed, had been the final straw. Her son, who was still just an infant, had followed her to the grave shortly afterwards. William grimaced as he recalled how heartbroken Nicholas had been, his pain compounded when his mother returned home in the early autumn of 1634, crippled, her health broken by incarceration. Apparently, the scream she let out when she learnt of her grandson's death could be heard for miles around. Since then, the Dickensons had locked themselves away in their farm on the heights, a shattered family, shrouded in misery and grief.

"Is she better now?"

"Yes." He told himself that the lies were for her own good.

"William, I am dying." Her voice was beginning to fade.

He clutched her hands tighter. "No, you can't. You can't die now. What about us, what about the time we should have together?"

She gave him another small smile. "I am the last one. It ends with me. It ends…" her breathing became increasingly laboured and she gasped hopelessly.

William drew himself closer, stroking her forehead. It burned ferociously. "What do you mean, Jennet? What ends with you?"

"Live a good life, and remember me."

Tears streamed down William's face as he laid his head on her shoulder. He couldn't bear to watch her face as she struggled to take her final breaths. "No," he kept saying. "No, you can't, not yet. I love you."

"I love you," she whispered. Then she was gone.

She was buried on the twenty-second of December 1636, at St Mary's in Newchurch-in-Pendle. It had been a cold, calm day, the heavy snowfall of the previous night still lying on the ground. William remembered the journey there, walking carefully with John along the white roads; his feet numb with cold, his mind numb with shock. It had only been three years since they had married at the same church. Only three years, and now she was dead. In his mind's eye, he kept seeing her that day; her long hair flowing freely around her shoulders, a beaming smile on her lips. She had been so happy. He had been so happy. Now he felt sure that he would never know happiness again.

Her funeral had been a quiet ceremony, with only the minister and a handful of people in attendance. Mainly friends of his, he had realised, for most of her family and friends were now dead. As her body was committed to the frozen earth, he had noticed Alice standing a little behind the mourners, her face well-concealed under a heavy shawl. For a moment she had caught his eye, her expression conveying sadness, sympathy, perhaps even remorse. He had given her a hard, cold look. He knew it wasn't godly to behave that way but he couldn't help it; however small her contribution might have been, however long ago it was, he held her in some way responsible for what had happened to Jennet. Looking at her then, shoulders hunched, her face strained and weary, he suspected that she felt that she was responsible, too.

He hadn't been able to afford much with which to mark Jennet's grave; a simple, wooden cross was all she had, and in time that would rot away to nothing. It was carved simply with the words "Jennet Sellers, alias Device." He had agonised over which name to use. Part of him wanted to bury her as Jennet Braithwaite, so that the world would know she was his wife, so that everyone would have to acknowledge his pain at losing her. However, in the end he had settled upon her two family names. It wasn't the usual way of things, he knew that, but then Jennet's life had been far from ordinary. After her death, he had thought continually upon her words – "I am the last one. It ends with me." When it had dawned upon him that she had meant the last of her family, he had known what to do. The best way to honour her memory was to call her what she was – a Device, and a Sellers. She was the last one; she was the last of them to die. The world needed to know that if there was ever to be any hope of ending such needless suffering.

William looked up and across the vast, blue ocean. He breathed in deeply, smelling the salt which lingered in the air. The journey had been difficult; there was illness below decks and he had found himself regularly plagued by sea sickness. Nevertheless, the further they got from England, the better he felt, as though an enormous burden began to lift from his shoulders. He had left Pendle straight after her burial. He found he could no longer bear to be there without her; every tree, every lane, every rolling hill finding some way to provoke a memory of their time together. It was too painful, too raw. So he did what had always come naturally to him: he wandered on to the next place.

Initially, he had intended to go to London just as he and Jennet had always planned. As he made his way southwards, however, he realised that he no longer had an appetite for the big city. A place which had once represented work, opportunity, and a degree of religious liberty to him, now felt like just another part of England, just another place which had brought Jennet suffering and hardship. Instead, six months ago, he had found himself in Ipswich, on the eastern coast of the country. A sea port, much like the one he had grown up in, filled with the eclectic mix of folk which he would expect to find anywhere which served as both an entrance and an exit to the world beyond.

There, he met a group of godly folk, people of all sorts of radical religious persuasions who felt that they no longer fitted in England; that in matters of faith there was an irreparable chasm between them and their mother country. Many of them were talking about leaving, about sailing for America. By then, England was abuzz with talk of war; the Scots were threatening to rise in rebellion against the King's church reforms and the King, who hadn't called a parliament for almost a decade, was increasingly seen as a tyrant. In Ipswich, many of the assembled godly folk felt that England was drifting back towards the Church of Rome, and that they needed to go somewhere else to create the sort of land they wished to live in.

The mention of war had made William shudder: he had seen enough threatened violence, enough suffering, enough death. He had experienced more loss and heartbreak than any man should have to endure. So, when the group of one hundred pilgrims, as they called themselves, decided to sail the Dilligent to the American east coast, he decided to join them. There was nothing left for him in England now.

He looked out to sea once more, trying to peer beyond the

horizon, trying to imagine what lay before him. He wondered what America was like. Was it really the godly utopia which the folk around him were anticipating? They were due to dock in the harbour of a town called Boston at the beginning of August. He supposed they would all find out soon enough if it was the heaven that they had hoped and dreamed of.

William smiled wryly to himself. He had once hoped to attain heaven on earth. He was beyond heaven's reach now; his dreams of heaven had died, feverishly in his bed, almost two years before. All he sought was a place which was not infected with fear of witchcraft, where there were no more ludicrous accusations between neighbours, no more crude trials at the Assizes. No more cries of being damned or cursed every time an old woman uttered a few ill-tempered words. No more threats of the gallows every time someone's cow or child died. No more filthy prisons in which the incarcerated must pay their keep or never hope to be set free. If America, if Boston could give him that then he might, in time, learn to be at peace once again.

"It ends with me," she had said.

Had it?

William sighed. Only time would tell.

The End

AUTHOR'S NOTES

This novel is a story about Jennet Device, the youngest daughter of Elizabeth Device and granddaughter of Elizabeth Southerns, alias Old Demdike, who were both accused of witchcraft in the Pendle witch hunt of 1612. Born in 1600 and therefore aged just twelve when the trials took place, Jennet is remembered by history as the child witness, the small girl who stood on a bench and delivered the damning testimony which sent her mother, brother, sister and countless others to the gallows.

As a writer, I found myself wondering what became of Jennet's life after the 1612 trial – where did she live and who with, how was she regarded by her community, and how did she cope with the knowledge of what she had done? I also found the idea of her becoming caught up in the 1634 trials irresistible; another trial, another child witness, and the former child witness becoming one of the accused – it is truly the stuff of stories. I found myself asking, how would she have reacted to this cruel but ironic turn of events? How would she have behaved during questioning and during her trial – would she have fought for her freedom or would she have surrendered willingly, feeling that after all these years she was getting what she deserved?

In terms of historical data, very little is known for certain about Jennet's life. We know from evidence given at the 1612 trials that there was some question over her legitimacy, and that it was widely believed that she was the daughter of a man named Sellers. I pursued this theory concerning Jennet's parentage in my first Witches of Pendle novel, *The Gisburn Witch*. In this novel I have advanced it further, assuming that after the trials she went to live with her father and changed her surname to Sellers which, over time, would have helped to disguise her true identity. The idea that she changed her name is supported by some evidence; in 1635, a Jennet Sellers alias Device was buried in Newchurch-in-Pendle.

Between 1612 and 1634, Jennet Device disappears entirely from the records. Then, the name is mentioned by a little boy, Edmund Robinson, as he gave some rather fanciful evidence to the local Justices of the Peace which would ultimately lead to a second round of witch trials in Pendle. There is no conclusive evidence that the Jennet Device mentioned by the boy is the same Jennet Device who had starred in the 1612 trials; indeed, as John A Clayton notes in his book *The Boy Witchfinder of Pendle Forest*, there may have been at least two Jennet Devices in the area at the time. Certainly, Clayton's research into the records indicates that this may have been the case; as aforementioned, there is a 1635 burial record for a Jennet Sellers alias Device, yet in August 1636 a Jennet Device was still languishing in prison in Lancaster. However, as Clayton also notes, it is possible that these are records of the same person, and that the burial record is incorrect and should read 1636 instead of 1635 – I opted for this version of events when writing the novel.

In order to create the story, I wove a number of other fictional elements in amongst the factual background to the 1634 trials. Although Jennet's Holgate relatives really existed, we don't know what sort of relationship, if any, she had with them or if she ever lived with them. The Holgates were also mentioned in Edmund Robinson's testimony but were never brought to trial; however, I decided to omit this detail from the story. William Braithwaite, the love of Jennet's life, is fictional, although he was an absolute pleasure to create and provided a perfect opportunity to explore the religious landscape in Pendle at the time and in particular, the Grindletonian beliefs to which he subscribed. I also felt it was important to give Jennet, who had suffered a great deal in her life, some happiness and something to live for. I felt the inclusion of Bess Hargreaves (nee Preston), a fictional character from *The Gisburn Witch*, provided a useful link to the first novel, as well as giving some further context for the depth of Jennet's guilt.

Goodwives Lund and Dickenson were real women who were tried in 1634, and Goodwife Lund does seem to have died in Lancaster gaol. Grace and Nicholas were the names of their respective children; however, their marriage and subsequent child are fictional, as is Grace's insanity and suicide. The journey to London did happen and Goodwife Dickenson, Mary Spencer and Margaret Johnson were three of the women who were questioned, examined by the King's physician and then taken before the King himself. The fourth woman was Jennet Hargreaves, into whose place I substituted Jennet Device/Sellers.

Tragically, the outcome for the accused was much as I described in the novel and although the intervention of the Privy Council did lead to the case against them falling apart, many of them remained in prison, probably as a result of being unable to pay their debts. Edmund Robinson senior, the man who seems to have used his son's tall tales to rid himself of disfavoured neighbours, was imprisoned, but not before his spiteful actions had ruined the lives of so many.

The northern authorities, meanwhile, showed themselves to have been as hell-bent on rooting out witches in 1634 as they had been in 1612, with no apparent regard for the strength of the evidence or the fact that it was coming mainly from a child. In the novel I suggest that the Justices of the Peace may have neglected to have the women properly examined for witch's marks before submitting these claims as evidence. This is mere fiction on my part, although certainly the examination conducted in London disproved these charges, which in itself underlines the lack of skill and diligence applied by the northern authorities. Sadly, it seems, lessons had not been learned.

If this novel has inspired an interest in the 1634 Pendle witch trials, I would recommend John A Clayton's book, *The Boy Witchfinder of Pendle Forest* as an excellent source of further information concerning some of the research I alluded to above. For more information about the 1612 trials and about the family of Jennet Device, I would recommend Clayton's other book, *The Lancashire Witch Conspiracy: A History of Pendle Forest and the Pendle Witch Trials*, as well as *The Lancashire Witch Craze: Jennet Preston and the Lancashire Witches, 1612* by Jonathan Lumby. For more information concerning Grindletonianism and radical religious beliefs during this period, I would recommend Christopher Hill's *The World Turned Upside Down: Radical Ideas during the English Revolution.*

ABOUT THE AUTHOR

Sarah L King has always loved writing and as a youth she flirted with poetry, some of which was published. In addition, she has always loved history which led to her obtaining a 1st Class Honours degree in the subject from Lancaster University in 2006.

In recent years, Sarah has merged her two passions together to bring some new, interesting historical fiction to the world. Her first novel, The Gisburn Witch, was published in 2015 and with her second novel, A Woman Named Sellers, she has continued her exploration of the Witches of Pendle.

Born in Nottinghamshire, England, Sarah has lived in several places but now resides in West Lothian, Scotland with her husband and two children. Her days are filled with trying to juggle her time between writing, working and looking after her children.

For further information please visit her website & blog at http://www.sarahlking.com/

Printed in Dunstable, United Kingdom

70302375R00204